THY WILL BE DONE

THY WILL BE DONE

To my dear friend Linda
with Love,

Wendy.

~~Wendy~~ Hayden Sadler

The Book Guild Ltd
Sussex, England

This book is a work of fiction. The characters and situations in this story are imaginary. No resemblance is intended between these characters and any real persons, either living or dead.

The Book Guild Ltd.
25 High Street,
Lewes, Sussex

First published 2000

Set in Baskerville
Typesetting by
SetSystems Ltd, Saffron Walden, Essex

Printed in Great Britain by
Antony Rowe Ltd, Chippenham, Wiltshire

A catalogue record for this book is
available from the British Library

ISBN 1 85776 432 3

Dedicated to
Elisa Cabasso
a true romantic;
a great influence in my life

ACKNOWLEDGEMENTS

A special thanks to Kent for his unerring faith in me, for his encouragement, patience, support and dedicated help. For someone who has never read a romantic novel in his life, apart from the classics, this must surely have been a labour of love.

To Rebecca and Kate a sincere thanks for all the hours so willingly given to objective and critical reading.

I owe a debt of gratitude to Dean Barrett, American author of *Hangman's Point* and *Kingdom of Make-Believe*, for all his kind interest and inspirational advice . . . from the beginning.

My sincere thanks also to Adil Iskaros and Laurence Viallon, for acquiring and verifying information relevant to sequences set in Paris.

Finally, my heartfelt thanks to those close friends who afforded me great moral support.

Family Tree

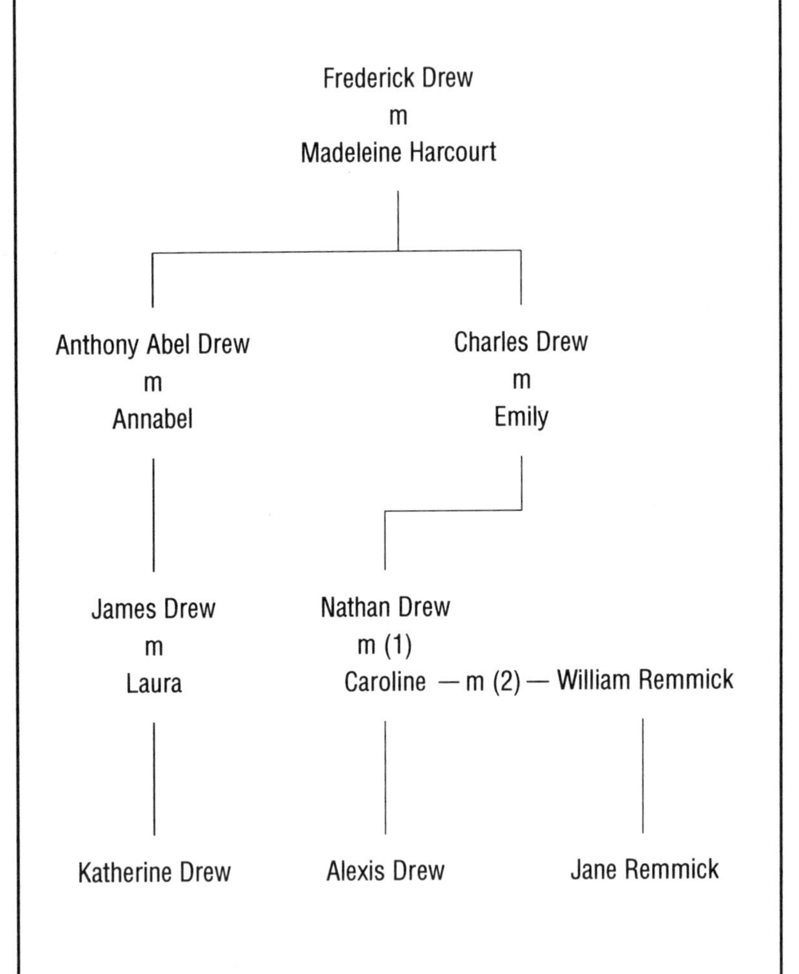
Frederick Drew
m
Madeleine Harcourt
Anthony Abel Drew
m
Annabel
Charles Drew
m
Emily
James Drew
m
Laura
Nathan Drew
m (1)
Caroline — m (2) — William Remmick
Katherine Drew
Alexis Drew
Jane Remmick

PART I

1

Katherine Drew was the first to enter the hall. She turned to the most prominent position at the banqueting table, a position she had assumed by right since the death of her grandfather. But, after a moment's hesitation, she changed direction and went instead to the shadowed, recessed window seat at the far end of the room. She chose this discreet vantage point, not because she was feeling shy or intimidated by the occasion and pending arrival of so many people, but because she wanted the opportunity to observe without being observed.

She had not long to wait. Slowly at first, the room began to fill with people. Moodily she watched, feeling the presence of so many to be a painful intrusion at a time when she most wanted solitude in which to mourn her loss. Although resentful of the disturbance caused by the reading of her grandfather's will, she could at least admit that it offered temporary distraction from the grief and self-pity of the last couple of weeks.

Her attention went to each new arrival in turn. A few she knew by name and some by sight only, but several Katherine had never seen before and she assumed they were her late grandfather's friends and business colleagues from London. Belligerently, she wondered where all these people had been when he was still alive to appreciate their company. She was, of course, well aware that, becoming reclusive after the death of his wife, followed soon after by the loss of her own parents, her grandfather had not particularly encouraged visitors. But, Katherine was in no mood to be reasonable.

Her gaze came to rest awhile on the staff of Ravenswood. Standing with their backs to an oak-panelled wall were Mr

Coteman, the estate comptroller, middle-aged and economical in every way, and the housekeeper's daily helper, gregarious, voluptuous Ellie, with the rosy cheeks and unruly, flyaway hair. Next to her stood Ned, the gardener, small, stooped and elderly, with cloth cap, baggy trousers and scuffed shoes. The housekeeper, Madge Johnson, was not yet in the room but her husband Reg, butler and chauffeur, smart in a dark suit, was silently standing guard over four empty chairs. Searching the room, his gaze came to rest on Katherine. He gave an almost imperceptible raise of the eyebrows. Katherine's slight shake of the head and adamant expression invited no argument, and so he moved his position to stand behind three chairs, thus leaving the fourth free.

Katherine assumed that the housekeeper was in the hall doing what she herself, as the new mistress of the house, should be doing: welcoming the guests and pointing them in the right direction. But, since she was not, as yet, officially mistress of Ravenswood, duty could wait while she followed her own more interesting inclinations.

Eventually, when there were no longer any new arrivals to observe and analyse, Katherine grew restless with waiting. Her gaze began to wander along the panelled walls, focusing in turn on the familiar ancestral portraits. The identity of each haughty face had been taught to her by her grandfather so that she could recite their history, lineage and relationship, each to the other and to herself. Although she had been known to pull faces and poke fun at some of her more austere-looking ancestors, she was immensely proud of that heritage.

Her admiring gaze came to rest on the small portrait of her great-grandmother, painted in her youth, just before her marriage to Frederick Drew, when she had still been Madeleine Harcourt. Although dressed in the height of late Victorian fashion, she had the kind of delicate, classical beauty that was timeless. Katherine had inherited the large eyes and spectacular colouring. For this she was thankful but how she wished she had inherited a few more of her great-grandmother's striking attributes.

Over the past couple of years, Katherine had watched her friends shoot up and fill out in all the right places while her own body had stubbornly remained dormant. She had allowed braces to be put on her teeth, top and bottom. Her long thick, beautiful chestnut hair, so like her great grandmother's and at one time the envy of all, had been badly and unevenly cut into an extremely short and unbecoming style. Her well-meaning school friend had not known when to lay down the scissors. The new look was supposed to have added age and the illusion of height, but she was sadly aware it had done neither of these things. In fact, it had quite the opposite effect, making her look more of a waif than ever. Now, her only redeeming feature was a pair of large, almond-shaped eyes, clear blue and fringed with thick, dark lashes.

Considering herself beyond redemption, Katherine had not taken much trouble over her appearance that morning, but had donned her one and only black dress, not out of hope that it would give her a degree of sophistication, but as a mark of respect to the memory of her grandfather.

With an inward sigh, she turned her attention to the ornate, cloisonné clock on the heavy, carved-wood mantelpiece. Its audible, monotonous tick drew attention to the approaching hour. A respectful hush settled over the room as, on time, Mr Fairfax, the solicitor, accompanied by two others, preceded Mrs Johnson into the room. While the housekeeper closed the dining-room door behind them, they made their way towards the chairs reserved by her husband.

Katherine already knew Mr Fairfax, a dapper, upright man with steel grey hair. Her attention quickly moved on to the tall, slim man at his side. He was considerably younger, probably somewhere in his mid-twenties and would, by most, be considered very handsome. Katherine, however, was at an age when the opposite sex had taken on a certain attraction, but also at an age when she considered anyone beyond their teens as having one foot in the grave. His dark good looks were, therefore, quite wasted on one so young. She did, however, notice and admire his worldly air of confidence and the way he moved with the easy, arrogant grace of one who knows his own worth. From the cut of his expensive suit and quality of shoes, she guessed he was no pauper.

Now that he had sat down next to the solicitor and turned his attention towards the attractive middle-aged lady seated on the other side of Mr Fairfax, Katherine could no longer get a clear view of his face.

Opening his briefcase, the solicitor extracted a file, which he placed on the table in front of him. Then, taking out a pair of gold-rimmed reading glasses, he perched them halfway down his nose, peered over the top, and searched the room. A slight frown marred his forehead until his gaze fell for a moment upon Katherine. Satisfied that the granddaughter of his late client and friend was present, he launched, without further delay, into the reading of the last will and testament of Anthony Abel Drew.

2

The November mist clung in patches to the gently undulating land. In places it resembled mere wisps of gossamer, in others it lay thick like a white shroud, impenetrable to the eye and dampening the sounds of the land. It moved as if stirring from a long sleep, reluctant to arise in answer to the weak call of a watery sun, swirling in slow motion, changing shape and creating an atmosphere eerie and strangely magical.

On higher ground, through the clearing haze, a grandiose late-seventeenth-century manor house of solid and durable Cotswold stone appeared. Where the sun was able to penetrate and touch its walls, it glowed warm and welcoming with the promise of comfort and luxury, its rambling size and architectural design reminiscent of the more gracious lifestyle of a bygone time.

Its many handsome rooms were of generous proportions and, somewhere along the path of time, numerous extensions had been added. The old stables across the cobbled courtyard at the back had, more recently, been converted into three garages and an office for the estate manager. A variety of climbing plants had been trained to meander around the large leaded windows and the arched stone entrance. In places, the Virginia creeper had found its way up as high as the attic windows where, clinging and weaving around the guttering, it threatened to reach out next for the gables and tall chimneys.

Parts of the estate were fairly wooded but the autumn winds had stripped the branches of all but their hardiest leaves, scattering them on the landscape to lie like a mottled brown carpet on an uneven floor. At one time, ravens had nested in some of the taller trees, thus giving their name to the house and property. With their decline in numbers, they had departed for the more natural habitat of rocky regions and there had been few ravens spotted in the treetops in recent years.

From the house and through the late morning mist a young girl came, pushing an old man in a wheelchair. Leaving the long straight drive, they took the winding path that skirted a small natural lake. When they came to an ornamental grey stone bench, they stopped. She seated herself on the cold slab half facing him, and together they looked back the way they had come, to Ravenswood: home to them both and to generations of their family before them.

Both granddaughter and grandfather sat for a while in comfortable silence, each wrapped in their own deep thoughts. The one was only 15 and just beginning life, while the other was nearly 70 years her senior and awaiting the inevitable conclusion of his.

Being an invalid did not come easily to Anthony Drew. He had enjoyed good health and an abundance of vitality all his days, never succumbing to anything more serious than the usual childhood illnesses. Throughout his adult years he had enjoyed a robust outdoor life, filling his free time with favourite sporting activities. Now, after two strokes in quick succession, he was feeling both his age and his mortality. He did not need his doctor to tell him that the next stroke would most probably be his last and so he had sent for his solicitor with the intention of updating his will. But how to update it was the problem that weighed so heavily upon his mind.

If only Annabel was still alive, he brooded, she would know what best to do for their granddaughter, but 13 years had passed already since her untimely death. So vividly etched were the memories of her last days that it was as if only yesterday she had lost her footing on the bottom few steps of the staircase and hit her head on the banister. Such a little knock it had seemed, with only a small lump to show for it. He remembered how, although badly shaken, Annabel had bravely made light of the fall. Later had come the complaints of headaches and nausea. Within a few hours she had died.

Anthony Drew was not a man to waste time on sentimentality. But, since his decline, he had allowed his thoughts to dwell more and more on the loss of his wife, and on the motorway accident which had claimed his son and daughter-in-law, leaving in his sole charge their only daughter, Katherine.

There had been Drews at Ravenswood for generations but now, upon his death and her eventual marriage, the name would cease to be. He looked at his only grandchild: heiress to Ravenswood, its estate and all his wealth, and he felt a deep concern for her future. A likely prey to every fortune hunter who crossed her path, and he would not be there to protect her. Anthony Drew prayed daily for a few more years of life. Every precious passing year gave Katherine added maturity to cope with all the changes his departure would bring but, sadly, he sensed his end was imminent. He sighed.

Startled by the sound, the girl searched her grandfather's face for signs of fatigue.

'I promised the Johnsons I wouldn't keep you out too long,' she murmured anxiously, wondering if she should return him to the house.

The old man frowned. 'They fuss too much,' he grumbled, but not unkindly, for he was fond of Reginald and Madge Johnson and well aware that, of late, he had given the domestic staff plenty of cause for concern over his fragile health. No, Anthony Drew was not yet ready to return to the house. He had come out into the crisp morning air with a purpose. He wanted to think and, if needs be, discuss with his granddaughter her future so that he could put his affairs into satisfactory order. He did not want to alarm her with talk of death. As it was, there had been too much evidence of it in her young life. But he had some important decisions to make, and only when he knew Katherine and Ravenswood were safe would he feel he could rest easy.

'Mr Fairfax will be coming to see me next week to discuss certain matters and, if necessary, to make a few changes to my will,' he told her, striving for a casual tone. He saw her move uneasily on the rough surface of the stone bench. He continued, 'Where Ravenswood is concerned, nothing will change. It will come to you,' he assured her. 'And, of course, you and the house will be well provided for . . . no need to worry about your future, my dear.'

'Don't let's talk about it, Grandpa,' the girl said in a small, worried voice. 'Nothing's going to happen to you.' Fiercely, with a note of pleading, she added, 'It can't . . . you're all I've got.' As if she had said too much, her eyes slid evasively away to focus on a couple of moorhens that had emerged from the reeds on the far side of the lake.

He knew the thought of losing him was a constant source of anxiety to her. But what could he do, what could he say to ease that anxiety?

'Not quite all you've got, my dear,' he said, gently, comfortingly. 'You're forgetting your aunt Caroline and her brood.'

She turned vivid blue eyes on him, full of intelligence. 'She's not a real aunt,' she corrected. 'She's one too many removed for that, and only related by marriage.'

'Well then, what about Alexis? You can't disown him,' he persevered, with a tolerant smile.

No, she could not disown him. As her second cousin he was her only remaining blood relative, apart from her grandfather.

'You probably don't remember,' the old man reflected, 'but you met them once.'

While her mind focused on the distant past, her eyes returned to watch the slow jerky progress of the moorhens and the slight ripple they left in their wake. Katherine did remember but, as she had been so young at the time, it was only a hazy recollection.

*

Eagerly, she had looked forward to meeting these distant, estranged relatives, only to be disappointed when they finally arrived at the manor house. No one had told her that Alexis was eight years her senior and almost in his teens. No fitting playmate for a little girl starved of young company.

Responding to a nudge from her mother, she had stepped forward to be introduced to her tall cousin with the penetrating eyes and Drew dark good looks. He had not talked down to her as others were apt to do with one so small, and when she had reached up to shake his hand, had not stooped condescendingly to her level. He had answered her smile with a confident one of his own and returned her frank look of appraisal before turning his attention to her grandfather.

Her aunt, on the other hand, had chucked her under the chin and said all a doting mother could wish to hear. Duty done, it seemed she had quickly lost interest. In awe of her cousin, wary of her aunt, Katherine had instinctively stayed out of their way and, for all she knew, had not been missed by either.

She had taken herself off to sit on the top step of the oak stairway that curved grandly up to the dim gallery landing and, from the shadows of her refuge, had surveyed, through the turned polished wood spindles, everyone's comings and goings in the hall below. With regret, Katherine had watched the housekeeper wheel the laden tea trolley in through the drawing-room door and, an hour later, wheel it back to the kitchen nearly empty. She had listened to the muffled, indistinguishable conversation of her parents, grandfather and their guests and then, just as she was beginning to grow bored and drowsy with waiting for them to go, the music had started.

Katherine had known instantly that it came from the revered grand piano in the drawing room. On a very few occasions she had been allowed to raise the lid and press the precious ivory keys, but never before had she heard it played like that.

The wondrous music, soft at first, and then gaining in strength, had floated up to fill the air with its poignant magic. The enchanting melody had affected her like a powerful drug, lulling her into a state of wellbeing and filling her young mind with elusive dreams. She had not wanted it to come to an end and when, inevitably, it did, there had been a feeling of deep disappointment, as if she had lost something precious and beautiful.

For a long time after their visit, Katherine thought it had been Aunt Caroline who had played the piano with so much flair and passion.

'Good heavens no, dear,' her mother had told her. 'That wasn't your aunt Caroline. She doesn't have nearly that much musical ability. It was Alexis. He seems to have inherited Frederick Drew's genius.' Seeing the blank look on her daughter's face, she had gone on to explain. 'His great-grandfather, darling . . . and yours too, for that matter.'

A few years later, after the death of her parents, her grandfather had looked up from an absorbing letter he had been reading at the breakfast table and, beaming with pleasure and pride, informed her, 'Young Alexis has won himself a scholarship to the Royal College of Music. That takes extraordinary talent, my dear.' Reading on, he said, 'His mother says he'll be studying the piano and violin.' Here, he had paused to reflect before adding, 'I didn't even know he played the violin and, come to think of it, I was under the impression Alexis was going to study law.'

With a worried scowl on his face, her grandfather had grumbled: 'There seems to be a lot I don't know about that boy.'

3

It very soon became clear to everyone, including Katherine, that the reading of the will was going to be a long-drawn-out procedure. There were pensions to certain members of staff, past and present, and legacies, some with provisos attached. There were donations to several favourite charities and small bequests to a few remaining friends whom Katherine had not only never seen before but had never even heard of. Companies, smallholdings, partnerships and stocks and shares were all mentioned, and it went on endlessly.

Katherine had known her grandfather was a wealthy man but, until now, had not known just how wealthy, nor had she realised the full extent of his business interests. She sighed at her ignorance.

Despite the open windows, the room was hot and stuffy, made worse by the midday sun, which now streamed through the south-facing casements. Even though determined not to miss a word, Katherine was finding it increasingly difficult to maintain concentration on what, at the moment, did not concern her. Her gaze strayed out to the well-maintained gardens to roam over the profusion of brightly coloured summer flowers. The blossom-scented air reminded her of her mother's perfume and, for an unguarded moment, her mind slipped back to the last time she had seen her parents, that fateful, tragic day, when she had been only eight years old.

Wistfully, she smiled to herself. How splendid they had looked all dressed up for dinner in London and a night at the theatre. Her mother, so pretty in a vibrant blue cashmere gown, her sleek golden curls loosely swept back and piled high on her head in the style she knew most suited her.

Carefully picking up one of her mother's blue sapphire and diamond earrings, Katherine had held it close to the dressing table lamp and, fascinated by the lights dancing in the facets of the gems, had asked, 'Will you wear these, Mummy?'

'Do you think I should, darling?' Laura had smiled, her attention divided between her daughter and her toilette.

'Yes,' Katherine had replied with certainty. 'The blue is exactly the same colour as your dress.'

'And her beautiful eyes,' her father had added, coming up behind his wife and kissing the side of her neck.

Katherine had carefully replaced the earrings before turning to her father, and saying, 'Me next, Daddy.'

Before the last words had passed her lips, she had been off across the room, running for safety, knowing she was far too ticklish to allow him to kiss her neck. When he caught her, she had dissolved into a fit of giggles, squirming until he let her go again.

Katherine found herself thinking how different it would have been if only her parents had lived to see this day. Her father would have been the rightful heir, but now, it would seem, she was, and the prospect frightened her.

Mr Fairfax had arrived at a place in the proceedings that was of concern to only a few; he therefore said to the room at large, 'You will be hearing from my office in due course. Now may I ask the following people to stay behind: Mr and Mrs Johnson, Mr Alexis Drew and Mrs Caroline Remmick . . . would you mind?' Looking across at Katherine, he gave a slight smile. Everyone else, thus so neatly dismissed, began to leave the room.

So it's true. That's who you are, Katherine told herself, now looking at Alexis Drew with keen curiosity, trying to see the boy in the man. In stature and colouring he was very much a Drew, but apart from the thick, almost black hair and eyes, there was little left of the boy for her to recognise. But then, that was hardly surprising, she told herself, since 11 years had passed since their paths had last crossed and she had been only five at the time.

Katherine transferred her scrutiny to the trim, sophisticated woman at his side. Caroline Remmick, immaculately turned out from head to toe, was as fair as her son was dark. Like him, she had an undeniable air of authority. Handsome people, Katherine allowed with a tinge of envy.

Sifting through family history Katherine recalled that Alexis' grandfather and her own had been brothers: offspring of Frederick and Madeleine Drew. The brothers had sired one son each: James and Nathan. Caroline's marriage to William Remmick so soon after the death of Nathan, and subsequent removal of herself and her son from Ravenswood, had been a bitter blow to Anthony Drew. Alexis had kept the family name but seen little of his great uncle in the ensuing years. As Katherine's second cousin, not only was he her only remaining blood relative, but the last male in a long line to carry the name of Drew.

When the dining-room door was at last closed to the outside world, Mr Fairfax peered over his glasses, and said, 'No doubt, you're all aware that Mr Drew rewrote a section of his will six months ago, soon after his second stroke. You may also be aware of the changes he made.' He searched each blank face before allowing his eyes to settle hopefully on the young man at his side, so that now, he was primarily addressing him.

With a slight shake of the head and glancing at his mother so as to include her in his reply, Alexis said, 'We knew nothing about my great-uncle's wills. He never mentioned them to us.'

It was the first time Katherine had heard his voice and although he had not raised it, his words carried clearly across the room. It was an arresting voice, cultured and masculine, with perfect diction.

'When Mr Drew mentioned your visit to Ravenswood last January, I assumed he invited you so he could discuss the changes he wanted to make,' the solicitor explained.

Alexis frowned. 'He may have intended to . . .' He paused a moment to reflect. 'But, as I remember it, our visit was purely a social one.'

Mr Fairfax looked down at the document. He seemed perplexed and it occurred to everyone that he was not at all comfortable with its contents. However, clearing his throat, he came to a decision. 'Well then, perhaps I had better get on with it,' he said. Picking up the document, he was about to commence reading when he evidently changed his mind. Laying it down once more, he said, 'It may be easier for some of you present if I merely explain at this stage and then leave you each a copy of the will to read at your own leisure.'

Since no one disagreed, he continued. 'What it amounts to is that the late Mr Drew has left Ravenswood with all its contents and estates to his granddaughter, Miss Katherine Drew. To his great nephew, Mr Alexis Drew, he has left his London town house, complete with contents. However, certain conditions have first to be met.' Here, he waited for a moment to allow these words to sink in.

When Mrs Remmick and her son had received Mr Fairfax's letters informing them of a death in the family and requesting their presence at Ravenswood, the likelihood of them being named as beneficiaries had indeed crossed their minds. It had not, however, occurred to either of them that Alexis was to inherit anything as valuable as Linnet House, along with its collection of beautiful and valuable antiques.

Caroline, marvelling at her son's good fortune, turned towards him eyes bright with elation. His expression, however, was guarded. Two words had caught his attention: *contents* and *conditions*. He had heard them quite clearly and was not a man to allow himself to get too excited without being in full possession of the facts. First he wanted to know if a certain very important item was listed among the contents of the house, and then he wanted to know exactly what the conditions of inheritance were. Warily, he waited.

Katherine had not realised she was holding her breath until she slowly released it, along with a great deal of accumulated tension. Light-headed with relief, she allowed a little smile of satisfaction to hover on her lips. Unaware of Alexis' scrutiny, she lovingly, possessively, stroked a hand along the wooden casement.

Ravenswood is mine, her dancing, triumphant eyes told the ancestral portraits, and it was as if, for once, even the cynics smiled their approval. She laughed at herself. Of course, Ravenswood was hers. It was always to have been hers. Had not her grandfather told her so? Had she ever had reason to doubt his word?

Naive and trusting, she paid scant attention to the solicitor, who had moved on to address Mr and Mrs Johnson.

'In addition to the pensions promised by your late employer, a very generous sum of money is to be settled on you both on condition that you complete, as previously agreed, ten more years of service to Miss Drew. I am to assure you that your pensions will not be affected if you decide, for reasons of your own, that you cannot stay on at Ravenswood.'

Mr Fairfax now turned to Caroline Remmick. 'Mr Drew's bequest to you, Mrs Remmick, is unconditional. However, it was his wish that you take a discreet interest in the welfare of Ravenswood and its staff, particularly during school term when Miss Drew will be away from home and unable to see to its management. He hoped you would do so until she reaches the age of twenty-one.'

Hearing only what she wanted to hear, giving not a moment's thought to the word 'conditions', Katherine was, as yet, oblivious to the bombshell which was about to drop.

But not so Alexis! Not a word, not a look escaped his

notice. Through alert, narrowed eyes, he watched the growing agitation of Mr Fairfax, saw him pause to nervously straighten his already straight tie, and he wondered.

'Now we come back to the conditions which I mentioned earlier,' the solicitor said. Glancing first at Katherine and then at Alexis, he managed to appear even more disconcerted than he had done previously. 'Before I continue, you should both know that I did not approve of these conditions and made my feelings perfectly clear to the late Mr Drew. He, however, was quite adamant and would not be dissuaded.' He paused to clear his throat.

By now, no one was particularly interested in whether or not Anthony Abel Drew had his solicitor's approval. Sensing something untoward, they were interested only to know what the conditions were. Impatiently, all willed him to continue.

Hesitantly, reluctantly, Mr Fairfax obliged. 'It was his wish that his granddaughter and Mr Alexis Drew should be . . . er . . . married to each other as soon as possible.'

The perpetual, slow rhythmic ticking of the clock sounded extraordinarily loud in the unnatural stillness of the room as five pairs of eyes turned to stare at Mr Fairfax in utter disbelief.

For once, Mr Johnson had allowed his professional deadpan expression to slip from his face. His wife, with mouth gaping, had staggered back to collapse into the nearest chair, where she now sat immobile. Mrs Remmick had sat bolt upright and, Fairfax noticed, was gripping the edge of the table so tightly that her knuckles had turned white. She was not, he judged, a woman to be long lost for words on any subject, especially one so close to home.

Briefly, the solicitor focused on the person whose interests most concerned him. The shock in Katherine's large, sensitive eyes, the pallor of her skin and the rigid outline of her light frame, showed clearly the state of her turbulent emotions. Clearly, on this particular subject, her grandfather had not consulted her. Indeed, unless he was much mistaken he had given not even a hint of his intentions. She had his sympathy.

Only Alexis, masking his true feelings, managed to appear unaffected.

Taking advantage of the stunned silence, dropping his eyes to focus on the document in front of him, Mr Fairfax quietly continued his task.

'Furthermore, you, Mr Drew, would be expected to oversee the financial and administrative responsibilities of both properties and investments, working in conjunction with the appointed trustees and the estate manager, Mr John Coteman.' He paused, but still no one spoke. 'It is also a condition of the will that you must, neither of you, seek a divorce before a period of seven years has expired; after which time, you are at liberty to do as you wish and Miss Drew may then assume the full responsibility of running her own affairs.'

He cleared his throat yet again. 'It's all detailed in legal terms but that's the brief outline.' As if wishing to excuse such folly, he went on, 'Granted, they are extraordinary conditions but, clearly, Mr Drew wanted to leave all he loved in safe capable hands.' Turning to the young man at his side, he observed, with a hint of apology, 'He must have formed a very high opinion of your ability and integrity during your brief meeting.'

At this moment, Alexis Drew did not give a damn for the good opinion of his great uncle. He gave no reply and, but for the scornful glint in his dark eyes, no hint of the temper he held tightly in check.

With an inner sigh, the solicitor continued to carry out his client's unorthodox wishes. 'It weighed heavily upon Anthony Drew's mind that after more than two hundred years he would be the last Drew at Ravenswood, unless you, his granddaughter and his brother's grandson, chose to carry on the family name, in which case, you would both have his blessing. He wanted you to know his feelings on this matter, but it was made quite clear it was not to be a condition of the will.'

Although delicately put, the meaning behind these words was clear to all. Katherine suddenly broke the long silence with an audible gasp, which resulted in everyone turning to look in her direction. Apart from Mr Fairfax, no one had, until then, paid her much attention but now all were truly aware of her presence.

Confused and bewildered, Katherine was having great difficulty believing her beloved grandfather had made marriage to this stranger a condition of her inheritance. That he had hoped for a perpetuation of the family name made matters a thousand times more humiliating. The imagined intimacy required between her and this man in order to fulfil those wishes caused her cheeks to redden in a deep blush of embarrassment. Involuntarily, her gaze crossed the room to the man who was expected to oblige. Their eyes locked, until his, breaking away, moved quickly, appraisingly, over her. To Katherine's chagrin, it seemed a hint of mockery appeared in their angry depths. Only too aware of her own lack of appeal, she guessed that none of his thoughts were likely to be complimentary to either her or the memory of her grandfather. Although bristling under such critical scrutiny, she felt she could not blame her cousin for what he must be thinking.

Through the tangle of her emotions, a few pertinent questions now arose, begging to be answered. Why had this man been appointed as her guardian when his mother so obviously was a more appropriate choice? How could her grandfather have made such outrageous conditions, and without so much as a hint to her of his intentions? And, how was she ever to find it in her heart to forgive him for this day's work?

Mrs Remmick was the first to speak. In tones of icy contempt, she expostulated, 'The will can't be legal, surely, Mr Fairfax?' Peering at Katherine through narrowed, speculative eyes, she tactlessly pointed out, 'The girl doesn't look old enough to be married. She's only a child.'

At the unfortunate choice of words, Katherine stiffened with indignation. Growing increasingly more sensitive by the minute, she was inclined to imagine slights at every turn, and was fast reaching the point of open retaliation. The solicitor, however, with his wary eye on the young girl, was quicker than she to respond. 'Katherine has just turned sixteen and is therefore legally old enough to marry,' he assured Mrs Remmick. 'The will is in order.'

'But they're related,' she argued. 'They can't possibly marry!'

'Distantly related,' the solicitor patiently corrected. 'There's no law to prevent it.'

'Immoral nonsense, the most ridiculous thing I've ever heard,' she bristled. 'Didn't anyone think to tell Anthony Drew that arranged marriages in this country are a thing of the past?' Her scornful tones seemed to suggest the solicitor should have done so. 'Surely that will would not hold up in court if my son decided to contest it?'

Mr Fairfax would like to have pointed out that the person in the strongest position to contest the will was Katherine. Since Alexis was only a great-nephew who had very recently become reacquainted with his wealthy, elderly and obviously ailing relative, Katherine might have a case for ousting him altogether. At this stage, he prudently decided to keep these thoughts to himself. He had been retained by Anthony Drew in a professional capacity for many years and had served him to the best of his ability, honestly and loyally. Somewhere along the way the two men had become friends. His late client had trusted him to carry out his wishes and that was what he fully intended to do.

With an impatient gesture of a hand, Alexis put a stop to further conversation. 'What if we refuse to marry?' he asked softly, his focus again on Katherine.

'Mr Drew foresaw that possibility,' replied Mr Fairfax. 'He drew up a contingency plan.' As he spoke, he reached down to take from his briefcase, a long white envelope on which the red sealing wax was clearly still intact.

'I'm not privy to the contents of this envelope and not at

liberty to open it unless one or both of you formally refuse the bequest under its present terms. I must warn you though, once opened, there's no going back . . .'

Alexis offered no comment. Instead, silently, he sat back in his chair and meditated on all that had transpired. His mother, however, still seeking a loophole, continued to discuss the situation with Mr Fairfax, while Mr and Mrs Johnson stood silently, wondering how all these troublesome revelations would affect their erstwhile orderly lives.

Although no one spoke to Katherine directly or asked for her opinion, she heard her name mentioned several times. She felt she might just as well not be in the room and found it thoroughly humiliating that these virtual strangers should feel free to discuss her future, the intimacies and delicacies of it, as if she had no say in the matter.

How dare that woman call me a *child*, she fumed to herself, grasping at trivialities rather than face up to the enormity of her predicament. How dare they treat me this way in my own home? Her mind was in total disarray. She could not think straight . . . could not think what options, if any, were open to her.

Of one thing she was sure, she would not marry this cousin. No one can force me to marry a man who must be a dozen years older than me, she raged to herself. It gave her perverse pleasure to grossly exaggerate the age gap between them.

As if magnetically drawn, Alexis once more met Katherine's stormy gaze, but this time his expression was unreadable. He was, in fact, only vaguely aware of her, his main focus being on memories of his last meeting with Anthony Drew. Their conversation, he recalled, had at times been rather like an interview. He now knew his great uncle had been assessing him, but he did not know what had prompted the old man to name him joint heir with his granddaughter. Nor did he understand why he had felt it necessary for them to marry.

Anthony Drew was not a man to do things without good reason. He had wanted something in return, and not just the successful running of this girl's affairs either. There were a number of people better qualified than he for the job. And, if he had merely required a guardian for his granddaughter, he would have appointed his mother, who was eminently more suitable to babysit a proud, rebellious teenager. No, there had been something else bothering the old man, of that he was quite sure, but what?

Leaving the question unanswered, he went on to recall how the old man had steered the conversation around to Linnet House, to its treasures, knowing that within its walls was one particular treasure he could depend upon as irresistible bait. A cynical smile curled his lips.

The wily old fox! Alexis told himself. He knew he had in that house the one thing for which I'd sell my soul . . .

4

Whilst Madge Johnson could sympathise with old Mr Drew's problems, she could not approve of his methods for solving them. She felt sure a clever man like him could have arrived at a happier conclusion for all if only he had given it a bit more thought. Alone with her husband in the kitchen, Madge aired her feelings.

'Well,' she huffed, as she went about the job of setting a tea tray, 'it's not for us to question the methods of our employer I'm sure, but he must have been very out of touch with the modern world. Fancy him telling Miss Katherine who she must marry,' she grumbled on indignantly. 'Have you ever heard of such a thing? It's not right, Reg.'

Reg nodded his agreement. He was a man of few words.

'There's going to be trouble,' Madge warned, warming to the subject. 'You know how stubborn she can be. Got a mind of her own, like her grandfather. If she decides against this marriage, nothing will change her mind, and then what's to become of her and Ravenswood . . . and if there's no Katherine and no Ravenswood, what's to become of us?'

There was no answer to that. Reg continued to keep his peace.

Tea tray in hand, Madge stopped at the door and turned an anxious face to her husband. 'She can't be turned out, can she Reg?' Not waiting for his reply, she answered herself, 'That's not very likely now . . . is it?'

In the driveway below, a car engine started up. Crossing to the window, Katherine was in time to see a BMW pull away from the house, skirt the lake and go out through the open wrought iron gates. She was not sorry to see Mr Fairfax go – he had been the bearer of bad news.

She hoped he had not forgotten his promise to leave her a copy of the will; maybe it would shed some light on her grandfather's reasons for wanting her married so soon. She was impatient to go in search but, so long as those two other cars remained in the drive, nothing was going to tempt her away from the safety of her bedroom.

The almost overwhelming desire to slam doors and throw things had long since subsided, along with the tears of frustration. But, under a thin veneer of calm, the confusion remained and, to her already numerous problems, she had acquired a throbbing headache.

Leaning her shoulder against the window frame and her head against the cool glass, her eyes went to the distant stone bench down by the lake, the bench where she and her grandfather had stopped to talk the last time he had been well enough to leave the house. She tried to remember their conversation, and subsequent conversations during her visits home from boarding school, to remember if he had given a clue as to his intentions. But there had been nothing, not a word, not a look.

Her unhappiness was like a physical pain, an ache in the chest. It seemed to her that she had lost everything in life that she most loved and valued: her parents, her grandfather; the security that came with their love and now, on top of all that, she was about to lose Ravenswood. If the only way she could keep her home was by marrying this man, then she had no choice but to give it up.

Young and romantic, she had woven such beautiful dreams for herself, and those dreams did not include marriage with Alexis Drew, a 24-year-old man of whom she knew very little.

I won't marry him, Katherine reassured herself, and no one can make me. But then, where would she live, and on what? Her parents had left her some money in trust, but she would not inherit it until she was 21. Another five years, she calculated – a lifetime, and what would she do until then? With a temporary lifting of spirits, Katherine remembered there was another will with which she could take her chances. Surely her grandfather would not have left her destitute? Surely he had loved her enough to leave her provided for, no matter what?

Only a few hours ago, she had trusted him completely, but now, she was not so sure she wanted to put that trust to the test.

Mrs Johnson placed the tea tray on the dressing table. Seeing the proud upward tilt of her young mistress's chin, the stiff straight back, she hesitated, at a loss for the right words. Cautiously, in her gentle Gloucestershire accent, she asked, 'Would it help to talk about it, my dear?'

Without turning from the window, Katherine shook her head. 'No, not yet, Mrs Johnson,' she replied in a carefully controlled voice.

'A problem shared is a problem halved, my granny used to say, so when you're feeling up to it we'll talk it through and then things won't seem half so bad, you'll see.' Mrs Johnson was not at all convinced by her own well-meaning words, but ... what else was there to say under the circumstances?

Madge would have stayed longer, offered more of Granny's wisdom, but she knew, without being told, that Katherine was in no mood to give it the attention it deserved. She wanted to be left alone. Besides, with two guests to look after, Madge had no time to linger above stairs.

Leaving the room, she quietly closed the door behind her. 'Poor lamb,' she muttered, as she hurried away, 'she's far too young to be married, especially to a man as worldly as that one.'

Katherine had not long been left alone with her distress, when Ellie put in an appearance. 'Mrs Johnson 'as asked

Mr Drew and Mrs Remmick if they would like to stay to supper before starting back to wherever they came from,' she breezily volunteered. Her cheeks were flushed with pleasure; a smile played on her lips. 'They said they would, miss, and asked if you would be joining them.'

Her voice was husky and her manner too restless, even for one as excitable as Ellie. Katherine gave the girl a curious stare. She recognised the symptoms; had seen them many times before.

Who on earth is it this time? Katherine wondered suspiciously, awed by the older girl's propensity for falling in and out of love. Her behaviour only that morning had seemed normal enough, so who, since then, had crossed her path? A name occurred to Katherine. She looked at Ellie with sharp disbelief. Surely not Alexis Drew? Despite her low spirits, Katherine almost found it within herself to laugh.

'I'll bring a tray up then, Miss Katherine, shall I?' asked the girl, completely misinterpreting Katherine's look and pre-empting a negative reply. She was eager to return to the vicinity of the guests, one in particular, and finding it hard to hide her impatience to be gone.

'Yes do that please, Ellie.' Katherine watched her hasty retreat and shrugged. Well, why shouldn't Ellie find him attractive? she asked herself. After all, she's nearer his age than I am. And, I suppose, he is good-looking . . . for a man of his age, she grudgingly allowed.

The other girl's interest did not surprise her, not really. Ellie was in love with the idea of being in love and her numerous amorous escapades, innocent or otherwise, had earned her a reputation in the village, where a secret was never a secret for long.

'She's never out with the same man more than a half-dozen times. Always swapping and changing,' she had overheard Mrs Johnson grumble on more than one occasion.

This time Ellie's fancies would do her no good. Alexis Drew was not some over-eager village boy and she was hardly his type . . . whatever his type might be. For a while, she pondered on the question of his type: elegant, sophisticated, beautiful, worldly, wealthy . . . catty, boring, vain, vacant . . .

Her vindictive thoughts were interrupted when Ellie returned with a tray and, again later, when it was taken away hardly touched.

Left to herself, with a mind that would not settle for long on anything that was not connected with the devastating revelations of the day, Katherine lay on the bed in the darkening room. She had not bothered to change nor did she switch on the lights. Emotionally drained, she wished the oblivion of sleep would come to the rescue, but for once it stubbornly refused to claim her. The room grew dark; time passed slowly. Then the music started.

From one of the open windows below, it floated up on the warm, scented evening breeze. Its strains came softly at first, the melody melancholy, haunting, caressing. Slowly it built up to a crescendo, before returning once more to its soft recurring theme. Wrapped in a spell of enchantment, the beautiful harmonies lulled and tranquillised her senses, restoring peace and serenity to her disorientated world.

A feeling of déjà vu was followed by vivid memories of a time, long ago, when she had sat upon the landing in a state of rapture, listening with a child's simple pleasure, knowing that all was right with her world and believing it would never be otherwise. Alexis had played with his heart and soul then, as he did now. Once again, when the music ceased, Katherine was aware of a sense of loss.

For the first time that day she felt relaxed. Falling into an exhausted sleep, nothing disturbed her again that night; not even the revving up and departure of one of the parked cars.

'I simply can't understand why Anthony Drew didn't make me the girl's guardian,' Caroline said, placing her aperitif on the pedestal table beside her armchair. 'I know we had our differences, but . . .' Seeing her son's quizzical expression, she hastened to add, 'Only personality clashes, darling, nothing serious.'

'I would never describe one of your personality clashes as *nothing serious*!' Alexis laughed.

'But he always had to have his own way,' she explained in self-defence.

'How provoking,' he affectionately teased.

'Well yes, as a matter of fact, it was. He liked to be in charge, make everyone's decisions for them . . . head of the family and all that nonsense,' she went on. 'He had some very old-fashioned ideas.'

'So it would seem,' murmured Alexis, his thoughts never far from the afternoon's astonishing turn of events.

'Which brings us back to the will.' Caroline frowned. 'What on earth possessed him?' Settling back in the chair and crossing one elegant leg over the other, she silently mulled the question over in her mind.

Glass in hand, Alexis strolled over to stand by the open drawing-room window. To the right, the sun was sinking towards the horizon, leaving a crimson and amethyst trail in its wake. Alexis was reminded of past sunsets seen from this same window. His nostalgic gaze moved on to trace the gentle curve of the land down to the lake, the land he had walked in his early youth, with his father, and sometimes his great-uncle. In that same lake he had fished, and on warm days, swum. The slight September breeze ruffled his hair, stirring him from his reveries. He raised the glass to his lips and returned his mind to his mother's question. What indeed, had possessed Anthony Drew? Alexis had already asked himself that same question. The answer still eluded him.

At *what* stage had his great uncle decided upon this course of action? he wondered. Could he have decided before January? No, he thought not. It was more likely that he had been toying with the idea of making his mother the girl's guardian but, as a consequence of their meeting, had changed his mind in favour of the son. But *what* exactly had brought about that change of mind?

Suddenly it all became clear: the answer so simple. 'Of course . . . that's it!' he exclaimed softly.

About to sip from her glass, Caroline paused to raise questioning brows.

'Think about it. As the law stands, with or without a guardian's consent, the girl can marry anyone she chooses just as soon as she reaches the age of eighteen. But, if she's *already* married, she would be tied up and out of harm's way for seven years – and, what's more, to a man of Anthony Drew's choosing.'

'To a man with integrity,' Caroline continued for him, 'who, being already wealthy in his own right, would not try to cheat his granddaughter out of her inheritance.'

In acknowledgement of the compliment, Alexis gave his mother a mock bow. Visualising the waif in question, he smiled. 'The failure of the marriage would be a foregone conclusion,' he went on. 'He could, therefore, safely assume we would be only too willing – anxious, even – to seek a divorce at the end of the seven years, by which time Katherine would be old enough and, hopefully, wise enough to take care of herself and her own affairs.'

'And, if you chose not to divorce,' Caroline took up again, 'even better. Katherine would have a husband of whom her grandfather approved and the name of Drew would be carried forward in perpetuity.' She gave a dry, humourless laugh. 'How neat and tidy! Well, Anthony Drew always was a manipulative old devil . . . never one to leave loose ends.' After a contemplative pause, she agreed, 'Yes . . . I do believe you're right, it fits the character of the man.'

Remembering the proud tilt of the girl's head, the clearly defined line of a stubborn jaw and the glint of wilful defiance which, on more than one occasion, had flashed in large, intelligent eyes, Alexis considered the old man had known what he was doing after all.

At this point Johnson entered the room to inform them that supper was served. They moved into the dining room where, at one end of the long table, two places had been set opposite each other. Caroline turned questioning eyes on the butler.

'Miss Katherine regrets she won't be able to join you. She sends her compliments,' he improvised, his face expressionless.

Like hell she does, Caroline told herself. It was obvious that the child did not wish to participate in their discussions, despite the fact that it concerned her future as much as it did her son's. Although tolerance was not one of Caroline's virtues, she allowed that the afternoon's proceedings would have been a daunting experience for a girl of Katherine's age and sheltered background. She therefore refrained from comment.

While they did justice to the housekeeper's cooking and a bottle of claret brought up by her husband from his late employer's well-stocked cellar, Caroline and Alexis continued their discussion. The evening wore on but, although they looked at the problem from every angle, nothing was resolved. Alexis decided that, on his return to London, he would consult with Irvine, his own solicitor, before making any irrevocable decisions.

Coffee and liqueurs were served in the drawing room, after which Alexis seated himself at the piano. Raising the fall, he let his long, supple fingers run up and down the ivory keyboard, and then he began to play Schubert's Impromptu in G flat major, one of several pieces he had been practising for a forthcoming concert tour.

Caroline, her head resting on the back of the armchair, closed her eyes and gave herself up to the music. How she loved to hear him play, this handsome, gifted son of hers.

As Alexis played, a part of his mind dwelt on Katherine. If he accepted the terms of the will, she would become his responsibility, and not a very attractive one at that. But, does that really matter? he asked himself. After all, we would be married in name only. No one's asking us to set up house together. And thank God for that, he told himself, visualising the rather unattractive proposition that was this distant cousin, to whom, before today, he had given not a thought: romantic or otherwise.

The wry smile that softened his face turned into a frown of discontent. But, supposing I want to marry before the seven years are over? What then? he asked himself. Oh hell! What a bloody awful decision to have to make.

In his heart, Alexis knew the decision had already been made. Seeking advice from Irvine was merely stalling. The temptation within Linnet House was enough to put a saint to the test and, God knew, he was no saint. A sardonic smile now replaced the frown. He did not doubt his great uncle had known that too.

Caroline had spent a comfortable night in one of the luxurious guest bedrooms. Not having come prepared, she had not really wanted to stay at Ravenswood but Alexis had persuaded her to do so.

Both breakfast and luncheon had come and gone without the appearance of Katherine, who, she knew from questioning the housekeeper, had gone out early that morning and only recently returned. Now, Caroline sat in the drawing room, impatiently drumming her long, manicured nails on the arm of the chair.

'Katherine, my dear, you're avoiding me,' she murmured to herself. For a moment she considered, and then, coming to a decision, rose to her expensively shod feet. 'I think it's time I paid you a little visit . . . we need to talk.' However, before Caroline could put her plan into action, the telephone rang.

She waited awhile, but when, after the fifth ring, no one had picked up any of the extensions, she decided that, since it could be the promised call from Alexis, she had better answer it herself.

The moment his cultured voice came on the line, she knew his interview with Irvine had not been encouraging.

'Maybe we have a case to take to court, but by waiting for

a hearing, we run the risk of losing everything,' she heard him say. 'The old boy put a time limit on our acceptance.'

'I see . . . well, you could call his bluff,' Caroline reminded her son. 'Refuse to marry his granddaughter and insist on reading the second will.'

'Katherine can't afford to take chances . . . She could find herself disinherited,' Alexis warned. 'Where would she live if not at Ravenswood?' He was remembering the girl's transparent relief and joy on hearing Fairfax's confirmation that she was to be mistress of the manor house. 'As her only relatives, we would feel responsible for her welfare.' She heard him laugh and say, 'And it would do her reputation no good to accept accommodation from me.'

Caroline was silent for a moment. An irritable frown creased her brow. 'I can do without the responsibility,' she replied, coolly, 'and may I point out that sharing the same great-grandparents doesn't make you responsible for the girl's welfare. You're not even first cousins. Besides,' she continued, 'I don't for a minute think her grandfather would leave her destitute, Alexis, he loved her too much. He had a lot of faults, but he wasn't heartless . . . not where she was concerned, anyway.'

'Even so, with that much at stake, only a fool would take chances.' He paused and then, in a thoughtful voice, added: 'I would be less than honest if I said Linnet House was not an important consideration.'

His mother sighed. 'Yes. It is beautiful. A great temptation, dear. Your father and I spent some very happy times in that house – we were young and life in the big city had its attractions,' she mused softly. Then, more soberly, she continued, 'Have you come to a decision then?'

'Yes,' he responded, sounding decisive but far from pleased. 'As far as I'm concerned, the old man may have his wish. I must have her answer tonight if possible, I leave for Budapest tomorrow.'

'When and where will the big occasion take place?' asked Caroline, as if the wedding was already a foregone conclusion.

'Ravenswood will do, and the sooner we get it over and done with the better,' was the cool reply. 'I'll be back from Budapest at the weekend and I don't go to Vienna until the end of the month, so let's say any time in between. And,' he warned, 'absolutely no fuss or announcements in *The Times*. It's a strange affair and we don't want any unwelcome publicity.'

'Am I to assume that I have the dubious pleasure of proposing to Katherine on your behalf?' asked Caroline, with little relish for the task.

'Under the circumstances, I'm sure you could do it more eloquently and persuasively than I, Mother dear,' he cajoled.

'I doubt that.' Caroline was well aware of the potency of her son's charm when he cared to use it. 'What if she refuses? What then?'

'For both our sakes, she had better not,' he replied.

5

The wedding day arrived, bringing with it a summer storm. All morning it rained steadily, with thunder a faraway threat but by lunchtime it was obviously moving in the direction of Ravenswood. The nearer it came, the darker the sky, the heavier the rain. The air was close and charged with static, and after each reverberating roll of thunder, the lightning streaked, illuminating in dazzling silver flashes everything for miles around. It was as if heaven itself was protesting against the marriage.

Watching in fascination from her bedroom window, Katherine forecast that if the storm continued on its present course, it would be directly overhead by two o'clock; an unwelcome guest come to the wedding to complain noisily. She shuddered at the thought, wondering if it was a bad omen sent to warn her that her next seven years werc going to be stormy ones.

Although she had a tendency to be a little superstitious, storms did not frighten her. They never had, not even as a little girl. She felt awe and admiration at the majesty and sheer power of them, but never fear.

Her father had once told her the old adage: 'God is moving his furniture around in heaven.' It certainly sounded that way and she had believed it at the time. Now she sat on one of the window seats in her bedroom and marvelled at the violence of the world outside her safe haven.

Katherine had been ready for the service for some time. She wore no special wedding dress, carried no bouquet of flowers, but she had paid a little extra attention to her appearance.

'Something old, something new, something borrowed,

something blue;' she recited the rhyme to herself wistfully. With wry amusement, it occurred to her that this was one superstition she could safely disregard. After all, she was not looking for happiness, or indeed, permanency in this union. A 'marriage of convenience' was what Mrs Remmick had called it, and Katherine intended it should never be anything else.

Three weeks before, Caroline Remmick had come uninvited into her bedroom. 'How charming,' she had commented, looking around at the feminine ornamentation and the handsome furniture. It was a spacious room, with a great deal of character, tastefully decorated in blending shades of nasturtium, peach and cream. The door to the ensuite bathroom was ajar and showed a marble interior luxuriously modernised in recent years at some considerable expense.

When Katherine did not immediately respond beyond polite formalities to her attempts at friendliness, Mrs Remmick wasted no more time on preliminaries, but crossed the room to a window seat, perched herself elegantly on the edge, and came straight to the point. Introducing the subject of the will, she talked convincingly and persuasively for a while before eventually concluding, 'So you see, in the long run, you've nothing to lose and everything to gain by marrying my son.'

Everything she said was true, but an element of doubt still lingered in Katherine's mind. 'And after? What then?' she asked suspiciously.

Understanding her, Mrs Remmick said, 'Why, you go your own separate ways, of course. No need to see each other again until the divorce. As for an heir, well, your grandfather may have mentioned it to Mr Fairfax in passing, but it could only have been a bit of wishful thinking. After all, he had the good sense and consideration not to write it into the will.'

That was true. And so too, was all she said concerning the awesome responsibility of running an estate the size of

Ravenswood. Why not let others look after her interests while, unencumbered, she completed her education?

It all sounded so simple and straightforward, the way Mrs Remmick put it, that it was easier to accept the solution offered than to turn it down. She and Alexis would be married, in name only, and Ravenswood would be hers. Alexis would not infringe upon her privacy but would quite likely move into Linnet House. They need not see each other again if they did not wish to, and at the end of seven years they would automatically file for divorce, probably on the grounds of incompatibility.

If Katherine agreed, Mrs Remmick would stay long enough to organise and attend the wedding, after which, everyone would depart to go their own separate ways. Katherine would then be free to return to boarding school to continue life as if nothing had happened, leaving her responsibilities in the capable hands of others for the next seven years.

Katherine could not visualise a future for herself that did not include Ravenswood. The manor house meant all the world to her. She had no choice but to put her trust in this man. No useful purpose would be served by delaying, and so she had given her consent and from then on done her best to keep her misgivings to herself.

'Now that's settled, my dear, you can't go on calling me Mrs Remmick, not if we're to become friends, which is very likely if I'm to take an interest in Ravenswood as your grandfather wanted.'

Katherine looked doubtfully at Caroline Remmick, hoping she was not going to suggest she call her anything as ludicrous as *mother*.

Divining the girl's thoughts, the older woman hastened on, 'May I suggest you call me Caroline, or even Aunt Caroline if you prefer. Our relationship to each other makes it acceptable, don't you think?'

So Aunt Caroline she had once more become. At first

Katherine had felt self-conscious using the title, but after a surprisingly short time it rolled off her tongue without a second thought, just as easily as when she had been a little girl.

Now, three weeks later, after much soul-searching, Katherine no longer had to ask herself if she could go through with the wedding. She knew she could. In fact, with so much at stake she was quite determined to do so. Only one thought continued to disturb her young and romantic heart: what if Mr Right came into her life before the seven years had passed?

Catching sight of her adolescent reflection in the window pane, Katherine sighed with discontent. Her gaze went beyond her reflection to refocus on the formal gardens below. It moved on, slowly sweeping over the uneven landscape of the storm-battered park to the distant wind-tossed woods. All was bathed in an eerie yellow light that looked so dramatically beautiful under the grey, rolling clouds.

'Maybe you're right, Grandpa. There are those who would marry me just to get their hands on Ravenswood,' she told his unseen presence. Then a thought occurred to her, and with a sad little smile she acknowledged that, by a quirk of fate, this was precisely what she was about to do herself: marry for Ravenswood!

Her attention was arrested by the arrival of a sleek, burgundy Jaguar. Knowing it to be the property of Alexis, she suffered a renewed attack of nerves. She watched its progress through the heavy rain, her eyes not leaving it for a second as it skirted the lake and turned up the wide drive towards the house. The nearer it came the more acute her pangs of anxiety.

Soon after the ringing of the doorbell, Mrs Johnson, in her Sunday best, came bustling into the room to inform her of the arrival of Mr Drew.

'Now let me look at you, Miss Katherine,' the housekeeper fussed affectionately, walking around her young mistress. 'Yes, yes. You look well,' she commented kindly but without too much real conviction, 'but wouldn't you like to wear something a little more cheerful for the occasion?' Under Katherine's chilly stare, Mrs Johnson hastened to add, 'No . . . well, you're still in mourning, I suppose.'

'Perhaps you should go and inform Mrs Remmick of her son's arrival,' Katherine suggested, irritably. 'I'll be down in just a minute.'

In an attempt to still the butterflies in her stomach, Katherine took a few deep breaths. They did not help. Think of it as a business contract, she commanded herself for the umpteenth time. That's all this marriage is . . . a business contract. But her nerves refused to be soothed and her rebellious thoughts raced on out of control. She still could not believe this was happening to her: marriage at 16, to a man she hardly knew, eight years her senior.

After a long last look at herself in the mirror, Katherine squared her shoulders and marched determinedly out of the room, along the gallery, down the wide staircase and into the empty hall below.

On hearing male voices issuing from the drawing room, she hesitated. All her newly acquired courage suddenly deserted her. Feeling wretchedly shy, she was now reluctant to enter the room without the support of her aunt's company. Resorting to delaying tactics, she quietly turned her footsteps in the direction of the study adjacent to the drawing room. From there, she could listen for the arrival of the older woman.

Katherine went to sit on the edge of one of the leather-upholstered easy chairs facing the solid Victorian desk, the one she used to occupy when visiting her grandfather for mid-afternoon coffee breaks. The connecting door to the drawing room was slightly ajar and she could quite clearly hear two men conversing in the other room.

An educated voice, unfamiliar to her, was saying, 'I must

admit, I had my doubts as to whether you would actually go through with this.'

'So did I, at one stage,' said the distinctive voice she recognised as belonging to Alexis Drew. 'But then, I asked myself *why not*? The rewards are handsome enough, after all, and it's not as if we're talking about a real marriage here . . . no one's expecting us to live together, thank God.' His laugh was not altogether pleasant.

'Was your great-uncle in the habit of playing with other peoples lives,' asked the stranger, 'or were the strokes responsible for this addle-brained scheme?'

Katherine scowled. She was not at all sure she liked to hear her grandfather talked about in this irreverent manner.

There was the sound of a glass being placed on a tabletop. 'He was known to be manipulative,' she heard her cousin reply. 'But as for addle-brained, no, Hugh, he was a single-minded man who knew exactly what he wanted.'

'A man not unlike yourself then?' the stranger chuckled. Apparently, not expecting a reply, he went on, 'I wish I had a relative to do as much for me, but I'm not sure I'd relish the terms. Tell me more about him, and the two houses.'

There was a pause while Alexis seemed to consider the request, then she heard him answer in an obliging drawl, 'Well now, let me see . . . first, you had better understand the family background. I'll start with Frederick Drew, his father.'

He stopped to allow for a roll of thunder. When the noise had abated sufficiently, he continued, 'That's the old reprobate up there . . . inveterate gambler and womaniser, with a penchant for making disastrous investments.'

Katherine knew he must be pointing to the large portrait of their haughty and exceptionally handsome great-grandfather. 'Dear Freddy,' he continued, 'was far more attracted to the high life of the big city than he ever was to playing the role of country squire. Never one to deny himself for long, he bought a London town house within a few months of coming into his inheritance, and into this house he installed his mistress, Arabella Haste.

'With his money and her good taste, the house was revamped from top to bottom. Since Freddy made no effort to balance the books, it was not long before his extravagances depleted the family coffers.' With wry humour, Alexis added, 'It was just as well my great-grandfather came to an early end.'

'Did he indeed? And what carried him off?' the stranger quizzed.

'A well-deserved dose of the pox,' was her cousin's flippant reply.

'Poetic justice then?' laughed his companion.

'You could say that. Whoever gave it to him, and apparently it was not Arabella, did everyone a huge favour, especially his long-suffering wife.'

Katherine was agog with interest. This was family history she had never heard before. It was unbelievable that any member of her illustrious ancestry could die of anything quite so vulgar as syphilis. She stifled the urge to giggle. Mrs Johnson must have decided that it was a skeleton best left locked in the family closet. Mischievously, Katherine made a mental note to ask her about it at the first opportunity.

Alexis' melodious voice drew her back to the conversation. 'Anthony Drew was quite young when his father turned up his toes,' she heard him say, 'only in his early twenties. Fortunately for everyone, Freddy's father took care of the future prosperity of the family by placing a large portion of his wealth in a trust, which was to bypass his son and eventually come to his grandsons Anthony and Charles.'

'Shrewd move,' the stranger responded.

'As it turned out,' Alexis agreed. 'But, if Freddy hadn't shuffled off this mortal coil when he did, the trusts would have been unlocked too late to save the family from ruin. Charles, my grandfather, took his smaller portion and, with his new bride Emily, went off to make his fortune in India, while Anthony Drew, being the heir, had no choice but to stay and pay off his father's debts. He was a natural businessman and no doubt his early taste of poverty was responsible for his determination to succeed.'

'It would also explain his rather excessive caution over his granddaughter's inheritance,' his friend surmised. 'I didn't realise you knew so much about him and the family history.'

'When my father was alive,' Alexis explained, 'we used to visit Ravenswood two or three times a year. Then, later, for a short time, my mother and I came to live here. When my mother remarried, we moved away. Up until then, my great uncle and I had been quite close, but after, we rarely saw each other.'

Katherine thought she detected a tinge of regret in his voice.

There followed a short pause, after which Alexis added: 'I suspect he and my mother fell out . . . they were never really comfortable with each other.'

Katherine, who had been listening intently to this dialogue, made a few rapid calculations and discovered Alexis Drew must have lived at Ravenswood when she herself had been a baby. She had not known. Her only memory of him was on that one later occasion when he had visited with his mother.

The man he had called Hugh reclaimed her attention by saying: 'This London town house must be quite something if you're prepared to go to such extremes for it.'

'You're mistaken. I never said I was putting myself through this farce for the sake of a house,' Alexis drawled.

'You're not?' his friend exclaimed. 'Then what the hell are you getting married for?'

A flash of lightning lit up the room. As she waited for the angry roll of thunder to pass, Katherine found herself asking that same question. So as not to miss a word of his reply, ears straining to hear above the noises of the elements, she arose from the chair and silently edged nearer to the open door.

'I'm not denying it's a beautiful property and a great temptation,' she heard Alexis say, 'but there is something in that house that means so much more to me than bricks and mortar.'

'For goodness' sake, what can mean more to you than a fabulous town house on Belgrave Square?' Hugh asked with an impatience almost equal to Katherine's.

'A grand piano Hugh . . . a *Steinway.*'

There was a pregnant silence before she heard Hugh exclaim, 'A piano! So that's it, Alexis. I might have known there was more at stake than a mere palatial town house. You've restored my faith in you,' he said with sarcastic humour.

'A Steinway? He's marrying me for a bloody piano!' Katherine muttered furiously under her breath.

'But, if you want a Steinway so badly, why don't you just go out and buy one?' Hugh wanted to know.

'I don't want just *any* Steinway. I want this *particular* Steinway,' Alexis said with feeling.

Hugh did not respond. He was obviously waiting to be enlightened – as, indeed, was Katherine.

Patiently, Alexis explained, 'My great-grandfather knew that, because the lady of the house was his mistress, and what's more, one that had been on the stage, polite society would snub his invitations. So he devised a plan to make his invitations irresistible.

'Apart from squandering the family fortune, he had another talent. He was a truly gifted pianist. I say *gifted* because I can't believe my great-grandfather ever worked really hard for anything in his life.' She heard the derision in his voice. 'It was a gift not entirely wasted, since Freddy used it lavishly to bring him into contact with the famous artistes of his day.

'From a well-publicised Sotheby auction, he bought a grand piano that was much celebrated for having once belonged to Liszt. It was said that on this piano, the great maestro had composed most of his later works. Freddy let it be known that he was the proud new owner and then invited his artistic friends to soirées at Linnet House. The word quickly got around that Freddy's lavish parties were frequented by famous and colourful people, and were a huge success. The moralists who might earlier have shunned an invitation soon sought one.

'I first pressed the keys of that piano when I was about four and found that, if I concentrated, it would play wondrous tunes to me. I thought it was magic. Fortunately, my parents saw it as talent and decided I was worthy of lessons.

'Each time I visited Linnet House, my great-uncle encouraged me to play that piano. I didn't need the encouragement: the Steinway was already my inspiration. I coveted it from the very beginning and now, at last, it's going to be mine,' Alexis purred.

'I don't mean to throw a damper on your enthusiasm but, are you absolutely sure this Steinway is still in Linnet House?' Hugh asked.

'Absolutely sure,' Alexis replied with total conviction.

To Katherine, this was all highly intriguing. No one had ever mentioned a Steinway before, but then, there seemed to be a number of fascinating things that people had neglected to mention to her.

While she was assessing all her newly acquired knowledge, the conversation in the drawing room moved on. With a jolt, her attention came back into focus when she heard the stranger say, 'You were never one to miss a trick with the ladies. Are you sure you wouldn't rather stay on here for the night and catch the morning flight? I can always get a lift back to London with Fairfax.' There was mischief in the tone of his voice and his meaning was unmistakable.

'Thanks, but no thanks,' was the emphatic reply. 'She's only a child and, for all my sins, no one ever accused me of being a cradle-snatcher.'

'Correct me if I'm wrong, but are you saying she's old enough to wed but not old enough to bed? I thought the legal age was sixteen for both,' his companion said, his humour evident.

'Indeed not, Hugh, my old friend, I'm saying no such thing,' Alexis laughed. 'But I am saying I might have difficulty rising to such a momentous occasion. You'll see what I mean when you meet her.'

'That bad, eh?' asked Hugh, chuckling over his friend's choice of words.

'That bad,' confirmed Alexis. 'And besides, the lovely Henrietta is threatening to join me in Vienna at the weekend.'

'You mean you're planning to take your lover on honeymoon instead of your child bride?'Hugh asked, mock incredulity in his voice. He did not wait for an answer, but went on to tease, 'That's novel behaviour indeed, even for you. And I thought, as a respectable married man, you would turn over a new leaf.'

'OK . . . enough wit,' Alexis laughed. 'Nice to know you find my demise so amusing.'

Katherine was by this time choked with indignation. That she should be the butt of their despicable humour was mortifying.

If this is how men talk between themselves, then I hate them . . . every one of them, and especially you, Alexis Drew, she fumed resentfully. Tears of humiliation filled her eyes and threatened to spill over onto her cheeks. How dare they joke at my expense, she seethed. I wouldn't have you, Alexis Drew, if you were the last man on earth. What arrogance! What conceit! Why, I'd like to . . . like to . . . But Katherine could not think of anything she would like to do to him that was quite terrible enough to fully avenge her injured pride.

One of these days she would find a way to make him sorry for the things he had said she promised herself, blinking back the tears. She was to hold that promise in her heart and nurture it for a long, long time.

The arresting sound of Caroline Remmick's stiletto heels beating a tattoo across the black and white marble floor put an end to the conversation.

Katherine waited only long enough to get her emotions

under control and then she, too, entered the drawing room. At a glance, she saw that all were immaculately dressed for the occasion. Feeling gauche, she now wished she had taken more trouble over her own appearance. With regret she remembered the occasion Aunt Caroline had looked in her wardrobe and, not finding an appropriate dress, had offered to buy one. Katherine knew from past experience that because of her size, she would not easily find something suitable in the ladies' department. Naturally, she had baulked at the embarrassment of having to resort to the children's section. Firmly, she had declined the offer. Her aunt had not insisted.

At her approach, the two men arose in polite greeting. Alexis introduced her to Hugh Bradford, who, it was explained, was to be a witness, along with Mr Fairfax. Although not exactly handsome, his features were regular and, she thought, quite pleasing. He was the shorter of the two men, and also the heavier as, unlike her cousin, he carried a little surplus weight. Even so, he was not fat.

The smile lines around his hazel eyes suggested he was a man who found much in life to laugh at. Bitterly, Katherine reminded herself that Hugh Bradford had just done quite a bit of that at her expense. A pity, she told herself. But for the remarks, she might have come to like him.

Although already aware of the lack of chemical reaction between Alexis and his young cousin, Hugh had not been prepared for just how mismatched they were. Already he regretted the rousting he had given his friend only minutes earlier.

Feeling compassion for the waif with the large tragic eyes, he hoped, for her sake, she was not harbouring romantic ambitions where Alexis was concerned. If so, she was going to get terribly hurt.

Both the Reverend Martins and Mr Fairfax arrived on time. After a brief exchange of pleasantries, it was agreed the nuptials should begin without delay.

The vicar was middle-aged and portly, with a round, ruddy face. An observer might be forgiven for thinking that the red nose and network of broken surface veins was due entirely to being out in all weathers visiting needy parishioners, but this was not so. The after-dinner tipples of port had much to answer for. His forgiving parishioners knew him to be a caring, intelligent man with a quick wit whose sermons were anything but dull.

The Reverend Martins had known the Drew family ever since his arrival in the community 11 years ago. They were not regular churchgoers but at least they put in an appearance at important festivals, came to all the charity fairs and were generous with their donations.

Whenever he'd had reason to call at Ravenswood, Anthony Drew had made him welcome and been most obliging with the port. In fact, he rather suspected the old gentleman had enjoyed the occasional drinking companion and the ensuing heated theological debates.

He had not had the pleasure of meeting Mrs Remmick before her visit to the vicarage three weeks previously. She had introduced herself and over a cup of tea given him a brief explanation of the will and its unusual conditions. The request that the wedding take place at Ravenswood and not on hallowed ground had come as a blessed relief. Although, privately, he thought it a very sorry situation, he had, nevertheless, agreed to read the marriage lines.

To suit the unusual circumstances, he had revised the service as much as possible. It occurred to him, however, that if he were to omit everything that was either irrelevant or inappropriate, not a lot would be left for him to say, and he did so like to hear the sound of his own voice.

If he were a superstitious man he would think that this storm was God's way of showing His disapproval. Fortunately, he was not a superstitious man, but he quickly crossed himself anyway.

*

The storm, continuing to rage unabated, moved ever closer to Ravenswood. The walls vibrated with each new clap of thunder, and occasionally the drawing-room lights flickered ominously, as if threatening to go out altogether.

As Katherine had earlier predicted, it was directly overhead during the service. The Reverend Martins had to pause several times to allow the noise to abate sufficiently for his voice to be heard.

As if caught up in a bad dream, Katherine went through the whole ceremony with the mechanical precision of a robot. Finally, with the gold band on her finger, the service came to an end.

'Now you may kiss the bride,' the vicar said.

At his side, Alexis felt the girl flinch at the inappropriate words. He was aware of her deep embarrassment: the confused, self-conscious way she continued to stare straight ahead. Someone should have warned the vicar to leave that bit out, he told himself, amused but careful not to show it.

Taking Katherine by the shoulders, he turned her towards him and then, gently but firmly, Alexis raised her chin so that he could brush her lips with his own. Looking down into the startled sapphire-blue eyes, he noted, and not for the first time, how expressive and sensitive they were.

If eyes are truly the mirror to one's soul, then you, little girl, must have a very beautiful soul, he reflected thoughtfully. These observations, however, were short-lived and very soon forgotten.

With the service over, the register signed and the certificate handed to the couple, the assembly quickly broke up.

Mr and Mrs Johnson, who had been present in the background, quietly left the room, but not before Katherine thought she glimpsed tears in Madge Johnson's eyes. The sheepish look cast at her exasperated mistress seemed to say: 'Sorry, but I always get emotional at weddings.'

The first to return was Mrs Johnson, with canapés and

finely cut sandwiches. Her husband followed closely behind, with crystal flutes of champagne on a silver tray.

'We didn't think a wedding cake necessary, under the circumstances,' the housekeeper said almost apologetically, in her soft rural accent. 'But Johnson thought it right to open a bottle of champagne to celebrate the occasion . . . Mr Drew would have expected it.'

With a sage nod, Reg Johnson accepted the credit inaccurately attributed to him. Whenever possible he left the talking to his wife, especially when he was in the role of Johnson the butler. With well practised, quiet dignity he went about his important duty.

This was hardly a happy occasion, but if anyone wondered what it was exactly they were being asked to celebrate, they refrained from asking. Just so long as no one suggests a toast to the happy couple, was a thought that passed through Katherine's mind.

At the first opportunity, she removed herself from Alexis' side. Pointedly turning her back on him and his friend, she went to talk to the vicar whom she had known most of her life and with whom she felt comfortable. Katherine was aware she was showing appalling bad manners, the reason for which none would understand. But she still seethed with resentment at the overheard conversation and did not care what anyone thought of her. Churlishly, she reminded herself that she already knew the opinions of two people in the room.

After a short while, the Reverend Martins and Mr Fairfax took their leave. For them it was a working day and both had appointments to keep. The other guests soon followed.

Katherine's farewell to Hugh Bradford was accomplished in a few bland words and, to Alexis, her manner was positively chilly. Although Hugh glanced at her askance, Alexis did not give her the satisfaction of appearing to notice anything amiss. On the contrary, he seemed not in the least perturbed by anything happening around him. His thoughts had, in fact, already moved on to other more important matters ahead. His absent-minded leave-taking reminded her of an adult who had no inclination to humour an ill-mannered child.

As Katherine watched them drive away, she noticed that the storm, which had taken so long to arrive, now no longer raged around them but was rapidly receding into the distance. It had left a vacuum in its wake, and that strange eerie yellow light that had so impressed her earlier still illuminated the rain-drenched landscape.

Katherine re-entered the house and, with quiet fascination, watched Johnson close and secure the heavy oak doors. She had seen him secure the house many times before but this time it seemed to her that his actions represented the shutting out of evil.

Turning away, her attention was next arrested by the loud, rhythmic ticking of the hall clock. Her gaze went to the mesmeric swinging of the heavy brass pendulum and then, travelling up, came to rest on the familiar white dial with its black hands and Roman numerals. With surprise she noted that, from the arrival of the first guest to the departure of the last, only 40 minutes had passed.

Our wedding ought to go into the *Guinness Book of Records* as the shortest ever, she thought, her humour bitter.

Slowly, with dignity, Katherine climbed the stairs. Too much had happened to her in too short a time, and nearly all of it had been bad. Now she felt an urgent need to put the unpleasantness behind her: to hasten back to Haldene Abbey to begin her two years in the sixth form.

On entering her bedroom, she removed the gold band Alexis had placed on her finger. Raising it to the light of the lamp, she slowly revolved it. Her luminous eyes held an unreadable expression. Then, with a lift of her proud chin, she tossed it carelessly into the open vanity case.

6

The sun had long since sunk below the horizon by the time the British Airways flight touched down on the runway of Vienna International Airport. A limousine was waiting to take Alexis to the luxurious Hotel Sacher Wien, in the heart of the city, where a prior booking had been made for four nights. By the time he had settled into his room, it was already too late for anything other than a nightcap in the hotel's Blue Bar.

The next morning, dressed casually and carrying his music scores in a zip-up leather folder, he walked across to the Vienna State Opera House opposite. At the magnificent main entrance, he came face to face with a poster of himself at the pianoforte. It was a dynamic black and white action shot of him in concert, wearing full formal evening wear, his dark features set in serious concentration, his thick hair slightly ruffled.

Alexis did not bother to read the words: they would say the usual things. His agents always did an excellent job on the advertising and press coverage before a concert, ensuring that, even before his arrival, his face and name were already familiar to the music lovers of the cities he visited.

Quickly, he studied the other posters and pictures. He had been guest soloist with the Wiener Philharmoniker once before, the conductor and some of the musicians were known to him.

On entering the auditorium, his ear was assailed by music. The orchestra, in rehearsal, was coming to the end of the Overture to *Die Fledermaus*, and so he went quietly and unobtrusively to a seat to listen while he waited. He was not left incognito for long. It was soon noticed that Alexis Drew had arrived and, to the conductor's chagrin, concentration among a couple of the younger female musicians broke down and the overture came to an untidy end.

Remembered for his charm and ready wit, for his professional dedication to his work, Alexis was both liked and respected by his fellow musicians. In him they recognised genius. It was rumoured he played the violin almost as well as he did the piano. Although none could claim to have heard him play this instrument, they were prepared to believe it – he did nothing by halves.

The orchestra had been practising together for days before Alexis' arrival and now they were ready to devote their time to him. Together, they worked steadily throughout the day. By late afternoon it was agreed everyone had earned a well-deserved break and need not return to the theatre until the following evening, when they would give the first of three performances.

Deciding to take a walk through the city, Alexis bypassed the Hotel Sacher. He had not gone far before he became aware that a member of the orchestra was following closely behind. He had recognised the pretty red-headed cellist from his last visit to Vienna, and had noted from the covert looks cast in his direction during rehearsals that she had lost much of her former shyness towards him.

The fact that he had forgotten her name, if he had ever known it, did not worry him. She would refresh his memory when she managed to catch up. Later, he was meeting the conductor and a few select guests for cocktails followed by dinner, but in the meantime he was not against feminine company, and so he slowed his pace to help her along.

'I think we are going in the same direction,' she told him in an accented voice made slightly breathless from the exertions of carrying a rather heavy and cumbersome instrument.

'So it would seem,' Alexis replied, a glint of amusement in his eyes, 'and since we are going in the same direction, whatever direction that may be, perhaps I had better carry that for you,' he offered, taking the burden from her.

'Oh, thank you. I'm Anita Hammen,' she introduced

herself, falling into step beside him. 'I already know your name, of course.' She smiled sweetly and provocatively up at him from under thick lashes. Not surprisingly, Alexis correctly predicted he was in for a most entertaining few days.

Each evening, with inspirational brilliance, he played to a packed house. After each performance, while the cellist waited for him in the wings, he honoured requests from the media for backstage interviews. The newspapers were full of glowing reports of outstanding performances adding to his growing worldwide renown.

His infidelity caused not the slightest qualms of conscience. His affair with Henrietta Maison was over, and his newly acquired obligations to Katherine extended no further than to her physical welfare and business interests. His career was on an upward spiral and his private life was still his own.

He was bringing back to England some very pleasant memories of Vienna, and as Alexis flew into Heathrow Airport, he noted with wry humour that not a hint remained of the stormy weather he had left behind him only a week earlier. The sun shone in the clear blue September sky and all was well with his world.

The luggage belonging to the first class passengers was the first to arrive on the turntable in the collection hall. Alexis had no trouble identifying his case and clearing customs. Retrieving his car from the long-term car park, he took the busy route to Henley.

An hour later, the Jaguar came to a standstill outside a sizeable cottage of outstanding character. Its mature and colourful gardens sloped down to the glistening waters of the River Thames. Alexis paused in the bright sunlight to savour the sounds and sights of home. Then, letting himself into the house, he put his case down in the hall and went in search of Jenny Simmons.

He found the petite, brunette secretary working over an

account book in the room they had set up as an office when he had first hired her two years previously.

'Welcome home, boss,' she greeted him warmly. Pushing the account book to one side, she said, 'Now you're here, that can wait until tomorrow.'

Swivelling round to face him, Jenny regarded her employer through critical hazel eyes. He looked a little tired, she decided. Concerts were debilitating things. The hours of preparation, the travelling and the tension always took their toll and, no doubt, Alexis had been burning the candle at both ends, as usual. Nothing wrong with him that a good night's sleep won't put right, she diagnosed.

'I'll get us some coffee and then . . .' – she looked at her watch – 'I've just got time to bring you up to date on a few things, if you're up to it.' She raised a quizzical brow.

He nodded. While she prepared the drinks, he flipped through a pile of mail and, at the same time, gave her an account of Vienna.

Jenny listened with intense interest to everything he said. She always did. She found him and the life he led quite fascinating. With every intention of becoming indispensable, she had quickly and efficiently learned to deal with the hundred and one things that make up the life of a celebrated virtuoso. Now, because of her fine management of his affairs, Alexis was free to devote his time to his music, to the hours of practice necessary before each engagement.

'The piano was tuned yesterday,' Jenny informed him, handing over a steaming mug, 'and Irvine wants to see you again . . . nothing pressing, but he wants your signature on another contract.' When Alexis raised questioning eyes, she said, 'Oh, nothing immediate. It's to do with next summer's South American tour. And while I remember, Hong Kong Arts Festival, end of February. They've put you in the Peninsula Hotel. OK?'

He remembered the splendid old colonial hotel from his last visit to Hong Kong: The huge foyer with rows of columns reaching up to high white and gold stucco ceilings, where, under the slowly revolving fans and among the pots of tall ferns, visitors to Hong Kong from all over the world came to take afternoon tea. The hotel was right opposite the Cultural Centre where he would be performing. Alexis nodded with satisfaction. 'Yes, fine,' he confirmed, pleased with the choice. 'Very convenient.'

He went through the incoming mail placed before him, noted the new entries in his diary, and signed a few waiting letters. After discussing several business propositions and social invitations, it was time for Jenny to conclude her work for the day.

'I've dug out the scores you wanted to go through for your next concerts. They're on the coffee table in the studio,' she called over her shoulder as she hurried off to collect her two young children from the local school.

Settling back in the padded swivel chair, Alexis laced his fingers together behind his head. Thoughtfully, he watched Jenny's departure from the window. At some time or other, he was going to have to put her in the picture with regard to Katherine Drew and the two properties. They would increase Jenny's workload to a certain extent. Not so much Ravenswood, as it was under the management of the capable John Coteman. But, since Coteman was now answerable to Alexis as well as the trustees, he was bound to phone from time to time and Jenny should know who he was. Then there was Katherine. He would have to enlist Jenny's help where she was concerned. After all, the girl was only 16 and, like any other 16-year-old, would need watching. He decided he would refer to her as his ward.

There would be school fees to take care of, plus bills and allowances. End of term reports had to be sent to someone. The headmistress of Haldene Abbey would have to be notified of the changed circumstances and she would want to know who to contact should problems arise. To her he would simply be known as Katherine's second cousin and next of kin. He was sure Mrs Johnson could be relied upon to notify him if she felt there was anything he needed to know. She already had his Henley telephone number and Jenny Simmons' name.

He was seeing Fairfax in the morning. By the end of the meeting he hoped to be in possession of the deeds and keys to Linnet House and to have all the information necessary for the task his great-uncle had entrusted to him. Anthony Drew's death had certainly given him much to think about, he told himself ruefully.

Alexis got to his feet and, stretching the tired muscles in his tall, lean body, strolled into the hall. Deciding the unpacking could wait a little longer, he bypassed the case and continued on through the lounge and into the studio extension beyond, where he clicked on the answerphone. While it whirred into life, spilling out the day's messages, Alexis drew back the sliding doors to the patio, admitting the warm summer breeze with its pot-pourri of summer scents. Arms folded across his chest, he leaned against the door frame and gazed out at the colourful garden, to the trees and river beyond.

The first few recorded messages were inconsequential; from people he did not know, asking him to give recitals or donate money to obscure charities.

Next, his mother's voice came on the line. 'It's me, darling. How did Vienna go? I don't know why I bother asking, I'm sure it all went well, it always does. I'm at Ravenswood learning the ropes,' she laughed. 'But only for the day. Mrs J. does an excellent job, she won't be needing me around much. Call me at home this evening about nine if you can.' The phone clicked and went on to the next message.

'Hi, Alexis! This is Julian. Just to let you know we're all congregating tonight at the Angel. Guess whose going to be there. Shelly . . . that gorgeous blonde. Remember her? Mind you, I don't know what I'm telling you for. If you turn up, I won't get a look-in!' His voice was good-natured. 'See you at eight-thirty?'

Alexis looked at his watch. He doubted he could stay awake that long. He smiled to himself. He would phone

Julian back; say he couldn't make it and that Shelly was all his, with his blessing.

The final message was from Henrietta Maison. She was clearly miffed. 'Why haven't you called?' she asked in a sulky tone. 'I can't sit around waiting all day so I'm going out with Jamie Evans. Give me a ring tomorrow.'

Alexis regarded the machine with disdain. 'Typical!' he said out loud. 'The concerts were a huge success. Thank you for asking, Henrietta.' He shrugged. Then, with the realisation that Jamie had saved him the trouble of having to return Henrietta's call, a hint of a sardonic smile crossed his handsome features.

He cast his mind back to the beginning of their six-month-long affair, to a time when she had been easy and interesting company. The traumas of a recent divorce had had a subduing effect, so that only later did her Jekyll and Hyde personality begin to show itself. By then, she and Alexis were already lovers. Here at least, they were compatible. They gave mutual pleasure, and were of equal experience and skill.

In those early days, Henrietta had repeatedly said she would never marry again. Since Alexis had no wish to change her mind on that score, he had been happy to believe in the sincerity of her words. It later transpired that Henrietta's disenchantment with marriage was mainly due to the inadequate size of the divorce settlement. Within a short space of time, she had philosophically recovered from the financial disappointment, and, with that recovery had come a change of heart regarding her marital aspirations.

As it happened, before Alexis could inform her that he was a lost cause, she had discovered it for herself, when she opened a file named 'Anthony Drew' and, uninvited, read its contents.

The workings of her mind were no mystery to Alexis. Knowing he was no longer available, or at least not for seven interminable years, Henrietta would already be casting around for a suitable successor to take his place – someone who would continue to open doors into affluent society. Only then would she willingly move on. With luck, Jamie Evans would prove to be just the right person to take his place.

A smile flickered across his face. Being married seems to have its advantages after all, he told himself.

Alexis turned his attention to more pressing matters. He was under contract to commence recording sessions with the London Symphony Orchestra in less than three weeks, followed, a couple of weeks later, by two concerts in Stockholm and another in Berlin. Such a gruelling schedule required hours of preparatory practice if he was to give his best, and he knew it was not in him to give less.

Going to the pile of music scores Jenny had placed on the coffee table, he flipped through the top few. Selecting one, he took it over to the piano and, propping it up in front of him began to play. But, for once, his heart was not in it, and he soon came to a halt.

His restless mind, refusing to be stilled, interfered with his concentration. An impatience to take possession of Linnet House was steadily growing within him, an impatience born of a burning desire to renew his acquaintance with the Steinway, the treasure for which he had paid so dear a price. Tomorrow, right after his meeting with Fairfax, he planned to go to Belgrave Square. He remembered that, before his departure to Vienna, Hugh had expressed an interest in visiting Linnet House. With this in mind he reached for the telephone and dialled Hugh Bradford's number.

Henrietta sat at her dressing table: her eyes focused on her image in the large oval mirror. A frown of discontent creased her brow. She had just returned home from what should have been an enjoyable and entertaining night out, but instead she had spent the entire evening thinking of one man while in the company of another.

'Damn you, Alexis Drew!' she said out loud. She did not seem able to get him out of her mind. The man was like a drug – the more she had of him, the more she wanted. What made this man so different from all the others in her life? she wondered.

He had deliberately discouraged her from flying out to be with him in Budapest and had made it clear he did not expect her to join him in Vienna either. She was also aware that he had returned to England early that afternoon but, so far, he had not called her. Now that she had simmered down, she regretted her impetuosity in leaving such a message on his answerphone but, even more, Henrietta regretted the tone she had used. It would not impress a man like him. Dismally, she wondered if he would phone her the next day. Hardly what one would call an eager and impatient lover, she told herself petulantly.

Several items of clothing lay discarded and scattered on the bedroom floor. That Henrietta had thrown them down so carelessly was a sign of her agitated state of mind. Running her fingers through her sleek golden curls, she raised her hair off her shoulders. Turning her head from left to right so that she could see her pale striking features from all angles, she critically surveyed her reflection through large, baby-blue eyes. Knowing herself to have the kind of looks that belied an innocence long gone, she allowed a little self-satisfied smile to play at the corners of her well-shaped mouth.

Rising from the stool, she stood back in order to see the whole of her reflected image. Releasing her hair, Henrietta ran the flat of her hands from her ample firm breasts down to her trim waist. There they came to a stop as, with a worried frown, she examined her hips. It was the one place she was prone to put on weight but, satisfied that they were proportionate to the rest of her body, her gaze travelled slowly on down the length of a long, shapely pair of legs. She liked what she saw: a good-looking woman in the prime of life.

'You were a lucky man, Alexis Drew,' she murmured,

reaching for the flimsy silk negligee. 'If only you had known it,' she added, a note of regret in her voice. As the folds of the gown fell softly around her, the smile hardened. 'Your loss will soon be another man's gain,' she promised herself.

Almost from the beginning, she had singled out Alexis to be husband number two. He was everything she wanted in a man: wealthy, handsome, caring, intelligent and successful. He had been her entrée into polite circles, into the glitzy glamour of a desirable world. His immense talent and stage presence were taking him rapidly to the top of his profession and she had fully intended to ride the crest of the wave along with him.

Henrietta had always relied heavily upon her good looks to get her what she wanted in life. She knew no surer, faster way to achieve her goals than to use her femininity to charm the opposite sex. Having had lovers before, during and after her three years of marriage to a man she thought of as a loser, she knew herself to be an experienced and skilful lover.

The way to a man's heart is through his stomach, went the saying; but she knew better. She had enjoyed more success feeding men's inflated egos, and the best place for that was in the bedroom.

Uncomplicated sex was all Henrietta had originally required out of her affair with Alexis. She had not intended to get emotionally involved with anyone so soon after her divorce but somehow it had happened. Being in love had made her vulnerable. Like a bad habit, it had clouded her judgement and been the cause of irrational behaviour. It was not she who had been in control of their affair, but Alexis, and she had not liked it. Having at last met her match, it was hardly surprising that Henrietta should have found him such an attractive challenge.

For some time, even before the discovery of his impending marriage, she had not felt confident about their relationship. It had obviously not been going anywhere. But then, she had to admit Alexis had never pretended that it was. Even so, Henrietta had allowed herself to hope.

Over the last few weeks he had not phoned her unless in answer to one of her calls, and she suspected that he did so only out of a sense of obligation. There was no doubt that Alexis had cooled towards her and it was only through her continual perseverance that they continued to see each other at all.

Good sex had always played an important part in their relationship. Recently, that was all they seemed to have left. Now that he was married, even that was over between them. Finding another man to fill the role of lover would not be difficult, but finding one as desirable and accomplished as Alexis . . . now that would be a different matter altogether. Despondently, she sighed.

7

The offices of Fairfax & Partners were situated in a remarkable row of premises just off Chancery Lane. The ancient beamed building, leaning precariously towards the narrow street, seemed to groan with the burden of old age. Within its gnarled wood portals, however, a professional decorator had taken a hand in blending the old with the new. The white-painted, uneven wattle and daub walls and the stained warped beams had been left intact and much of the sturdy furniture looked as if it had begun its life within the confines of these musty, impressive premises. Large floor-standing pot plants were a recent innovation in the reception area, their shiny green leaves healthy and fresh. Quality pictures hung on the walls, and there was both visual and audio evidence of modern office equipment in some of the rooms. Fitted carpets had been laid over the dipped and uneven wooden floor and, as Alexis followed Mr Fairfax to his office, this had an unsettling effect on his senses, so that he felt for all the world as if he was walking on the boards of a rolling ship.

The solicitor, in his usual orderly manner, had everything ready and waiting to be signed and sealed. Before Alexis had agreed to the terms under which he was to receive Linnet House, he had taken the precaution of refreshing his memory by viewing once more the exterior of the property. It was still much as he remembered and just one look had been enough to impress upon him how much he wanted to be its new owner.

'The premises are in good repair,' Mr Fairfax assured him. 'I don't think you'll find much wrong inside or out and, if you've had a chance to look through the inventory, you'll have seen how reasonably it's furnished,' he said with characteristic understatement.

Alexis had studied the list thoroughly, looking anxiously for the Steinway, and not until he was satisfied that it was still on the premises had he given his attention to the handsome antiques he vaguely remembered from his youth. He had not been through the solid doors of Linnet House since the death of his father, but the layout of the rooms and their opulent splendour had left a lasting impression upon his mind.

Whilst the solicitor flipped through files for relevant information, Alexis made notes of all he thought necessary to ensure the continued successful management of Ravenswood and its estate.

'John Coteman has been employed as comptroller for quite some considerable time,' Mr Fairfax told him, looking over his spectacles. 'In his latter years, Mr Drew left the running of things very much up to him. A capable administrator . . . worth his weight in gold.'

Alexis was pleased to hear it. He was quite busy enough with his own affairs to want to get too heavily involved in anyone else's but since, theoretically, Mr Coteman answered to him, Alexis felt the need to be well informed.

The solicitor went on to familiarise Alexis with the lucrative financial investments left by his great-uncle. Then, having acquired Alexis' signature on various documents, he handed over the keys to Linnet House, together with the deeds. With the formalities of the day over, Alexis accepted the solicitor's invitation to lunch in a nearby restaurant, where, over a light meal and a bottle of very palatable red wine, they progressed to first-name terms. It was in this congenial and relaxed atmosphere that Neil Fairfax added what little he knew to Alexis' already considerable knowledge of the history of Linnet House.

By the time they parted company, their respect for each other had grown. Any reservations Neil Fairfax may have felt concerning the will of his late client had been laid to rest. As he told his partner later in the day, 'The old fellow always was a good judge of character. He knew what he was about all right.'

With the deeds and keys now safely in his possession, Alexis made his way across London to Belgrave Square, where he found Hugh already waiting on the grey stone steps of the newly acquired house. Together they toured every room, from the attic to the ground floor, deliberately leaving to the last, heightening the expectation, the splendid drawing room, where Alexis' eyes immediately alighted on the piano.

Hugh followed the direction of his friend's gaze. 'Ah . . . the famous Steinway, I presume?' he said, in his best Watson to Sherlock tones.

'Yes, Hugh . . . the Steinway,' Alexis murmured, letting his fingers trail lovingly, almost caressingly, along the cool, polished wood. 'Exactly as I remember it.' Raising the lid, he set the prop in place so that, with shining, probing eyes, he could inspect the interior. Seemingly satisfied, he moved on round to raise the fall. Briefly, he paused to gaze nostalgically at the keyboard and then, concentrating on the sound, he ran expert fingers up and down the keys, rending the air with several variations of scales and arpeggios.

'Nothing that a little tuning won't put right.' He spoke softly, a smile on his lips.

Not having a trained ear, Hugh was deaf to the irregularities that were so obvious to Alexis. 'Very nice,' he muttered with genuine admiration, as much for the Steinway's elegant lines as for the sonority of its tone.

Closing the piano and leaving it as he had found it, Alexis turned. His gaze swept the room as if only just becoming aware that it held other treasures. All was as Anthony Drew had left it after his last visit, and Alexis felt the man's presence all around him. The armchair where he had habitually sat was slightly indented by his weight to the shape of his body. The drinks cabinet was well stocked, and the crystal decanters on the silver tray were topped up as if in readiness for the old gentleman's next unexpected visit. Much to the credit of the part-time housekeeper, the room had been dusted and aired and still had a lived-in feel about it.

While pouring a couple of drinks, Alexis wondered if Katherine had expected to inherit both houses. He felt no qualms about accepting the inheritance, after all, Frederick Drew had been as much his great-grandfather, and it was he who had purchased the house. Alexis admitted to himself that he had not actually detected any resentment on that score. Keeping Ravenswood had so obviously been Katherine's main concern. He judged they had both received their heart's desire.

'A very impressive little pad,' remarked Hugh, breaking in on his thoughts. 'You're a lucky fellow. I wish I had a rich relative to leave me half as much.' He was feeling somewhat overawed at the size and splendour of the rooms, and for once, was lost for adequate words.

Taking the proffered glass from Alexis, and leaving Anthony Drew's armchair for its new master, he went to sit in its twin on the other side of the white marble fireplace. 'Now you've got it, what are you going to do with it?' he quizzed.

'Good question. I've been asking myself the same thing – and so has my family,' Alexis added lightly. 'They seem to have taken to the idea of a London town house. My mother's already offered to find me a full complement of staff, to continue the tradition of keeping the house in readiness for visitors, no doubt,' he laughed. 'I've managed to convince her that the one I've inherited is more than adequate for my needs and the family's occasional stopovers. It's not as if any of us intend to take up full time residence here. Not yet, anyway.' He sipped his drink appreciatively, mentally congratulating his late relative on his good taste in whisky.

'I know it has a burglar alarm system, but even so, your mother's suggestion might not be such a bad idea,' Hugh said. 'I'm not sure I'd want to leave a house like this empty for too long.' His eyes swept meaningfully around the valuable collector's items.

'Actually, I don't intend to,' Alexis assured him. 'I mean to divide my time fairly equally between here and Henley, and that way I can keep Jenny on. She'd be hard to replace.' Thoughtfully, he continued, 'But I do seem to be spending more and more time in London, so this "little pad" as you called it, should come in very handy. I won't have to drive backwards and forwards to Henley at all hours of the night and day.'

'Yes, I can see it's going to have its advantages, especially last thing at night, when it comes to "your place or mine?"' his friend grinned knowingly.

'*Au contraire*,' Alexis contradicted. 'Henley has a definite advantage. The distance means I can say, "Your place not mine", and that saves waking up in the morning to the startling realisation that you've acquired a house guest.'

'True,' Hugh laughed in agreement. 'Never thought of that.' With an expansive wave of the hand, he inquired: 'Does Henrietta know about all this?'

'She knows.' A wicked glint of humour appeared in Alexis' eyes and a smile curved his lips. 'It would seem that her love for me is not exactly of an enduring nature. I'm not worth waiting seven years for.'

'Well, what a surprise,' Hugh chuckled.

'Drink up, Hugh,' Alexis encouraged. 'I want to go out on the town to celebrate.'

'And what would you like to celebrate? Farewell to Henrietta or hello to Katherine?' asked Hugh, enjoying himself immensely. 'Or perhaps we should celebrate your acquisition of Linnet House.'

'None of those things,' Alexis said, placing his empty glass on the table and rising. 'Let's celebrate . . . the Steinway.'

8

Like the other sixth-form students at Haldene Abbey, Samantha Scott was in the habit of pinning newspaper and magazine cuttings of the opposite sex on her study wall, together with photographs of family and friends.

This morning, before going off to the lecture hall, Samantha took down an old cutting to make room for a new one. Stepping back, she paused to admire its handsome subject through lively, appreciative green eyes.

'Eat your hearts out, girls, when you see this one,' she muttered to herself. An attractive, if somewhat smug smile spread across her regular features.

Becoming aware of the shortage of time, she hastily, in obedience to school rules, clipped her sleek blonde hair back at the nape of her neck and, gathering up her books, made for the door. There, she turned and blew a kiss to her latest heart-throb before rushing off.

At the beginning of the autumn term, on returning to boarding school, Katherine had looked for the rooming list for Caldwell House, the sixth-form building. It informed her she was to share a bedroom and study with Samantha Scott; a prospect she did not find appealing.

The girls had known each other since their enrolment at the school at the tender ages of 11, but had always kept to their own circle of friends. Apart from a love of art, they seemed to have little else in common.

Katherine, having come through her formative years mostly in the company of adults, had acquired mature common sense quite missing in Samantha. However, the tragic losses in her life had undermined both Katherine's security and self-esteem, taking their toll on her personality. Samantha, on the other hand, came from a secure background, had physically developed early, and was a carefree, fun-loving extrovert.

Since the two girls were so diverse in temperament and looks, it was a foregone conclusion that they were going to influence each other dramatically, one way or another. The housemistress responsible for putting them together held her breath and awaited the outcome.

As expected, both girls had initially eyed each other with misgivings and, for the first month or so, held each other in abeyance. An understanding and a compromise had first to be reached before a friendship could develop. They were not long in coming.

Katherine was first through the study door. Coming face to face with the new picture, she stopped dead in her tracks. Her books fell with a thud to the floor as she gaped hypnotically at the handsome, familiar features.

It didn't take a genius to realise that something was wrong. 'What's the matter?' asked Samantha, her penetrating gaze shifting from her friend's stricken face to the picture.

Flustered, Katherine quickly stooped to retrieve her scattered property. 'Nothing's the matter, I just dropped my books,' she muttered.

'So I see,' Samantha commented dryly, 'but as for there being nothing the matter, I don't believe a word of it.' Her gaze lingered on Katherine's pale face a moment longer, then, turning away, she put the kettle on and began to prepare a couple of mugs. 'I'm going to make some tea and then you can tell me all about it,'

With shaking hands, Katherine piled the books on her desk. 'There's nothing to tell,' she replied, with an unconvincing attempt at nonchalance.

'Of course there's something to tell. Any fool can see that,' Samantha contradicted. A thought occurred to her.

Leaving the mugs, she went to rummage in a drawer for the magazine from which she had taken the picture. Finding it, she placed the magazine on one of the desks and opened it at the mutilated page. After reading the article, she looked thoughtfully at Katherine, and said, 'Now there's a thing. Isn't that an extraordinary coincidence? His name happens to be Drew, just like yours. Alexis Drew. A concert pianist.' Samantha ran an inquisitive eye over the picture. 'Beautiful artistic hands,' she murmured appreciatively and then, looking at Katherine's hands, added, 'not unlike yours really. A family trait?' she asked. Getting no response, she continued, 'He has the same family name as you. Is he related?'

Continuing to fuss over the books, eyes averted, Katherine again did not answer. She was remembering snippets of conversation overheard between Alexis and his friend; words that had lost none of their power to wound.

'Well, I know you don't have any brothers, so what is he? A cousin?' Samantha persevered.

Katherine knew there would be no let-up until she had given an adequate answer. Angered by memories, feeling cornered, she answered irritably, 'A second cousin, if you must know. Now, will you let it go?'

Here was intrigue indeed. Samantha could not possibly let it go. She commented, 'To cause such a response, he must be either a much loved second cousin or a much hated one.' She waited.

Katherine scowled. 'He's neither, I . . . I hardly know him,' she muttered, still keeping her eyes lowered.

Mystified, it was now Samantha's turn to frown. 'He's a second cousin, you hardly know him, and yet he causes you to drop your books and stutter like a two year old. Why?'

'Well actually, he's my guardian . . . and we don't get on together,' Katherine snapped, hoping this simplified explanation would put an end to the subject. 'Not that it's any of your business,' she added.

'Well, lucky you!' Samantha murmured under her breath, not at all daunted by Katherine's tone. With a surge of optimism, she wondered if there was any likelihood of meeting this incredibly handsome relative on Open Day. She placed one of the steaming mugs in Katherine's hands and with indomitable curiosity ordered, 'Here, drink this and tell me all about it.'

Katherine stubbornly refused.

Samantha tried a different approach. 'All this term, there's been something wrong with you,' she accused, 'and I'm not the only one to notice, so there's no use denying it. Preoccupied . . . jumpy . . . not a lot of fun to be with.' She paused and then said softly, with encouraging sincerity, 'I'd like to help, Katherine . . . really I would. But I can't help unless you tell me what's wrong.'

Katherine hesitated. She was sorely in need of a confidante; she had thought so, and wished for one, since the reading of her grandfather's will. Her gaze turned to the cutting of Alexis and before she could change her mind, responded in a whisper, 'I'm . . . married to him.'

She did not expect to be believed and was, therefore, not surprised to hear Samantha say, 'You can't be.'

'I knew you wouldn't believe me,' Katherine muttered with a shrug, already regretting her impetuosity.

There was silence, while Samantha stared at her. Finally, breaking eye contact, she raised incredulous eyes to the picture of the celebrated concert pianist.

'I did hear you right? You did say you were married to him?' she asked, sure there must be some mistake.

Katherine nodded.

Samantha was clearly stunned. How could plain, dull Katherine Drew possibly be married to a man of this calibre, she was asking herself, and at only 16? If it was true, then she had stolen a march on them all. Who out of their friends was going to believe it?

'But you said you hardly know him . . . how can you be married to him if you hardly know him?' she questioned. 'Tell me.'

Katherine did, to the last detail, leaving nothing out.

When she had finished, her friend said with a dreamy

sigh, and to Katherine's utter astonishment, 'That's the most romantic story I've ever heard. Why has nothing like that ever happened to me?'

From there on, life for Katherine began to improve. She had a confidante, and one who viewed the world very differently from herself. Seeing her unusual situation through a second pair of eyes altered her perspective on life.

Neither she nor Samantha had heard of there ever having been a married student at the school and were, therefore, in no doubt that if the truth were known, Katherine would be asked to leave. They saw no reason to jeopardise her future by making her affairs public and agreed to remain silent on the subject.

However, Samantha had no intention of allowing Katherine to wallow in self-pity. To that end, making no secret of the fact that she found Alexis Drew devastatingly attractive, she insisted his picture stay on the wall. And whenever she came across other pictures and articles, whether Katherine liked it or not, she brought them to her notice and discussed them quite openly and naturally.

With the latest cutting in hand, careful not to spoil the outline of Alexis, Samantha snipped his beautiful, radiant partner out of the picture. Crumpling the unwanted paper into a ball, she tossed the reminder of his romantic life into the waste-paper basket. 'I think I'll marry him myself when he's free,' she mused, dreamily.

'You're welcome to him,' was the flippant retort, 'but don't you think he's a bit too old for you?'

'Too old? You must be kidding – he's only twenty-four,' Samantha exclaimed. 'Why settle for the boys when you can have a man?'

'What use is a man whose only interest is a Steinway piano?' Katherine demanded petulantly.

'So, he married you for a Steinway,' Samantha giggled. 'At least that's original. If you were in Arabia, you'd probably have been married for a flea-bitten, mangy old camel. A Steinway's a definite improvement . . . got more class.'

'Thanks, Sam,' Katherine said archly, a quirk of a smile on her lips, 'that's reassuring to know. Now I feel a whole heap better!'

Katherine was not always quite so easily mollified, however, and there were times when she seemed to take pleasure in wallowing in grievances.

Samantha was not unsympathetic, but as far as she could see, everyone had got what they wanted, even if it had all come about in a rather unorthodox manner.

'Just so long as he doesn't ask for a divorce too soon – or, for that matter, refuse the divorce when the time comes,' she told her friend, 'I can see no reason to fuss.'

Samantha felt her friend had the wrong approach to life, took everything far too seriously. It was time she lightened up. With enthusiasm and her usual boundless energy, Samantha set about the task of reforming Katherine.

The days when they had been required to wear the smart red and charcoal-grey school uniform were over. Sixth-form students were permitted to wear what was referred to as 'mufti': smart casual clothes of their own choosing, with the school blazer. Although Katherine was interested in fashion, she did not extend that interest to her own wardrobe. On their weekend walks into one or other of the villages, she had been quite happy to throw her school cloak over her shoulders, but now Samantha would have none of it.

'That looked very becoming on you last year,' said she, eyeing her friend critically, 'but this year you've outgrown it both in stature and seniority. Hasn't anyone told you that we sixth formers don't have to wear school uniform any more? Give it to one of the younger students.'

Seeing Katherine hesitate, she quickly warned, 'I'm not walking down the road with you if you wear that.'

‘OK. If it means that much to you,’ Katherine sighed, tossing the cloak aside in favour of the blazer.

Discreetly, Samantha began to influence what clothes Katherine purchased in the village shops and weekend market. She could do nothing about her friend’s height and shape, or rather, continued lack of either, but she could make sure she wore nothing to highlight her disadvantages.

No longer allowed to sit quietly in the background, Katherine once more joined in with the activities and debates of their friends. Steadily gaining in confidence, her latent personality began to develop, bringing her unexpected popularity.

Attending heavily supervised mixed socials was, however, one activity Katherine refused to take part in. Whether at Haldene, or at one of the nearby boys’ colleges, no amount of coaxing would induce her to change her mind. It was not that she was afraid to dance. She had learned by emulating the other girls and was a very good dancer. It was just that she knew she was not attractive to the opposite sex and had no desire to spend the evening sitting with the wallflowers, waiting to be asked.

On such occasions as these, Katherine either slipped away through the cloistered archways to walk in the grounds beyond, or took refuge in the dark corner of her favourite pew in the silent old abbey.

Influence was not all one-sided. Katherine’s gentler, calmer nature had a restraining effect on the excitable Samantha, whose impulsive tendencies invited trouble. Katherine knew where to draw the line and, with quiet strength, nearly always succeeded in doing so, for them both.

The housemistress responsible for putting the two girls together noted with satisfaction that, while Katherine now occasionally allowed herself to be led astray, Samantha was not nearly so troublesome. The influence the girls were having on each other created the healthy balance she had hoped for.

*

At the end of the first term in Caldwell House, Katherine was faced with the depressing prospect of Christmas at Ravenswood, without the presence of her grandfather. His death and all that had occurred after it were still too fresh in her mind.

Samantha, knowing Katherine's reluctance to return to the scene of so much unhappiness, and naturally curious to see the old manor house of which she had heard so much, sought and received the consent of her parents to accompany her friend to Ravenswood. There, with Samantha much awed by the attentions of the staff and the splendour of Katherine's home, they spent the first week of the holidays together.

On Christmas Eve, Reg Johnson drove them to Surrey, where they enjoyed the remainder of the festive season with Samantha's parents and her older brother James.

This happy solution set the precedent for all the other holidays that followed.

On such visits to Ravenswood, the staff offered snippets of information regarding Alexis and his mother. But, to Katherine's relief and Samantha's chagrin, they had either just been or were expected at some future date. Consequently, although Samantha was keen to meet these relatives of Katherine, and more particularly Alexis, the opportunity never arose and she had to be content with second-hand accounts.

The romantically inclined Ellie did not need much encouragement to talk on the subject of Mr Drew but, unfortunately, her knowledge of him was more limited than she would have liked since, during his infrequent visits, he spent most of his time with Mr Coteman.

Occasionally, Caroline telephoned Katherine to inquire after her well-being. And, whilst she never visited when she knew Katherine had company, she did appear briefly during some of her weekend exeats – usually around teatime – and was careful never to outstay her welcome. Both she and Alexis were true to their promise not to infringe on Katherine's privacy.

The last two years at the Abbey flew by. They were happy times for Katherine. In her final year, after 18 long tedious months, the disfiguring braces were eventually removed to reveal perfectly straight teeth, the envy of all those who had needed but declined the services of the orthodontist.

When her helpful friend, the amateur hairdresser, suggested she try to remedy the earlier disaster she had made of cutting Katherine's hair, Katherine tactfully declined the offer. Professional services were sought but not until her hair had become quite long again.

When all her friends had long since stopped growing, it was noticed that Katherine had at last achieved an average height and was slowly but surely beginning to fill out in the right places. With the approach of advanced level examinations, however, no one had much time to marvel over this late phenomenon. The pressures of work were such that even Samantha had to put aside her busy social life.

Towards the end, they were all working at fever pitch, showing suicidal tendencies and voicing death wishes, in the theatrical tones that only sixth-form females seem able to accomplish. The exam dates came and went, and so did the stress. Miraculously, all psychological tension ceased in a remarkably short space of time and was replaced by a festive mood while desks, lockers and rooms were emptied and trunks packed.

Cars of all makes, colours and sizes arrived, filling car parks to capacity, overflowing into drive-ways, and onto the edge of the playing field and parkland.

Addresses and telephone numbers were exchanged and tearful farewells said with affectionate hugs until, eventually, one by one, the loaded cars departed, removing the girls and their trunks, each to their own destination. Most would be returning at the beginning of the next term, but for Katherine and her sixth-form friends their days at Haldene Abbey had come to an end.

9

The Bentley sped along the busy highway, steadily increasing the distance between Katherine and Haldene Abbey. She had left the nest many times before, but this was different – there was no going back, the door had closed behind her.

A sense of bereavement stayed with her for a while, but slowly, with the passing of miles and time, her melancholy lifted and melted away. Now, as she gazed through the car window, it was as if she were being reborn into a dazzling new world where everything was possible and she was on the verge of something new and wonderful.

The brightness of the sun's rays intensified the vivid June colours of the countryside. Katherine lowered the window, letting in the warm afternoon air to blow across her face and whip her long heavy chestnut curls back off her brow and shoulders. With closed eyes, she savoured the mixed perfumes of the passing hedgerows, fields and country gardens. By the time Johnson turned the Bentley in through the gates of Ravenswood, her spirits were soaring high.

The next few days passed quietly. It was a settling-in time for the young mistress of the manor. With Ellie's help, she unpacked her trunk and stowed it away in one of the attic rooms.

Roaming through the house, Katherine found simple pleasures in touching much loved objects, listening to familiar sounds, like the faint clatter of pots and pans coming from the vicinity of the kitchen and Ellie in a distant room singing off-key above the noise of the vacuum cleaner.

Initially, she avoided the drawing room. It brought back too many disturbing memories; ones best forgotten. But, with time, Katherine found she could again pass through its door with no more than a moment's distress.

When the midsummer weather permitted, Katherine took her meals on the patio, after which, she would draw whatever took her fancy. The pages of her sketchpad filled rapidly with such things as Ned under an old cloth cap, pushing a wheelbarrow through the vegetable patch, and Mr Johnson in work clothes, polishing imaginary marks off the already spotless Bentley. Then there was the housekeeper's lazy, unsociable tabby cat lying on the warm paving, eyes closed, with chin and fluffy tummy turned up to catch the heat of the sun.

When the occasional summer shower kept her indoors, she played her grandfather's classical music or browsed through the books in the library. Sometimes she was drawn to the kitchen by appetising smells and would either help Mrs Johnson and Ellie with whatever they were about, or just sit and drink tea while catching up on the local gossip.

On one such occasion, when sitting at the kitchen table leisurely shelling peas with Ellie, the older girl said to her, 'After all the 'ard work of those exams, you won't know what t' do with yourself any more.'

'Oh, I've got a few things planned, Ellie,' Katherine smiled. Following Ellie's example, waiting until the housekeeper had turned her back, she popped a few more peas into her mouth. 'I've arranged to have driving lessons, for a start.'

'Driving lessons!' the housekeeper said in a startled voice. The clatter of dishes at the kitchen sink came to an abrupt halt as she turned to stare at Katherine, a look of incredulous surprise on her face. 'And what do you want with driving lessons when you've got Johnson to chauffeur you around?' she asked, wiping wet hands on her apron. 'Anyway, that big Bentley's no car for a young lady like you to be driving around the countryside.'

'No, Mrs Johnson. I wasn't thinking of driving the Bentley,' Katherine corrected, laughing at such an incongruous idea. 'I thought I'd phone Mr Fairfax and ask him if he could arrange for me to have a car of my own. Something smaller and a lot more practical.'

'What will you do with the Bentley then?' asked Mrs Johnson suspiciously. Knowing the car to be her husband's pride and joy, she was apprehensive for him.

'Nothing at all. What *should* I do with the Bentley? It still has its uses, and in any case how would Johnson get around without it?' Katherine asked soothingly.

The housekeeper was visibly relieved. Now her attention was free to turn to other matters. Her eyes went to the heap of opened pods lying on the table. As she mentally compared them with the diminutive quantity of peas in the pan, her eyebrows rose. She picked up the saucepan and, tipping it slightly, looked from its meagre contents to each of the grinning girls in turn. 'Just enough for Reg and me, I see. But then, you two won't mind will you, since you've already had your supper!'

In the afternoon, Katherine made her telephone call to Neil Fairfax. He did not sound at all surprised by her request. In fact, he seemed to think it quite reasonable that she should want the independence a car would bring.

'Have you got Mr Drew's telephone number?' he asked.

'Yes,' came Katherine's guarded reply.

'Give him a ring, and ask him. Let him know exactly what you have in mind. I'm sure he'll agree to it.'

'Agree!' she exclaimed, open rebellion in her tone of voice. 'Why does he have to agree?'

'If your grandfather was alive, you would ask him,' he pointed out, not unreasonably.

'That's different,' Katherine shot back, her resentment turning into anger. It hurt her pride to have to ask Alexis Drew for anything.

'Not really, my dear. Just think of Mr Drew as standing in for him.'

There was silence while Katherine mulled over his words. After a moment, in a resolute voice, she said, 'I'll leave the matter in your hands, Mr Fairfax. You discuss it with him.' Before he could object, she hurried on, 'You said to tell him what I had in mind. Well, I'd like something smallish and reliable, red or white, and I'd like it in time for my eighteenth birthday which is on the twenty-eighth of July.' After a moment's pause she said, tongue in cheek, 'Mercedes Sports would just about fit the bill, and naturally, I'd like it to be new but, since beggars can't be choosers, I'll have to accept what I'm given.' She ended the sentence on a hint of bitter sarcasm and then, changing her tone, said sweetly, 'I appreciate your help, Mr Fairfax.'

Before he could reply, the line went dead and he was left gazing at the handset. The message is clear, he reflected thoughtfully: I'm no longer a child, so handle with care. With an indulgent smile, he returned the handset to its cradle.

Much to her annoyance, Mr Fairfax failed to phone back. Although, several times, she came close to calling the solicitor to ask the outcome of his conversation with Alexis, pride prevented her from actually doing so. She was damned if she was going to ask him again for a car. If necessary, she would save from her allowance until she could afford to buy for herself a little second-hand runabout.

Regardless of the eventual outcome, Katherine took driving lessons, passing the test at the first attempt.

The twentieth-eighth arrived, along with several cards, which the housekeeper placed on the breakfast table with four parcels of various shapes and sizes.

While Mrs Johnson and Ellie kept her company, she dealt first with the cards. Mr and Mrs Fairfax had remembered her birthday, so had the vicar, and there were several from school friends. After reading each aloud, she handed them to Ellie, who took them over to display on the sideboard. The last one to be opened was from the Remmicks. She read the affectionate message and noted from the handwriting that it had been written by Aunt Caroline, who had signed it from all the members of her family, except Alexis.

She focused briefly on the name of Aunt Caroline's daughter from her second marriage. She had been told that Jane was in her second year at St Andrews University in Scotland. Katherine wondered what she was like and if they would ever meet.

Next, Katherine turned her attention to the parcels. She recognised the handwriting on all but one, and this she put aside to open last. There was a compact that held a selection of eyeshadows from Ellie and a pot of African violets from Ned. The Johnsons had given her a box of Rowley watercolour paints and, from Samantha, there was an exquisite pair of silver filigree earrings.

The fourth present came inside a brown padded envelope. Now, drawing it towards her, she paused to study the distinctive handwriting. From the bold style, she guessed, it had been written by a man.

'Don't keep us in suspense,' Ellie begged. 'We've been trying to guess who that one's from ever since it arrived.'

Katherine too was mystified. Without further delay, she opened the packet and removed a box, beautifully gift-wrapped in purple and gold diagonal-striped paper and tied round with gold ribbon. Threaded onto the ribbon was a small gold card – inside was a message in the same artistic hand: *Best Wishes on your 18th Birthday, Alexis.*

'It seems a shame to spoil such beautiful wrapping,' Ellie sighed sadly, but was nonetheless impatient to discover its contents.

Katherine remembered that Alexis had not sent her a present for her seventeenth birthday and wondered why he should do so now. Perhaps he had not known the date of her birthday the previous year, whereas Mr Fairfax would have brought it to his attention recently, when passing on her message about the car. On the other hand, maybe he regarded 18 as a milestone and therefore a birthday to be remembered.

These thoughts ran quickly through her mind and were

followed by another, less charitable one. More likely, this is the consolation present for the car he is not going to let me have, she told herself peevishly.

Katherine removed the wrapping to disclose a box containing a bottle of Miss Dior perfume. The exquisite bottle held an essence fragrant and subtle which exactly suited her skin. With glowing eyes, she held up her wrist to Mrs Johnson and Ellie. The former gave it an unceremonious sniff before pronouncing her verdict: 'A very nice scent, dear.'

Ellie, however, resurrecting her infatuation for Katherine's wealthy and handsome cousin, went into starry-eyed raptures and said she wished someone would send her such a romantic present. 'Even better than chocolates and flowers,' she declared dreamily. 'Lasts longer too.' To herself, she added, Costs more an' all!

By mid-afternoon Katherine had given up all hope of hearing anything from Mr Fairfax with regard to a car. Grudgingly, she decided to dismiss the whole thing from her mind, at least for the time being. She promised herself, however, that as she was not yet ready to sacrifice so large a portion of her allowance for so expensive a purchase, the next time she spoke to him she would be a lot more assertive.

At about four the housekeeper came to the drawing room to inform Katherine there was a man at the door, asking for her by name.

'Ms Katherine Drew?' asked the man. On seeing her nod, he thrust out a clipboard and said, 'Sign here, please.'

'What am I signing for?' Katherine wanted to know. She assumed he must have a registered parcel to deliver but could see no evidence of it.

Noting her mystified expression, he smiled sheepishly and said, 'Sorry, miss. I thought you was expecting the delivery.' He stepped back so she could see beyond him and into the drive.

Katherine gasped, for there was a white Mercedes sports

car neatly parked and the man was holding out a set of keys as if he was giving them to her. 'For me?' she asked, hesitantly.

'If your name's Katherine Drew, and this is Ravenswood,' he stated with a grin. 'Since it ain't Christmas, it's my guess it's your birthday, Miss.'

'It is,' she managed to acknowledge; her eyes still focused on the car.

As if in a dream, Katherine walked down the steps and into the drive, taking the keys from the man as she passed. This could not be true. She had not expected a Mercedes: not really. Mr Fairfax must have taken her request literally, or had he repeated their conversation word for word to Alexis Drew, and had it been Alexis who had taken them literally?

Who cares? she thought. This is the car of my dreams and I only hope I don't wake up to discover that a dream is all this is.

All of a sudden, the car was surrounded by people. Reg Johnson was the first to materialise. Garden shears in hand, he popped out from behind a hedge on the west side of the building. Mrs Johnson and Ellie came out of the house and down the steps, and even old Ned came doddering out of nowhere, dislodging his cloth cap from the centre of his head and causing it to bob up and down as he scratched his balding pate in wonderment. 'Well, I never did,' he kept muttering.

'It's fully taxed and insured for a year, Miss,' the delivery-man told her. 'Now, if I can just have your signature here.' Ten minutes later, with the clipboard and documents safely stowed in a canvas bag and the work plates tucked under his arm, the man asked Reg for directions to the nearest station or main road.

'The station's not far. I'll take you,' Katherine volunteered, 'and then you can check me out on the controls and some of these buttons and dials,' she added hopefully.

*

From the station, feeling her new-found freedom and independence, Katherine continued on. She put her foot down on the accelerator. With the surge of power, she discovered the pleasure and exhilaration of being behind the wheel of a fast car. Her recent resentments of Alexis Drew and Neil Fairfax melted away, her hurt pride temporarily forgotten.

It was sometime later that she reluctantly turned for home. The Johnsons would be worried if she was gone too long and, fearing the worst, would get the Bentley out to come looking for her. As it was, Johnson stood in the driveway, watching for her return.

When she came to a stop, he surprised her by opening the door and easing his tall bulk into the passenger seat. With a rare grin and attempt at humour, he chuckled, 'You call this sardine can a car? It's all right for the likes of you, Miss Katherine, but I can't get my knees down from under my chin.'

'You're exaggerating!' she admonished him, laughing happily.

He was aware of the pleasant smell of newness and his hands stroked the dark leather dashboard and upholstery lovingly. There was a gleam of admiration in his eyes. 'It's not a patch on the Bentley, but I'm going to like being driven for a change, even if it's only round the back to show you where to garage it,' he grinned wickedly.

10

'A Mercedes!' Samantha gasped into the phone, on hearing about the car. 'I wish someone would take me literally when I ask for something.' As an afterthought, she asked, 'Who's paying for it?'

'I am, of course,' Katherine replied, a little on her dignity, and then added lamely, 'Alexis had to OK it so that Mr Fairfax could take the money out of my trust fund.' It still galled her to think that anything she wanted beyond her allowance had first to be approved by this virtual stranger, but right now, she was too happy to dwell on resentments.

'Now you've got wheels, would you like to drive yourself down for the weekend?' Samantha asked. 'My parents have organised a big surprise evening for James's twenty-first. They said to ask you if you would like to come. A sort of belated birthday treat for you too.'

'I'd love to.' Katherine's eager reply was spontaneous. She always enjoyed being with the Scotts; they treated her like family. Their house had become a second home to her over the past couple of years.

As they happily chattered on, contributing handsomely to the profits of British Telecom, both girls were oblivious as to just how big a surprise the birthday treat held in store for them.

Katherine made the journey to Sunningdale in Surrey as planned, arriving at Ivy House late in the afternoon. By the time she had cut the engine and climbed out of the car, the whole family had come out onto the shingle drive.

'Welcome, shrimp,' James grinned, tousling her hair playfully in his usual patronising fashion. Looking her up and down, he remarked, 'I see you've finally decided to grow a bit. I'll have to find a new name for you.' His attention then homed in on the car. 'And what have we here?' he murmured, wandering over to join his father.

Samantha, staring at the car, was, for once, temporarily rendered speechless. An admiring, 'Wow!' was all she could manage.

Arms folded, looking and sounding for all the world like car sales representatives, the two men walked all around the gleaming Mercedes, peering at it from every angle, determined that nothing should escape their attention.

Watching them, from the steps of the house, Katherine noticed, and not for the first time, how alike father and son were. They had the same slim build, warm hazel eyes and regular clean-cut features. But whilst the older man's hair had turned a distinguished pepper and salt, James's was dark auburn.

'It's a lovely car, dear, and I'm very happy for you,' Mrs Scott told the proud owner, but there was reservation in her voice and she wore a worried expression. 'It looks very fast. You will drive carefully, won't you? No accidents.'

As her mother retreated into the house, Samantha rolled her eyes in amusement and whispered to Katherine, 'Have you attempted to break the sound barrier yet?'

Katherine laughed. 'Give me time!' she whispered back, poking her friend in the ribs.

The younger members of the family would have insisted on a ride right then if it was not so late in the afternoon. Instead, Samantha linked her arm through Katherine's and led her into the house, while James followed with her holdall, still talking cars with his father.

In the drawing room, they helped themselves to tea and cake from the trolley. Seeing that James had not cut himself a slice of cake, Katherine asked: 'Aren't you having any?'

'No. Samantha made it,' James informed her matter-of-factly, as if that explained everything.

Puzzled, Katherine inspected the slice on her plate and

noticed that the doughy centre had not risen. 'It looks like her handiwork,' she laughed.

'There's nothing wrong with that cake,' Samantha stated defensively. 'It's supposed to be like that . . . holds more cream on top.' A grin appeared along with a couple of dimples.

'A good camouflage job, little sister,' James teased affectionately, 'but I think I'll pass up on the instant indigestion!'

They talked and joked for a while but, because of the lateness of the hour, did not linger too long over tea.

There was no need for anyone to tell Katherine which guest room she would be occupying. She always had the same room. In fact, it was habitually referred to as Katherine's room. The teal blue décor, the pine furniture and the view of the patio, pool and gardens exactly suited her tastes. She felt almost as much at home in this room as in her own.

After unpacking, Katherine prepared herself for the evening's entertainment. She had brought with her for the occasion a burgundy silk shift dress and matching court shoes. With these she wore Samantha's birthday present: the silver filigree earrings.

Mascara and lipstick were all Katherine usually applied by way of make-up, but now she had the compact of eyeshadows given to her by Ellie. Leaning nearer to the mirror, she cautiously experimented with a couple of blending shades and, observing the effect, was pleased with the way they emphasised the size and colour of her eyes.

Next, she took up the exquisite bottle of perfume. Slowly, she revolved it, watching the light catch in the facets of the glass and dance in the pale amber depths of the precious liquid. Because she had never owned an expensive perfume before, the gift pleased her – thrilled her, in fact. But then, because of the identity of the sender, it also had the power to make her feel uneasy.

Her thoughts lingered on the dark, handsome image of her cousin. Through the media she had followed, with a wide range of changing emotions, his kaleidoscopic career and social life. In what far corner of the world was he tonight? she wondered wistfully. Was he perhaps in a magnificent theatre somewhere in Europe, playing to an enraptured audience, or was he somewhere on the Mediterranean, partying the night away on the private yacht of a fabulously wealthy friend? Was he alone . . . or in the arms of a beautiful woman?

'Right,' beamed Mr Scott. 'Let's away.' But away to where, neither he nor his wife would say.

However, the minute he steered the car onto the M3, the party knew they were bound for London and the guessing game began. Still neither parent could be inveigled into saying where they were going or what the evening held in store for them. When, 40 minutes later, a parking place was sought in the vicinity of the Royal Albert Hall; it became apparent where the entertainment was to commence.

Finding a space large enough to accommodate a Rover proved to be a bit of a problem, and one that took longer to resolve than expected. They arrived at the concert hall with only enough time to buy programmes and take their seats in the auditorium before the doors were closed. Here, their ears were immediately assailed by a cacophony of sounds coming from the stage, but as the musicians finished tuning their instruments, the jarring and disturbing noises died away. Their seats were excellent, being in the middle and just far enough back to offer the full benefits of good acoustics and a clear view of the orchestra.

This was Katherine's first London concert. Enthralled, she used the minutes before the lights were dimmed to gaze around her. The hall was filled to capacity.

To enthusiastic applause, the first violinist walked onto the stage and took his place and then, soon after, to louder applause, the conductor followed.

Although she could not put a name to it, the music was familiar to her. Her grandfather had enjoyed the classics and over the years built up an extensive collection of albums. In his lifetime the manor house had been filled with music, and she had come home every holiday to enchanting strains of classical melodies.

Katherine had long ago become aware of the pleasurable drug-like effect certain music had upon her senses and, for the next hour or so, she willingly gave herself up to it. At the end of the performance, she was awakened from her trance by the clamorous applause of an appreciative audience.

During the interval, the small party followed the jostling crowd into the bar and, while James and his father battled for drinks, the ladies scanned their programmes and discussed the performance.

'Here we are,' said Samantha, finding the appropriate page. 'We've been listening to the London Symphony Orchestra playing Mozart's Symphony No.40.'

Leafing through her own programme, Katherine came to a photograph of the conductor and a written tribute to his achievements and contributions to the arts. If the drinks had arrived only one minute later she might have turned to the next page. Instead, tucking the programme under her arm, she gave herself up to her companions and to James's increasing attentions, until the second bell rang, recalling them to their seats.

The lights in the auditorium dimmed. To applause, the conductor returned to the stage, but this time there was another man with him. Tall and lean, he was, like the other musicians, elegantly attired in formal tailcoat. As recognition dawned, Katherine gave an involuntary gasp, for she was looking at none other than Alexis Drew.

Samantha, aware of her friend's startled reaction, quickly realised the cause of it and placed a comforting hand on her arm. James, on Katherine's other side, was oblivious to her distress or he might have welcomed the excuse to offer similar comfort, for he had become increasingly aware of his sister's friend on this visit. Unfortunately for him, he noticed nothing amiss and his attention remained focused on the orchestra.

When the maestri reached the centre of the stage, they bowed to the house. The conductor then turned to take his place on the platform while the other walked over to the grand piano which, now that the orchestra had regrouped themselves, could be seen to be in a prominent position. Bowing to the applauding audience once more, Alexis seated himself before the keyboard.

The conductor raised his baton and kept it poised until the hall was absolutely silent. Then, bringing it down, the music began. Rachmaninov's Piano Concerto No.1 filled the auditorium.

As she watched, Katherine realised she had never seen Alexis play before, heard him yes, but never actually seen him. Never witnessed his total involvement in his music. She knew he must be in continual visual contact with the conductor, must be conversant with every note played by the other musicians, and yet, so absorbed did he appear that he gave no indication that he was aware of anything beyond the music he produced.

With the magic of the concerto filling the air, the shock of seeing Alexis again gradually left her. The enchantment of the evening returned, transporting her into a fantasy dream world full of heightened emotions. Katherine did not know how long he cast his rapturous spell but, to her, it seemed like only a moment in time and in that brief moment there was, for her, only Alexis and his music. All else in that vast splendid hall was temporarily obliterated from her consciousness until he played the last note, and the wild applause of the audience propelled her back to the realities of her surroundings.

The thunderous clapping and chanting for more brought the young virtuoso back onto the stage a number of times. He had won their hearts with his brilliant performance and easy charismatic presence. Graciously submitting to pressure, he resumed his seat at the piano. A hush fell over the exultant audience. Once more, the conductor's poised baton came down and the pianist, accompanied by the orchestra, commenced playing an étude, which Katherine recognised as Chopin's Revolutionary.

This time, while she listened, Katherine studied the man to whom she was doubly linked; whose path had crossed briefly with her own on three memorable occasions. Somehow, the Alexis Drew of Ravenswood did not quite equate with the Alexis Drew of the Royal Albert Hall. She could not define the difference in him, and yet in some subtle way he had changed. It was as if she was seeing him for the first time. This brilliant, enigmatic man was devastatingly attractive. Just watching him made her feel weak, caused all sorts of strange and exciting sensations to churn through her. Two years before, he had not seemed to have these qualities and neither had the sight of him affected her in anything like the same way.

Hypnotised, she studied the supple hands that moved rapidly over the keyboard; the body that swayed unconsciously to the rapturous sounds they produced. He was not old. How could she possibly have thought so? An astonishing realisation came to Katherine: it was not he who had changed, but she. Casting her mind back in time, Katherine remembered that at 16, she had been too hurt to notice anything good about him and too young to be aware of him in the physical sense.

Well, she had grown up a bit since then, come a long way. But then, upon reflection, she thought perhaps she had not come nearly far enough, not if she was harbouring any hopes where he was concerned. This last thought startled her. Harbouring hopes? Surely not. She did not even like him, had disliked him on sight . . . and more so after hearing his opinions on her. There never was, nor ever would be, a future for them. Besides, he had a sophistication and polish she could never hope to acquire. He lived in a different world to hers – moved in different circles. He was, and always would be, way beyond her reach.

I made so little impression on you, that we could pass in the street and you would not know me, Katherine told herself sadly. You, on the other hand, are unforgettable. I would know you anywhere.

Eventually the music came to an end, but still the audience was reluctant to let the soloist go. After numerous noisy and persistent ovations, the conductor and pianist took their final bow and left the stage, not to return. The rest of the orchestra soon followed.

With his unexpected re-entry into her life, Alexis Drew had rekindled in Katherine a multitude of conflicting emotions. For a short space of time, he had lit up her world with his presence, captivated her with his music. Now, all too soon he had walked out of her life again and, but for the new memories of an unforgettable evening, was leaving her world an emptier place.

The party went on to a small but busy late night Portuguese restaurant, where they wined and dined by candlelight. If Katherine seemed a little subdued and preoccupied, no one appeared to notice except Samantha, who cast worried looks at her from time to time.

Two courses came and went and during these, the main topic of conversation was their visit to the Royal Albert Hall: the conductor, the music, and, of course, the pianist.

It was after the main course had been cleared away and they were waiting for dessert that Mr Scott said, 'Not a particularly common name, Drew. No relation to you, Katherine, I suppose?'

It was inevitable that at some time the question would be asked; however, the timely arrival of a pre-ordered birthday cake saved Katherine from having to reply. To a chorus of 'Happy Birthday', their jovial waiter set the cake down in front of James. When the candles had been blown out and the first incision made, the waiter reclaimed the cake to cut and serve.

'There's nothing I like better than a slice of well-risen cake!' said James, glancing at his sister out of the corner of his eye. Then, as if he had just had an afterthought, he looked doubtfully at the slice on his plate. Prodding it with his cake fork, he quizzed, 'Not one you brought along for the occasion, is it, Samantha?'

'Oh no, dear,' his mother assured him quite seriously. 'Your father ordered it when he made the booking.'

Mirth erupted from the younger members of the party. The wine was beginning to have an uplifting effect.

Towards the end of the evening, toasts were drunk to James and, belatedly, to Katherine. As his parents had already given him a Tag Heuer watch earlier in the day, only presents from Samantha and Katherine were still to be opened. His sister's came first. She had chosen to give him a Gold Cross ballpoint pen.

Removing it from its presentation case, he brought it closer to the candlelight, the better to see it. 'Is this a hint that I don't write to you often enough?' he teased. As he gave her a hug and an appreciative kiss on the cheek, Katherine, looking on, found herself thinking, and not for the first time, how lucky Samantha was to have a brother, and one like James.

Returning the pen to its bed of velvet, he next took up Katherine's present. The removal of the ribbon and paper exposed a black box that had obviously come from a jewellery shop. Holding the little cubic box between thumb and index finger, he surveyed it for a moment with interest and then, looking across the table at Katherine, he asked in a teasing voice: 'Could this possibly be a proposal of marriage, I wonder?' Although he was only joking, his eyes lingered on her flirtatiously.

'No! It couldn't possibly be,' Katherine laughed back at him. 'But you never know, maybe next leap year . . .'

'Is that a promise?' he quizzed.

His parents laughed at the couple but his sister was alerted to something she had not noticed before, and her eyes went with interest from her brother to her friend.

Opening the box, James revealed a small nicely understated onyx and gold tie stud.

'Now you would really much rather have that, wouldn't you?' It was Katherine's turn to tease.

'Oh, I think I can manage to wait until the next twenty-ninth of February,' he grinned. 'Until then, I'll wear this as a token of your esteem and good intentions.'

As the box was passed around for everyone to admire, he came around the table to give Katherine what his sister perceived to be more than just a brotherly hug. His brief kiss found its way, not to her cheek, but to her lips.

It was already late morning when Katherine stirred. Her first lucid thought was that she did not want to wake up, not yet anyway. She was on the brink of a momentous discovery, and if only she could go back to sleep again, she would be able to re-enter the realms of fantasy where her dream would continue to unfold. Losing the struggle, she slowly, reluctantly surfaced.

Katherine stretched lazily and then, with a jolt that brought her suddenly to full consciousness, memories of the Royal Albert Hall and the pianist came flooding vividly back to her. Pictures began to go through her mind like a film running in slow motion. She revelled in the remembrance, allowing herself to recall every detail, from the moment Alexis had walked out of the wings into the spotlight to the moment he took his final bow.

Some instinct warned Katherine against romanticising, for where this particular man was concerned, there was no hope that anything good would come of such dreaming. But they brought so much pleasure; she had not the will to take heed of her own warnings.

Katherine wondered if there would be anything about his performance in the morning papers. Or, she asked herself, did critics only write about artists when they could find fault? Well, they would be disappointed in this instance, for they could not possibly have found fault in last night's performance, of that she was certain.

She no longer had any desire to waste the morning in

bed. Life was too exciting, too full of surprises. Hurriedly she dressed in jeans and sweater and went in search of the rest of the family. Following the sound of voices and the aroma of fresh coffee, she found Samantha and James in the kitchen, discussing plans for the day ahead.

Samantha, now on the alert, noted the subtle changes that came over her brother with the appearance of Katherine. His shift in posture, the way his expressive eyes followed her across the room, his sudden increase in animation and attention, and the very fact that he was prepared to give up his whole day to their entertainment, told reams. No, she had not been mistaken in thinking that her big brother had become very much enamoured of Katherine. Now, as she looked more closely at her friend, she saw what it was that her brother had been the first to notice.

Time had been very kind to Katherine. All the changes to her appearance over the past two years had been for the better. She had grown taller and acquired the kind of figure found on the pages of glossy magazines. Her lustrous curls were now long and a perfect frame for her oval face with its high cheekbones, vivid blue eyes and generous, well-shaped lips.

Samantha recalled that some of their school friends who earlier on had been so pleased with themselves, had not known when to stop filling out and had taken to moaning and groaning every time they caught sight of themselves in a mirror.

'Puppy fat,' Matron and the housemistress had called it. 'It will go,' they had assured the afflicted. In many cases, it had not. The dreaded word 'diet' had been added to the girls' daily vocabulary, and the treacherous word had found its way into conversations with ever increasing frequency. Katherine, a late developer, looked as if she would never have to consider dieting. Who at the age of 16 would have thought to call her lucky?

Katherine brought a cup of coffee over to the table and then, recognising Mrs Scott's writing on a note propped up against the sugar bowl, raised questioning eyes.

‘We’ve been deserted for the pleasures of the golf club. They won’t be back for lunch. “Help yourselves” is the message,’ Samantha informed her.

‘We’re discussing the merits of a pub lunch and, since my old banger is temporarily off the road, the added attraction of a ride in your car,’ James grinned. ‘How about it?’

‘Suits me,’ Katherine agreed. Although she had set her seal of approval on the suggestion, secretly she was disappointed that a tête-à-tête with Samantha would now have to wait.

With a favourite pub in mind, they decided to drive into Windsor. Samantha, being the smaller of the two passengers, squeezed into the back of the car, leaving the front passenger seat for her brother. To her amusement his right arm casually snaked its way along the back of Katherine’s seat, where it came to rest for the duration of the journey. Katherine seemed not to notice.

As was expected and hoped for, the pub was full to overflowing with young people: mostly students in the holiday mood. Having battled at the dim, smoky bar for beers and ploughman’s, they then juggled their booty back through the crowd and out into the garden. For a moment they stood blinking in the bright sunshine, searching for familiar faces to join, or an empty table. They were almost immediately espied by a group of friends.

One of the men, a newcomer to the group, made the mistake of looking too keenly at Katherine. This caused James to drape a proprietary arm around her shoulders before introducing her and his sister. Having staked his claim in this way, the next couple of hours passed pleasantly and uneventfully, until the group broke up.

Still Katherine seemed to have noticed nothing in James’s manner to suggest that his interest in her was anything other than brotherly. Oh Katherine! Do wake up! Samantha willed.

She felt no concern for her brother over his infatuation, nor did she have any intention of telling him that their friend was unavailable. Knowing James, his ailment was only temporary anyway, and if a serious attachment developed between them, then time would eventually remedy Katherine's situation. As for Alexis Drew, well, he had been pictured in the morning paper with yet another beautiful young hopeful at his side. What is sauce for the goose, is sauce for the gander, Samantha quoted to herself.

That night, at the supper table, James suggested they drive over to the Showcase to see what films were showing.

'With so many screens to choose from, there's bound to be something on worth seeing!' he pointed out. 'If we go early, we could book for one of the late performances and have a couple while we wait.'

'Count me out. I don't feel like seeing a film,' Samantha replied. 'But don't let that stop the two of you if you want to go.'

Although Katherine, as driver, had not had much to drink at lunchtime, she had been drinking wine with the evening meal. Hoping for an opportunity to talk alone with Samantha, she used this as an excuse. 'I'm over the top for driving,' she stated, 'and I don't particularly want to go out again.'

As for his parents, they declared they had had their quota of fresh air and exercise for one day, walking round an 18-golf course. 'Don't look at us! We're not going anywhere tonight except up those stairs to bed,' Mrs Scott informed him.

'Some of us know when we've had enough,' his father said, and then asked good-naturedly, 'and when was the last time you had a good night's sleep?'

At this point James laid his napkin down on the table and went to answer the hall telephone. Presently he returned, looking very pleased with life. 'Well, if you're all quite sure you don't want my company this evening, then I might as well have a night out with the boys,' he happily informed them.

Now Samantha had not exactly declined a night out with the boys, just an evening out playing gooseberry to her brother and best friend. This was a different matter altogether. It had all the right ingredients for a fun evening.

'Boys . . .' murmured Samantha. She looked at James hopefully but he was already closing the door behind him with an, 'Enjoy your dull evening!' flung over his shoulder.

There was a light tap at the door and Samantha's fair head appeared, followed by her dressing gown clad form. 'Can I come in?' she asked.

'Looks to me like you're already in,' laughed Katherine, pleased to see her.

'I thought you might like to talk about last night,' Samantha said, never one to beat about the bush. Throwing herself face down on the double bed alongside her friend, she continued, 'Honestly, I had no idea what my parents had in store for us. But I have to admit, if I had known, I probably wouldn't have told you. You might have ducked out.'

'Probably,' Katherine agreed. 'Anyway, it doesn't matter. It was just a bit of a shock because it was unexpected. It shouldn't have been, really. Something like that was bound to happen sooner or later.'

Seeing one of the *Sunday Telegraph* supplements lying open on her friend's lap, Samantha asked, 'I suppose you've already seen the picture of him?'

For a moment, their eyes locked, and then, with renewed interest, Katherine turned her attention back to the paper and once more began searching through its pages. 'No I haven't,' she replied. 'By *him* I assume you mean Alexis? I hope the critics did him justice?'

'Well, actually, it's not about last night's performance,' Samantha said. 'It's about his love life and, as usual, the papers have got it all wrong again.'

Katherine found the society page and the photograph, which was one of three others. The caption read: *Celebrated pianist Alexis Drew was one of the 300 guests invited to the*

Dorchester Hotel last Friday evening to help celebrate the twenty-first birthday of Miss Sara Collins. Friends say they have been seeing a lot of each other over the past few weeks. Could there soon be cause for a second celebration?

As Katherine's eyes lingered over the picture of what appeared to be a very happy couple, a frown spread across her brow. Slowly but firmly, she closed the paper and, folding it in half, dropped it on the floor by the side of the bed.

These articles had never bothered Katherine in the past, and there had been quite a number of them, but this one was the exception, Samantha observed, and wondered why. After a short pause, Samantha decided to change the subject. 'What did you get for your birthday, besides the car?' she asked.

Katherine had already thanked her for the silver earrings and had shown her appreciation by wearing them the night before, and so she talked about her other presents and cards. Lastly, casually, she mentioned the perfume from Alexis, indicating with a careless wave of the hand the bottle on the dressing table.

'So that's what you were wearing last night – I meant to ask,' Samantha said, impressed. Getting up, she crossed to the dressing table and, taking the ornate bottle in her hand, thoughtfully commented, 'An exotic present.'

Feeling vaguely uneasy, Katherine agreed. Because she and Alexis had been forced upon each other, it embarrassed her to receive any kind of attention from him. Perfume seemed a rather intimate gift to send under their peculiar circumstances, rather like sending red roses, and she was sure Samantha thought so too. Of course, it was possible, even probable, he had not given the choice of gift a great deal of consideration. He might even have left the selection up to his secretary, if he had one. Uncharitably, she told herself he was obviously a man much used to women, who probably thought nothing of giving perfume to all his girlfriends. As for sending her a present at all, well, he very likely saw the chore as just another tiresome responsibility inherited along with Linnet House.

Having replaced the little bottle, Samantha turned speculative eyes on Katherine, and asked, 'Are you absolutely sure Alexis will agree to a divorce when the time comes?' To herself: she thought but did not say – and are you absolutely sure you will want one?

The question took Katherine by surprise. 'Yes. Of course he'll agree. Why shouldn't he?'

'Well, it seems to me that, as things are, he more or less has everything he could possibly want in life. He has the Steinway, Linnet House, Ravenswood and his and your finances under his control. Furthermore, he has a presentable wife to give him children, and all the mistresses he wants. In other words, he can have his cake and eat it. What more can any man ask for?'

Katherine laughed, genuinely amused by such a ludicrous suggestion. 'You were not at Ravenswood for the reading of my grandfather's will. You did not witness his shocked reaction when he saw who he was expected to marry. You were not present at Ravenswood on the day of the wedding, and did not hear what he said about me to Hugh Bradford.' There was now little humour in her voice. 'Believe me, he's already counting the days to freedom,' she said, resentment creeping in. 'You saw him, Sam. Why should a man like that settle for someone like me?'

Samantha impatiently brushed her friend's words aside. 'Have you looked at yourself in the mirror recently?' she asked. Taking Katherine by the wrist, she pulled her off the bed and over to the full-length mirror. 'That all happened two years ago,' Samantha told her. 'You're not the same person any more. You've changed so much, I doubt if he'd even recognise you, and you're still changing. Look at yourself.'

Giving her reflection a sceptical glance, Katherine remained unconvinced. Then, recovering her sense of humour, she laughed, 'In that case, I'd better stay out of sight until he's signed the divorce papers.'

'That might not be such a bad idea,' Samantha replied. Realising Katherine was not taking the matter of her looks very seriously, she pointed out, 'Don't you notice the attention you arouse when you walk into a room? Even James is sitting up and taking notice.'

'James?' she said, with a mixture of surprise and doubt. Turning back to the mirror, Katherine cocked her head on one side and gave her reflection a little more consideration. 'I guess I've grown a bit taller, filled out here and there and, of course, those hideous braces have gone,' she finally conceded.

Laughing at her friend's modesty, Samantha said, 'What you really mean is, you've shot up and have somehow managed to acquire a super figure and a great pair of legs. The rest of you is not so bad either.' There was a lot more she could have added, but instead she said, 'And that's all I'm going to say, because I've already paid you enough compliments and I don't want them to go to your head.'

At the Scotts' insistence, Katherine stayed an extra day at Ivy House. Before her departure, a date was set for Samantha to visit Ravenswood and, although James said nothing on the subject, the girls suspected that, this time, he too had hoped to be invited.

On the drive home, Katherine had ample time to reflect on her conversation with Samantha on the subject of Alexis. She did not really doubt that he would give her a divorce when the time came but, even so, her friend's suggestions disturbed her. In fact, the very word 'divorce' disturbed her.

Lots of things had disturbed her over the past week: the arrival of the perfume, James's attentions, the concert, the newspaper picture and her conversations with Samantha. On top of all that, people were beginning to treat her differently. They seemed so much more aware of her presence. The change in peoples' attitude had to be attributable to the change in her appearance. Did they really find her interesting? Had she actually become attractive?

Katherine had thought of herself as plain for so long that she now had no confidence or belief in what her reflection so clearly told her. There was no doubting, however, that James found her attractive. His interest had become far from brotherly. Now that she no longer felt threatened by his close proximity, she could smile and admit to feeling flattered. Maybe, Katherine told herself, she could get used to that kind of attention . . . although, perhaps, not from James.

Her thoughts turned next to the picture of Alexis with the pretty debutante. She had seen him featured with other girls before and never felt more than a mild irritation. This time it was different. The picture had really upset her, and still did. Everything seemed to have changed since the night of the concert and now she would have to come to terms with a whole set of new emotions. Far better for her if she had never seen him again.

Irritated with her train of thought, Katherine was relieved when the gates of Ravenswood came into sight. As she slowed the car to make the left-hand turn, she was surprised to see a deep burgundy-coloured Jaguar pass through the open gates and turn onto the road ahead. Katherine could not immediately place the car but knew she had seen it somewhere before.

As the car passed, for a fleeting moment Katherine had a clear view of the driver. He was none other than the man who had, over the past few days, monopolised her every thought. Sitting beside him in the passenger seat was a young woman with a lovely, animated smile. Her fair head was turned to him and, although his eyes were on the road ahead, from his attentive expression, Katherine could tell his attention was all, affectionately, hers.

The thought that he should have the audacity to bring one of his numerous girlfriends to Ravenswood, her home, suddenly filled Katherine with indignant fury. How dare he flaunt this girl in front of the staff, and under her nose! The thought that there might have been others coming and going in her absence over the last couple of years further fuelled her rage. *And so much for Sara Collins*, she told herself with disgust.

Driving the car round to the back of the house, she locked it in the garage. Still fuming, and with a face like thunder, Katherine let herself into the manor via one of the back doors. Before she could get further than the hall, she came face to face with an excited and ecstatic Mrs Johnson.

'Oh Miss Katherine, you're back at last,' she beamed at her young mistress. 'What a pity you decided to stay longer with your friends – now you've missed Mr Drew. He only left five minutes ago. What a shame.'

'What was he doing here?' Katherine asked a little too sharply, trying to hide an anger now complicated by feelings of disappointment – a disappointment she had no wish to acknowledge, even to herself.

'He had business to discuss with Mr Coteman,' the housekeeper breezed on, unaware of Katherine's turbulent emotions. 'They were in his office for some time and then he brought the young lady over to be introduced and to ask if I would show her round the house. She seemed very impressed and was particularly interested in the portraits, wanting to know who everyone was. They hoped to find you home. I said you'd be back sometime this afternoon, but after tea they said they really had to go.' She sighed. 'They'd be so disappointed if they knew they'd only just missed you.'

Katherine did not respond to Mrs Johnson's enthusiasm. She was telling herself she was not in the least bit sorry to have missed them.

The housekeeper, at last noticing her lack of animation, refrained from further comment, except to say, 'Oh well. It can't be helped now.' Changing the subject, she said, 'While you freshen up, I'll go and see what I've got for your supper.'

The very last thing on Katherine's mind was supper. She would much rather have taken her disappointment, bruised ego and volatile temper up to her room but, before she could say anything, Mrs Johnson had disappeared in the direction of the kitchen.

'I used to think this a very lonely place for you,' the housekeeper later told Katherine, as she placed supper on the table. 'It was such a shame there was never anyone of your own age to play with when you were growing up. Now that young lady who was here today is only a couple of years older than you. She would have made just the right kind of playmate. It's a pity, for your sake, your grandfather didn't invite her to visit Ravenswood during the holidays.'

Katherine was mystified. Whatever was Mrs Johnson talking about? 'Why should my grandfather have wanted to invite her, a stranger, over to play with me?' she inquired, amazed.

'Well, if he had invited her, she wouldn't have been a stranger, now would she?' Mrs Johnson asked reasonably, seeming surprised at the question. 'Well, after all, you are related – slightly – even if only through marriage.'

'Who and what are you talking about?' Katherine asked, by now totally bewildered, aware she had lost the thread of the conversation somewhere along the way.

'Why Jane Remmick, of course. The young lady Mr Drew brought to meet you. His half-sister!'

11

Hugh's day in court had been a difficult one. He had won his client's case in the end, only to be informed by the man's smug smile and incautious words that he had, in fact, been guilty all along of date rape. Hugh had begun to suspect as much but had not liked having his doubts confirmed. Feeling contaminated by association, and in need of decent, uplifting company, he had called Alexis.

It was a warm evening and the friends decided to take advantage of the weather by dining al fresco at their favourite Greek restaurant, where the wrought iron tables and chairs spilled out onto the pavement in front.

The restaurant was situated on a quiet one-way road, partly residential. Only occasionally did a vehicle pass and fleetingly obscure the view of the railed garden opposite. It was hard to believe that running parallel only a couple of streets away was Knightsbridge, with its department stores and the noise and fumes of a steady stream of evening traffic.

Here, removed from it all, couples strolled arm in arm along the pavements, smiling at the world around them for no apparent reason, as people tend to do in the summer, when the days are long, the sky clear blue and the weather perfect.

The two men, casually dressed in jeans and sweaters, relaxed over a bottle of red wine delivered to their table by the talkative owner himself. Nikolai hovered for a few minutes of conversation before bustling off to take orders from a nearby table.

'Working on your next concert?' Hugh asked, glancing at Alexis over the top of his menu.

'Yes. I've one coming up at the Barbican at the end of

the month and then I'm going to give myself a rest from concerts,' Alexis replied. Having made his choice from the menu, he closed it and placed it on the table in front of him.

He had not actually said, 'I'm resting', which was the performer's way of saying: 'I haven't any work right now', but Hugh wondered if that was what he meant. He thought this most unlikely, but he asked anyway. 'Running out of concert bookings?'

Alexis smiled at the question. He had turned a number of offers down recently. 'No, it's not like that,' he replied. He moved his chair back from the table a little so that he could lounge in a more comfortable position.

'I've done so many concerts in the last couple of years that I feel as if I ought to be branching out and exploring other avenues for my talents,' he explained. 'I want to do something new and creative. After all, I don't need the money. Job satisfaction and success will do.'

'Exactly what do you have in mind?' Hugh was curious to know.

The warm breeze ruffled Alexis' dark hair. He unconsciously raked his fingers through it. 'Like taking on more recording sessions, for instance, and writing more musical compositions for agencies,' he replied. 'It seems they never have enough good suppliers, or so I'm told. I believe it, since my answerphone is constantly cluttered up with their messages.'

Seeing that Hugh was ready, he motioned to the hovering waiter to come over and take their orders. Then, picking up the threads of their conversation, he continued, 'There seems to be a shortage of all sorts of music. Ballads, was today's request. Last week I was asked if I would like to try my hand at writing the background music for a BBC play.' He thought about that for a moment. 'An interesting challenge. I might accept it.'

The conversation came to a temporary halt while the waiter refilled their wineglasses. Alexis then continued, 'I've also been asked to join forces with Jamieson and Welbeck to work on the music for a stage show.'

Hugh was impressed. He had heard of the playwright and lyricist. Who had not?

'Illustrious company you're keeping these days,' he commented. Hugh did not doubt that whatever Alexis put his mind to would bring just rewards. He had the Midas touch. He had a shrewd business brain and had always known where he was going and what he wanted. Not for him the confinement of an office or the job of defending misfits and miscreants in stuffy courtrooms filled with equally stuffy officials.

Alexis studied his friend for a moment, then quietly remarked: 'You look like you've had a bad day.'

'I got someone off who deserved to be locked up,' Hugh stated flatly, looking somewhat disheartened. 'Some rich bastard who owns an art gallery. It happens sometimes.'

'That's what comes of being too good at your job,' Alexis remarked lightly, but seeing his friend really was troubled, he asked more seriously, 'What happened?'

Hugh gave him a brief outline of the case. 'Unfortunately he's the type who's likely to do it again, and it will be on my conscience because I got the fellow off,' he concluded with a disconsolate sigh.

'Too bad,' Alexis sympathised. 'But no point in blaming yourself, you don't write the law, you just uphold it.'

The waiter arrived with their orders. After his retreat, Hugh changed the subject by asking, 'How was your visit to Ravenswood? Did you see your cousin?' He refrained from using the word *wife.* It seemed an inappropriate word under the circumstances.

'No, she was away visiting friends in Surrey. A pity, Jane particularly wanted to meet her.' Alexis' expression softened at the mention of his half sister.

Jane was about to enter her third and final year at St Andrew's University and he had not seen as much of her as he would have liked over the past two years. Too often he had been on tour abroad when Jane had come south for the holidays. During those two years she had done a lot of growing up. No longer an adolescent, she was quick-witted and level-headed, and he had enjoyed her company immensely.

He had seen Henrietta only once since his return from Vienna, and on that occasion had taken her to a cocktail party, where he had introduced her to a number of wealthy acquaintances. Not having received any more telephone calls since, he assumed, with satisfaction, that she had found his successor.

Only recently, the tabloid press had mistakenly linked his name with Sara Collins' and he determined that in future, when he needed a partner to take to official engagements, if Jane was home and available he would invite her to accompany him. He would introduce his sister only as Jane Remmick, and omit to mention their relationship. Both he and Jane would find it very amusing to see what the press managed to make of them and their future together.

'Do you remember Mrs Johnson?' Alexis asked, turning his attention back to his table companion. When Hugh looked blank, he went on, 'The housekeeper at Ravenswood.' When enlightenment dawned, he continued, 'She told me Katherine had applied to study at Central Saint Martins and was almost certain to be accepted.'

'Good for Katherine,' Hugh approved. 'That's one of the best art colleges in England.' After a moment's thought, he added sceptically, 'I must say, she didn't look the arty kind, but then, come to think of it, she didn't really look any kind.'

'Hidden talents, maybe?' Alexis suggested. 'If this school friend of hers, Samantha Scott, also manages to get into Saint Martins, they mean to share an apartment together.'

'Makes sense,' Hugh nodded.

'That's what I thought, but Mrs Johnson had other ideas,' Alexis replied. 'She was clearly not in favour of letting two inexperienced hothouse plants loose alone in London.' Remembering their conversation, he chuckled. 'City survival, it would seem, was not on the convent's curriculum and, to hear her talk, you'd think Katherine had yet to discover the existence of a second gender.'

'If this friend looks anything like Katherine, they'll both be perfectly safe,' Hugh grinned.

Their main course arrived, filling the air with the appetising aroma of Mediterranean spices. The solicitous waiter hovered over them, refilling their glasses.

Alexis waited for him to withdraw and then, on a more sombre note, continued: 'I do believe she expects me to keep an eye on the girl.' He meditated on the glass in his hands, then, looking over the rim, asked somewhat belligerently: 'And when does she think I'm going to find the time, let alone the inclination, to babysit an eighteen-year-old student?'

'If the eighteen-year-old were anyone other than this eighteen-year-old, you'd jump at the chance to show her the wicked ways of the world,' scoffed Hugh.

Alexis laughed. 'True,' he acknowledged, honestly.

'What about your mother? Can't she help out?'

'I've already discussed it with her but, in a few weeks' time, she's leaving on her annual summer migration to Saint Tropez,' Alexis replied. 'She's willing to help out when she gets back but what happens in the meantime, or when she makes her winter migration to the ski slopes of Klosters?'

After a moment's thought, Hugh commented, 'You're lucky Mrs Johnson didn't ask you to accommodate Katherine at Linnet House. After all,' he threw in, 'there's no shortage of space.'

'Scandalous!' Alexis exclaimed in mock indignation. 'What would the neighbours say?'

'What could they say? It's all legal and above board,' Hugh reminded him.

'There are some things best forgotten,' Alexis replied, with a grimace of distaste. 'Anyway, I've got a better solution to the problem.'

'Tell me more.'

Alexis sat back, a smug look on his face. 'What do you do with unwanted work when you don't have time to deal with it?' he asked.

Hugh waited for the answer.

'You delegate it to someone else, of course,' he stated, with a flourish of an artistic hand.

'Of course. Now why didn't I think of that,' Hugh grinned. Suddenly, as an unwelcome thought occurred to him, his amusement evaporated and a frown creased his brow. He asked suspiciously, 'You're not thinking of delegating the work to me, I hope?'

'That's taken the complacent smile off your face,' Alexis teased. 'No, Hugh. Rest easy. I hadn't given you a thought . . . until now, that is.' With humour, he asked, 'I suppose you don't want the job?'

'You suppose absolutely right. In this, you're on your own.' Hugh relaxed, obviously relieved.

'Too bad. Now I'll have to go through the Yellow Pages and find someone who specialises in babysitting rich teenage girls.' As an afterthought, he asked doubtfully, 'I suppose such a person does exist?'

'Without a doubt,' Hugh assured him. He could think of a number of trusted people his firm used on a regular basis who would willingly take on such an assignment. He considered each in turn. 'There are such things as bodyguards, of course, but that's not quite what you had in mind, I take it? Besides, Katherine might object very strongly to having a muscleman move in with her – but then, again, she might not.'

'According to Mrs Johnson, she wouldn't know what to do with one!' Alexis smiled wryly. 'No, that's not quite what I had in mind for her.' He deliberated a moment. 'I want someone more discreet than a bodyguard. So discreet, in fact, that she doesn't even know she's being watched over.'

His eyes went fleetingly to two passing girls who, by casting lingering, flirtatious looks in their direction, were doing their best to catch his and Hugh's attention.

He smiled absent-mindedly but disappointed them by

turning his attention back to his table companion. 'He or she need only report to me if and when problems occur,' he continued, 'and that way, Katherine can still enjoy an independent and private life.'

'Doesn't sound too independent and private to me,' Hugh commented.

'We all have to answer to someone,' Alexis pointed out, somewhat flippantly.

'True,' agreed Hugh. 'Well, it just so happens I know the right man for the job: Quentin Smith of Smith and Son. He's a retired policeman who's prepared to turn his years of accumulated talents to just about anything legitimate.'

Seeing they had finished eating, the waiter came over and removed their plates. They ordered coffee but not liqueur. They knew from past experience that Nikolai would present them each with a glass of ouzo, compliments of the house.

It was approaching ten o'clock, the summer evening light had faded and lighting-up had taken place all over London. The two men watched the frenzied activity of the insects attracted to the glow of a nearby Victorian street lamp.

Hugh resumed their conversation. 'Quentin Smith has done a lot of good work for my firm over the last few years, from the most ordinary to the most extraordinary. Despite the somewhat distinctive name, in appearance he's completely nondescript. And therein lies his greatest strength: his ability to pass unnoticed in a crowd. We've commissioned him to find missing persons, tail unfaithful spouses, guard battered girlfriends, etc. This, however, may be a first!'

Soon after nine the following morning, Quentin Smith telephoned for an appointment. At ten, he was on the stone doorstep of Linnet House. He prided himself on being quick off the mark.

The door was opened by a small middle-aged lady with faded hair and watery, suspicious eyes. Like a badge of office, a yellow duster hung half out of a pocket of her pale green overall.

After he had given his name and assured her he had an appointment, the housekeeper looked him up and down, and said without a hint of welcome, 'You'd better come in then.' Mrs Stewart led him across the marble floor of an impressive hall to a study, where Alexis was putting together information useful to the interview.

'Quentin Smith, sir,' the man introduced himself, putting out a hand as he approached. 'You must be Mr Drew. Hope I can be of service,' he said in a voice that held a trace of a Cockney accent.

'I hope so too,' Alexis responded, shaking the extended hand. Introductions over, he invited his visitor to be seated facing him across the large leather-topped desk.

The detective's gaze flickered admiringly around the room, along the tall, solid-oak bookcases, over the silk damask curtains, antique furniture and Persian carpets. All spoke of tasteful, genteel wealth. In an instant, his attention came to rest on the man behind the desk. Voice, dress, manners – all declared him to be a man born to his present privileged station in life.

He had not needed to be told the identity of Alexis Drew. He already knew him to be a brilliant and celebrated concert pianist. He had seen him perform on television and, only recently, had noticed his face on a poster advertising a concert at the Barbican. He was on the covers of cassettes, CDs and records, some of which Quentin Smith had in his own private collection. And with equal frequency he appeared in the entertainment pages and society gossip columns of the press.

While all this was flashing through Quentin Smith's mind, Alexis was telling himself that Hugh was absolutely right when he said the only memorable thing about the man was his name. In height and physiognomy, Smith was no sinister Hollywood interpretation of a typical private eye. In fact, every line on his round face appeared to go up. This would have been testimonial to a sunny, cheerful disposition but for the eyes, which, Alexis noted, were hard and shrewd. Smith had been recommended as discreet and trustworthy. Hugh might have added also that he was not a man to cross.

The detective listened attentively to the facts, and to an outline of requirements. Since it was not a particularly taxing assignment for someone of his varied and extensive talents, he readily agreed to take on the job. He asked a few relevant questions, made notes in a pocketbook and, when he had finished, asked for a photograph of the young lady; one he could take away.

There was only one in the house, and that was a school photograph of Katherine wearing her charcoal grey and red school uniform. It was in a silver frame and had been on the desk when Alexis took possession of the house. No doubt put there by her doting grandfather in the days when he had been well enough to visit London. Not needing a constant reminder that he was married to a schoolgirl, Alexis had removed it.

Now, taking it out of the drawer, he handed it to the detective, saying, 'That's the only photograph I have of her. It was probably taken a year or two before the wedding, but I don't expect she's changed much . . . at least, she hadn't last time I saw her. Appears to be a good likeness. Take it if it's of any use to you.'

Quentin Smith studied the photograph of the girl, whose only remarkable feature was a pair of startling blue almond shaped eyes. Their size and innocence dominated her young face. The words *child bride* came unbidden to mind. Taking into consideration what he had been told, he calculated that there was probably about eight years between her and his client, but in experience probably a whole lifetime.

Poor little sod doesn't stand a chance being married to someone like him, he reflected, removing the picture from the frame. Stands to reason that with his looks and money, he's never going to limit himself to just one girl and certainly not one as ordinary as this.

*

The next morning, Alexis drove out to Henley. The time had come to take his secretary into his full confidence and tell her of his marital status. Alexis did this by simply handing Jenny an unabridged copy of the will and, when she had finished reading it, a copy of the wedding certificate. Arms folded, leaning against the tall filing cabinet, Alexis watched her reactions with interest.

A series of fleeting expressions crossed Jenny's face. She had thought she knew all there was to know about her employer, but this was obviously not so. She was pleased he could not see into her heart, could not know the emotional turmoil he was putting her through.

Almost from the beginning, Jenny had been more than a little in love with Alexis Drew. Initially she had thought it infatuation and told herself it would pass. When it did not, she thought it would be impossible to continue to work for him under the circumstances. But he was away much of the time, leaving her to run the office on her own during those long periods of absence. Somehow Jenny settled into the job and learned to live with her feelings. The work and the hours suited her, and she and her husband Jim needed the money to keep up the mortgage payments on their modest house.

If Alexis was aware of her deep feelings for him, he showed not a sign of it. His attitude towards her was, and always had been, friendly, appreciative and strictly businesslike.

Jenny laid the documents down on the desk and looked to Alexis for further enlightenment. She knew him well enough to know he would not have taken her into his confidence on such a strange and personal matter without good reason.

'As you can see from the will, Katherine's grandfather expected me to look after her as well as her interests,' he said, 'but I'm so often tied up with work or out of the country on tour, that I'm not really in a position to do the job properly. Katherine doesn't have anyone else except my mother, and she's too often abroad herself to be of much help. Anyway, she sees Katherine as my responsibility, as does Mrs Johnson, the housekeeper. In fact, everyone sees her as my responsibility.' He paused to consider and then, amused, added, 'Well, I suppose legally, she is.'

'She's eighteen,' Jenny reminded him. 'From what I understand, that makes her legally responsible for herself.'

'Yes, but as you can see by that innocuous looking little scrap of paper, in the eyes of the law, she's my wife. In any case I obligated myself the moment I accepted the terms of the will,' he pointed out.

'What are you going to do about it?' Jenny asked, knowing he was leading up to something.

'I've been in touch with a reputable detective agency called Smith and Son, and yesterday interviewed the owner: a man by the name of Quentin Smith. He's agreed to keep a discreet eye on Katherine. I've told him that I don't want her privacy violated unnecessarily – I'm only interested in her welfare.'

Pulling out a drawer in the filing cabinet, Alexis extracted a new file, on which he wrote the name of Katherine Drew. Placing it in front of Jenny, he instructed, 'Every month he'll send you a report. Just read them through and then file them in there. There's no need for me to see them unless you think there's something I should know about.'

'What sort of things would you consider you needed to know?' Jenny asked.

He paused to consider. 'Accidents, illnesses, financial difficulties, drug abuse. Anything really serious,' he told her.

'OK,' Jenny agreed, and then as an afterthought asked, 'Do you want to know if she gets into any heavy relationships – you know, affairs?'

For a moment, Alexis seemed surprised by her question. It was as if the idea that Katherine might have an affair had not previously entered his mind. A smile hovered on his lips as he turned the question over in his mind. 'No,' he eventually replied, with an amused shrug. 'Affairs are her business. Just so long as she doesn't get herself into trouble.'

'Well, let's hope the girl knows all about contraception, then we can continue to enjoy a trouble-free existence.' She laughed.

When Jenny came to pack up her work for the day, Alexis was still on her mind. No angel himself, she was pleased he was not going to inflict double standards on Katherine. She remembered he had made no pretence at wanting Katherine for himself, and yet, strangely, the suggestion that she might have an affair had surprised him, amused him, even. She wondered why.

12

Neither Katherine nor Samantha had lived in a city before, nor had they ever been without adult control. Suddenly finding themselves free from restrictions, they wilfully set out to take full advantage of their new found freedom. They went out late, returned late, went to bed late and slept late. They subsisted on junk food, and when they overdosed on alcohol, which they occasionally did, they would fall up the steep stairway to their apartment, giggling and alternately noisily hushing each other as they went. No sober person could have understood their conversation or brand of humour, but to each other they made perfectly good sense. Finding their keys usually necessitated the turning out of pockets and bags, but finding the keyhole was not so easily achieved and always initiated fresh waves of hysterical giggling.

The discovery that they were not blessed with a natural immunity to the morning-after syndrome came as a surprise to them both. Disprin, Alka-Seltzer and vitamin C were new additions to the bathroom cabinet.

If Madge Johnson could have seen their rapid decline in standards, she would have considered her very worst fears well founded.

Weeks before, and after several day trips into London, the girls had found an apartment near the art college. It was not luxurious, neither was it huge, but it was affordable, newly decorated and offered the privacy of separate bedrooms.

Since the new tenants did not intend to live in impoverished student squalor, they had agreed they would not put anything into the apartment that did not blend with the existing décor. Consequently, backwards and forwards they had gone, to scavenge in the attic rooms of Ravenswood and the loft of Ivy House. Items that had not seen the light of day for years were brought out of trunks and dark dusty corners to be cleaned, polished and admired. Bit by bit, these rediscovered treasures had been transported into London, to be hauled up the four flights of stairs. The apartment at Marlow Place became a hive of enthusiastic activity as the girls hung pictures on walls, positioned ornaments, scattered cushions and found places for all those necessities they had not previously missed in their lives but now felt were essential to their happiness and well-being.

Since parking facilities did not come with the property, Katherine was not able to keep her car with her. Reluctantly, she left it garaged at Ravenswood, to be used only during holidays and weekend visits. Now, with two cars to clean and polish, Johnson was in his element, the duster ever at the ready.

Initially, the car was missed but, because of the location of their new home, the girls soon found they could manage very well without it. After all, Marlow Place was only a short distance from Central Saint Martins, was conveniently situated on several good bus routes, and was near the underground and main line stations. The girls had only to step outside to find themselves surrounded by shops, popular pubs, clubs and restaurants. Also within walking distance were large and beautiful parks, the River Thames, art galleries and theatres. It appeared as if the whole busy, bustling, noisy city was on their very own doorstep.

Setting up surveillance on Katherine's activities presented few problems. Quentin Smith assumed that a block of apartments the size of Marlow Place would have a maintenance manager, and it was this person's services he meant to enlist, but first he needed to know what the man looked like. Approaching the entrance, he found and rang the doorbell labelled *Caretaker* and then, without waiting for a reply, removed himself to the telephone booth across the street, where he could observe without being observed.

A rather scruffy middle aged individual came to the door, squinted suspiciously up and down the street and then, muttering irritably to himself, retreated back into the building. All Quentin Smith now had to do was wait patiently for the man to reappear. From the shape of his distended midriff, he anticipated the caretaker would do so around pub opening time. The appointed hour brought him from his lair. Smith's patient vigilance paid off as he had hoped it would.

The detective followed him into one of the local pubs. Sitting next to him at the bar, he struck up an uninspiring conversation about the exorbitant price of beer and cigarettes. Smith introduced himself and learned that his drinking partner went by the name of Becket. He bought him his next pint and then, noting the nicotine stains on his right hand, left his cigarette packet open on the counter, generously indicating that Becket could help himself. While they progressed to the subject of horse racing and betting shops, the caretaker warmed to his new-found friend. After all, here was a man who was generous to a fault and spoke the same language as him.

Quentin Smith, on the other hand, was not so enamoured of his companion. But then, he told himself, a smart appearance and good manners were not requirements of the simple task he had in mind for him. And he was, after all, the only man in the right position to do the job. Becket, he concluded, would have to do.

By the time they were on their third round, also bought by Quentin Smith, Becket was listening to a definition of the various aspects of detective work. Smith told him about some of the more interesting assignments he had found himself on, and let him know that he often worked in conjunction with social workers. Playing on the sympathies of the man, he pointed out what a tough life it was for the youth of today, and elaborated on some of the problems and pitfalls they had to face, especially those left alone in the world to fend for themselves.

He overestimated the simplicity of the man. Becket was not of a similar opinion and did not hesitate to disagree with him. He thought the youth of today had it far too easy.

'The only kids I come into contact with lead the life of Riley!' he grunted into his beer. 'I'm the manager of a block of apartments that's full of art students, being so near Saint Martins an' being on their list of suitable accommodation an' all,' he said, puffing himself up importantly. 'Most of 'em gets 'anded those grants, and where do you think those grants come from? From the likes o' you an' me!' he said, looking up with belligerent eyes. 'You an' me,' he repeated for emphasis. 'The bloody taxpayer, of course, that's where! And where do you think them grants goes?' Without waiting for a reply, he went on to inform him, 'On booze and cigarettes! Booze and cigarettes! I ask you. What a bloody waste o' money.' Then, while Quentin Smith struggled to keep a straight face, Becket took a gulp of beer and followed that with another drag from his cigarette.

'Manager, eh!' Smith said, trying to sound suitably impressed and endeavouring to get back onto safer ground. 'That's a big responsibility. I hope they pay you well for it?'

Becket grunted but did not reply. He did not want his generous companion to think he was too well off, or he might be expected to buy the next round.

After a slight pause, the detective continued, 'What block of apartments do you manage then?'

'Marlow Place, in Gordon Square,' was the subdued and gloomy reply, for Marlow Place was a very ordinary building and not really much to brag about.

'Marlow Place, you say?' said Smith, feigning surprise. 'What a coincidence. One of my young ladies lives there.'

'Oh yeah?' Becket muttered, managing to look just a little bit interested.

'Now there's a sad case,' Smith told him. 'Poor little mite lost both her parents when she was very young and, but for this one guardian, she's alone in the world. He's a good bloke, this guardian of hers, and he really worries about her welfare but he's hardly ever in the country to keep an eye on her, so I do his job for him.'

'One o' them rich geysers, eh? Do you get paid for your trouble?' Becket asked with avaricious curiosity.

'Of course I do, my friend.' Then he added as an apparent afterthought, 'You know, someone like you could be a great help to me. You're in a position to keep an eye on the young lady – make sure no harm comes to her, and you'd be doing me and her guardian a really good deed.'

In Becket's books, 'good deeds' were for Boy Scouts. He was not a Boy Scout and never had been. He looked doubtful, and started to say, 'Well I dunno abou' tha' . . . I'm a busy ma—'

Smoothly, Smith cut in, 'And there'd be a bit of money in it for you, naturally.'

The fish took the bait. 'Who's the girl and what d' you want me t' do for you?' he asked.

Quentin Smith told him and explained the sort of information he was after. He warned Becket that the girl must not know anyone was looking out for her; young people took exception if they thought their independence was under threat, and if she took exception, their job would be finished. 'I just want to know she's OK. No accidents, not doing anything seriously out of order.'

He then handed over his business card, having first underlined his mobile telephone number. 'You can get me on that night and day,' he said.

He left behind him a very self-satisfied Becket, muttering that he ought to be getting back to his responsibilities, but showing no signs of hurrying over his unfinished pint. Wondering just how reliable the caretaker really was, the detective waited and watched from across the street.

Ted Hunter was, like Quentin Smith, an ex-policeman. They had known each other while on the force but had not got around to forging a friendship until after their retirement.

Although 12 years junior to Ted in age, Quentin Smith had outranked him. Ted bore no grudge but it did make friendship difficult. It was not until Quentin Smith opted for an early retirement at about the same time as Ted's became due that the men finally got around to a friendly pint together.

Initially, Ted had had no ambition for the future. His pension was modest but adequate, and he had looked forward to nothing more stressful than supporting the local football team and a stroll to the corner pub for a pint and a game of darts with his friend.

Quentin, on the other hand, had always had a great deal of ambition. He had applied for early retirement with the intention of taking all his accumulated experience into his own private venture.

It was not long before Ted began to grow weary of the idle life. 'I envy you your get-up-and-go,' he had once confided over the froth of his beer. 'A full time job is out of the question, but there are times when I feel I could do with something to keep the brain ticking over.'

Quentin did not forget those words. Ted may not have been one of the leading lights in the department, but he had proved his worth and been regarded as a steady and reliable member of the team. From thereon, when overloaded with work, he recruited Ted's services. Ted was grateful. It gave him back his dwindling self-esteem, made him feel he still had something useful to contribute to life and, he had to admit, the extra money came in very handy.

It was an easy step to the discovery that one of Ted's numerous relatives, a hairdresser called Anne Hunter, had a boyfriend who had just enrolled as a new student at Saint Martins College. Her help was enlisted.

'If you can get David to take you to some of the pubs and clubs those students frequent, you might get a chance to meet and strike up a friendship with this Katherine,' Ted encouraged his niece.

'I'm not sure I'd want anyone watching out for me, Uncle

Ted,' Anne told him doubtfully, pushing her long, multicoloured hair extensions back off her shoulders.

'But that's just it, love – you have got someone watching out for you,' her uncle was quick to point out. 'You've got a whole host of family doing just that. You're lucky. This kid's got no one, but now she's got us. Right?'

When put like that, it did not sound so bad. Anne nodded agreement. She was, in fact, pleased to be of assistance to this much-revered uncle. He had never asked for her help before and she felt honoured.

Having set the wheels in motion, all that was left for Quentin Smith to do was harvest the information, combine it into a monthly report and send a copy off to his client's secretary, Mrs Simmons.

13

By the time Saint Martins College opened its doors, the novelty of having so much unaccustomed freedom had worn a little thin. Katherine and Samantha were ready to settle into a slightly more moderate existence.

Coming from the country, and from a disciplined, traditional boarding school for girls, straight into a busy art college, was bound to be a bit of a culture shock for Katherine. For the first time, she found herself constantly in the company of men her own age and among people from all walks of life. The mixture of accents, backgrounds, dress and conventions made her feel strange, like an alien just dropped in from another planet. Samantha, on the other hand, with her less restricted background and indomitable personality, was not in the least bit daunted. Taking the changes in her stride, she was in her element and, with her usual impetuosity, threw herself into anything and everything that was going. Katherine suffered by comparison. She had no immediate desire to be the life and soul of the classroom, studio or party and was, for the time being, happy to stay quietly in the background and observe.

Hiding her shyness behind an aloof, confident veneer, she gave the impression of being proud, haughty and a bit of a loner. The other girls were too busy finding their own level and circle of friends to give Katherine much thought, except to note that she had good looks and figure and, if she was not so staid in dress, would be serious competition. The boys, however, took the trouble to give her more attention and found her cool stand-offishness a definite turn on. Unfortunately for them, though, it also succeeded in keeping them at arm's length.

With the passing of time, Katherine adjusted to her new

life and to the people she shared it with. Influenced by the outlandish apparel of her peer group, she soon adopted a mode of dress more suited to a trendy art student. The flowing fabrics and dark dramatic colours favoured by her met with approval and admiration.

Although not overtalkative, it was generally felt that what she had to say was worth listening too. More so as, with maturity, her voice had taken on a husky quality that was thought to be seductive and appealing. Glimpses of a multifaceted personality were beginning to materialise, along with new mannerisms both charming and alluring. It was only a matter of time before Katherine's assumed confidence became genuine and on those social occasions when wine brought her defences down, she laughed and flirted outrageously along with the rest.

Drawing the line at any deep relationships only seemed to add to her appeal. It was not that she was against the idea of having an affair, it was simply that there was no one she cared for enough, and something within her rebelled against indulging in casual sex.

For some, like Katherine, it was a time for physical and mental growth; for all, it was a time for forging new friendships. In their first year, she and Samantha seemed to spend as much time in other people's apartments as in their own. When in to callers, they laughingly complained their apartment resembled Waterloo Station during rush hour.

From the beginning, one of their more frequent callers was David Darnley and his girlfriend, Anne Hunter. Anne had made Katherine's acquaintance within the first week of the first term. Meeting Katherine through David had been so simple, requiring neither effort nor ingenuity. David was everyone's friend: a real socialite to be found wherever the masses gathered. A friendship between the girls had quickly developed and, although initially contrived, it was sincerely felt.

*

Katherine did not meet Jeremy Grierson until the beginning of the spring term. Life drawing was new on the curriculum, and his name appeared on the timetable as tutor. Having gone initially to the wrong studio, she arrived ten minutes late for the first lesson. Instruction had already been given and the project started and so, as unobtrusively as possible, Katherine went to the seat Samantha had predictably saved for her.

Taking sketchpad and equipment out of her folder, she looked down on the forum to see whom she was supposed to be sketching. The subject was a large, handsome and voluptuous middle-aged lady reclining on large cushions. The studio lights were aimed to highlight, from all angles, her ample curves, and to show every fold of surplus flesh. In startled amazement Katherine's jaw dropped open. There appeared to be acres of the woman, and she was as naked as the day she was born.

She saw at a glance that the model was an incredibly good subject to draw, but Katherine had been unprepared for such blatant nudity. Of course she knew what life drawing meant, but somehow she had not expected to see so much uncovered flesh all in one go. She had expected a little more subtlety – partial nudity . . . a drape of fabric strategically placed, perhaps. Her assumptions, she now realised, had been ridiculously naïve.

Jeremy Grierson had become aware of Katherine the moment she came through the door. But then, he had noticed her before, many times, in the corridors of the college. With an artist's eye, he had seen the perfect bone structure of a fascinating face.

With interest, he had watched her cross the studio and go quietly to a seat. He had also observed her reaction to Lily. It amused him to imagine what her response was going to be next week when confronted with Allen. This was obviously her first life drawing class. He had seen similar reactions to nudity before. They did not last: the students soon became blasé.

Jeremy gave her a moment to collect her wits before

approaching to issue the same instructions he had already given the rest of the class. After one initial fleeting embarrassed look at him, Katherine lowered her eyes and kept them fixed firmly on her sketchpad while she listened.

I do believe we have a virgin in our midst, Jeremy told himself with cynical humour. How refreshing! His attention soon turned to other matters, however, and he spent the rest of the tutorial going around the class assessing work and offering advice.

Eventually, he returned to Katherine. Gazing down on her sketchpad, he was pleasantly surprised by the quality of her work. Virtue *and* talent, he concluded. Doubly refreshing!

The following week, with impatient curiosity, Jeremy watched for the arrival of Katherine. As he had earlier predicted, when her eyes came to rest on Allen, she was even more embarrassed. If his guess was right, not only was she a virgin, but she had never before seen a naked man.

Unaware she was being closely observed, Katherine was having her own private thoughts on the matter. She had seen partial nudity in films and in magazines. There were paintings of the gods exhibited in the art galleries and pictures of nude statues in her book on mythology. Not all wore fig leaves. This was quite different, this was total nudity in the flesh, and the model seemed to have no modesty. He was obviously proud of his assets and, peeping with discreet curiosity from under thick, dark lashes, it appeared to Katherine, not without good reason.

The students often took a break to wander around the studio and peer at each other's work. Every class has its jester and David Darnley was theirs. He meandered his way around the room, observing and quietly commenting on his friends' sketches, until he eventually came to Katherine. Folding his arms across his chest, he silently studied her drawing. After a moment, he cocked his head on one side as if to view the picture upside down. Next he studied the model through half closed eyes, and then, looking back at the drawing again, said with a straight face, 'Well, well. Isn't that interesting?'

'What is?' Katherine asked, puzzled.

'I was just wondering why, when everyone else has drawn it pointing down, you've drawn it pointing up!' he pondered thoughtfully. 'Definitely Freudian . . . A deep insatiable need, perhaps?'

The students on each side of Katherine heard his comment and moved closer to take a look at Katherine's sketch.

Jason grinned wickedly. 'Maybe it's the only way she's ever seen it before,' he suggested with a knowing wink.

'B-but I haven't!' denied Katherine in some confusion.

'Haven't what?' quizzed David. 'Drawn it pointing up or seen it any other way?'

Before she could answer, Spike interrupted with, 'Na, what she means is she prefers it that way – makes a more appealing picture,' he suggested helpfully.

'But I don't prefer it that way,' Katherine flustered.

'You don't?' exclaimed David, 'I thought all girls preferred it that way.' All three looked at her in mock astonishment.

Jeremy, silently working only a few paces away, had overheard most of this dialogue. Keeping his face averted, he struggled to suppress the urge to laugh.

Her tormentors were not so successful. The corners of their mouths were beginning to twitch with irrepressible humour. Katherine realised she was being wound up.

They would all have disintegrated into fits of raucous laughter had they not been afraid of offending the dignity of the model.

Jeremy Grierson was not much older than his students were but his superior artistic skill set him distinctly apart.

He had himself formerly been a student at Saint Martins and one of its shining lights. So much so, that when he applied for the post of tutor only three years after leaving, it was a foregone conclusion that he would get the job. He was immensely proud to have been selected out of so many applicants and quite determined to give satisfaction. Tutoring, however, was not Jeremy's prime ambition in life, but for the time being it gave him a regular income and enough free hours in which to pursue his real interest.

Jeremy enjoyed pure art in its various forms, but what he wanted to be most of all was a portrait painter. In order to receive commissions he had first to become known. He needed publicity, good publicity, and lots of it. If that meant kowtowing to the likes of Rodney Harrington, well, so be it.

Jeremy had just begun working towards an exhibition to be held at an art gallery on Lexington Crescent. Rodney Harrington was the owner of the gallery and the self appointed art director. With infuriating condescension, Harrington had agreed to exhibit half a dozen of the artist's paintings if they came up to expectation.

Since Harrington always did everything on a grand scale, Jeremy knew this exhibition could prove to be the big break he was looking for. The gallery was large, plush and well known in the art world. Anyone who was anyone would be invited to attend the opening night, but what was more important: all the top art critics would be invited. Through their columns he hoped his talent would receive recognition, and through their personal recommendations the longed-for commissions.

The subjects for the half dozen canvases were to be Jeremy's own choice, and he was looking for interesting faces. Katherine had such a face, and he had known from the moment he first set eyes on her that he wanted to paint her portrait. From the day she had come to him for her first tutorial and gone through a kaleidoscope of emotions at the sight of Lily, he had become obsessed by his desire to capture her on canvas. While she sketched in the studio, absorbed in her work, he had done preliminary drawings of her face at all angles, in different moods, and in varying lights. Jeremy had taken these preliminaries home with him to his studio apartment and, in the evenings, used them to begin work on a canvas. He knew he would eventually need more than just drawings to do her justice; he would need the girl herself to sit for him.

On the day of Katherine's last lesson before the end of term, aware he would not be teaching her again, Jeremy asked if she would stay behind after class for a private word.

Katherine did initially wonder why she had been singled out, but concluded he wanted to talk about her work. She arranged to catch up with Samantha later and, as her fellow students packed up their equipment and filed out of the studio in their usual rowdy, disorderly fashion, she lingered behind.

Her eyes focused on Jeremy: tall and lean, with unruly, dark Titian curls and warm amber eyes. He favoured casual shirts tucked into well-fitted black jeans; wide, silver buckled belts; loose-fitting jumpers and hiking boots. As she watched him stow his artwork away, Katherine wondered, and not for the first time, about his private life.

He occasionally frequented the same pubs as the students, usually with his own group of friends. When on his own, he sometimes came over to join them. A very private person, not particularly communicative on any subject other than art, he gave the impression of being deep and intense. He had no recognisable accent, and it now occurred to Katherine that not once during the whole term had she heard him raise his voice. Attention and respect had been earned, and freely given.

Katherine was aware that some of the girls regarded Jeremy as attractive, but he showed no romantic interest in them or any other female. Very little was known about his private life, although he was believed to be unattached. She attributed much of this attraction to his air of mystery and unobtainability. His lack of interest in women inevitably aroused speculation that he might be gay. Katherine had heard this question raised a few times but had not given it much thought.

Having finished his task, Jeremy came over and, perching on the edge of a table, came straight to the point. 'I would like to do a portrait of you,' he stated, fixing her with speculative eyes. 'I've been given the opportunity to enter some of my work in an art exhibition: about half a dozen pieces or so. I've got the best part of a year to put a collection together and I wondered if you would sit for me, at my studio, after the summer holidays?' He waited for her reply.

The request took Katherine by surprise and she wondered what had prompted him to single her out for the honour. For honour it was. She knew, as did everyone else at Saint Martins, that Jeremy Grierson was a superb artist. Although she had never actually seen any of his finished work, each quick demonstration sketch done for the benefit of the class had been impressive proof of his artistic ability.

Her instincts told her that he was a man to be trusted, that his request was genuine and not just an excuse to get her into his studio. Even so, there was a question that needed to be asked. She hesitated for a moment, not knowing quite how to put it. Lost for the right words, and feeling rather foolish, she eventually inquired, 'With my clothes on?'

The question and her way of asking amused him, but he was careful not to smile or allow his gaze to waver. He merely shrugged. 'If you prefer.'

PART II

14

The summer was long and hot, and although there were those who complained about the soaring temperatures and high humidity, Katherine was not one of them.

Dressed in brief shorts and skimpy T-shirts, she spent many contented hours roaming the grounds of Ravenswood. Sometimes she settled on grass or boulder to capture on canvas the magnificent landscape and sometimes she swam in a secluded part of the lake. More often than not she took a picnic with her and was gone for hours, returning to the house only when the light began to fade. There were days when, with flowers for the family vault, Katherine walked the short distance to the village church, stopping occasionally to chat with a familiar face. Her skin took on a golden tan and her long limbs glowed with health and vitality.

The Reverend Martins was pleased to see her in church on two consecutive Sundays. When she failed to appear again, he sadly told himself that if only her late grandfather was still around to bring out the port, he would drive over to Ravenswood to give her church attendance some encouragement.

There were days when Katherine either visited school friends who lived within striking distance of Ravenswood or drove into one of the nearby towns to browse around the department stores and boutiques. Since her enrolment at Saint Martins, she had developed a keen interest in fashion and invariably ended up studying garments in the couturier departments. When tempted to buy one of these expensive creations, she would quickly remind herself that they did not go with the student image she had created for herself and would look ridiculously out of place in an art college.

It was while she was away on a day-long outing that Alexis made one of his periodic calls on the manor house. Katherine did not hear about it until well into the evening, when Mrs Johnson brought coffee to her in the drawing room.

'He was with Mr Coteman a couple of hours, and then he came in to see me,' the housekeeper told her, looking pleased. 'Johnson offered him a drink from the cabinet, of course, but he said he wouldn't because he'd got a long drive ahead of him.' She thought for a moment. 'I think he said he was on his way to York: and something about a charity performance. Anyway, I gave him tea and some of my fruit cake instead. He always likes my fruit cake,' she beamed proudly.

About to leave the room, Mrs Johnson paused at the door to say, 'Before he went, he asked after you, said he was sorry to have missed you and to give you his regards.'

Katherine was burning with curiosity. There were so many questions she wanted to ask, but the door was closing behind the housekeeper and she was too proud to call her back.

All the following day, with a radiant smile on her face, Ellie went around singing love songs to the air. Not once did she mention Alexis, preferring to keep the intoxicating memory of his visit to herself. Katherine was longing to ask questions, but again was too proud to do so. Eventually, irritated beyond endurance, she took to avoiding the lovelorn Ellie.

For the next couple of days, Katherine suffered severe mood swings, and on several occasions, inexplicable sighs escaped her lips.

Must be coming down with flu, the observant Mrs Johnson told her husband.

Only Katherine knew she was suffering from nothing more than a bad dose of disappointment.

When the Scotts had invited her to join them on a holiday abroad, Katherine had declined the offer for several reasons. A desire to see Alexis again had been one of them.

Since their paths had already crossed three times at Ravenswood, it seemed logical to conclude that Ravenswood was where their paths were most likely to cross again. He had come, and she had missed him.

James was another reason why Katherine had not wished to impose herself upon the Scotts. They had been in each other's company at Marlow Place and Ivy House on several occasions throughout the past year. Since his feelings towards her had shown no sign of returning to their former more casual condition, Katherine had felt, and continued to feel, uncomfortable in his company. Whilst she loved James dearly, she knew it to be the wrong kind of love. Clearly not the kind he wanted from her.

James had already been in and out of a number of relationships, all of them deep and meaningful at the time. Katherine, at 20, had not had any affairs at all. This was mainly because she still had not met anyone with whom she wished to be on intimate terms. Well, perhaps there was one, she admitted to herself in a rare honest moment, but he had made it abundantly clear from the start that he was not interested in her.

A desire to learn a little about the running of her affairs had been another reason for Katherine wishing to stay at home. When she had gone to Mr Coteman's office to ask questions, he had answered them, and been as willing to instruct as she had been to learn. Katherine had accompanied him on business calls to some of the nearer properties belonging to the Ravenswood estate. It seemed perfectly natural to all that she should be with Mr Coteman, taking an interest in her tenants and business concerns.

Oh why couldn't Alexis have chosen to visit on a day I was in the office, she moaned to herself, and why on earth didn't Mr Coteman tell me he was expecting a visit from him?

On a number of occasions, the comptroller touched on his discussions with Alexis and later in the week mentioned a telephone call he had received. But, although Katherine lived in hope, Alexis did not come again to Ravenswood while she was there and neither did he phone the house.

Students were pouring back into London for the start of the new academic year, and all too many of them were finding their way to the apartment on the fourth floor of Marlow Place, or so it seemed to the disgruntled Becket. For hours on end, students sat around listening to music, drinking, smoking and swapping holiday experiences.

'Wha's wrong wi' usin' the pub?' the caretaker was heard to mutter on a number of occasions.

The reopening of Saint Martins eventually put a stop to the stream of traffic, and peace was once more restored to Sid Becket's life.

Having completed their year of general art, the second year students were now required to specialise. Katherine chose fashion design and Samantha, textile design, so that now, for the first time, the two girls were going in different directions. By day, they saw little of each other, except when they met for lunch or passed each other in the busy corridors. Most evenings and weekends, however, they continued to enjoy a social life together.

As it happened, Katherine did not begin her sittings for Jeremy until after the Christmas break. They had not been able to synchronise their busy timetables until then, and now Jeremy was keen to get started on the new preliminary sketches.

Anticipating she might have difficulty finding his apartment, he arranged to meet her out of college. Together, in the light cast by the street lamps, neon signs and passing traffic, they walked the short distance in the cold, damp, January air.

His studio proved to be a large barn of a place on the top floor of an old residential building. The whole of one wall had been knocked out and replaced with huge plate-glass windows, as had a part of the high ceiling, so that by day the room would be suffused with natural light. Leaving

Jeremy to turn up the heating and switch on the table lamps, Katherine went to gaze out over an uneven sea of dark grey slate rooftops broken in places by the warm glow of the illuminated streets of London. Her gaze travelled up to the skylight, to marvel at the silver radiance of the full moon and a million tiny stars.

With the completion of the window conversion, inspiration appeared to have run out, for Katherine could detect no further evidence of modernisation and improvement to the apartment. Large unframed paintings hid portions of scarred walls, while oddments of rugs did much to obliterate the dull, creaking floorboards from view.

That half of the apartment she saw, had been kept strictly as a work studio, and it was from here the pungent smell of oil paint and turpentine permeated the air. She took in the battered tallboy which housed an untidy assortment of art equipment; the canvases of varying sizes stacked against a wall; the paint-splattered easel and a couple of powerful free-standing photographic lamps. There was a rather grand stone fireplace under a large ornate mirror, and a Victorian chaise longue partly covered by a colourful embroidered and fringed shawl.

Her attention turned next to the other end of the apartment, to the curious selection of old furniture and ornamentation. There was something distinctly Jeremy about the more beautiful pieces of artwork; the alabaster sculptures were undoubtedly his own creations. His work, in the same recognisable style, lined the corridors of Saint Martins.

'I love your apartment, Jeremy,' she said softly, taking one of the steaming mugs from his outstretched hand, 'and this – it's fascinating.' She turned to gaze through one of the windows at the miracle beyond. 'I could never get tired of such a view.'

Her eyes locked with his and she heard him say, 'I'm pleased you like it, since for the next few months you'll be spending quite a bit of time up here.'

15

'Enough's enough! Give me a break, Katherine,' Samantha begged. 'College all week, art galleries at weekends. I want to do something else for a change.' Hearing no opposition coming from her companion, she relaxed into thoughtful contemplation, and then, with a face illuminated by a pleasurable idea, she piped up with, 'Harrods! I haven't been to Harrods for years.'

Inwardly, Katherine groaned. Shopping with Samantha was definitely not her favourite pastime. She would not be content until she had visited several of the huge departments, whereas Katherine, because of her studies, was really only interested in high fashion. However, because Samantha rarely pressed for her company on these expeditions, she had not the heart to say no. Perhaps Samantha was right, she told herself. A distraction from work would probably do them good.

Knowing when to give in gracefully, Katherine replied cheerfully enough, 'OK. Harrods it is, then.'

Early in the afternoon, they took the underground to Knightsbridge. As it was a Saturday, the store was crowded. After little more than three hours, the usually indomitable Samantha was ready to give up the struggle for survival and suggested, much to Katherine's relief, that they beat a retreat.

They found a little coffee shop situated a short distance away down one of the side streets and, occupying a table for two by the window, ordered cappuccinos.

'Well, that was a good afternoon's work,' said Samantha, pleased with her purchases. Taking a parcel out of a small but bulging carrier bag, she extracted from the wrapping a pair of handsome ethnic earrings. Pushing her strawberry-blonde hair back out of the way, she held them to her ears for appraisal.

Regarding them with a critical eye, Katherine approved, 'They're lovely, Sam.' Sighing, she said, 'I could have spent a fortune in there. I've never seen so many fabulous things under one roof. It was like Aladdin's cave.' She surprised herself with such words. They made her realise she was not, after all, an indifferent shopper.

After the coffees had been set down on the table, Samantha asked, 'What do you want to do now?'

Katherine thought for a moment. The afternoon was still quite young, it was a warm and gloriously sunny day, and she did not yet feel ready to head for home.

'A walk in Hyde Park?' she suggested hopefully, wondering if they would find any artwork exhibited along the wrought-iron railings and on the pavement stalls.

'Oh no you don't,' cautioned Samantha, reading her mind. 'This is a day off from art. Remember?'

Caught out, Katherine smiled sheepishly, 'All right, this is your day, you make a suggestion. I'll go along with whatever you want.'

'Promise?' Samantha asked, looking at her in a curious way.

'I have a feeling I'm going to regret having said that,' Katherine retorted, studying her friend through narrowed, suspicious eyes. 'You've got something up your sleeve,' she accused.

'There's a place very near here I've heard a great deal about but never seen,' Samantha replied thoughtfully, 'and frankly I'm more than a little curious.' Knowing Katherine would not like her suggestion she hesitated, but only for a moment. 'Linnet House,' she said with enthusiasm, 'Let's go take a look at Linnet House.'

Caught off guard, Katherine gave a start. A flicker of irritation crossed her lovely features, but she said nothing.

After a short pause, Samantha went on, 'Aren't you just a little bit curious? After all, the house has been in your family quite a long time and you said yourself you've never seen it.'

'I don't know where it is,' Katherine demurred, feeling the onset of butterflies in her stomach as she always did at the mention of anything that reminded her of Alexis. With agitated fingers, she pushed a stray curl back off her face.

'I know where it is. Belgrave Square is no more than a five-minute walk from here. How about it?' Samantha asked encouragingly.

With moody downcast eyes, Katherine thought for a moment. Although her parents had visited the house on many occasions and talked quite a lot about it, she had not been with them. Yes, Katherine had to admit, she was curious to see it for herself, even if only from the outside.

'If you really want to . . .' she agreed, somewhat reluctantly. 'But don't think for a minute that we're going to knock on any doors, Sam,' she warned.

'The thought never crossed my mind,' Samantha assured her with a grin. 'But if he was my cousin . . .'

'Second cousin!'

'. . . second cousin then, I'd think nothing of paying my respects whilst in the neighbourhood.' Checked by Katherine's withering look, she stopped, hastily put her hand up and said, 'Word of honour, no courtesy calls.'

In the past, they had only ever been to Knightsbridge to visit the huge museums, and for the shopping. They had never made any detours that took them beyond the main roads. However, since Samantha had found Belgrave Square on a map some time ago, she knew the direction they should take.

The further they moved away from the stores, the quieter and more impressively grand appeared the well-kept streets and residential town houses. When they came to Belgrave Square it seemed to them to be the most impressive of all and they stopped to stare at the tall white houses, with their wide stone steps leading up, between handsome columns, to the brass trimmed doors. The garden onto which the houses faced was well cared for; its flower borders along the paths neat, the benches nestling in among the tall shrubs, inviting. Through the surrounding black wrought iron railings, the gentle breeze was mildly scented from summer blooms. The whole square had an almost sleepy quality about it: even the birds and the butterflies seemed languid. Expensive cars were parked in the spaces designated to 'Resident Permit Holders Only'.

'Not bad! Not bad at all!' Samantha approved, slowly letting out her breath. After a moment, she asked, 'What number are we looking for?'

It was only then that Katherine realised she did not know the number, only the name of the house. Perplexed, both girls looked at the size of the square and at how many houses there were set back along its pavements.

'We won't find it by standing here gawking,' said Samantha, eager to begin the search. 'Come on, let's make a start.'

Together they walked along the wide pavement, looking up in turn at each house. With each step, Katherine's feelings grew more at odds with their surroundings. This was a smart part of town, frequented by conservatively dressed people and she was aware that, in their rather unorthodox clothes, she and Samantha looked out of harmony with the setting, and therefore, immediately noticeable. This was Alexis' territory. At this very moment, he could be looking down at them from one of the windows, scornfully aware of their presence.

'Why don't we give this up?' she suggested, a testy edge to her voice. 'It could take ages to get around all these houses and there's no guarantee the name is even on display for us to find,' she pointed out.

Samantha would have none of it. 'Very true, but we've come this far, I'm not going to give up at the first hurdle. We've lots of time. If it's here, we'll find it.'

They had already completed two sides of the square and were a third of the way along the brighter sunnier side, when Katherine saw the name Linnet House. It was clearly worked into a leaded stained glass window, shaped like an open fan over a solid white door.

Putting a restraining hand on Samantha's arm, they slowed their pace to gaze up at the grand exterior. Unlike some of its neighbours, this house had not been turned into an embassy or converted into luxury apartments and offices. It looked what it was – a private residence of a wealthy family. Through the tall sash windows, beyond the heavy, luxurious drapes, were glimpses of ornate plaster-work, crystal chandeliers and the expansive sweep of a large, green fern.

So this was the town house bought by Great-Grandfather Frederick to accommodate his mistress; the house her parents had loved and talked of in such glowing terms; the same house her grandfather had lived in when not at Ravenswood. Katherine longed to walk up the steps, as they had done, go through the front door and into the same rooms, to stand where they had stood, to gaze on all they had loved. Would it, just for a moment, turn back the clock, bring them close to her once more?

Just as they were almost abreast of Linnet House, the door opened and a man appeared. An open-necked white shirt tucked into close fitting Levi's showed to advantage his strong athletic build. He carried a sports bag and squash racquet.

Both girls recognised him instantly as Alexis Drew. His sudden appearance left them no time to retreat without drawing attention to themselves, and so they did the only thing they could under the circumstances: they continued to walk slowly along the pavement.

Deeply embarrassed, Katherine fervently prayed he had not witnessed their gawking at Linnet House. In an agony of torment she wondered what on earth she was going to say to him, how she was going to explain their presence in Belgrave Square.

She need not have worried. The man came down the steps and, just for a moment, as he crossed the pavement he raised striking dark eyes to look straight at them. A flicker of a lazy smile passed across the handsome features; a courteous, absent-minded smile. In a moment he had passed by, without hesitation or hint of recognition, and no backward glance. With long, purposeful strides he crossed the road to the burgundy Jaguar Katherine remembered so well.

As they watched him drive away, Samantha broke the silence with an exasperated gasp. 'Why on earth didn't you speak to him?' she asked, turning to stare at Katherine. 'You're related, after all, and in more ways than one, I might add. It would have been the most natural thing in the world, under the circumstances.'

Seeing him again had deeply disturbed Katherine, and far more than she cared to admit. 'Natural!' she retorted. 'There's nothing natural about our relationship, nor, for that matter, is there anything natural about the circumstances under which we find ourselves practically on his doorstep!' Katherine reminded her bitterly. 'Besides,' she added lamely, 'he didn't know me from Adam.'

Her heart was pounding and she was aware that, although relieved not to have had to explain their presence, she was also deeply disappointed that he had not recognised her. She hated herself for these mixed feelings and, as always, was unwilling to analyse them.

'Did you really expect him to recognise you without a bit of help?' Samantha questioned, turning bright, quizzical eyes on her friend. 'He hasn't seen you in years, and at the time you were knee-high to a grasshopper, and about as pretty as one,' she reminded her. 'Just look how much you've changed since then.'

16

Eighteen months had passed since Quentin Smith's meeting with Alexis Drew. Apart from his monthly reports, there had been no reason to communicate further with his client. Now it was time to compile another report.

Open on the desk in front of him was the file named 'Katherine Drew', and in his hands a routine letter from Ted Hunter. As he opened the single folded sheet of paper, a photograph dropped out onto the desk. He picked it up and glanced at it.

The picture had clearly been taken in a crowded pub. The main subjects, two men and a woman, were sitting companionably at a table. Relaxed and happy, all three were smiling for the photographer. Laying the photograph aside, Smith turned his attention to the neatly typed letter.

Dear Quentin,

Re: Katherine Drew

I'm pleased to be able to report that no calamities beyond the normal have befallen the young lady.

Miss Drew made two trips out of London: one on the second Sunday of the month when she went with her flat mate to Sunningdale to visit her friend's family. Brother James was also visiting for the weekend on that occasion.

As previously mentioned, he has stayed at Marlow Place a few times and has apparently shown more than just a passing interest in Miss Drew. He made another visit this month but, according to Anne, she continues to give him no encouragement of a romantic nature.

The second journey out of town was to Ravenwood, where she spent the third weekend of the month.

She made the usual round of pubs, clubs and parties. A bit of high jinx from time to time but nothing serious. No evidence of drug abuse, but it does sound as if she and friend have been a little over-indulgent with the liquid intake and the late nights this month. Despite all, they don't appear to have forgotten their way home, to their own beds, unaccompanied.

As you know, now that David Darnley is on a different course to Miss Drew, there is no way of getting regular detailed information on her progress in college. But my niece assures me the young lady has a lot of talent and is reputed to be doing very well in fashion design. It would seem she made the right choice.

I understand that Jeremy Grierson, her tutor, is painting a portrait of Miss Drew that he plans to exhibit in a prestigious art gallery on Lexington Crescent in a few months' time, along with half a dozen other pictures. The gallery is owned by a man called Rodney Harrington, who, I'm told, is well known in the art world, though not much liked.

She goes over to Grierson's studio apartment on an average of two evenings a week, and sometimes for a few hours during the weekend. His apartment is on the top floor of 39D Princeton Street. Anne assures me there is no romantic attachment between them: Grierson's only love is his work.

With so little to report, I would have phoned the information through to you this time but, as you can see, I needed to enclose the photograph. Grierson is the man on the right of Katherine Drew and you will probably recognise the other as David Darnley. Anne took the photograph in the White Hart on Southampton Row. They use the pub as a meeting place most Friday nights, where they down a couple of pints before moving on to other things.

Sincerely,

Ted.

Quentin Smith retrieved the photograph and, this time, gave it his full attention. It was the girl who claimed his interest. Surely there must be some mistake here. This was not Katherine Drew – well, not the Katherine Drew he knew, anyway.

He leafed through the accumulated contents of the file until he came to the photograph given to him by his client at their one and only meeting. Placing it alongside the new photograph, he compared its likeness.

He could see it now: the two faces did bear a resemblance. It could be her, but he would never have guessed if Ted had not pointed it out to him. The girl had undergone a marked change, all for the better, and he marvelled at what a few years had done for her.

The detective wondered at what stage the change had taken place: before or after the wedding. He thought that if she had matured before the wedding, then the child bride may not have come as such a shock to Alexis Drew as he had originally supposed. With a frown, he shook his head. That was not possible. He remembered being told that, although the photograph had been taken a year or two before, it was a good likeness. 'She hasn't changed much,' Alexis Drew had said. If that was so, then the metamorphosis had come later and her husband was unaware of what she looked like today.

He pondered the question for a moment and then told himself his client must know by now. After all, he and the girl were related to each other, and not only through marriage. They were sure to be in touch from time to time.

His eyes went next to the man sitting on her right, Jeremy Grierson. So this was the tutor mentioned in past reports. Smith briefly noted the slim build and fairly regular facial features. There was a hint of sensuality about the mouth, and a certain sensitivity in the eyes. He suspected that some girls might find these qualities appealing. There was nothing there to give alarm: he looked pleasant enough. Neither the mode of dress nor the length of his hair perturbed Quentin Smith. From what he could see, 90 per cent of the pupils and staff at art colleges dressed outlandishly. It seemed to go with the vocation.

Nothing to worry about there, he told himself. Tossing the photograph aside for the time being, he proceeded to give his full attention to the writing of the report.

The main source of Jeremy's disappointment was his portrait of Katherine. It had not come up to expectation, and so, at the last minute, he decided to withhold it from the exhibition. It was to have been his pièce de résistance, but there was a certain something missing and he was not quite sure what that something was.

Rodney Harrington accepted four of his best canvases and hung them alongside the work of other aspiring artists. On the big night, Jeremy's paintings were well received by the guests, and before the end of the exhibition three had sold at the asking price. He and his work got a mention in the art section of a couple of small-time papers but, even so, Jeremy was disappointed. He had hoped for more. Harrington, on the other hand, seemed satisfied and agreed to review more of his work for a future exhibition. Recognising real talent when he saw it, he intended to keep a watchful eye on the progress of Jeremy Grierson's career.

Jeremy now had a whole year in which to paint another portrait of Katherine, if she was still willing to sit for him.

Over the past few months, he and Katherine had become friends and comfortable in each other's company. Their conversations on art invariably turned into a casual lesson, followed by Jeremy giving a demonstration in answer to a question. After work on her portrait they would cook supper together, and then, while they dined with a bottle of wine, their conversation would turn to a whole range of topics.

Although, like Katherine, Jeremy was inclined to be secretive, he had eventually talked a little about his past. His mother had been a single parent, he told her, who, rather than struggle to make ends meet, had given him into care. He had been farmed out to a succession of foster parents until the social services and the law dictated that he had at last reached an age where he could be expected to take responsibility for his own welfare. A government scholarship, he told her, had brought him to Saint Martins, where with equal energy he had thrown himself in to both work and a string of casual relationships. From the moment of joining the staff, despite continued ample opportunity, he had carefully avoided the complications of physical involvement with the students. 'Not so easy,' he had laughed. 'Some can be very determined.'

Although Katherine talked freely of Haldene Abbey, of Ravenswood and her family, not once did she mention Alexis Drew; there were some secrets she would not share.

The portrait of Katherine had not received its finishing touch until the end of the spring term. She thought it wonderful and could not understand Jeremy's disappointment.

'You're just being modest!' she laughed at him. When he denied this, she said more seriously, 'Then you can't see how good it is because you're too close to it.'

He shook his head at that too and continued to look morose.

Katherine had studied the portrait more closely. 'You can't be dissatisfied, I don't believe you, Jeremy.'

Clearly, Jeremy did mean what he said and did not seem likely to change his opinion.

With a sigh, Katherine had agreed to sit for a new portrait. Her assurances that she did not mind were sincere, she had enjoyed their evenings together. They had become very much a part of the pattern of her life.

Her evening desertions of Samantha caused no pangs of conscience. After all, Samantha was rarely home herself these days. She was seeing a lot of a fellow student: quite literally, if she was to be believed.

Work, therefore, commenced on the new canvas in the

October, right after the summer holidays and, as before, Jeremy began by sketching preliminaries.

Although, by now, Jeremy's knowledge of Katherine was quite extensive, he constantly had the feeling there was more to know about her – much more. It was there: a sadness that sometimes came into her eyes, when her thoughts carried her off to some remote time and place where none could follow.

He suspected she was still a virgin: that it was the child and not the woman in her that he had captured on canvas. He wondered if this was the reason for his dissatisfaction with the portrait.

Katherine was beautiful, but how much more beautiful she would be if sexually awoken. He wanted her to look for him as a woman in love looks at her lover: eyes dreamy, lips parted in sensual promise, that glorious mane of hair loose and tousled around naked shoulders, and a wistful smile to suggest possession of an intimate secret.

But, he reminded himself, she was not a fulfilled woman and not likely to become one, because she was spending so much time with him. His thoughts had been bordering on the erotic and he was taken by surprise when he realised they had the power to arouse him.

So lost in thought was Jeremy that he was unaware he had stopped working and that his gaze had, for some time, been fixed on Katherine.

Silently, she returned his gaze, and waited.

Jeremy laid down his pencil and, going over to the chaise longue where Katherine held her pose, murmured, 'I want to try something new.' Taking her by the hands, he gently raised her to her feet and led her over to the chiselled stone fireplace.

It was apparent from the way the long, silk dressing gown skimmed over her slender form that she wore nothing underneath. He had requested this because it made a difference to the way the soft fabric draped over her body. Uncomplaining, she had yielded to his wishes. It was the nearest she had come to nudity for any of the sketches.

Now he turned her so that, when he repositioned his easel, she would be three-quarters facing him, while the other side of her face would be reflected in the heavy, gilt-framed mirror. Raising her left arm, he positioned it so that it rested along the mantelpiece, her fingers on the handle of a silver mirror. Then, he lifted her right hand so that the fingertips rested lightly on the edge of the shelf, almost touching her other hand. He tousled her hair so that it cascaded in disarray over her shoulders and down her back. Taking a step backwards, he paused to survey the overall affect. So far, he was satisfied.

Next, gently, intentionally, he untied the belt, letting it fall to the floor. The kimono fell apart as he knew it would. The soft silk slipped down over her right shoulder, coming to rest in the crook of an arm, leaving her partially exposed.

Katherine's first startled reaction was to clutch at the falling fabric, but he placed a firm, restraining hand on her arm, preventing her from doing so. He did not look at her body but only into her eyes until the first awkward moments of overwhelming shyness had passed. It was as if he was willing her, pleading with her, not to move. Although not a word had passed between them, she understood perfectly all that he was asking of her.

After a moment, feeling no further resistance, he slowly removed his hand. Holding his breath, afraid she might change her mind and rearrange the robe, he moved back. The pose was exactly what he wanted, the expression one he had not seen on her face before.

Turning away, he adjusted the lights and, when he had finished, their effect was dramatic. Still she had not moved, still she watched him. Silently, he released his breath; slowly, he allowed himself to relax, but the air between them remained charged.

Jeremy drew only one preliminary, which he worked on for half an hour at fever pitch. He was now unbearably impatient to get started on the main canvas. Laying the finished sketch aside, he took up the prepared canvas and placed it on the easel. Silently, he worked on, non-stop, until it occurred to him that Katherine must be desperately in need of a rest. Reluctantly he placed his brushes in a jar of turpentine and, taking the canvas from the easel, turned it to the wall. He did not want her to see the work in progress. Not this time.

For more than an hour, Katherine had been wrapped in her own deep thoughts. In an impersonal sort of way, she had always thought Jeremy an attractive man, but in all the time they had known each other, he had never given any indication that he was sexually interested in her. That he had made no advances towards her had been a relief, as she had experienced no really deep stirrings of desire for him. Why then, she asked herself, was she feeling like this now? It was almost as if she were willing, longing even, for something to happen between them.

Although she had been watching him through the mirror, their eyes meeting whenever he glanced up, Katherine was not aware that he had finished work for the evening until he stooped to pick up her belt. Now her eyes wavered and she moved uncertainly, as if she had just awoken and was disorientated.

He pulled the gown up over her shoulders, concealing her once more from his sight. In doing so, he was conscious of her nipples, erect with desire, pressing against the soft fabric of the silk. Instinctively he knew that it would be easy to take advantage of her, if he wished to. He had not made love for some time and never for the right reasons. But then, he had not, until now, met a girl like Katherine Drew.

Hesitantly, she turned towards him, placed her hands on his chest, slowly moving them up until her arms were around his neck. There was shy invitation in her eyes.

Fleetingly, Jeremy wondered about the moral ethics of involvement between a tutor and former pupil. He knew that if he was going to draw back, it must be now. He hesitated too long, already beginning to lack the will to do so. Sliding his hands under the folds of her gown, he pulled her to him. Their lips came together in a tender, exploratory kiss. She gasped at the new and sensuous pleasure of his uninhibited touch. If their minds told them it was not too late to draw back, their bodies told them otherwise.

Their meetings went on much as before but now a new dimension had been added to their relationship. All the qualities he had wanted to see in Katherine were there. Added to that was the transformation that had taken place within himself. As if a veil had been lifted from his eyes, he found he was able to paint this woman as he had never been able to paint a woman before. He saw her and the world through the eyes of a man in love and, through this newly discovered emotion, he began to paint with his heart.

The portrait was completed by the end of Katherine's third and final year at Saint Martins College. Even Jeremy was awed by his magnificent achievement. Impatiently he waited for the day when he could launch his masterpiece on the world.

Katherine was a little apprehensive about being exposed to public gaze but gave her consent anyway. It was too late to do otherwise. She did, however, exact conditions. Jeremy had to promise the portrait would under no circumstances be sold for public exhibition, but only to a private collector. She also asked him not to disclose her true identity. If asked, he was to give her name as Madeleine Harcourt. Secretly she prayed that her great-grandmother would, under the circumstances, forgive her the liberty of making so free with her name.

17

'The most exciting thing about life is the never knowing what's around the corner,' Katherine had said to Samantha, when telling her about the new collection that she was helping to put together for the Paris Spring Show.

She had barely completed her three months' probationary period with Veronique Couture and was living in a state of excited euphoria. She was not to know that, after such a short time as a trainee designer, her days with the prestigious company were about to come to an abrupt end. Nor could she know that she was approaching a major turning point in her life.

This particular morning, Katherine made a point of arriving early at the workshop over the ground-floor showroom on Great Portland Street. She hoped to get off to a good start on the line of garments awaiting her attention before the rest of the staff arrived to disrupt her day. Unfortunately, she was not the only one to be full of good early-bird intentions. Before she could even get the door open, she was assailed by the raised, anxious voice of Madame Veronique.

'Silly, thoughtless girl!' Madame was wailing in true tragic operatic tones. ' 'Ow could she do this to me? Ungrateful girl. Now what am I to do?' she was asking Michael, the showroom manager.

'Call the model agency for a replacement?' Michael asked hopefully.

'And 'oo do you think they 'ave to send? Any model worth 'aving ees already booked out by now! It ees the 'eight of the season,' the woman moaned in her heavily accented voice. 'So irresponsible of 'er to let us down like this.' As her agitation increased, so did her French gestures: her busy hands emphasised her every word.

'What's happened?' whispered Katherine to a young seamstress with a round face and large dancing eyes whom she knew only as Angela.

'Ava's had the audacity to break her ankle. Don't ask me how, that's all I know,' the girl whispered back, grinning mischievously, but making sure she could not be seen by either Madame or Michael. She turned her attention back to the job of removing the overnight dust covers from several rails of sample garments.

Oh hell! It's going to be one of those days, Katherine told herself, eyeing her employer warily.

Madame Veronique was known to be French by birth and had been heard to refer to the south of France as home, but an olive complexion, dark eyes and black hair gave a hint of a Moorish connection somewhere along the line. The youthful looks and figure that belied her 60-odd years were due, so Katherine had been told, to a Bedfordshire health farm and the medical profession. The observant might notice the small, too perfect nose and the fine skin slightly too taut over high cheekbones. The presence of liver spots on the backs of her perfectly manicured hands told a more honest tale of passing time.

For a few minutes, with mounting unease, Katherine listened to the commotion. Then, feeling the urge to distance herself from the dramatics, she turned her attention towards the rail of garments she had set aside the night before. She reached for a flame-red, chiffon evening gown and was about to hand it to a seamstress with instructions, when Madame's arresting voice called out, 'Stop!'

Katherine turned to see who she was addressing and was surprised to discover all eyes, including Madame's, fixed on herself.

'Come 'ere!' her employer demanded.

To hear was to obey, so Katherine, still holding the gown, went forward, but with some trepidation. Now what? she asked herself.

Taking the fabulous garment out of her hands, Madame Veronique held it up against Katherine's tall, slender form. Through narrowed eyes, she regarded her silently for a moment. 'Yes. Yes. I do think you weel do very nicely,' she murmured to the charged air around her. 'You weel simply 'ave to do. Pretty face, good figure and legs, almost tall enough, and I'm sure we can do something with this 'air,' she said, holding up a long lock and letting it fall from her fingers. Turning to her assistant she asked: 'What do you theenk, Michael?'

Before the startled man could reply, she had thrust the evening gown into his arms and turned back to Katherine.

'My dear, you are going to be our latest recruit,' Madame declared with a Gallic flourish of her heavily ringed hands.

Suspicion began to dawn on the incredulous Katherine. 'Do you mean model?' she asked sceptically.

'*Mais oui!* But of course I mean model,' Madame replied.

'But I don't want to be a model. I'm a designer,' Katherine stated, hoping that would settle the matter.

'No more a designer. Now you are a model.' The tone of Madame's voice was final and invited no further argument.

She walked all around the bewildered girl, looking her up and down as if she was an inanimate piece of merchandise. 'We could do with a little less bosom 'ere and another inch or two in 'eight, but I suppose we cannot do anything about that,' she complained to Michael.

Katherine did not consider herself to be over-endowed or short, so these remarks took her quite by surprise until she remembered that most models were inclined to be rather flat-chested and at least 5 feet 9 inches tall. She had no desire to be either of these things and would like to have said as much, but Madame was saying, 'You must 'ave a new name. We already 'ave a Katerina.'

Katherine had no intentions of becoming a model, so when, on an impulse, she said, 'Madeleine Harcourt,' she took herself quite by surprise. For a moment she allowed herself to hope that Madame had not heard her, but unfortunately the lady had, and her next words confirmed it.

'Good. From now on you will be known as Madeleine. We will not need the 'arcour',' she stated imperiously.

'What's wrong with Harcourt?' Katherine wanted to know, staring at her in bewilderment.

'Nothing at all *chérie*, but Madeleine – it ees enough, 'arcour' ees quite unnecessary. People weel remember Madeleine, it has that *je ne sais quoi*, and it is French!' she stated with another Continental flourish of her bejewelled hands.

'But Madame, I don't want to be a model,' the girl tried once more.

'Nonsense. Every girl wants to be a model. Now that ees settled, ees it not?' The question was not an invitation to argue the point. One simply did not argue with Madame Veronique, or plain Vera as she was affectionately called behind her back.

Turning dark piercing eyes on Michael, Madame said, 'I must see the garments on 'er immediately. If there are any alterations to be made, they must take priority. *Oui*, Michael?' With one last theatrical flourish she breezed off in the direction of her office.

Madeleine glowered after her. I won't do it, she told herself truculently.

Michael sighed at the unforeseen turn of events. The day had already threatened to be a difficult one without Ava's accident adding to their last-minute problems.

He usually spent a large proportion of his day downstairs in the elegant showroom, tending to the needs of wealthy private customers and retail buyers or sorting out orders for delivery. But today, he feared he would not have much time for the showroom.

Michael moved his slight, dapper frame into action. 'Angela. Collect all Ava's gowns together and bring them to the fitting room.' Angela, at the tender age of 19, was an experienced hand. She had been with Veronique Couture since leaving school at the age of 16. After three years as a seamstress-cum-Girl-Friday, she did not need to be told to bring all the necessary implements for making alterations.

With a marked lack of enthusiasm, Katherine turned to assist Angela.

'Not you Ka— Madeleine,' Michael snapped. 'You come with me.'

He gave no sign of noticing her reluctance to follow him to the fitting room. The needs of Veronique Couture took precedence over all else and this girl's needs and feelings were of little consequence right now. A catastrophe had been averted and that was all that mattered.

'Take those hideous bags off,' he instructed Katherine, with no attention to tact. He took a wrap dressing gown off a peg and handed it to her.

Hideous? Katherine asked herself, appraising the mirrored image of cabled woollen over long, dark skirt. *Ordinary* maybe, but surely not hideous. However, she did as he commanded and donned the dressing gown.

It was well known that Michael was gay: he made no secret of it. She knew her body would not interest him in the least. He had never so much as raised an eyebrow at any of the models in their various stages of undress. The girls never remarked upon his presence in the changing rooms, nor challenged his right to be there. He was the most important member of the team: the hub of the wheel. Michael knew everything there was to know about feminine garments and could be a godsend in a crisis, especially during the whirlwind activities of a fashion show, when time was short between changes and things were most likely to go wrong. A zip might get stuck, a button fall off, or a necessary accessory go missing. Michael could always be counted upon to keep a clear head in a crisis.

'Sit down.' He indicated to one of the chairs in front of the long wall mirror. Taking up a brush, he began rearranging her hair with dextrous fingers, this way and that, surveying the effects in the mirror. Finally, laying the brush down, he said with some severity, 'You should be ashamed of yourself.'

'Why? What do you mean?' Katherine asked, quite taken aback by the abrupt words.

'With all your fashion training and obvious talents, how can you allow yourself to go around looking the way you do?' He scowled at her. 'If only you would take the trouble to apply some of that creative know-how to yourself, you'd be beautiful. What an utter waste.'

Katherine appraised her reflection. Beautiful? she asked herself. There was honest doubt in her eyes.

Labouring the point, Michael continued, 'Well, look at yourself. You're wearing hardly any make-up, you haven't done anything remarkable with that fabulous hair and, as for your clothes, they don't give even a hint of what you're hiding under them. I can't understand your lack of personal interest. It's as if you don't want to be noticed.'

Katherine continued to regard herself in the mirror. Until now, she had been quite satisfied with the way she looked. After all, most of her college friends had dressed more or less as she did, and those she had kept in touch with still dressed this way. All except for Samantha, perhaps. Now she came to think of it, her friend had gradually changed her mode of dress since leaving Saint Martins.

Now it had been pointed out to Katherine, she had to admit that Michael was right. Not a great deal of her creative ability went on herself.

Michael reclaimed her attention. 'When you left that college of yours, you should have left the student look behind. You're out in the real world now.' He waited for his words to sink in and then, taking her by the arm, he said a little more kindly, 'Get up and walk across the room.'

Self-consciously, Katherine did as he asked, but she had covered only half the distance before he said with exasperation, 'Not like that! Stand up straight, tuck your derrière in and put your shoulders back.'

He watched her for a moment and then said, 'Look, do it like this.' Michael began to pace across the room giving an excellent demonstration of how a model should walk, and several interesting turns. So professional was he that it did not occur to Katherine to laugh at his exaggerated feminine movements. She copied him as best she could.

The girl's a natural, Michael thought, Madame was not wrong. She'll do very nicely. Aloud he said, 'You'll have plenty of time to practise during rehearsals when we get to Paris. I'll instruct the other girls to teach you. Don't worry, you'll be all right,' he assured her. 'The experts will be on hand to take care of your hair and make-up. Right now, our main concern is getting those dresses altered in time.'

As if on cue, Angela chose that moment to push a rail of garments through the door and into the room.

'You're a lucky girl, Madeleine,' Michael said, already sounding comfortable with her new name. 'This is your big break. There are not too many who get to start at the top.'

He eyed her enviously. Her raw equipment was sensational and, if that was not enough, she had a fabulously husky voice to go with it. Even without knowing how to use and enhance those God-given assets, the girl oozed sex appeal.

'I keep trying to tell you, I don't want to be a model,' she obstinately reminded him. 'But maybe I'll do it just this once to help out,' she condescended, knowing she was fighting a losing battle.

'We'll see,' was his only comment. To himself he said, silly girl doesn't recognise her potential. Once she's up there on the catwalk under the bright lights; gets a taste for the glamour and glitz; sees herself in the press – she'll change her tune.

The journey home in the rush-hour traffic did nothing to improve Katherine's humour. To make matters worse, when she complained to Samantha about the day's disaster, she did not get the sympathy she expected.

In the middle of their conversation Anne Hunter, resplendent with sandy hair streaked red and green, unexpectedly turned up on the doorstep bearing gifts. There was no need for her to announce the contents of the bulging carrier bag. The pungent aroma of fish and chips permeating the air did a rather thorough job of announcing themselves.

'I've brought supper,' she declared happily in tones that would have been more appropriate if she had come bearing champagne and caviar.

Out came the plates, wine, napkins and cutlery. Over their greasy feast, Katherine told Anne of her misfortune.

Anne stared in disbelief. 'You're mad!' she declared, not mincing words. 'Most of us would kill to be in your shoes.'

'Give it a try,' Samantha advised. 'If it doesn't work out, you can always return to designing. You'll have lost nothing.'

After supper the three friends went through Katherine's meagre wardrobe with the hope of finding apparel suitable for Paris. Within five minutes, they agreed she was one of the few who could legitimately claim to have nothing to wear.

'An interesting collection, but hardly suitable for a model on her way to the top,' Samantha commented disparagingly. 'You should have come shopping with me last weekend.'

'Wish I had,' Katherine gloomily admitted.

'For what it's worth, you're welcome to borrow anything I've got . . . if it fits, that is,' Samantha added, assessing Katherine's willowy figure while at the same time making a mental note to cut down on the snacks.

'I'd offer, but I know I've got nothing suitable,' Anne sighed, knowing that the garish colours in her bizarre collection would not appeal to Katherine.

'That's very generous, but I think it's time I took some of that good advice you keep handing out, Sam,' Katherine responded. 'I'm going on a shopping spree first thing in the morning.'

'Now you're talking. And while you're in the mood for a little free advice, how about treating yourself to a whole new set of make-up?' Samantha added, turning her pert little nose up at the remnants lying on the dressing table. 'I can't remember the last time you bought any.'

'If you insist, but you're bound to find fault with whatever I bring back,' Katherine laughed, feeling better now that she had come to a decision.

'I know you can be trusted to pick your own wardrobe after all, clothes are your business and it's something you happen to be very good at, but make-up . . .?' Samantha shook her blonde head doubtfully. 'You're right, I'm not sure you should be let loose on your own in the cosmetic department. I'll come with you,' she said, grabbing at the excuse for another shopping spree. 'You'll need a second opinion and an extra pair of hands to help carry all your purchases. I'll enjoy spending someone else's money for a change,' she grinned.

'Hair and nails are my department,' chipped in Anne, admiring her splendid set of bright green nails. 'I'll come over Saturday evening if you like, and give you a manicure and crash course on hair care and styling.'

Eyeing the colourful nails and hair, Katherine teased, 'The traffic light look wouldn't suit me . . . just so long as you know that.'

Samantha, behind a desk piled high with catalogues and swatches, could not concentrate. The Monday morning blues had accompanied her to work. She suspected her feelings of anticlimax were the result of so much activity over the weekend. Now all she could think about was Katherine on her way to Heathrow airport and the empty apartment that would be waiting for her at the end of the day. Samantha was not overly fond of her own company. She needed people and the stimulus of romance. A month had passed since ending her last affair and there was still no one new to make her pulse race.

At least, she consoled herself, she was happy with the way her career was shaping up. Since joining Howard and Anderson Interior Design, she had successfully completed her probationary period and was now on the permanent staff, with a substantial increase in salary and responsibility. The company specialised in refurbishing apartments for wealthy overseas landlords. It had several overseas offices and Samantha had every reason to believe that business would one day take her to those offices.

Samantha pulled her diary towards her to check the time of an afternoon appointment. It was an important appointment and one over which she felt some apprehension. Right after lunch she was scheduled to meet John Howard and, with him, visit a luxury apartment in Mayfair. John Howard was the only son of the company's senior partner. She had not yet met him, and was not at all sure that she wanted to meet him. If he was anything like his overbearing father, he would be difficult to work for.

John Howard had spent the past three months in Saudi Arabia, opening and establishing a new branch. He had recently engaged and trained a local businessman to take over, leaving him free to return to the London office.

In order to give herself confidence, Samantha had taken extra care over her grooming that morning. There was something to be said for power dressing. People reacted to appearances, and she wanted the right reaction – to be taken seriously and treated with respect.

So far, she had only been allowed to work on small, uninspiring properties and always on a tight budget. This apartment, however, was said to have fabulous potential, and its wealthy Arab owner was allowing them a handsome budget. While John Howard worked on the structural renovations, she, with his guidance, would be working on the interior design and soft furnishings. Over the next few days they would be putting together a package of ideas and estimates to send to the Jeddah office for client approval.

It had been made clear that every move she wanted to make and every penny of company money she wanted to spend would first have to meet with John's approval. She only hoped he had a talent worthy of respect.

Without much enthusiasm, Samantha put her mind to

the task at hand and worked steadily through the morning. Satisfied with her achievements, with lunch in mind, she closed a catalogue and pushed it back out of the way. In doing so, she inadvertently knocked over a pile of leaflets, which fell onto the floor between the wall and the back of the desk.

'Damn!' she muttered, in frustration. Knowing she was not up to moving the heavy desk, she pulled the chair out of the way, got down onto hands and knees and, with tightly clad bottom in the air, crawled under the desk.

'Anything I can do to help?' asked an amused, very masculine voice from the doorway.

Wriggling back out into the open, Samantha looked to see who owned the unfamiliar voice. The first thing she noticed about him was his colouring: how blonde his hair, how blue his eyes against a sun bronzed skin. He was smart, attractive and confident, and, Samantha judged, just about the right age. Unbelievable, she groaned to herself. The best-looking man I've seen in months, and he catches me with my rump in the air.

'I dropped some papers,' she flustered, hurriedly coming to her feet.

'So I see,' he murmured, looking highly entertained and eyeing the untidy mass of literature in her hands. 'If this is your office, you must be Samantha Scott,' he said, glancing from her to the nameplate on the door. 'I'm John Howard.'

18

She was a vision in cream and taupe: colours that worked like magic with her ivory skin and chestnut hair. Everything about her looked expensive and stylish: make-up artistically applied, curls taken up high in elegant twist, nails manicured.

Standing near the British Airways check-in counter with his entourage, Michael was slow to recognise the girl he now thought of as Madeleine. It seemed she had taken his harsh criticism very much to heart, as he had meant her to. He marvelled at the transformation and thought how pleased Madame Veronique would be with the miracle walking so confidently towards him.

Whilst waiting for the flight, Michael gave the other models a brief outline of Katherine's history with strict instructions to help her learn the ropes. Though Abigail, the in-house model, was the obvious choice of tutor, it was Isabel, a young flaxen-haired English model, and a West Indian girl called Katerina, who took the job to heart. They arranged to sit with her in the aircraft so they could answer her questions.

Katherine was impatient to add to her knowledge of what awaited them in Paris. She was being asked to participate in something new and alien and was nervous about her capabilities to appear professional among the professionals. She had her pride.

'First we'll be working in the Pavillon Gabriel,' Isabel told her, over the drone of the engines. 'It's on the Avenue Gabriel, near the Champs-Elysées, and it's fabulous for haute couture, since only the big fashion houses can afford it. You'll see what I mean. We'll be showing the exclusive, top-of-the-range collection there tomorrow. Then, on

Thursday, Friday and Saturday we're doing morning and afternoon shows at a trade fair.' She grimaced.

Katherine saw the look and waited.

'Well,' Katerina chipped in, 'it won't be anything like working at the Pavillon Gabriel . . . a bit of a comedown, but only in comparison. Less exclusive,' she explained, 'more the ready-to-wear range. Anyone in the rag trade can attend the exhibition centre.'

Katherine had been working on the evening gowns for the past two months and knew the two collections more intimately than her companions. Also, from her involvement in the planning and overheard conversations, she had acquired a certain amount of information about the forthcoming events. Even so, she let them talk on without too much interruption, pleased to be able to add, no matter how little, to her knowledge of what lay ahead.

As she listened, her anxiety grew. 'How will I know what to do?' she asked.

'Oh, don't worry about that,' was Isabel's breezy response. 'We'll have plenty of time to rehearse in the morning. We'll teach you all you need to know.'

'In the morning!' gasped Katherine. 'You mean I've only got the morning to learn everything?'

'Nothing to worry about,' was Katerina's blasé reply. 'It's easy.' After a pause, she grinned. 'You look the part, so you're halfway there already. You can bluff your way through the rest.'

'Just like that!' Katherine said, seeing nothing but disaster ahead. 'Thanks for the vote of confidence. I only hope I don't let you down by falling flat on my face!'

The team booked into a small but select hotel within walking distance of the Pavillon Gabriel. Before parting company with them for the evening, Michael ordered, 'In the dining room at seven-thirty for an early breakfast and,' he warned, 'be sure you come down with everything you need because we'll be leaving right after.'

In response to Katherine's appeal, her tutors came to her room. After explaining the layout of the Salon Alcazar as they remembered it, they proceeded to give her a crash course.

'Don't walk out into the spotlight until Michael tells you to,' Isabel warned her, 'and don't rush as if trying to break a track record. It's a nervous reaction to walk too fast. Oh, and make sure you wash your hair in the morning ready for the hairdresser, then all she'll have to do is set it on heated rollers.'

'Tomorrow will be easy,' Katerina told her. 'Amongst the guests there will only be a few specially selected fashion editors and their photographers and, although the photographers will want to take pictures of the collection, Madame will be the one giving all the interviews.'

'You'll have to be on your guard at the trade fair though,' warned Isabel. 'There's sure to be a mass of press – and television cameras too. Don't relax in public, you never know when a camera might catch you out, and be very careful what you say if you don't want to be quoted out of context. Every gown you model is fabulous even if you hate it.'

The next morning, Katherine entered the Pavillon Gabriel. As they passed, through open doors, she could see into large luxurious salons. All were beehives of activity in varying stages of preparation for luncheon guests. To Katherine, each room she glimpsed was impressive in its own individual way, but none as impressive as the Salon Alcazar.

The dining room, large and luxurious, was a study of blue and white. Lavish folds of silk curtains hung at the windows and along the wall behind the raised dais. Flowers and plants were everywhere: on tables, in hanging baskets and on pedestals, their bright splashes of colour a cheerful contrast to the predominant theme. Tables were lavishly laid with porcelain, crystal and silver. Lights, like stars, dotted the high ceiling. Among these were the spotlights.

From the steps of the dais, through the centre of the room, a wide expanse of floor had been left clear of tables for the models to walk. Katherine stared at it mesmerised, her stomach doing somersaults. Tearing her eyes away, she followed the example of her companions and put her holdall down out of the way in a corner of the room.

Madame Veronique, stunningly groomed as always, was near the music centre, discussing her requirements with a technician. Her favourite perfume wafted on the air as if in competition with the fragrance of the floral arrangements.

'Our Vera looks as if she has just come back from one of her health-farm vacations,' Abigail giggled in a conspiratorial whisper.

Madame's greeting to the group was an imperious flutter of a heavily ringed hand which seemed also to be the signal for Michael to waste no time in setting the girls to serious rehearsal. Giving admirable demonstrations along with instructions, he soon had them all moving to the music, doing exactly what he wanted.

With encouragement and back-up, it quickly became apparent that the fledgling, Madeleine, had natural flair and, provided she kept her head, would not let them down.

Finally, looking at his watch, Michael gave the order for the girls to go and get ready.

The spacious changing room resembled a hairdressing salon, with its strongly lit wall mirrors, tables and rows of chairs. Territorial instincts took each girl to an area of her own choosing, where she immediately staked her claim by settling her belongings. Katherine followed suit.

The gowns, so secretly manufactured and guarded throughout the past months, were hanging on long chrome railings. The designer fussed over the assistants, who were removing the plastic covers and arranging the garments in order of appearance. The hairdresser and make-up artist, working as a well-practised team, attended the needs of each model in turn.

From the dining room, along the corridor, new sounds began to drift into the changing-room. A hum of conversation, steadily growing in volume, announced the arrival of the luncheon guests.

In a stunning organza gown, Katherine was at last ready and waiting to step into the spotlight.

The salon had filled up with distinguished sophisticates, but Madame Veronique, as she welcomed her guests, outshone them all. The glitterati of Paris had come to dine in the Salon Alkazar with one aim: to see the unveiling of her new collection of eveningwear. With her designer, and her most important clients, she sat at one of the tables and, holding court throughout the luncheon, waited for her approaching moment of triumph.

When the dessert had finally been removed and coffee served, the brilliant spotlights were turned onto the dais. The girls, resplendent in eveningwear ranging from mini cocktail dresses through to full ballgowns, waited behind the curtain for Michael to give them their cue.

After his short introductory speech, they heard him say, '. . . and now, ladies and gentlemen, what you've all been waiting for . . .' Suddenly the music became upbeat, the tempo pulsating. 'It is my great pleasure,' he announced, 'to present the exclusive premier collection of Veronique Couture.'

While waiting for her big moment, despite all the preparation, Madeleine experienced severe stage fright. Stepping out onto the dais, she suddenly found herself blinded by a blaze of lights and flashing cameras. Panic threatened to overwhelm her. After only a moment, her eyes adjusted, though her audience remained a blur. If she could not hear the loud pounding of her heart above the rhythmic music, she could certainly feel it. The long walk down the room seemed endless, and before she found herself safely backstage again, she had asked herself a dozen times what she was doing in a fashion show, and one of this high calibre.

To her amazement and utter relief, 45 minutes later, it had all gone without a hitch. She had not disgraced herself by tripping on the step and falling flat on her face as earlier predicted, and although her legs had felt wobbly, her knees had not actually knocked together; they only felt as if they had. During the pandemonium of lightning changes, zips had not broken, accessories had not gone missing, dresses had not been torn and no unforeseen calamity had occurred.

With each appearance Katherine had felt a little less panic-stricken, until the required poise of Madeleine overtook the reservations of Katherine and sheer exhilaration eclipsed her fears.

As rehearsed, on completion of the finale the models stayed on the dais while Madame Veronique and her top designer, to tumultuous applause, left their tables for the spotlight.

Hugging an enormous bouquet of flowers to her ample bosom, Madame basked in the glory of her success. Her gracious smile swept around the enthusiastic audience, acknowledging with a great show of appreciation their tribute to her genius. Turning a brilliant smile on her team, with a generous flourish of a hand, she included them all in her triumph.

Just for a moment, her Moorish eyes came to rest on the radiant beauty in the flame chiffon ballgown. 'Well done, *ma chérie*,' she whispered under her breath.

The next three days passed in a whirl of activity but it seemed to Katherine that far more time went into preparing than into the actual performance. She and the other girls spent hours in hair rollers, applying make-up and painting their nails. While all this was going on, they were repeatedly interrupted by calls to appear for rehearsals because Madame, being the perfectionist that she was, constantly wanted to change things for the better.

There were twice as many gowns in the less expensive

and more eccentric ready-to-wear collection and, so that the show did not drag on too long, the girls were now required to appear in twos and threes.

They did two long shows a day to packed audiences. Every type of person connected with the fashion industry seemed to be present at the exhibition centre.

Constantly pretending to be a professional, accepted as such, Katherine felt and became the part. By the last day, beginning to think of herself as Madeleine, she had to admit she was sorry her short-lived career as a fashion model was coming to an end. She had thoroughly enjoyed the crowds of noisy enthusiastic buyers, the bright lights, the flashing cameras, the animated attention of the photographers and reporters, the fabulous gowns, and all the fuss made of her and the other girls. The glamour of the past five days had made her feel special, and she had revelled in it all in a way she had not expected. Now she felt sad, for she did not want it to come to an end.

Any misgivings Michael may have felt where Madeleine was concerned were laid to rest after the first show. Through subsequent shows, he had watched her with growing admiration. And he had watched the response of the audience. She had bewitched them all. Whatever it was that made a model special, that made one stand out above all others, she had it. An inner glow, a lithesome grace, a mystical smile? This girl who, before last week, no one had heard of, had already caused a stir in the fashion world.

Every day, Michael had meticulously gone through all the papers and magazines he could lay his hands on, looking for publicity of value to Veronique Couture. Madeleine had featured several times already, and in each case she had proved to be extraordinarily photogenic.

He was aware that she was being talked about, had been photographed for the fashion editorials of several newspapers and top magazines, and been singled out for television interviews that would eventually be edited for programmes on the trade fair. Not only did she delight the eye, but also her husky voice recorded well. When interviewed, she had answered intelligently, never careless or flippant with her words.

As Michael had foreseen, Madeleine was revelling in the high life. Who would not delight in the adulation? She was, after all, only human. Her days as a designer were surely over; after this past week, Madeleine could never return to the nine-to-five existence of Katherine.

He would talk to Madame about the girl's future just as soon as they returned to the London showroom. He did not want her poached from under their noses.

Within a few short days Michael would regret that he delayed so long.

Cameron Knight was the art director of a large London-based advertising company. Belle Laurie Cosmetics had commissioned his agency to launch worldwide a new range of cosmetics and skincare products. All had been going smoothly and according to plan until he came up against a stumbling block: a very important stumbling block. He had been unable to find the right face to launch the advertising campaign.

There were lots of beautiful women in the world to choose from, but this one had to be a woman with a difference. He was not exactly sure what he was looking for, but instinct would tell him when he found her. He knew only that she had to be the kind of woman capable of setting trends; the kind of woman men admired and other women wanted to emulate. She had to be well-spoken, sound intelligent, move with easy grace, have a fabulous, well-proportioned figure, be alluring and sensual in front of a camera, and possess beauty of an unusual kind. A tall order to fill, and he was beginning to think he had set himself an impossible task. He wondered if this miracle of perfection really existed outside his own imagination.

Finding the right person for this promotion was the sole

purpose of Cameron's visit to the Paris trade fair, and with him he had brought Tom Flanagan, a keen, up-and-coming freelance photographer.

Cameron thought the trade fair would be an obvious place to search, as some of the world's most beautiful women would be present. However, many of the models that might have interested Cameron Knight were either already too well known, or else they fitted the mould of today's modern woman. He wanted a whole new look.

For three days he had mingled with the crowd, hunting without success for that special face. He had systematically searched the stands for beautiful models and visited the rooms where the shows took place. Discouraged, feeling he was wasting valuable time, Cameron decided to take an early flight back to England. When he voiced his decision to Tom, the young sandy-haired photographer was more than a little disappointed. Unlike Cameron Knight, the opportunity to travel, especially at company expense, did not present itself very often. This was his first visit to this particular trade fair, and he was getting some very worthwhile shots – fashion shots he felt sure he could sell to the photographic agencies.

Besides, he was enjoying himself. Carrying photographic equipment around his neck; so obviously a photographer, had its definite advantages where some of the aspiring young models were concerned. Eager for publicity that would further their careers, they were keen to be photographed, and very friendly. The more responsive had parted with their home numbers as well as their agency numbers. Yes, Tom was enjoying himself immensely, and in no hurry to quit the field.

'There's only one more show on our agenda for the day,' Tom informed Cameron, glancing at his notes. 'It's just about to start. Do you want to stay for that?'

Cameron did not miss the hopeful note in the young man's voice. Looking at his watch he considered for a moment and then, with a resigned shrug, said, 'OK. Lead on. We've seen so many, what's one more?'

But for Tom, Cameron Knight might have missed the collection of Veronique Couture. If he had, he would not have seen the girl who commandeered his attention from the moment she walked onto the catwalk.

'My God, I do believe we've found her, Tom!' he declared. Excited, he turned to the photographer, but Tom's artistic eye had seen quite clearly what Cameron Knight had seen. With a surge of energy, he had already swung into action. Each time the girl passed him, the flashlight worked overtime. He got full-length action shots of her from all angles and then he zoomed in to get head and shoulder shots. By the time he had finished, three whole reels of film had been used up.

When the show was over, the room was cleared of all but the news media and camera crews. Madame Veronique, Michael and the models made themselves available for interview. Good publicity was absolutely essential to fame and sales, and Madame wanted her fair share of both.

Over the years she had cultivated a wonderful theatrical manner and a flamboyant but elegant mode of dress. Madame, at such moments as this, was rather larger than life, and the press surrounding her and Michael loved her for it.

Without hesitation, Cameron and Tom made straight for the only person in the room that interested them. They were, however, not the only ones to single out Madeleine. Hanging back, unperturbed, Cameron was content to listen and observe while she replied to the questions of others.

He learned that Madeleine was employed on the permanent staff of Veronique Couture. He assumed, therefore, as did everyone else, that she was an in-house model. The address of the London showroom was listed in the programme he carried, and he rightly surmised that finding her again would present no problem.

He was impressed with the way she calmly handled herself in front of the media: the intelligent, articulate answers, the effortless charm. He imagined her background had much to do with the cultured voice and the quiet gentility.

He wondered if everyone around him was as acutely aware of her alluring qualities as he was. Looking keenly into the faces of the hovering journalists and photographers, a satisfied smile spread across his face.

19

It was already well into the evening by the time Katherine arrived at Marlow Place. As she was letting herself in through the main entrance, Mr Becket shuffled out of his caretaker's flat.

Strange how he always manages to put in an appearance whenever Samantha and I are passing, Katherine told herself, regarding him warily.

She also questioned his occasional visits up to their apartment to inquire into their well-being. Sticking his sizeable nose around the door, he would ask gruffly if everything was in order. If they happened to mention the likes of dripping taps and loose floorboards, he would nod his head and say he would look into it, but he never did. Although not in the least bit helpful, he was always polite, and therein lay the big mystery. The good Becket was not nearly as polite with other tenants, and that was a known fact.

When she had mentioned this to Samantha, her friend had merely replied with a grin, 'Well, aren't we the lucky ones?'

''Ave you been away, Miss?' the caretaker asked the obvious, eyeing the suitcase and smart apparel with some suspicion.

'I've just returned from Paris, Mr Becket.'

'What they got over there that we haven't then?' he wanted to know.

'Just a business trip,' she informed him, moving towards the stairs.

A likely story, he told himself. A business trip sounded too tame. There had to be a man involved somewhere. A good-looking girl like that was sure to be up to no good. If he could get her talking, he might learn something Smith would pay extra to hear.

'Want some 'elp with that case, miss?' he uncharacteristically volunteered. Scratching his beer protuberance, he summed up the weight of the case and decided to carry the duty-free carrier bag instead. Katherine was not keen to have either his help or company.

'Oh, no thank you, Mr Becket. It really isn't that heavy. I can manage,' she insisted, proceeding to heave her belongings up the many flights of stairs.

Pushing open the door to her apartment, she was greeted by Samantha, Anne, David and Jeremy. 'What's this, the welcoming committee, or did you all just happen to drop by?' she asked, beaming with pleasure.

'Well, just look at you!' Anne exclaimed scanning Katherine from head to toe. 'Did some fairy godmother wave a magic wand?'

None of her friends had ever seen her looking quite as elegant as she did at that moment. She knew she looked good and could not help feeling pleased with herself. After pushing the door shut with an expensively shod foot, she deposited her case up against the wall and proceeded to execute an exaggerated modelling turn for her admiring audience.

'Wow . . . you look fantastic!' David exclaimed with a touch too much enthusiasm for Anne's liking.

'Your tongue's hanging out and you're drooling,' she told him with mock severity, throwing a well-aimed cushion at his head.

Kicking off her shoes, Katherine padded across the lounge to sit next to Jeremy on the sofa.

'Details,' demanded Samantha with eager curiosity. 'We want all the details from day one onwards, and don't miss anything out.'

'My head is still spinning,' Katherine complained. 'I don't think I can remember half of what happened.' But, after Jeremy had put a glass of wine in her hand, she did her best to oblige, despite the constant interruptions.

The newspaper cuttings caused comment from all round.

'You're so photogenic,' gasped Anne, eyes round with admiration.

'Never mind the model,' Samantha exclaimed irreverently. 'Just look at that fabulous dress! Dare I be so vulgar as to ask how much it costs?' She raised hopeful eyes. Before Katherine could reply that she had not the faintest idea, Samantha had turned her attention back to the cutting, and groaned, 'Forget I even asked that question. It wouldn't look anything like that on me.'

Jeremy was quieter than usual. Ever since Katherine's arrival he had watched and listened, but said little. Of late, he had become aware of a cooling in their relationship. Despite all his efforts, the gulf between them had increased. He had always known Katherine did not really belong in his world. With the versatility of youth, she had thrown on a Bohemian cloak in order to identify with an alien background and peer group. Now that this phase of her life was coming to an end, she was ready to cast off that cloak and move on. He was equally certain that where this new Madeleine was going there would be no place for him.

Feeling his gaze upon her, turning to him, Katherine was startled to see the sadness in his eyes.

Reaching for her hand, Jeremy placed a kiss on her open palm: a kiss as tender as the wistful expression in his amber eyes.

Intuitively she knew he was already mourning her loss. She did not want to cause Jeremy unnecessary grief. There would be no slow painful drawing apart before the final breaking up, no pretence of feelings that were not there, no time for disillusionment and quarrels. They would part quickly she determined. . . . right after the exhibition.

Towards the end of the week, Katherine and Jeremy called in to Harrington's gallery to deliver the completed canvases.

Katherine had met Rodney Harrington a couple of times before: an insensitive man who liked to pipe the tune while others danced. She guessed he might have been good looking in his youth, but now, in middle age, he wore all the signs of an over indulgent lifestyle. She had not liked him then and, watching him approach, she knew instinctively she was going to like him even less now.

His gaze, flickering over Jeremy's paintings, came quickly to rest on her portrait. Now in no apparent hurry to be done, he leisurely examined it in detail. Eventually, raising hooded eyes to linger on Katherine in a way that made her feel she was being mentally undressed, he muttered so that only she could hear, 'Lovely, my dear Madeleine. Quite lovely.'

Attention and admiration was something Katherine was now quite used to, but this was different. This man made her flesh crawl.

It was decided that Jeremy's exhibits would be grouped together in the section reserved for aspiring unknowns. But, because of its dramatic quality and size, the portrait of Madeleine Harcourt would take pride of place on a wall nearby, where it would be spot-lit from above. This rather exposed and exalted position did not appeal to Katherine's sense of modesty. With great difficulty, however, she refrained from comment.

Insisting on directing the hanging of the canvas himself, Harrington further embarrassed her by repeatedly standing back to appraise the positioning and angle of the light. Each time he stepped back, his appreciation for the portrait grew, and for all the wrong reasons. Infuriated, Katherine treated his attempts at conversation with chilly politeness. Harrington seemed to take pleasure in her discomfort.

Mavis Ford, his personal assistant, summed up the situation at a glance. She had been with Harrington a long time and was the only female member of staff who felt safe alone in his company. She knew he was only ever attracted to pretty young things, especially those who gave the impression of vulnerability. Mavis was secure in the knowledge that she was not pretty, young or vulnerable. Madeleine Harcourt, on the other hand, was in a category all of her own and had quite clearly been targeted. Coming to the rescue, she invited Madeleine to return with her to her office for coffee.

When Jeremy was ready to leave, he put his head round the door, and Katherine went with him.

She would not have accompanied Jeremy to the gallery the following day had her help not been required in transporting the remaining paintings. The gilded wood frames, being both cumbersome and heavy, needed the careful handling of two pairs of hands.

They deposited their burdens against the wall on which they were to be exhibited. Recognising Katherine's aversion to Rodney Harrington, Jeremy went alone in search of his patron, leaving Katherine to retreat, as before, to Mavis Ford's office.

Over recent years, nasty rumours about Harrington had circulated among the staff. To the first few, Mavis had given little credence, but later she had begun to suspect the validity of some of those rumours. A warning to Madeleine was on Mavis's lips but, out of loyalty, she hesitated, not liking to speak ill of her employer. The conversation moved on; the moment to speak up was lost. Later, Mavis was to regret that moment of indecision.

In a quiet corner of a pub just off Charing Cross Road, Katherine and Samantha sat at a wooden table. A little light music played in the background. At the bar were several rowdy regulars. Because of its proximity to Marlow Place and the hairdressing salon, it was a convenient place for an occasional early evening rendezvous.

It was not long before Anne entered the pub. The bright green streaks still remained in her hair but the red had gone, to be replaced with a liberal spray of fine silver glitter. Her nail extensions sported green varnish frosted with silver.

'We won't need a Christmas tree this year,' Katherine whispered, stifling the urge to giggle. 'We'll invite Anne over to stand in the corner. The angel can go on top of her head and the presents can hang from her upturned fingers.'

Anne brought her beer over from the bar. Turning her head from side to side and flashing her nails under their noses, she spoiled their tenuous self-control by asking, 'Well, what do you think?'

They choked on their mirth.

It was some time later that Anne got around to asking Katherine, 'Whatever happened to that portrait of you . . . the new one?' There had been no mention of it in recent months.

'Oh, that's at Rodney Harrington's gallery. We took it over yesterday.' Seeing Anne's blank expression, Katherine explained, 'The exhibition begins tomorrow evening.'

Samantha pulled a face at the mention of Harrington. She had met him briefly the previous year, at the time of Jeremy's last showing, and had not liked him very much.

'Just being near that man was enough to give me the creeps,' she shuddered. 'The way he kept leering at me, I thought I must have forgotten to do my buttons up,' she said glancing down at her ample breasts. 'Such a lecher!' She grimaced. 'And he's so condescending to Jeremy. Why does Jeremy have anything to do with him? There must be others willing to exhibit his work.'

'Jeremy dislikes him too, but as he says, no one puts on an exhibition quite like he does,' Katherine quoted. 'He's the best, and anyone who is anyone in the art world will be at the opening, including the critics. This could be Jeremy's big break.'

Katherine narrowed her eyes against the irritating effects of cigarette smoke wafting across from two newcomers at a nearby table. From the way the men were eyeing the three girls, it appeared there had been motive behind their choice of table.

Avoiding eye contact, Katherine turned her attention back to her friends. 'He's been burning the midnight oil for months preparing for this show,' she continued. 'If anyone can get recognition for Jeremy, Harrington can.' She looked slightly troubled. 'Jeremy promised faithfully he wouldn't sell my portrait for public exhibition.' Katherine paused to reflect and then in more subdued, confidential tones continued, 'Sometimes I regret sitting for that wretched picture.'

'Why? Because of what you forgot to cover up, and now you're feeling bashful?' Samantha laughed over the rim of her glass at her friend's modesty.

Anne's antenna went up. This was something she had not heard before. 'You've posed nude for Jeremy? Eh . . . how nude is nude?' she asked.

'Quite nude,' Katherine admitted, unable to look her in the eye. With assumed nonchalance, her gaze wandered evasively around the interior of the room, along dark beams, over reproduction pictures and nicotine-stained curtains.

Leaning forward, Anne waved the palm of her hand in front of Katherine's face to catch her attention and, when she had it, she raised her eyebrows in silent, persistent question.

'Posing semi-nude wasn't my original intention, but somehow it just happened,' Katherine said defensively. 'Well, you know what it was like in college; there were always nude models around the place. We didn't think anything of it at the time, but now . . . well, I'm not so sure I like the idea of it being me on display in the altogether.' She shifted uncomfortably in her seat.

Samantha regarded her friend's worried face. 'Better not sell it to a private collector either, or it might end up on some pervert's bedroom wall. Then there's no knowing what might take place under your immortalised gaze!'

Katherine looked startled. 'Perish the thought,' she said with a shudder, but her anxiety passed when she saw the merriment in Samantha's green eyes.

'You shouldn't take life so seriously. After all, it's only an oil painting, not some pornographic photograph,' Samantha laughed.

'What time does the exhibition start?' asked Anne.

'Six o'clock, but I'm afraid the first night is by invitation only,' Katherine told her apologetically.

Anne shrugged. 'We've got all week to visit.'

Katherine assumed that by *we,* Anne meant her and David. Well, that was all right; David was an artist too and quite used to nudity.

As they were in her line of vision, it was hard for Katherine to avoid noticing the two men at the nearby table. One of them tilted a glass towards her in appreciative salutation. Not wanting to encourage them by noticing the gesture, she refocused on Anne, who was asking, 'Are you going to the exhibition?'

'Tomorrow night only. I don't really want to, but Jeremy's asked for my support,' Katherine said moodily, playing with the stem of her glass. 'He's on edge. What the critics have to say could make or break him. Naturally, after all his hard work, he's nervous about the outcome.' She shrugged and continued doubtfully, 'I'm not sure how my presence is going to help anyone to reach a favourable verdict.'

Anne Hunter stayed only five more minutes before excusing herself. She had an important telephone call to make to her uncle. A nude portrait of Katherine on public display was something he might want to hear about. Anne was not to know that, by leaving early, she would miss a vital part of the conversation.

Lingering over their unfinished drinks, Samantha asked, 'So, despite your aversion to Harrington, you plan to be at the opening?'

'Yes, I guess so,' Katherine replied unenthusiastically and then, brightening up, asked, 'Did I tell you I had Jeremy enter me in the catalogue under a pseudonym?'

'Oh? And what name are you known by this time?' Samantha questioned.

'The same one I used for modelling – Madeleine Harcourt. Did I tell you, it's the maiden name of one of my illustrious ancestors?' Rolling her sparkling eyes as if to heaven, she murmured, 'May my great-grandmother forgive me for making so free with her good name. At least,' she continued, 'if the critics do give Jeremy a write-up, no one will see my real name in print.' Laughing, she added, 'We wouldn't want the good nuns of Haldene Abbey to think me a fallen woman.' Putting a hand up, Katherine continued, 'Yes, I know. As you so rightly pointed out, it's only an oil painting, but I don't want anyone I know rushing over to the gallery to leer at me in the altogether. OK?'

'How good a likeness is it?' Samantha wanted to know.

'Too good,' she answered, with a sigh. 'Unfortunately, Jeremy's no latter-day Picasso. He painted all my parts in proportion and in the right places.' Seeing movement out of the corner of her eye, Katherine merrily warned, 'Whoops! Here comes trouble.' She had been keeping a wary watch on their neighbours, who were now beginning to show certain familiar signs of intent. 'Time to drink up and beat a hasty retreat.'

20

On entering the study, the flashing message light on the answerphone was the first thing Alexis saw. He had been out since early morning at a studio, recording for Decca. His theme and background music for the new Duane Harrison movie had been accepted, provided he agreed to play the long, haunting melodies himself. With secret satisfaction, he had agreed to the conditions: he would never have trusted anyone else to record them.

It had been an all-day session, making him late home. Hugh was expected at any minute, but that did not hurry him. Hugh would not mind waiting while he showered and changed. He would fix them both a drink and make himself at home, as he always did.

As Alexis clicked on the answerphone, a stream of names immediately ran through his mind, but the first message came from someone who did not belong to any of them. For a moment, he failed to recognise the voice. After all, three years had passed since he had interviewed Quentin Smith, and they had not spoken to each other since. There had been very few occasions when Smith had needed to contact Mrs Simmons and on none of those occasions had there been a need to trouble Alexis. Because of this, he listened to the message with curiosity rather than concern.

Quentin Smith gave his name and telephone number, and then went on to say: 'As you already know from previous reports, Miss Drew has, for some months, been having her portrait painted by an artist friend and tutor. This portrait is going to be on show at Harrington's Art Gallery on Lexington Crescent.

'The exhibition opens tonight at seven p.m. and I really think that, under the circumstances, you should go and see it. No need for me to explain further, you'll see why when you get there.

I would have given you more warning, but I've only just become aware of this new development myself.'

There was a click and the line went dead.

Since Jenny Simmons had not once drawn his attention to any of Smith's reports, Alexis had been only too happy to assume that all was well in that quarter. He had never so much as taken the file out of the cabinet, let alone the reports out of the file. He therefore knew nothing whatever about a portrait.

Puzzled by Smith's words, Alexis played the message through again. Looking at his watch, he scowled, wondering what could be so special about a portrait that made it necessary for him to drop everything at a moment's notice to go traipsing off to some art gallery, probably on the other side of London. If Quentin Smith was thinking he would want to buy the portrait just because the girl was his wife, then he was much mistaken.

His thoughts faltered over the word *wife*. It always rankled when applied to Katherine. In truth, though, he had to admit, apart from the occasional visit or telephone call to Ravenswood, marriage to his cousin had not made much difference to his life. In the past five years or so, she had not presented him with a single problem, and he had needed to give her no more than a passing thought. Women had continued to float in and out of his life, but he had not wanted to marry any of them. He shrugged. Even in that she had not been an obstacle.

With a decided lack of enthusiasm, Alexis turned to the bookcase and reached for the *London A-Z*. He and Hugh had made plans to spend the evening with friends at the Reform Club on Pall Mall. If Lexington Crescent was not too far out of their way, they would have time to call in at the gallery. Otherwise, a visit would have to wait.

*

The gallery was in a state of readiness by the time Katherine and Jeremy stepped through its doors and onto the thick plush carpet. Pictures of all media, subjects, shapes and sizes hung on the vast expanses of pale walls and screens. A variety of intricate sculptures, some fabulous, some ugly, but all intriguing, stood on plinths in safe locations. The rooms were ablaze with lights so that no object of art was left in shadow. Many of their fellow artists had already arrived. With the staff, they stood in small groups, and while they awaited the arrival of the guests, discussed art in general and the merits of some of the exhibits.

Espying Katherine, Mavis detached herself and hurried across the room. 'You look wonderful Madeleine,' she said, gazing enviously at the short black cocktail dress that hugged every perfect curve of her slender form. Although there was not much of the dress, it looked very expensive and she concluded that, whilst Madeleine may not have received value for money where the amount of fabric was concerned, what the garment lacked in quantity it clearly gained in quality and style.

'How on earth did you manage to get your hair up like that?' she asked, standing back to inspect the Grecian hairstyle which somehow managed to defy gravity with the aid of just one ornamental clasp.

Mavis had been content with her own appearance, but now felt as if she had gone up into the attic to raid granny's ancient trunk. With the arrival of the first guests, she excused herself and hurried away.

'She's right,' Jeremy murmured. 'You do look wonderful.' Katherine glimpsed the raw emotion in his eyes, before he turned away.

The gallery began to fill, slowly at first and then more rapidly, with people of all ages and from all walks of life. The one thing most of these potential customers appeared to have in common was money and, by the look of them, Katherine observed, lots of it.

Over a number of years, Harrington had compiled and updated an extensive invitation list. A jealously guarded secret, Mavis had told her, which many of his competitors would give much to get their hands on. Only Harrington and she had access to it.

Members of staff mingled sociably with the guests, answering questions and steering them in the direction of artists and exhibits. Hired professional caterers in formal black and white, balancing trays of champagne and canapés, wove their way through the galleries, now a-hum with polite conversation.

For some time, the evening progressed well. Jeremy's work was generating more than its share of interest, especially his portrait of Madeleine. Katherine suspected the interest in her portrait was due as much to her state of undress as to the artist's skill. No man who passed within visual range could keep his eyes from the portrait or having recognised her as the model, completely conceal his interest in her. She suppressed a smile. The champagne, the conversation of art lovers and the atmosphere were lightening her mood. She was enjoying herself. Art was Katherine's subject, and a subject she knew well. Using her knowledge and charm, she endeavoured, for Jeremy's sake, to say all the right things. She prayed the critics would favour his work and put into print all the things he longed to read. If the critics were of the same opinion as these wealthy patrons, then Jeremy should be in for some good reviews, Katherine told herself, but . . . you never could tell. There was an abundance of talent on display and only a few artists could hope to get any kind of a mention.

Her gaze, travelling beyond her immediate circle, came to rest on a face in the crowd. With a start, she realised she was the focus of Harrington's attention. How long, she wondered, had be been watching her with that predatory look in his eyes, no doubt comparing the portrait above with the reality. It seemed to Katherine as if he had been making a dark promise and now, with raised glass, was sealing a pact with the devil. With a shiver of revulsion, she pointedly turned her back on him and gave her full and animated attention to the surprised and flattered young man at her side.

Later, when she dared to look again, Harrington was no longer to be seen. Nevertheless, she moved away from the all too revealing portrait and went to stand in the vicinity of Jeremy's other work.

From time to time Mavis flitted past. A few friendly words passed quickly between them, but the older woman, being on duty, could not stop. Several times more, Harrington came too close for comfort and it was with relief that Katherine eventually espied him through the crowd, accompanying guests up the wide sweeping staircase to the upper gallery.

Harrington's attention had spoiled her evening. Glancing distractedly at the wall clock behind the man who had for the past 15 minutes been monopolising her time, Katherine noted wearily that it was not nearly as late as she would like it to be. Another 15 minutes and, she promised herself, she would desert her post.

The two men were about to enter Harrington's art gallery on Lexington Crescent when, with a sudden audible intake of breath, Hugh stopped short. Taking a step back, he took another look at the name over its portals, scowled, and swore softly.

'What's the matter?' Alexis asked, following the direction of his focus.

'That's the matter,' Hugh said, pointing at the name *Harrington's*. 'I once got a fellow by the name of Harrington off a date-rape charge. He owned an art gallery. Could be the same man.'

'I remember you mentioning it. About two years ago . . . at Nikolils, wasn't it?' Alexis replied. 'Said he was as guilty as sin.'

Still scowling, Hugh followed Alexis through the double doors.

That neither had invitations to attend the opening night

of Harrington's prestigious exhibition perturbed them not at all. Immaculately attired, they knew they looked like wealthy art patrons. Under the circumstances, it was unlikely they would find themselves turned away at the door. In this they proved to be right. Having produced cards for the attractive receptionist, they were supplied with catalogues and admitted with a welcoming smile.

Passing through the open double doors into the floodlit gallery beyond, they were immediately confronted by a noisy throng of some of London's smartest and wealthiest citizens. Even though guests were still arriving, it was apparent that there was already no shortage within.

Accepting champagne from a passing waiter, the two men mingled freely with the crowd, taking in their opulent surroundings, the ambience of the gallery and the quality of the artwork. As was to be expected, not all the exhibits appealed to Alexis' taste. Some even raised questions and doubts in his mind, causing him to look at Hugh in quizzical amusement. Even so, they acknowledged it to be an impressive display.

'Without the name of the artist, this is going to be a bit like looking for a needle in a haystack,' Alexis observed, and then added, 'unless the name of the model is listed in the catalogue.'

Both men scrutinised their catalogues from cover to cover, but it soon became apparent that the name Katherine Drew was not listed.

'Why on earth didn't Smith give you the name of the artist?' Hugh wanted to know. 'Their names are always listed. Smith's usually very thorough in his work.'

'And so he was this time,' Alexis assured him. 'No doubt he put it in his last report but, short of driving all the way out to Henley, there's no way I can get that information at this late date.'

They soon discovered from the catalogue, and from observation, that there were two large galleries: one above the other. They agreed that unless they were prepared to take all night looking for the portrait, they had better split up for the search.

'You do remember what she looks like, don't you?' Alexis asked.

'Unforgettable!' Hugh grinned at his recollections of the dumpy little teenager with the silver tram-tracks on her teeth and the large soulful eyes. 'Once seen never to be forgotten. Right?'

'Right,' Alexis agreed, smiling at his own indelible memories. 'This shouldn't take too long. I'll take the upper floor, if you'll work your way around this one,' he said, already turning towards the wide sweeping staircase.

Nearly half an hour had passed by the time they met again at the bottom of the stairs. Neither had been successful in their search.

'If I didn't know better, I'd say Smith was an idiot.' Alexis scowled irritably.

'If he says there's a portrait of Katherine Drew in the exhibition, then it's bound to be here somewhere,' Hugh stated with certainty. 'But I can't for the life of me see a painting anywhere that looks remotely like her.'

Alexis regarded his watch. 'Look, we still have time, and I hate to admit defeat, so how about you take the upper floor this time and I look around down here? We must have missed it.'

There were, in fact, very few portraits on the ground floor and Alexis studied each one in turn very carefully. None of them was Katherine Drew.

While he waited for Hugh to return, he accepted another glass of champagne from a circulating waiter, and let his gaze sweep around the room for any nook or cranny he might have missed.

His attention was drawn to a portrait of a beautiful, half-naked young woman, a portrait he had noticed earlier and studied with a little more interest than the others. He approached it once more. If he was going to wait for Hugh, he could think of no better place to while away the time.

The painting was in deep, dramatic colours, as if the

room had been in darkness and, the subject alone illuminated by a solitary lamp. Against the sombre brown shadows of the background and the rich burgundy folds of her robe: her ivory skin glowed translucent.

The girl stood in front of a stone fireplace, three-quarters facing the artist and partly reflected in the mirror. Her long and abundant hair, a deep, rich chestnut, hung over her shoulders and cascaded down her back in long, lustrous, spiral curls. Such hair might have given her an untamed look, but for the soft expression in her wistful deep-blue eyes that spoke of love, promise and sensuality, as did her slightly parted lips.

The model was wearing only an exotic flowing silk gown, which had fallen open and off a shoulder to reveal one side of a perfect body. Alexis let his eyes travel from the exquisite face, slowly downwards over the exposed curves. They took in every detail, from the smooth, sculptured lines of a bared shoulder and arm, to a firm high breast, flat stomach and thigh, and then on down the full length of a long shapely leg.

So perfect was the subject that Alexis could not help wondering if the artist, in order to portray such perfection, had allowed himself a certain amount of poetic licence.

Arriving at last at the bottom of the canvas, his focus went to the signature in the right-hand corner, where he read the name, Jeremy Grierson.

Opening his catalogue to the appropriate page, Alexis found the name, along with a brief resumé of the man's background and impressive art qualifications. There was also a list of his exhibits and their asking prices. Apart from that, there was little else to be learned about Jeremy Grierson.

He knew he would not buy the painting. As much as he admired it, he saw no point in owning a portrait of someone he did not know. Even so, for some reason this girl fascinated him.

Returning his attention to the portrait, he found himself studying the eyes of the subject. It was the eyes that had first attracted him and now, once more, they seemed to command his attention. Strangely, they reminded him of a pair of beautiful eyes he had seen before, but he could not place where or when. He studied the girl's exquisite features until, reluctantly, he had to admit that, as she had an unforgettable face, if he had ever seen her before, he would most assuredly remember the occasion in every detail. Inwardly, he laughed at himself for his wishful thinking.

Looking again at the catalogue, Alexis noted that, apart from her name, which was Madeleine Harcourt, no other information had been given. He toyed awhile with the name. His memory stirred. There was something vaguely familiar about it. He knew he had heard it at sometime, somewhere, but no matter how hard he tried, he simply could not remember the occasion.

Closing the catalogue, he looked again at the picture, and once more those compelling eyes drew him like a magnet. He felt sure he did not know the girl and yet . . . there was something about her.

He shrugged. Farewell, Madeleine Harcourt, he said to himself, raising the champagne flute to his lips.

He was about to turn away when suddenly it hit him like a bolt from the blue exactly who it was that she resembled. An ancestor of his whose portrait hung in a shadowed recess in the dining hall of Ravenswood. Jane, on her visit to the manor house, had commented on the beauty of the subject. The similarity between the women in the two portraits was uncanny: same skin, same hair colouring, same refined bone structure and eyes. Undoubtedly, that was who this Madeleine Harcourt reminded him of. His great-grandmother – and, it dawned on him, Katherine's too. Before his great-grandmother had married Frederick Drew, her maiden name, so Mrs Johnson had told them, had been . . . Madeleine Harcourt: the same name as the artist's model. This was too much of a coincidence.

Realising the truth, he stared at the telltale eyes in the portrait. Katherine had eyes like that. He had admired them: the only redeeming feature he had admired. With a frown of concentration, he turned his memory back five years, to the nondescript little 16-year-old-schoolgirl Katherine, with the funny haircut and the orthodontic braces, for whom he had felt sorry. She would be 21 by now, he calculated, about the age of the girl in the portrait.

So this was what Quentin Smith had wanted him to see! This is the portrait of Katherine Drew, he told himself incredulously. Take away the braces, grow the hair, add some height and curves, and what have you got? This very beautiful and desirable young woman, he concluded.

Once more his discerning eyes swept slowly and thoughtfully down over the perfect body, and as they did so, a hint of a sardonic smile shadowed his handsome features. If this was really Katherine Drew, then this woman was his wife. For once, the thought pleased him, intrigued and amused him even. He had never had any desire to know Katherine the schoolgirl, but Katherine the woman was quite another matter.

He remembered that Jenny Simmons had said to him only recently, 'Mr Smith has sent an up-to-date photograph of Katherine, if you want to see it.'

'Fine. Put it in the file and I'll look at it later,' he had replied without much interest, and had promptly forgotten all about it.

He was still deep in reflection when Hugh found him. Clapping Alexis on the back he said airily, with a grin, 'Naughty but nice. Trust you to find the most interesting woman in the room . . . *and* the one with the least on.'Hugh noticed that his friend's dark eyes sparkled as if he had just understood the point of a very good joke. Looking inquiringly at Alexis and then at the painting, he asked, 'Am I missing something here?'

'No, Hugh. I'm the one missing something,' Alexis murmured, 'but I intend to put that right – and very soon.' With his eyes still focused on the portrait, he asked, 'Don't you recognise her?'

'No, but I wish I did,' Hugh answered. Glancing at Alexis, he asked quizzically, 'Should I?'

'She's listed as Madeleine Harcourt,' Alexis informed him.

'Never heard of her,' his friend replied, shaking his head regretfully.

'No, you wouldn't have, but look carefully at the eyes,' he ordered.

'I'm looking at them, *and* at the rest of her too.' There was open admiration in Hugh's voice.

'The *eyes*, Hugh. Look again!' Alexis commanded.

Hugh looked searchingly and after a while replied firmly, 'Never seen the lady before in my life. If I had, I'm quite sure I'd remember. However, if you'd like to introduce us I'd be more than happy to know her.' Running lascivious eyes over the model's exposed curves, he added, 'Every lovely inch of her.'

'So would I,' mused Alexis.

'Ah! But you're a married man,' Hugh gloated.

'So I am,' Alexis agreed, looking smug.

'That makes her off-limits where you're concerned,' Hugh reminded him.

'*Au contraire.* That makes her off-limits to you,' Alexis countered.

Hugh raised an inquiring eyebrow at his friend. He was not sure he quite understood the reasoning behind those words. 'You've lost me,' he admitted. 'You're going to have to explain?'

'Very well, Hugh,' Alexis replied. With a flourish of a hand towards the portrait, he informed his friend, 'That lady, my dear fellow, is my wife.'

'Your . . . what did you say?' There was confusion in Hugh's voice.

'You heard me right,' Alexis stated. 'Madeleine Harcourt and Katherine Drew are one and the same.'

'That's Katherine?' Hugh asked doubtfully. 'Never!' He stared at the portrait through narrowed eyes, and then, shaking his head, said, 'Can't be – looks nothing like her. This girl's got hair, a whole thick mane of it, and no tram-tracks.'

'Hair grows, and braces come off after a year or two,' Alexis reminded him.

'But this girl's got a figure,' protested Hugh.

'She grew up,' Alexis countered patiently.

'That must be the understatement of the year.' His companion finally gave up but continued to stare.

'If we occupy this spot any longer we'll be had up for vagrancy,' Alexis laughed. 'So when you feel able to drag your eyes away from my wife, perhaps you'd like to go over to that receptionist, who seems to be showing more than an ordinary interest in you, and purchase the portrait for me.'

That did the trick. With hopeful interest, Hugh's attention was diverted to the pretty receptionist.

'Just say you're acting for a private collector and give her some fictitious name to put on the bill of sale. Have the portrait delivered to your own address, not mine, and say the purchaser is leaving the country tomorrow so that it's imperative that it's delivered first thing in the morning. I see no reason for it to remain on display any longer than necessary.'

'They won't like having it removed before the last day of the show,' Hugh warned. 'They'd rather put a sold sticker on it and leave it where it is.'

'No doubt you're right, but if they want to make the sale, they'll have to agree,' Alexis stated firmly. 'Pay them their asking price and if they become difficult offer more. I mean to have the portrait, Hugh, and I want it off that wall tonight.' Before Hugh could move away, Alexis placed a restraining hand on his arm. 'See if you can find out if this Grierson has painted any more pictures of Madeleine Harcourt of a similar nature. If so, I want those too.' Alexis watched his friend cover the short distance to the open doorway and approach the smiling receptionist. During their brief conversation, the smile faded and she shook her head. Leaving Hugh, she entered the gallery and approached a small group of people standing not far from Alexis, where she stopped to converse with one of the men and the woman at his side. After a short conversation, the receptionist retraced her steps to where Hugh waited. When Alexis saw him hand over his credit card and was satisfied that the purchase had been made, he turned his attention once more to the couple, knowing that he was looking at Jeremy Grierson – and Katherine Drew.

With a critical eye, he studied the girl. There was no faulting her dress sense: she looked expensive and a far cry from the trendy art student he might have expected. The portrait had not lied, she was indeed stunningly beautiful and did appear to have a perfect figure.

He focused next on her companion. An interesting face: sensitive features without being effeminate. He was unconventional in his attire for an evening such as this. But then, the artist probably did not own a lounge suit let alone a dinner jacket. The body language between artist and model told Alexis that they were very good friends; possibly lovers, even. He was surprised that he found the thought so disturbing.

Alexis strolled across to look at Grierson's exhibits. He did not need to be told that the oils all bore the same signature. They had an unmistakable style of their own.

When Grierson looked with interest in his direction, Alexis remarked in all sincerity, 'Good . . . very good. An appealing technique.'

Jeremy moved away from the group to talk to the newcomer. 'Thank you. I'm pleased you like my work,' he said with modesty, thus introducing himself as the artist and at the same time acknowledging the compliment.

'Then you must be . . . Jeremy Grierson,' Alexis said glancing at his open catalogue. 'I'm very pleased to meet you.' He extended a hand. 'I'm Alexis Drew.'

It crossed Alexis' mind that if the artist and the model were on intimate terms, Grierson might know enough of her past to recognise his name. The artist showed no sign of doing so. There were some secrets then that Katherine preferred to keep to herself, and Alexis Drew was one of them.

They had not been in conversation for long when Alexis,

watching from the corner of an eye, saw Katherine move away from her present company and turn in their direction. Jeremy, also aware of her approach, put out an arm, and in comfortable familiarity drew her towards them.

'Madeleine, come and meet Mr Alexis Drew. This is Madeleine Harcourt,' he said by way of introduction.

Alexis turned to face her. Their eyes locked and held. He was sure he heard a sharp intake of breath and saw, just for a moment, the shock of recognition in the girl's blue eyes. He regarded her with impassive interest, wondering if she would acknowledge him to her lover. He waited for her to lead the way.

After only a moment's hesitation, she offered a cool, smooth hand, and said, 'I'm pleased to meet you, Mr Drew.' Her slightly husky voice pleased him. It was cultured and in harmony with her appearance.

It was obvious then that she did not wish to acknowledge her acquaintance with him. Alexis was amused to go along with her decision. If she chose to keep secrets from her lover, that was her business. When, a few minutes later, Jeremy was drawn away by a talkative guest, Alexis fully expected Katherine to admit recognition. Still she said nothing. Only then did it occur to him that she thought she had not been recognised and preferred to keep it that way.

He decided to have a little fun of his own. Looking slightly puzzled, he asked nonchalantly, 'Haven't I seen you somewhere before?' Before she could reply, he continued, 'Oh yes, of course, I remember now, you're the model in that delightful portrait over there, aren't you?' He indicated the one he was referring to.

The girl blushed and lowered her eyes. 'Yes,' she admitted. 'I'm pleased you like it.'

Alexis wondered why, if she was so modest, she had posed for the portrait at all. Had she done it for Grierson, to please him because they were lovers? Her expression in the portrait suggested the possibility. The thought disconcerted him . . . annoyed him even. He wanted the answers to a great many questions, but now was not the time to ask. At any minute Hugh might join them and spoil it all by unwittingly saying the wrong things. Reluctantly he began to take his leave.

'It's been a pleasure meeting you, Madeleine,' he said. 'I hope we'll meet again.'

'I don't think that's very likely, Mr Drew,' she demurred, with a cool smile.

'Oh? And why do you say that?' Alexis inquired.

'Because we move in different circles,' she suggested.

That can soon be remedied, he told himself, but to her, he replied, 'It's a small world ...... you never know.' Then, with a calculating look in his dark eyes and a faint smile on his lips, he walked away.

After a leisurely dinner at the Reform Club, Alexis drove to his cottage in Henley to collect the file containing Quentin Smith's reports.

At that time of night traffic was sparse. Even so, it was already gone two in the morning by the time he re-entered London.

Letting himself into Linnet House, he passed quickly through the hall and into the study, where he threw off his jacket, loosened his tie and the top button of his shirt. Settling into the large leather chair that had once belonged to Anthony Drew, and Frederick before him, he laid the file on the desk, opened it, and began to read.

For the first time, he was deeply interested in what it contained. He had to know everything there was to know about Katherine: her successes and failures, what made her laugh and cry, how she filled her free time and, more importantly, with whom.

Recalling the portrait, he visualised the sensuous look in those large, expressive eyes, and the inviting lips so seductively parted. Moodily, he asked himself if her thoughts had been all for the artist, or for some other lover about whom he had yet to learn.

Alexis did not concern himself over the ethical rights and wrongs of reading about Katherine's private life. If he had felt any qualms of conscience, it would not have made any difference; he would have read the reports anyway. This was more than idle curiosity. This was an urgent need to build a bridge across the years.

Nearly two hours had passed by the time he laid down the last report. His eyes focused on the photograph of Katherine, the one Jenny had tried to draw his attention to the previous month. He picked it up, and leaning back in the chair, studied it closely. According to the date and information written lightly in pencil on the back, it had been taken very recently. No more than six months ago, he calculated, which meant it had been taken towards the end of her final year at Saint Martins. With her long, burnished curls, hoop earrings and bizarre student clothes, she resembled an exotic Gypsy girl, and an incredibly appealing one at that.

The young Katherine had done well throughout her school years. Her reports and advanced level passes in English, history and art proved she was no slouch. Sadly he wondered who, if anyone, had gone to Haldene Abbey on Speech Day to see her collect her certificates. Maybe his mother had, but she had not mentioned it to him. He should have been there for her. Too late, he felt her isolation through those early years.

After Haldene, she could have retreated to her country home to live in idle luxury, but instead she had chosen to go on to make her mark at Saint Martins. Eventually, leaving well qualified and highly thought of, she had walked straight into a plum position as a trainee designer with Veronique Couture. On top of that success, she had been asked to take part in several Paris fashion shows. From the enclosed cuttings, it was clear she had made a success out of that venture too.

He asked himself if he was entirely to blame for neglecting her. After all, Katherine had made it abundantly clear she did not expect their paths to cross again. At the time he had understood her outrage and humiliation, had been aware she was using those emotions to fuel her resentment towards her grandfather and himself.

Did she think he had used his influence over Anthony Drew to gain his own lucrative ends? He had not troubled to explain that the strange turn of events had taken him as much by surprise as they had her. In fact, now he came to think about it, he had not taken the trouble to say much to her about anything.

With a terrible feeling of loss and time wasted, Alexis asked himself how he could have been so negligent as to have allowed Smith's reports to be filed away without giving them so much as a glance. The responsibility should have been his but he had given it to Jenny Simmons and felt few pangs of conscience in doing so.

His great uncle had left him a fortune in the shape of Linnet House and its priceless contents. All he had asked in return for his generosity was the safe keeping of his granddaughter and her inheritance. That his great uncle had asked him to do this in a rather unorthodox fashion was neither here nor there. Alexis had accepted the terms and, in so doing, had given his promise to carry out the old gentleman's wishes.

Alexis now reflected over the direction his train of thoughts had taken. When the girl had been a plain, unattractive and petulant child, he had not allowed such thoughts to encroach upon his conscience. But now that the same girl had miraculously turned into a highly desirable and interesting woman, he found himself suddenly willing to admit he had not been doing his duty by her. A cynical smile passed fleetingly across his face as he considered his hypocrisy.

Slowly, his mind's eye travelled over the perfect features and figure in Grierson's portrait. Then he visualised its flesh and blood counterpart, and he found himself wondering how those lips might respond to a kiss, and that body to the caresses of a lover. He had a burning desire to know more about the passionate side of Katherine's nature.

Disappointingly, there was little information on that subject. Quentin Smith had been particularly discreet, but then Alexis remembered telling both him and Jenny that Katherine's love affairs were to remain her own business, unless she ran into difficulties. It would seem they had taken him at his word. That was as it should be. He did not want the whole world privy to her personal life. He was the only one who had the right to know, and that right, he had to admit, was a rather tenuous one.

Several masculine names were mentioned but there was nothing to suggest that any of those men had been more to her than just friends. Even though the reports on Jeremy Grierson had been worded with respectful discretion, the duration and nature of the friendship left Alexis in little doubt that they were or had been lovers. Regrettably, there was nothing in any of the reports to indicate that the affair was now over.

He scowled at the thought of Katherine in the arms of another, yet he knew he had no right to feel possessive over her. Their marriage had not meant to bind them to each other in that way. Choosing freedom, they had gone in different directions, neither wanting nor expecting anything from the other: not even friendship.

Now, after the evening's astonishing revelations, Alexis knew for a certainty that he was going to bring about a few changes. He closed the file. Lacing his fingers together behind his head, he leaned back in the chair. His eyes narrowed, his handsome features set into hard, determined lines. She was not for Grierson. If her affair with the artist was not already over, he would put an end to it – and the sooner he did so, the better.

21

'Damn the man!' she said out loud, slamming the cupboard door. Katherine would have been more guarded with her tongue and temper if she had known that Samantha, drawn out of her bedroom by the inviting aroma of the fresh coffee, was just about to enter the kitchen.

Such an outburst from her usually mild-mannered friend would normally have startled Samantha, but having been out late the night before with John Howard, she was still in a state of blissful euphoria and not yet fully awake to a new day.

'To whom are we referring?' she asked languidly.

Katherine looked disconcerted. She did not want to answer. Anything she said now would invite further questioning, when all she wanted was to forget that last night had ever happened. One look at Samantha's face told her she was indulging in wishful thinking. She was not going to be allowed to forget, and so she answered curtly, 'Alexis Drew.'

Samantha had not heard that name mentioned in quite a while. Surprised, she raised her eyebrows. 'Oh? And what has he done to disturb the peace?' she wanted to know.

'Reappeared. That's what he's done,' Katherine informed her, shrugging her hair back off her shoulders in a gesture of annoyance. Sleep had been a long time coming to her overactive mind, and when it had, she had slept badly. Tired and irritable, everything annoyed her this morning.

Burning with curiosity, Samantha waited for her friend to continue.

Grudgingly, Katherine muttered, 'He was at the exhibition last night. Would you believe, of all the places in London from which to choose, he chose to be at Harrington's Art Gallery. Oh, why did he have to go there of all places, and last night of all nights?' she wailed.

Enlightenment dawned. 'He saw the portrait, right?' Samantha grinned merrily.

'Right,' Katherine confirmed, but saw nothing to smile about.

'And he recognised you?'

'Well . . . not exactly.' She deliberated over her words, a scowl on her face. 'Unfortunately, he recognised me from the portrait, but he didn't actually recognise me, if you know what I mean.'

'I think I'm beginning to get the gist of the conversation,' Samantha replied, her green eyes sparkling with humour.

'Sam, this is not a laughing matter,' Katherine rebuked her. 'I was introduced as Madeleine Harcourt and, would you believe, he didn't bat an eyelid over the name.'

Seeing her friend's look of scepticism, Katherine insisted, 'Honestly, he had no idea who I was.'

'And you didn't enlighten him, I suppose?'

'No. Well, how could I. He'd seen the portrait.'

'So what? If I had a body like yours, I'd bare all for a dozen portraits, and be proud of it,' Samantha said, striking up a sexy pose, and sticking out her bottom lip into a pronounced pout.

'You don't mean it,' Katherine was trying hard not to laugh at her friend's ridiculous posturing.

'Oh yes I do,' Samantha airily assured her. Dropping the pose, she assumed normality once more. 'But no one's ever offered to immortalise my rather generous curves on canvas.'

Putting one of the steaming mugs into the other girl's hand, Katherine led the way into the lounge. 'You've got a great figure, Sam, and you know it. It's always got you more than your fair share of attention.'

'I'm not complaining,' Samantha grinned contentedly. 'OK. I'm all ears now, and you've got my serious, undivided attention.' Balancing the mug carefully, she settled herself into one of the armchairs across from Katherine, who had gone to sit on the sofa.

Katherine fell into a silent reverie, reliving once more those disturbing few moments of numbing shock when her heart had skipped a beat, the blood had pounded in her head, and her legs had felt as if they were about to collapse beneath her. She remembered how Alexis had looked at her without a hint of recognition. And how it had flashed through her confused mind that, since he had neither recognised her outside Linnet House nor questioned her introduction as Madeleine Harcourt, it was possible, indeed, quite probable, he did not know who she was. At that point, Samantha's words had come floating back: 'He hasn't seen you in years, and at the time you were knee high to a grasshopper and about as pretty as one. Just look how much you've changed.'

'So? What happened after you were introduced as Madeleine Harcourt?' Samantha asked impatiently.

Katherine remembered that he had smiled at her, but it had been an impersonal sort of smile. It was then that she had made the split second decision that prompted her next action.

'Well, I just stuck out my hand and said, "I'm pleased to meet you, Mr Drew,"' Katherine answered lamely.

Katherine remembered that he had held her hand just a little too long, until she had hesitantly removed it, that he had continued to regard her with a smile playing at the corners of his beautiful mouth. Was this what Samantha wanted to hear? she wondered. And that he spoke to her with easy nonchalance in that deep, melodious voice that she remembered so well from the past?

'He must have said something, even if you lost your tongue,' Samantha insisted, watching her friend suspiciously.

'Yes. Actually, he did,' she replied crossly. 'He said, "Haven't I seen you somewhere before?" For a moment I thought he had recognised me. I mean, really recognised me, until he said, "Oh yes, aren't you the model in that delightful portrait I've just been admiring?" Oh Sam, I could have died of embarrassment. I didn't know where to put my eyes so I stood there like a dummy staring at the carpet, and when I looked up he was getting ready to move on. I must have managed to hold his attention for all of two minutes . . . what an air-head he must have thought me!'

'And then what happened? He didn't just walk off and leave you, surely?' Samantha insisted.

'Oh, he said something about it being a pleasure to have met me and how he hoped we'd meet again, or some such thing . . . Not quite the sentiments I remember him sharing with Hugh Bradford five years ago.' After a moment's resentful recollection, she continued indignantly, 'We'll meet again all right, but the next time, it will be over divorce proceedings!' As an afterthought, she added hotly. 'How I wish I had thought to say that to him.'

Seeing amusement in Samantha's eyes, Katherine stubbornly determined to say no more on the subject. However, she could not prevent herself from recalling to mind, as she had done over and over throughout her sleepless night, his exact words, said with such devastating charm: 'It's been a pleasure to meet you, Madeleine. I hope we will meet again.' And, after her negative response, the way he had for a moment regarded her through thoughtful dark eyes before replying in a voice like velvet, 'It's a small world . . . you never know.'

She thought she had detected a hint of promise in his parting smile as he had, once more, walked casually out of her life.

22

A meeting was in progress at Earl and Harrow Advertising, and had been all morning. The staff around the boardroom table were in fine humour and, for the most part, the meeting had been both interesting and entertaining. They were a team of men and women chosen for their creativity and their literary and artistic talents, and they worked well together.

They had arrived at the most important issue to be discussed on the morning's agenda: the account of Belle Laurie Cosmetics. Earl and Harrow had worked hard to get this account and, so far, had achieved a good working relationship with the company's own in-house advertising department. All the work they had undertaken for them to date had met with their client's approval.

Isabelle Laurie had founded the company in the 1940s, and the product had originally been sold in exclusive shops at prices only affordable by the wealthy. Bought as much for the prestige of its name and the beauty and elegance of its containers as for the product itself, it had done well and made its founder a very prosperous woman. Noting the changing world around her, Isabelle Laurie was quick to take advantage of the advent of an expanding breed of modern career women who had money in their bank accounts and a strong desire to pamper themselves. A new range of commodities went into production, to be sold at more affordable prices, in more practical containers and in more accessible shops. Sales went up, but that was already some time ago and demand for new wonder products did not end there. It was time to introduce yet another new line.

The designs for the labels and packaging had already

come off the drawing board. The silver filigree work embossed on a white background gave it a touch of sensuality, the black print, strength. It was hoped that these qualities would appeal to the modern woman.

The factory was ready to start mass production. The sales representatives were poised to tote the samples to the wholesale suppliers and they, in their turn, were waiting to take orders from the retailers. The advertising campaign had been planned down to the last detail. Everyone involved was standing by ready to swing into action. But there was one problem: no one, so far, had been able come up with the right face to launch the campaign.

Cameron Knight had looked tirelessly through countless portfolios delivered to his office courtesy of London's top modelling agencies and, when that failed to turn up the right person, he had gone further afield and applied to the theatrical agencies. He had searched for that special someone even in the crowded streets of London, in pubs and restaurants and on the platforms of the underground during rush hour, but all to no avail. Now, thanks to the Paris Trade Fair, he had found her. From his transparent demeanour, it was obvious to all at the meeting he had something up his sleeve that was making him feel more than a little pleased with himself.

'You're in a rare good mood this morning, Cameron,' one of his female colleagues teased. 'You're about to tell us you've found her.'

'Am I that obvious?' He smiled smugly. Absent mindedly, he turned his pencil over and over between his fingers, tapping the ends alternately on the notepad in front. Enjoying the moment of suspense, he took time to gaze leisurely around the table at the six pairs of eyes focused on his, before saying, 'Yes, you're right. I've found her . . . at the Paris Trade Fair.'

'Do get on with it, Cameron,' someone prompted with good humour.

Laying the pencil down, he lounged back in his chair and unhurriedly came to the point. 'The girl is fresh out of art college,' he told them, 'and has been a trainee designer for a London based company called Veronique Couture for the past few months. When one of their models had to drop out at the last minute, she was roped in to take her place on the catwalk. 'From what I heard, she'd never had any training or experience in her life, but you'd never have known it from her performance. You should have seen her; she was fantastic!

'Before this, she was an unknown but, believe me, she's not likely to stay that way for long, so if we decide we want her, we had better move fast.' Cameron paused for emphasis, his face serious. He wanted them to understand the need for a quick decision. 'She caused quite a stir, and I'm sure that, if Veronique Couture have not already signed her up, one of the bigger and better fashion houses will waste no time in doing so.'

Cameron Knight reached down to open his briefcase and from it he extracted a large brown envelope. 'This is the face we've been looking for. She's got the lot. I could go on waxing lyrical, but I won't keep you waiting any longer. You shall judge for yourselves.'

With this, he removed a dozen or so enlarged photographs from the envelope, together with some magazine cuttings, and, leaning forward, scattered them down the middle of the boardroom table. There was a hush as they were picked up, examined, and slowly passed from hand to hand.

Eventually Cameron broke the silence. He had been watching their expressions and now he triumphantly commented, 'Well, I don't think I need to ask you what you think – your faces say it all.'

He gave them a couple of minutes to discuss the pictures amongst themselves, and then he said, 'Although I haven't personally spoken to her, I did have a chance to listen to her talking to the media. The lady has class and intelligence and, if that isn't enough, she also has a superb voice.'

'Really? In what way superb?' one of the men queried.

'Soft . . . husky . . . incredibly sexy,' Cameron replied.

Exaggerated groans of ecstasy came from the men, and one was heard to mutter, 'Not only does she please the eye but we can get orgasms just listening to her!'

'Can't wait to make her acquaintance!' grinned his neighbour.

'Poor things, it's the only way they can get it these days,' chortled one of the women to another.

Cameron waited for the banter to end, then on a serious note warned, 'She's destined for higher things, so we and Belle Laurie need to come to a quick decision.'

'This girl's a trainee designer, you say? If she takes her career seriously, she might not want it disrupted,' one of the team remarked.

Cameron looked mildly surprised. This was a point that had not previously crossed his mind. 'What? And turn her back on fame and fortune? I don't think that's very likely,' he said. He paused a moment to consider the possibility, before saying with a careless shrug of the shoulders, 'We'll just have to make sure our offer is too good to refuse.' After a moment, Cameron continued, 'I understand that Belle Laurie is still not one hundred per cent happy about the name they chose for the new range. Should the contract go to this young lady, they may like to reconsider and name the product after her.'

'And her name is . . .?' asked a colleague.

Picking up the nearest photograph, Cameron gazed at the beautiful face and replied, 'Her name is Madeleine.'

'I would like time to think about it,' Katherine had said to Michael, when he broached the subject of a modelling contract with Veronique Couture, and that was what she had been doing all morning: thinking about it instead of concentrating on the new designs.

She had not received any extra salary for her part in the Paris show. For that matter, Katherine had no idea what the job should have paid; she had not thought to ask Isabel or Katerina to clarify that aspect of a model's life. She considered that, under the circumstances, Madame had been more than fair as she had paid all her expenses in Paris, and had given her a number of beautiful and expensive gowns out of the stockroom to compensate. It had been one of those fabulous little numbers Katherine had worn to the art exhibition.

The exhibition was something else not easily forgotten. Every time she thought of that evening, Alexis came to mind, and then her heartbeat would play tricks and her stomach would churn over in a most uncomfortable way. That he had seen the portrait continued to cause her embarrassment. Each time she remembered the way he had directed his interested gaze towards it, she would feel herself blush and her imagination would run riot. It was as if she could feel that gaze like a gentle caress upon her body, and she revelled and delighted in each imagined touch.

For days now, Katherine had found herself floating in and out of a dream world, unable to concentrate for long on what she was supposed to be doing. Thinking their young designer was daydreaming over her involvement in the Paris shows, the staff teased her, but Katherine knew better. That had been a truly novel experience, but it was over now and her chosen career was back on course.

Paris might have been followed by feelings of anticlimax if it had not been for that chance meeting at Harrington's Art Gallery where Alexis had once more walked in and out of her life, turning it upside down, creating emotional chaos where there had been calm. Now, like a fascinating daemon, his image kept materialising at unexpected moments. For the hundredth time that day, Katherine banished him from her thoughts, knowing full well he would soon return to torment her over again. Peace would come in time: past experience told her so.

The ringing of the telephone interrupted her turbulent thoughts. Taking her eyes from the sketchpad, Katherine reached to answer it.

'A Mr Knight to speak to you, Madeleine,' said the girl on the switchboard.

Since her return from Paris, everyone at Veronique Couture had taken to using her assumed name. She had grown used to it.

'This is . . . Madeleine Harcourt,' Katherine said, after a slight hesitation. 'Can I help you?'

'I hope so,' said a confident voice. 'I'm Cameron Knight and I'm the Art Director for the Earl and Harrow advertising agency. I was at the trade fair in Paris last week and happened to see you there, on the catwalk.' Afraid she might get the wrong idea and hang up, he hastened to add, 'I have a business proposition I would like to put to you. One I think you might find very interesting. Could we meet to discuss it?'

There was a short silence while Katherine thought about what he had said.

He waited.

'Mr Knight, you're probably under the misconception that I'm a fashion model. Actually, I'm really a designer for Veronique Couture. I just filled in at the last minute because a model dropped out,' she informed him, honestly.

To her surprise, he replied, 'Yes I know, but I would still like to talk business.'

'No,' she said decisively. 'I don't think so, Mr Knight, not unless you're thinking of offering me a career move in my real line of work.'

'A few minutes of your time. That's all I'm asking for,' he said persuasively. 'Look, it's nearly five-thirty. I'll drop everything and come over to you. OK? We'll find somewhere nearby to drink and talk. No pressure, no obligation, and if you're still not interested then I'll take no for an answer, and move on.' He waited for her reply.

'OK,' she finally relented. 'But I'm in the middle of something I want to complete today . . . I should be finished by about seven,' she told him, feeling little enthusiasm for the meeting.

It took longer than the proposed few minutes to win her

over but, as Cameron anticipated, the carrot he dangled in front of her proved to be an irresistible temptation. Katherine agreed to visit Earl and Harrow the following day to talk matters over in more detail.

Katherine had arrived at yet another turning point in her life.

23

Although he had Katherine's Marlow Place address, Alexis felt he could hardly just turn up on her doorstep and say, 'Hi, Madeleine. Remember me?' For a start, she would want to know how he had come by her address. He could not own to having a file that contained it, and a lot more information besides. Nor could he claim to have got it out of the telephone directory, as she was listed under the name of Katherine Drew, and he was not supposed to know that Madeleine and Katherine were one and the same person.

Alexis had spent the day at a recording studio only a few minutes' walk from Lexington Crescent. The session had gone well, finishing earlier than anticipated and leaving him with time on his hands. It occurred to him that, as it was now the last day of the exhibition, Madeleine might well be at the gallery, if only to help Grierson remove his unsold paintings. On the off chance, he called in.

The same young attractive receptionist Alexis remembered from his previous visit was at the desk, in conversation with a man whose tone and air of patronising superiority announced to anyone who cared to listen that he was the man in charge. Seeing Alexis approach, Susan flashed him a smile of recognition.

'Mr Drew, isn't it?' she said by way of welcome. Although she prided herself on having a good memory for names and faces, Susan had not needed to make a conscious effort to remember this man. Indeed, she had been having a difficult time forgetting him. Although his friend had not made quite the same impact, he too was memorable, for he at least had appeared to notice her.

'This is Mr Alexis Drew,' said Susan to the man at her

side, and to Alexis, 'Mr Rodney Harrington, our Executive Art Director.'

The man extended a hand, which to Alexis' firm grip felt weak and slightly clammy to the touch. 'Pleased to meet you,' Harrington said. His memory stirred. He had noted the new names on the guest list. 'You were here for the first night of the exhibition,' he recalled. 'Sorry we didn't get a chance to meet then.'

By the time Harrington had finished this sentence, he had managed to place the name Alexis Drew, and knew him to be well known in the music world. Noting the expensive clothes and gold Rolex watch, he was sufficiently satisfied with the credentials to warrant the turning on of the renowned Harrington charm. The man obviously had money and plenty of it, and was therefore a potential customer of the highest calibre. 'Pleased you could join us for the opening.'

'Wouldn't have missed it for the world,' Alexis commented, thinking of Madeleine.

'It was a huge success, and I'm pleased to say we had some excellent reviews,' Harrington boasted. There was a slight question in the way he now regarded Alexis. He was wondering what had brought him back to the gallery again so soon and hoping he had returned to make a purchase.

Divining Harrington's thoughts, Alexis informed him, 'I'm looking for a birthday present for my sister. Mind if I look around?' He had not actually come in with the intention of purchasing anything but it was true, it would soon be Jane's birthday and the gift of a picture, under the present circumstances, seemed a very good idea.

'Not at all, Mr Drew. Please feel free,' Harrington replied, with an amiable smile and an expansive wave of a hand. This was the Executive Art Director at his most charming.

As Alexis moved into the gallery, the man fell into step at his side. On this occasion, movement around the room was not hampered by a surfeit of guests. In fact, the contrast between this and his previous visit was markedly noticeable. It was fairly late in the afternoon, most of the visitors had already gone or were leaving. There were no waiters and trays of which to be wary, no noisy chatter, glittering jewellery or evening attire. There were now blank spaces where artwork had once been on display, and *sold* stickers on many of the exhibits still awaiting delivery to their new owners.

Slowly they moved around the gallery. While on the lookout for Madeleine, Alexis allowed Harrington to regale him with the extensive range of his professional knowledge. There was no doubt he knew his subject, but there was condescension for the layman in the way he spoke that made him disagreeable to his listener.

The wall where the portrait of Madeleine had once hung was now blank, and the spotlight which had illuminated it to such dramatic effect turned off. As they approached, Alexis noticed the eyes of the other man fasten on the empty space, and the scowl of discontent that flickered across his face.

'A fine up-and-coming artist, that Jeremy Grierson,' Harrington muttered. 'Unknown, but I doubt if he will be for long. He got excellent reviews, you know, especially for the nude. You may have noticed it. It hung there,' he paused to indicate the blank space with a nod.

'Yes. I remember it well,' Alexis replied. A smile hovered at the corners of his mouth as he thought of the portrait now hanging safely on the study wall in Linnet House, delivered with the compliments of Hugh Bradford.

If Harrington had known this, his thoughts might not have been quite so transparent. 'Beautiful painting. Exquisite model. Pity I let it go, could have sold it a dozen times over for twice the price.' Aroused by the remembrance of the subject, he absent-mindedly ran his tongue along his fleshy lips. 'Wouldn't have minded giving it houseroom myself.'

Alexis had no intentions of discussing this particular portrait with the likes of Rodney Harrington, to whom he was fast developing an aversion. Now he knew Madeleine was not present, he saw no reason to inflict himself further with this man's company. Turning away, he strode in the direction of Grierson's remaining work. He already knew which painting he wanted. It had made a lasting impression on him and he was pleased, although surprised, to see the oil still available.

However, before he could indicate his choice, a woman approached to inform Harrington that Lady Mellingson was on the telephone. With a show of reluctance, he excused himself and hurried away.

Remaining to take her employer's place, the woman introduced herself as Mavis Ford. 'I'm Mr Harrington's personal assistant,' she enlightened him.

Alexis introduced himself, but really, there was no need. Mavis remembered him quite clearly from his previous visit.

Finding time, at last, to talk to Madeleine, Mavis had come to her side just in time to see this man walk away. She remembered the dazed and vulnerable look on the young girl's face as she watched him disappear into the crowd.

'Who was that?' Mavis had asked, intrigued.

'Alexis Drew,' Madeleine had whispered, her voice dreamy.

'Alexis Drew?' There had been a familiar ring to the name. 'Do you mean the pianist?' Mavis had inquired, a little thrill running through her as it always did whenever she came into contact with a celebrity.

'Yes, that's right,' the girl had confirmed, still not giving her full attention to Mavis.

Mavis had thought he looked vaguely familiar. 'Are you acquainted with him?'

'Acquainted?' Madeleine had murmured looking thoughtful. 'Yes. I suppose *acquainted* is an appropriate word.' Her brooding gaze had remained turned in the direction the man had taken, although the crowd had long since swallowed him up.

'Really? How long have you known each other?' Mavis had quizzed, eager to hear more about this strikingly handsome and successful man.

'Oh, we go back a long, long way,' had been the absent-minded reply. Then, as if making a mental effort to pull herself together, Madeleine had refocused her attention onto Mavis and deliberately changed the subject.

Now, with the subject of her curiosity once more back in the gallery, Mavis saw an opportunity for further enlightenment.

To Alexis, her arrival on the scene was timely, and her company a most welcome exchange for Harrington's. He decided to linger a little longer.

Harrington, he had already observed, liked to surround himself with the young and attractive, a mould into which Mavis Ford did not fit. However, drawing her into conversation, he soon discovered her true value. She had an in-depth knowledge of art that probably made her as indispensable to Harrington as Jenny was to him. As she warmed to her subject, he found himself listening with a genuine interest he had not felt with her employer.

Bringing her around to the subject of Jeremy Grierson's exhibits, Alexis remarked that there had been more of the artist's work on show when he had last visited.

'Oh yes,' responded Mavis, 'but his best pieces sold very quickly. They all stayed on show to the public until this morning, though.' Quickly, she corrected herself, 'Well, all but one, I should say.' Sensing his special interest in the paintings, she continued, 'That particular one was bought on the first night by a private collector from abroad. Apparently, he was leaving the country the next day and wanted to take it with him. A pity, really . . . it was the artist's best work. Fortunately, the critics did see it before it was removed, and it got him several excellent reviews.'

'Which picture was that?' Alexis asked, wanting to keep her talking on the subject in the hope she would tell him something he did not already know about Grierson and his beautiful model.

'The large one. The semi-nude that hung over there,' she

replied, turning to gaze in the direction of the blank wall. 'You know, the one of your friend . . . Madeleine Harcourt.' Her pause invited comment.

That this woman was aware of his acquaintance with Madeleine came as a surprise. Must have seen us talking together and just assumed, he told himself. Perhaps, if he encouraged her belief in the friendship, she might be more inclined to talk openly about the model and artist.

'Ah yes, of course, I remember it,' he said. 'A very beautiful portrait. A shame it had to come down so soon. Has Grierson painted any others of Madeleine?'

'Not that I know of, and now there are not likely to be any more,' Mavis volunteered.

Alexis looked at her questioningly and waited.

'Well, I mean, they don't see much of each other now that she's finished art school, do they?'

'Yet they appear to have remained on good terms,' he ventured, remembering the easy familiarity they had shared. 'They might still find time and inclination to work together.'

'I don't think that's likely,' Mavis went on, 'not now it's all over between them. It's not as if Madeleine is, or ever was, an artist's model by profession.' Mavis talked on, unaware she was telling him exactly what he wanted to hear. 'And besides, she has her own career to think about now.'

Taking no chances, Alexis said, 'If any more of Grierson's work goes on sale, perhaps you'd let me know.' He offered his business card.

'Your name should already be on our guest list,' Mavis said, 'but I'll make sure.' In fact, she knew it was. She had entered the details herself, copying them from the card he had left with Susan on the opening night.

Accepting the new offering anyway, she slipped it into her jacket pocket. Mavis collected celebrity's cards the way other people collected autographs, and this little treasure was destined for her own private collection.

'Jeremy Grierson's been invited to exhibit his work here on a regular basis,' she informed him conversationally. 'But some of his best will be kept back for our next show. I'll personally make sure you get an invitation, Mr Drew.'

As they talked, he studied one of the two remaining oils. Of Jeremy Grierson's half-dozen exhibits, it was the only still life. It featured slices of watermelon inside, and spilling out of, a crystal bowl that stood on a highly polished mahogany table. A lace-edged ecru napkin lay in gentle folds in front and to one side of the bowl. The rows of shiny dark-brown pips embedded in the bright orange-red flesh of the fruit and the yellow blotches in its thick green skin were pleasing splashes of contrasting colours. The brightness of the fruit, the transparency of the glass with the light bouncing off its multifacets and the dark sheen of the wooden table, gave the oil a wonderful blend of vibrant colours and an interesting array of mirrored reflections.

This was the painting Alexis bought for his sister. It was the painting which had caught his eye when in the gallery last, but at that time the portrait of Madeleine Harcourt had been uppermost in his mind, allowing little room for interest to develop in anything else.

Although Madeleine was not present, he was pleased he had made the effort to visit the gallery. If he had learned nothing else, he now knew there had indeed been an affair between model and artist, that it had run its full course and was truly over. A whole phase of her life, it would seem, had come to an end and it was probable that no more portraits of her would be found upon these walls. He doubted that anything further would be gained by a future revisit to Harrington's Art Gallery.

Maybe now was a good time to make one of his periodic visits to Ravenswood. A business call on Mr Coteman must surely be about due. But, no sooner had this thought entered his head than he dismissed it. Madeleine would be revealed as Katherine and that would spoil the enjoyable little subterfuge they had entered into. He now realised that if, in the near future, he were to make any forays into the Cotswolds, he would first have to make sure she was not there.

It would appear that neither the gallery nor Ravenswood held an immediate solution to his problem. He would have to think of another way to renew his acquaintance with Madeleine Harcourt.

24

Life was indeed moving on for Madeleine. In fact, she thought it was all moving on rather too fast. She had met and received the unanimous approval of the directors of Earl and Harrow, and been driven to the headquarters of Belle Laurie Cosmetics in Slough. Ms Laurie herself had flown in from Rome that morning, reputedly in a foul mood over the delay of the promotion. In her luxurious office, Madeleine was introduced to the entrepreneur and the executive members of her staff.

'Perfect!' Ms Laurie had pronounced, speaking for all and smiling for the first time that day. Cameron was congratulated on his find and given the go-ahead to get her under contract as quickly as possible.

Madeleine was having difficulty grasping the magnitude of the offer that had, unsolicited, dropped into her lap. Elation, however, was marred by concern at being thrust into a world she knew little about, with no guarantee she would come up to everyone's expectations. Hesitant to take the plunge, she questioned the logic of putting an end to a promising career for a contract that was only going to last six months.

Her lack of enthusiasm was noted by Cameron and his colleagues, and misconstrued. Perhaps Madeleine was unimpressed with the financial terms offered, or maybe she had received a better offer from someone else. For fear of losing her, new terms were agreed which far exceeded the original. It was, in truth, more in keeping with what a professional model could expect had the deal gone through an agency, and Madeleine, having telephoned Isabel and Katerina, now knew enough to be aware of this. Nevertheless, the new offer took her breath away. Cameron Knight had led her to believe that financially it would be well worth her while, but the value that had now been placed upon her seemed exorbitant and way beyond anything she could hope to earn as a designer for many years to come. Under the circumstances, she decided to say not another word on the subject of the career she was planning to relinquish.

Because of time already lost, Earl and Harrow were in a hurry to get the show on the road. However, a month's notice either way was the unwritten understanding between Veronique Couture and its less senior members of staff. Since Madame was not at all happy to be losing Madeleine, either as a promising designer or as a catwalk model for her future shows, she was disinclined to be accommodating over the leaving date. Madeleine was politely adamant that she would not be signing a modelling contract with Veronique Couture. And so, after much debate with Michael, Madame, at her most melodramatic, finally agreed to release her immediately on the understanding that she would model for them at next year's Paris Trade Fair.

Fearing fame would vastly increase the value of Madeleine services, she quickly stressed: 'For the same fee we pay the other models, of course.'

Madeleine agreed, and was happy to do so. She had enjoyed the work and, besides, her contract with Belle Laurie would be over by then and she could well find herself walking the pavement looking for a job. No point in burning her bridges with the couturier as either designer or catwalk model.

After the terms had been thoroughly discussed with Earl and Harrow and the papers drawn up, Madeleine agreed to sign, but not until Mr Fairfax had seen a draft and made amendments to some of the small print. When he had read the amount offered, his eyebrows rose halfway to his hair-line. 'We're in the wrong business!' he later told his partner.

*

Belle Laurie supplied all the garments and accessories for the photographic sessions and for the filming of the television commercials. They also supplied Madeleine with an exclusive range of suitable garments, from swimsuit to ballgown, for those occasions when she would find herself in the public limelight.

Left in the care of others, she saw little of Cameron in the ensuing days. He was busy putting into action all Earl and Harrow's carefully laid plans.

While all this activity was going on, Madeleine was expected to give her attention to the acquisition of her new and extensive wardrobe, be patient, and continue to look beautiful. She soon grew bored with trying on gowns and her patience wore rather thin. When one of London's top professional fashion photographers was finally called in to take promotional stills of her in the new gowns, the boredom became a thing of the past. Madeleine threw herself wholeheartedly into the photographic sessions. In front of a lens, she came alive, was truly professional and extraordinarily photogenic.

This was not Madeleine's idea of living a useful life but, as she cheerfully told Samantha, 'If they wanted to pay me an astronomical fee for enjoying myself, who am I to complain?'

Within a couple of weeks of signing the contract, Madeleine was on her way to Germany, accompanied by Cameron Knight, Tom Flanagan the photographer, and a girl not much older than herself, called Sally Piper. From the beginning, Sally had been put in charge of the wardrobe, make-up and hairdressing. Thrown so much together, a comfortable working relationship had quickly developed between the team.

By now, all were aware of her real name, but had become so used to calling her Madeleine that it felt strange to call her anything else. Besides, the name Madeleine had been added to the packaging and written into the commercial scripts. For her to revert back to the name of Katherine did not serve anyone's purpose.

Since the night of the art exhibition, she had seen nothing further of Alexis. She had not expected to, not really, but she had allowed herself to dream, and now the dreams would not be put aside. He was like a dark, mischievous phantom who walked in and out of her life wreaking havoc at will: a phantom over whom she had no control.

Fanning the flames of early resentments to use as an antidote against him, Madeleine frequently deliberately rekindled memories of that long ago conversation at Ravenswood between him and Hugh Bradford. In doing so, she unwittingly resurrected another bitter memory. Alexis had clearly said that within days of the wedding, some woman called Henrietta would be joining him in Vienna.

At the time, she had not cared enough to give it more than a passing thought, but somewhere along the way her feelings towards Alexis had undergone a change. Whilst the hurt inflicted by his criticism of her had somewhat diminished, the knowledge that another woman had shared his bed now filled her with pangs of jealousy.

They were eight days in Germany and most of the shooting took place in a modern luxurious office, on a launch on the Rhine and in a beautiful fairy tale Gothic castle in the Black Forest. The filming was taken out of sequence. But Madeleine knew, when the footage was edited, it would show her as a successful jet-setting business executive with a wealthy and romantic private life who, naturally, owed all that beauty, success and popularity to her usage of Belle Laurie's new range of cosmetics.

The German male model hired to play the aristocratic supporting role was blond, blue eyed and very aware of his personal appeal. Cameron counteracted his interest in Madeleine by deliberately monopolising her company both on and off the set. Consequently, Jurgen found, to his intense frustration, that he was never alone with her for more than a few minutes at a time.

'What an efficient chaperon Cameron makes,' Sally commented to Madeleine, much amused. 'By the way he's behaving, anyone would think you were his kid sister. Quite commendable if one didn't know he had ulterior motives of his own.'

'Jurgen's a bit obvious,' Madeleine agreed, 'but I'm sure you've got Cameron all wrong. He's just looking after company business – probably afraid I'll elope before the end of the contract,' she laughed.

'Believe what you will,' Sally told her breezily, 'but, all the same, someone should tell poor Jurgen he's wasting his time. He'll never get past Cameron. I know; I've seen him in action before.'

They were up and out early each morning and, unless they were expected at a promotional dinner or reception, often did not return to the hotel until the light began to fail. Everything she said and did before the cameras was carefully supervised by Cameron, as was everything she said and did in public. He was a patient director who knew exactly what he wanted and how to get it.

Thrust into an exciting new world, kept busy by a hectic schedule, by day there was now little time to indulge in fanciful thoughts of Alexis. At night, however, alone in the dark with nothing to occupy her mind, wistful thoughts of him returned to torment her. She wondered where he was, what he was doing, and what he thought of her . . . if, indeed, he thought of her at all.

25

Through no fault of his own, the series of recording sessions had not continued to run smoothly. Two vital days had been lost and other work needing Alexis' urgent attention had piled up. There was a deadline on an overture not quite completed for the BBC. By the time he put the finishing touches to that, attended a meeting with the Ravenswood trustees and brought his own affairs up to date, a fortnight had passed and it was time to depart on the next European tour.

Although frustrated, Alexis could philosophically console himself that, since he and Katherine were tied to each other for at least another year, there was no desperate hurry to manipulate a meeting between them. It could safely wait for his return.

The tour took him first to Madrid, and then on to Monaco. In these two destinations, Alexis stayed at the villas of friends, as he did in so many of the places he visited. There were many, especially in the south of France, who would not think of allowing him to book into a hotel if they knew he was to perform in their city.

A week after his arrival in Monaco and a few days before he was due to leave for Paris, a young domestic brought a telephone out to where he lounged at the pool-side. It was Jenny calling to keep him up-to-date on his complex business and social affairs. They conversed for a few minutes, but this time there was little that could not wait for his return to Henley. About to ring off, she remembered something. 'Oh yes, I nearly forgot to tell you, Mr Smith sent a final report. I guess it crossed with your letter telling him his services were no longer required. I've read it through and all appears to be OK. Nothing there to worry about.'

Since Alexis had never shown the slightest interest before, Jenny was surprised when, snapping out of his lethargy, he asked what it contained.

'Quite interesting, really. Katherine no longer works for Veronique Couture but now has a six-month contract with Earl and Harrow advertising agency.'

'Doing what exactly?' he wanted to know. Although his eyes were on a flock of little sparrows bravely pecking at remnant crumbs on a nearby table, his attention was focused entirely on what Jenny had to tell him.

'She's been chosen to launch a new range of cosmetics for a company called Belle Laurie. They're going to use her for all the advertising,' Jenny told him. 'Lucky girl, or should I say, clever girl. Seems to have a good head for business – it looks like she's got herself a lucrative deal.' There was an audible rustle of paper while Jenny scanned the report for anything of interest. 'Apparently a man named Cameron Knight spotted her at the Paris Trade Fair.'

Alexis sat up, the sudden movement causing the sparrows to fly off in alarm. He was familiar with the agency, had used their professional expertise a few times in the past. A number of its directors and employees were known to him, but Cameron Knight he was sure he had never met. The name, however, had a familiar ring to it. Racking his brain, Alexis tried to remember where and when he had heard it, but the memory eluded him. He knew only that it had been mentioned in derogatory terms

Jenny was talking again. 'They've been filming and promoting in Germany for a week but now they're in Paris. Next week they go on to Rome. Want to know any more?' she asked.

'Yes. Is Cameron Knight with her?' he inquired, raising his voice above the drone of a light sea-rescue plane.

'Cameron Knight, a photographer called Tom Flanagan, and a girl who looks after the wardrobe, hairdressing, make-up, etc. No name given for her.'

'Does Smith say what hotel they're booked into?' he asked.

'Let me see . . . Yes the Hotel Regent's Garden and it's on the Rue Pierre-Demours. For some reason, Katherine's going under the name of Madeleine Harcourt.' She paused. 'Now why would she want to do that, I wonder?'

To answer that question would mean explaining the nature of the portrait. Alexis let it pass. 'Good,' he said, and then instructed, 'See if you can bring my flight forward to tomorrow and change my reservation over to the Hotel Regent's Garden.'

'You'll be lucky, Alexis, it's the height of the season,' she replied, her voice laden with doubt. 'But I'll do my best. Call you later.'

The telephone conversation gave him plenty to think about. Restlessly, Alexis arose from the sun-lounger and, feeling the warm mosaics under his bare feet, strolled over to stand with his hands on the rail at the far end of the pool. With the salty sea breeze on his face and ruffling his dark hair, he looked down on the bright, azure-blue waters of the bay below. Boats were out, their colourful sails catching the Mediterranean breeze. The water-skiers and windsurfers too were taking advantage of a fairly calm sea, and the yachts and schooners of the wealthy ploughed in and out: moorings were never vacant for long. Tanned, skimpily clad bodies sunbathed or strolled along the beach and, in the distance, youths played an energetic, rowdy game of volleyball.

Gazing with unseeing eyes, Alexis was for once not fully aware of the beauty of the privileged world around him. His mind was on other things and would have remained so if a familiar voice had not said in French, 'By the way you are gazing at the beach, I think she must be very special.'

Simone, his hostess, came to stand at his side. Like him, she wore only swimwear and sunglasses. Her slender limbs were nearly as darkly tanned as his own.

'Who are we looking at?' she laughed, leaning forward to peer down on the sandy expanse. Her long, black hair brushed against the back of his hand, erotic and teasing.

Enjoying the sensation, he left his hand on the rail. 'No-one at all, Simone,' he replied in her own language, a smile on his lips. 'I was just thinking I may have to leave you and Henri a little earlier than planned.'

'How much earlier?' she asked, too quickly; for as much as she adored her husband, having Alexis' company brought a certain potent magic into her life.

Aware of the aura of restless passion surrounding Simone, Alexis turned his thoughts to his friend Henri. Reluctantly removing his hand from the rail, he admitted to himself that it was, indeed, time to move on. 'I may have to leave for Paris tomorrow,' he told her gently.

'Oh Alexis, you can't mean it,' Simone cried, turning to stare at him. 'We have not seen you for ages and you talk of going so soon, Henri and the children will be disappointed and I will be heartbroken.' Her large, tragic eyes implored him to stay. 'You said there were five days before your first concert in Paris,' she reminded him. 'What takes you away from us so soon – nothing serious, I hope?'

He ran the back of a finger down her cheek, amused yet touched to be so clearly in favour. 'Nothing to worry about, Simone, but there is someone I must see who will be in Paris for only a short time.'

Searching his face, she quietly asked, 'Is she very beautiful?'

'Yes,' he replied, 'she is very beautiful.'

'Is she your lover?'

Alexis laughed softly. 'Simone,' he said, gently, 'you French think of nothing but love.'

Unashamedly, her candid gaze moved admiringly over his lean, taught body. With a teasing, coquettish smile, she asked, 'Is there anything more important to think about?'

*

Within the hour, while Alexis was preparing for dinner at the Hôtel de Paris with a party of friends, followed by an evening in the Casino, Jenny telephoned again.

'You've got the luck of the devil. I've managed to get you on an earlier flight and, as for the hotel, they had a last minute cancellation, so you're in,' she told him, her voice triumphant. 'I have arranged for a limousine to collect you from the airport. I'm about to fax you all the details.'

He thanked Jenny and hung up. Suddenly he was very much looking forward to a weekend in Paris.

It was not until he was airborne the next day that Alexis remembered what he had heard about Cameron Knight. The stewardess was bringing around a tray of champagne soon after take-off and, as she put the glass in his hand, it jogged his memory. The previous year, at a business-related cocktail party, he had found himself talking to one of the directors of Earl and Harrow. A waiter had come by with a tray of champagne and Bob Shore had taken a couple of glasses and handed one to him. Spotting a colleague entering the room with a sultry brunette on his arm, his companion had chuckled, 'Another aspiring young model no doubt. I wonder what he's promised this one. Centrefold in next month's issue of *Playboy* magazine perhaps.'

Alexis had studied the girl for a moment. 'I'd subscribe to a copy,' he had approved.

'Me too. I wouldn't mind being in his shoes, but not if his wife ever catches him at it,' Tom had grinned. 'His reputation with women is known to everyone except Joanne, and God help him if she ever finds out. He'd be for the chop, and it wouldn't be his head leaving his body either.'

Amused, Alexis had shifted his attention back to the couple, and asked, 'Who is he?'

Tom had looked surprised. 'Cameron Knight . . . one of our directors. I thought you knew him, but then, come to think of it, Chris Ladbroke handled your account.'

The conversation had then turned to more serious topics

until other colleagues and acquaintances claimed their attention. Promptly forgetting Cameron Knight, Alexis had not given him another thought until Jenny's phone call. Now, he found his thoughts did not bode well for the man if he had encroached upon what Alexis was beginning to consider his own personal property.

It was late afternoon by the time he arrived at the small exclusive hotel, only a short distance from the Arc de Triomphe and the Champs-Elysées. It was tucked behind a high wall, accessible through tall gates that opened into a garden and a paved courtyard that allowed for the parking of only about eight cars.

As the hotel limousine turned in through the gates, Alexis saw that, despite the Anglified name, the exterior of the hotel was delightfully old Parisian.

The tall, white shuttered windows showed that, including the attic rooms, the hotel was only four floors high. It looked as if it might at one time have been the residence of a noble family. Alexis was later to learn that the hotel had been built by Napoleon III for his personal physician.

The marble-floored lobby was cool and airy, its ceilings high and decorated with elaborate plasterwork. One splendid illumination hung from the centre of the ceiling, suspended by wrought-iron chains. Tall potted ferns stood each side of the main entrance and another near the reception desk. The restaurant, coffee shop, paved courtyards and gardens were all situated off the central lobby, as were the stairs and the single antique lift.

Having completed the formalities of checking-in, Alexis was shown to an en suite room. Here, too, was the spacious elegance of old-world charm, with high ceilings, mahogany bow-fronted furniture, heavy fabrics of rich colours, and fine old paintings grown dark with age.

Crossing to the French windows that opened on to a wrought-iron enclosed veranda, he looked down onto a paved patio in a charming ivy-mantled walled garden at the rear of the hotel. Guests sat at tables under bright sunshades, enjoying late tea or early cocktails. The girl he had trained himself to think of as Madeleine did not appear to be among them. This observation brought his thoughts back to the reason for his being in this particular hotel, and he returned to the bedroom. Quickly he showered and changed, then descended the stairs to the lobby.

The atmosphere, tranquil and intimate, had none of the impersonal bustle found in the large modern hotels Alexis usually inhabited. The restaurant, although open for dinner guests, was, because of the early hour, still empty. At a glance he saw that Madeleine was neither in the coffee shop or bar and concluded she must be still out on location or in her room preparing for the evening's entertainment. Either way, she would eventually have to pass through the lobby and, clearly, the bar offered the best vantage point from which to watch.

Seating himself at a table near the door and under a slowly revolving fan, Alexis ordered an anise and waited. After two cocktails and 40 minutes, his patience was rewarded. Madeleine, Cameron Knight and Tom the photographer, identifiable by the camera equipment strewn around his neck, entered the lobby through the main entrance.

They stopped briefly to confer, before parting company with the photographer. Turning in the direction of the bar, Cameron took his companion's hand in his. Alexis watched to see if Madeleine would pull her hand away. She did not. With hard, appraising eyes he searched for further signs of familiarity between them. As he did so, he knew that he would not give her up without a fight, and never to this man.

When had he become so possessive? he wondered. The portrait flashed before his inner eye and he knew it was when he had made the astonishing discovery that the ravishing woman in the portrait and the funny little oddity with whom he had gone through the marriage vows were one and the same.

As they were about to pass his table, Alexis came slowly but purposefully to his feet. 'Madeleine. Madeleine Harcourt isn't it?' he asked, feigning surprise and forcing a smile to his face. 'What a small world we live in!'

So unexpected was the appearance of Alexis that Madeleine gave an involuntary start and, at the same time, tugged her hand out of Cameron's as if caught indulging in an indecent act. This put her companion on the alert. He looked sharply from one to the other, but there was nothing to be learned from their expressions.

In a barely controlled voice, heart beating erratically, Madeleine introduced the men to each other.

'I know the name. Concert pianist and songwriter – or should I say composer?' Cameron asked, shaking hands.

'I answer to both,' came the congenial reply.

'Earl and Harrow handled your advertising at one time, I believe.'

'Yes, that's right,' acknowledged Alexis. 'So you're with Earl and Harrow? Won't you join me in a drink?' he invited. Before either could refuse, he had pulled out a chair for Madeleine and summoned the waiter. 'What brings you to Paris?' he went on to ask with polite interest.

Cameron replied to his question and did most of the talking, while Madeleine listened, joining in only when courtesy made it necessary. Occasionally she glanced at Alexis, but seemed content to give most of her attention to her drink. She was, in fact, remembering how overawed she had always felt in the presence of this worldly sophisticate, and today was no different. Try as she might, she could not think of anything intelligent to contribute to the conversation. Madeleine deeply resented his power to inflict these feelings of inadequacy on her, and was wondering moodily why he was the only one who ever seemed to affect her in this way.

Alexis, in the meantime, was still studying the couple for signs of intimacy. Apart from the fact that they had been holding hands earlier, there was now nothing in their demeanour to suggest a deep involvement.

The conversation flowed amicably for about half an hour before Cameron volunteered the information that they had finished their work in Paris and would soon be going on to Rome. Some sixth sense must have warned him that there was something here he did not understand. It prompted him to add, 'Tom and Sally will be flying out tonight, but we don't need to be in Rome until Tuesday. We thought we'd stay on here and enjoy a romantic weekend in Paris.'

With these words, his hand moved across the table to cover Madeleine's. The gesture was proprietorial, the accompanying smile, smug, and the message unmistakable. He was warning Alexis off, telling him that she was his or soon would be.

Cameron shifted his adoring focus to Madeleine, but his suggestive words and familiar behaviour only served to irritate her. Avoiding eye contact with him, she cast an agitated look at Alexis. Her body language clearly told a story quite different from Cameron's and, for the first time in a while, Alexis felt the tension leave him. Unwittingly she had told him what he wanted to know.

Declining the reciprocal offer of a drink, Alexis set his empty glass down. Rising, he said to Cameron, 'I must go. I have an important telephone call to make. It's been a pleasure meeting you.' Then, with a smile that did not quite reach his eyes, he said to both, 'Enjoy your *romantic* weekend in Paris.'

At these words, as if stung, for the second time Madeleine abruptly withdrew her hand from under Cameron's. A distinctly stormy expression crossed her face, an expression familiar to Alexis that brought back memories of an irate schoolgirl.

Yes, enjoy your romantic weekend, Alexis added to himself as he left the bar, but only in your dreams, Cameron Knight!

*

Returning to his room, Alexis telephoned Jenny Simmons. After a brief conversation, he instructed, 'Mark it urgent and send it immediately.'

An hour later he went down to the lobby, where from a discreet position he was able to watch the departure of Tom and Sally, and it was with deep satisfaction that he saw a disgruntled Cameron Knight and his luggage depart along with them.

With a sardonic smile on his face, Alexis placed a call through to Madeleine's room. 'I think Cameron must have had a last-minute change of plan,' he purred. 'I've just seen him leave the hotel with his suitcases. Nothing serious, I hope?' he inquired, managing to sound suitably concerned.

'I don't really know,' she replied, her voice mystified. 'A message arrived from the London office to say he was needed urgently in Rome, but it didn't say why. He tried to get some information over the phone, but at this late hour there wasn't anyone in either the London or Rome offices to give him any answers, and he was running out of time.'

So far, so good, Alexis congratulated himself. 'I sincerely hope he'll be able to get a flight out of Paris at such short notice,' he said, this time with genuine concern.

'That's no problem; he can use Tom's ticket if the flight's full,' she informed him. 'Tom won't mind, but Cameron isn't very happy over the last minute changes.'

No, I bet he's not, thought Alexis, remembering Cameron's romantic inclinations. With a glint of satisfaction in his dark eyes, he said, 'Too bad for Cameron, but we should not let this spoil your weekend in Paris. Since you're now here on your own, perhaps you would let me take you to dinner tonight?'

Although her heart was beating wildly and she longed to accept, Madeleine did not immediately respond to the invitation. His conversation with Hugh Bradford echoed down through the years, as did the name Henrietta and a host of other feminine names with which his had been linked. Petulantly, she wondered if he had ever had any difficulty rising to the occasion with any of them. She remembered also, his declaration that it had taken a Steinway to bribe him into marriage. How humiliating, she told herself for the hundredth time!

Breaking the silence between them, Alexis said, persuasively, 'Nobody should ever dine alone, and certainly not in Paris.'

The thought of a whole evening in his company, overwhelmed and tongue-tied, filled her with apprehension, but being with him also had its undeniable attractions. Temptation overrode apprehension. Out of pride, however, she deliberated a moment longer. When she accepted, she told herself she did so only because she was unable to find a plausible excuse for turning him down.

As agreed, Alexis was waiting in the lobby at 8.30. He had not said where he was taking her but from his dark lounge suit it was obviously somewhere fairly sophisticated. Madeleine was relieved she had chosen to wear a dress chic in its simplicity, and that she had taken care over selecting just the right accessories. She felt childishly happy to see the warm approval in his eyes.

In case either Cameron or Tom should return to foil his plans, he took her without delay to the waiting hotel limousine.

'You wish to be taken to the Restaurant Julien, on the Rue du Faubourg Saint-Denis, monsieur?' The uniformed chauffeur asked in his own language for confirmation of his orders.

Madeleine felt she should not have been surprised when Alexis answered in flawless French. It seemed this man was never content to do anything by halves.

Ten minutes later they arrived at a typical Parisian restaurant, there before the turn of the century. It did not appear to be in the best part of Paris, but stepping through its double doors, Madeleine found herself entering a different world. It was clear from the warm greeting they received that Alexis was not unknown to the staff. Following the waiter, they threaded their way through the crowded, popular dining hall, past a mahogany bar to a well-placed table.

Removing the *Reservé* card, the waiter seated them and then while Alexis ordered aperitifs, Madeleine took time to look around at the delightful Art Nouveau mirrors and murals, at the stained-glass skylights, and to feel the intriguing ambience of a busy brasserie.

Both were aware that if things were different between them, they would have much in common to talk about but, afraid that with one slip of the tongue they would give themselves away, they could converse only in the guarded language of strangers. Over aperitifs, and while they ordered from the menu, Madeleine said little, leaving Alexis to take the lead and converse smoothly on inconsequential things.

Eventually, he brought the conversation around to Cameron Knight. 'Since Cameron's been summoned to Rome and not back to London, we must assume that all's well with his wife and children,' he casually suggested. Actually he had no idea if the man had any children, but he tossed them in anyway, for good measure.

'Cameron's married?' she asked, making no secret of her surprise. 'He never mentioned it. Are you sure?' Her gaze was direct; blue eyes wide and questioning.

'Yes, quite sure,' he said, meeting her gaze. 'We have mutual friends at Earl and Harrow and Joanne was mentioned a couple of times in passing.'

Remembering Cameron's suggestive behaviour in the hotel bar, and fearing the inaccurate conclusion Alexis must have drawn, she endeavoured to put matters straight.

'Well, I suppose there's no reason why he should tell me anything about his private life – we're only working colleagues, after all,' she informed him keeping her voice matter-of-fact. She would have liked to point out that Cameron was not the only man guilty of duplicity, but then she remembered that she too was not without guilt. She almost giggled at the thought that they were all three married and not one of them prepared to admit it.

The humour of the situation was not lost on Alexis either but, like Madeleine, he was not in a position to share the joke.

The waiter temporarily interrupted them. When they were able to resume conversation, Madeleine adroitly changed the subject.

'You haven't yet said why you're in Paris,' she prompted.

'I'm on tour,' he responded. 'Madrid, Monte Carlo, Paris, Milan . . . solo concerts, mostly private. For music societies, conservatoires and for the wealthy aristocracy and their guests,' he explained. 'Only until the end of the month and then I'll be back in England to join forces with a team to work on a musical.'

For some time, they kept to safe subjects. Only once did Madeleine come close to tripping herself up and that was when Alexis asked her, 'Do you play an instrument or sing?'

'Unfortunately, no,' she sighed regretfully. 'My great grandfather was a gifted pianist, I believe, but I didn't inherit any of his talent, it all went to – ' With a jolt, she realised what she had so nearly said and finished lamely, 'To other members of the family.' She looked searchingly at Alexis, but he seemed not to have noticed anything amiss. She breathed a silent sigh of relief, but mentally she was back on guard, once more picking her words with care, letting him do most of the talking.

Eventually, he murmured, 'Do you realise, all evening I've answered your questions, while you've told me little about yourself?'

'What do you want to know?' she asked softly, that note of caution again in her voice.

'Anything you care to tell me,' he replied encouragingly.

Madeleine realised that this was her opportunity to sweep all secrets aside: to divulge her true identity, but even as the thought crossed her mind, she knew she lacked the courage to do so. She was afraid of his response. The evening had been full of enchantment and Madeleine did not want to say anything that might break the spell. Not tonight, she told herself. I'll tell him the unabridged version another time . . . if there is another time.

'There's not much to tell really,' she demurred. 'My parents died when I was young. I have no close relatives. When I was eleven, I went to boarding school, and later, into the fashion industry.' She ended there, looked away as if to say: and that's all there is to know about me.

'I'm sorry to hear you haven't any family,' Alexis sympathised. Since she hardly knew his mother and himself, it was not surprising she did not consider them to be close relatives, but he thought it lamentable.

'It all happened a long time ago,' she shrugged carelessly.

He did not miss the hurt that had been there, just for a second, in her eyes.

'Before you went into fashion, when your parents were alive, where was home?' he asked.

Madeleine was not at all happy about this question. She did not want to tell blatant lies, but she could hardly say Ravenswood. If she gave the name of the village instead, he would be sure to suspect. Frantically she searched her brain for an answer. 'My family had a house in London,' she replied truthfully.

Alexis decided to ask no more questions but, one day, he promised himself, she would embellish upon the tale and fill in all the gaps.

They talked on into the night; the courses came and went. The wine, the golden hue of flickering candlelight and the soft background music all combined to have a mellowing effect upon her senses. Alexis watched her inhibitions slowly melt away until her gaze no longer wavered when she looked at him.

Unconsciously, her eyes followed the contours of his handsome features and came to rest on his lips. Acutely aware of his masculine appeal, she was remembering an afternoon long ago at Ravenswood when those lips had gently touched her own, throwing her into confusion. Carried away by her memories, she was unaware that a wistful, seductive smile, so like the one in the portrait, had spread across her face.

Intrigued and aroused, Alexis silently watched her unfold like a flower to the light. He had, throughout the evening, studied all the little mannerisms that made up the fascinating whole that was this woman, and he marvelled that she was his, albeit in name only. That knowledge intensified his growing desire for her. Whether that desire was born out of their peculiar circumstances, the intimacy of the moment or from the pleasure of the hunt, he cared not but knew only that he must have her – would have her – sooner or later.

As arranged, the limousine returned to the restaurant to collect and transport them back to the hotel. They alighted in the floodlit courtyard. As they approached the steps leading up to the entrance, Madeleine's foot suddenly turned over on the uneven cobbles, causing her to lurch against Alexis. His arm went out to steady her, and for a moment he held her close. Regaining her balance, a little flustered, Madeleine moved away. Her ankle was none the worse for the jolt and they continued on, but he kept his arm around her waist until they gained the lobby.

The strong coffee, fresh night air, the journey back to the hotel and the sudden jolt had combined to have a sobering effect on Madeleine's senses. Now she told herself that although she had already literally fallen into his arms, it would not happen again. As far as Alexis was aware, he was a married man enjoying a night out with a single girl. Tonight he had mentioned Cameron Knight's marital status but had conveniently neglected to say anything about his own. No doubt he had hopes of all-night entertainment. Well, she had no intention of joining the ranks of his easy conquests.

Her suspicions increased when, bypassing the bar, he insisted on accompanying her safely to her room. When, with a wary look in her eyes, she turned at the door to thank him for the evening, he surprised her by making no attempt to kiss her. He further surprised her when, taking the key from her hand, he opened the door and with a casual, 'Goodnight,' turned away leaving her to enter the room alone.

For quite some time now Madeleine had been receiving more than her fair share of masculine attention. It was, therefore, only natural that she should be aware of her own appeal. She had long ago assumed that Alexis was not a man to deny himself where women were concerned. That he, of all people, had neither wanted to kiss her nor invite himself into her room was a blow to her self-esteem.

Huffily, Madeleine consoled herself that if he had tried to take advantage, she would most certainly have rejected him – only he had not given her that pleasure. What was even worse, he had not said anything about seeing her again.

In the darkness of her room, lonely in the large bed, Madeleine relived their evening together. She remembering the feel of a strong, steadying arm around her waist, the sensual lips, the long, artistic fingers curved around a wineglass. She wondered how it would be to lie in those arms, to feel the passion of those lips upon her own, and the caress of his hands upon her body.

The next morning, Alexis went down to breakfast early. Being one of the first to enter the dining room, he had the choice of tables and again he chose to sit where he had a clear view of the lobby, just in case Madeleine chose to avoid the dining room.

By the time she put in an appearance, the room had filled up so that there were no longer any empty tables, and Alexis was already on his second cup of coffee. Coming to his feet, he pulled out a chair. Having had a bad night on his account, she longed to refuse his offer, but after another quick glance around the busy dining room, she thought it prudent to accept.

Like him, Madeleine wore sweater and jeans. Her hair was swept up into a ponytail and she had applied hardly any make-up. Despite her lack of sleep she looked as fresh as a daisy.

'Tom's in the hotel,' she informed him as soon as they were settled. 'He had to give his ticket up to Cameron. There were a couple of cancellations on one of today's late-afternoon flights, so our bookings have been brought forward.'

Alexis was annoyed by this piece of unwelcome news and even more annoyed to see the sandy-haired topic of their conversation enter the room. Situated where they were, Tom could not fail to notice them. With no more formality than a cheery good morning, he pulled out a seat and joined them.

Tom knew immediately to whom he was being introduced. He recognised both the face and the name. Searching his memory for something he had heard recently, he remembered that Alexis Drew had written the music for the new Duane Harrison movie. The premiere was scheduled for Leicester Square sometime in December. Anyone connected with the film would soon become newsworthy.

Always on the lookout for interesting shots for his agent's photographic library, Tom was never one to miss a monetary opportunity. An idea immediately began to form in his fertile brain, but since Alexis Drew did not look the kind to court publicity, he had the good sense to keep his thoughts to himself.

'We've got all morning and most of the afternoon. What shall we do with so much time on our hands?' he asked jauntily. 'I know it's Sunday but don't anybody suggest we go to church.' Tom showed no signs of knowing that three was a crowd. He looked at the couple with cheerful anticipation of an interesting day.

Alexis realised that he could not very well exclude Tom from his plans. If he did, it was highly likely that Madeleine would feel honour bound to spend the day with the young photographer. He therefore said with well-controlled amiability, 'Since Madeleine has not yet had the opportunity to see the sights of Paris, I thought we might behave like tourists and do the usual rounds.' When neither disagreed with this suggestion, he continued, 'We're within walking distance of the Arc de Triomphe and the same distance again on to the Eiffel Tower. From there we can take a taxi to the Tuileries, dine al fresco, see the glass pyramid, pay our respects to the *Mona Lisa* in the Louvre, pass back through the gardens and end up on the Champs-Elysées for sundowners before returning to the hotel.'

All that Alexis suggested truly appealed to Madeleine, but for his and Tom's sake she hesitated. 'You must have seen these sights countless times before,' she said, looking from one to the other. 'Are you sure you wouldn't rather do something different?'

'I haven't done the circuit for years,' Alexis assured her. 'Not since I did it in school uniform. It will be a trip down memory lane.'

'Sounds good to me,' Tom enthused. 'When do we leave?'

They were on their way within half an hour and it was soon clear that Alexis was equally familiar with the city as the language. Abashed, neither Madeleine nor Tom felt inclined to use their inadequate French in his hearing.

As Alexis had warned, it was a long walk and, because of the time limitation, they were never able to stay long in any one place. By mutual consent, they agreed to content themselves with only looking up at the dizzying heights of the Eiffel Tower and not down from it.

Tom turned out to be energetic and congenial company, willing to participate in anything that was going. His camera was constantly aimed at something or other, but when he endeavoured to get a few shots of Alexis and Madeleine together, Alexis turning away at the crucial moment foiled each attempt. Undeterred, Tom waited for an opportunity to zoom in on them from a distance.

Knowing how much pleasure the Louvre would give Madeleine, Alexis had carefully arranged their time so that she could pass along its galleries without too much haste. When confronted with the *Mona Lisa,* Madeleine was amazed to find it was in fact, much smaller than expected. Its diminutive size, however, diminished neither its beauty nor her delight in seeing it.

Later, when they walked through the Tuileries, Madeleine could not keep from daydreaming about all the court aristocrats who, down through the ages, had walked the same ground. By this time, Tom was impatiently looking forward to the promised aperitifs and so, leaving the gardens behind them, they passed the Concorde Obelisque and entered the Champs-Élysées. The young photographer was all for stopping at the first pavement café they came to, but Alexis would not hear of it.

'Every first time visitor to Paris absolutely must have a drink at Fouquets,' he said. 'I would never forgive myself if Madeleine missed this opportunity.' Knowing the price of the drinks would be exorbitant, he added: 'My treat.'

Although Alexis had seen it all before, he had derived much pleasure in seeing Madeleine spellbound by Paris, just as he had been when seeing it for the first time. For her, it had been an unforgettable day even though, with Tom's presence, it had lacked the magic of the night before. Not an intimate glance, word or touch had passed between her and Alexis and, when they finally parted in the lobby of the hotel, he made no reference to seeing her again, and neither did he ask for her address or telephone number.

Baffled and confused by his apparent indifference and her own erratic feelings, Madeleine tried to convince herself she did not care, in fact hoped never to see him again. She was not to know he was already in possession of her address and telephone number, and a lot more information besides.

Later, on the flight to Rome, while Madeleine stared fretfully out of the window, Tom was in fine fettle. He too had enjoyed the day and accomplished an afternoon's work. It was not the tourist-type photographs that put a smile on his boyish, freckled face, but the photographs of Madeleine and Alexis together. With the new movie about to be released and Madeleine's face about to launch a world-wide campaign, there was no knowing how newsworthy these two were going to become. Photographs of them together might be marketable to the gossip tabloids, and with the right carefully selected words, a whole range of interesting connotations could be applied to their being together for a weekend in Paris.

Tom saw no harm in a little publicity to help boost his bank account and Madeleine's career, just so long as Earl and Harrow did not trace the photographs back to him.

PART III

26

Because twice recently Alexis had come unexpectedly into her life, Madeleine had not been able to shake off the feeling that at any moment he would reappear and whisk her around the sights of Rome. But, of course, he had not and she realised that for him to put in another appearance would be too much of a coincidence. Even so, she could not help the persistent, unsettling feelings of expectancy.

After so many weeks of jet-setting around Europe, the novelty of living out of a suitcase and in luxury hotels had begun to wear a little thin and she had looked forward to coming home, no doubt because she knew that after Milan, it was where Alexis planned to be.

Now, back in England, Earl and Harrow did not need her for the next few weeks.

'There won't be anything for you to do for a while, so you might as well put your feet up and take advantage of the lull before the storm,' Cameron advised before they parted company at the airport.

'Is that what you're going to do?' she asked him.

'That I should be so lucky!' he laughed. 'No, dear heart. I've got my work cut out for me making sure everything's ready in time for the big launch date. I'm destined for the office.'

Taking Cameron at his word, Madeleine spent the weekend at Marlow Place. She and Samantha had so much to tell each other that it seemed they hardly stopped talking long enough to draw breath.

'So when am I going to meet the new man in your life?' Madeleine asked, when Samantha had finished telling her about her blossoming romance with John Howard.

'Soon,' was the promise. 'I'll bring him home after work one evening.'

In Madeleine's long absence, the lovers had spent quite a bit of time at Marlow Place. Now that Madeleine was home, Samantha suspected it would be more convenient all round if they used his apartment more. She wondered if John would ask her to move in with him, and then wondered how she would reply if he did.

Turning the conversation, she remarked, 'I still can't get over the coincidence of Alexis booking into the same hotel as you.'

'Just as well he did, or I wouldn't have known Cameron Knight was married,' Madeleine retorted. 'He doesn't wear a wedding ring and I don't suppose he would have volunteered the information. As it turned out, the knowledge was a useful weapon for keeping him at arm's length.' She grinned mischievously. 'Each time he got a little too interested, I simply tossed the name Joanne into the conversation. Worked a real treat.'

'When you told me about him, I thought you were going to have real problems,' Samantha said, referring to one of their numerous telephone conversations. 'I'm surprised he was so easy to handle.'

'Well actually, he wasn't that easy to handle,' Madeleine corrected. 'Cameron tends to think he's irresistible to the opposite sex. He took a bit of convincing that we don't all think he's God's gift.' She recalled all those times that his eyes had shown a desire for more than just platonic friendship. On those occasions she had treated him with light-hearted humour and a heavy measure of caution.

'Why didn't Sally tell you he was married?' Samantha asked.

'She said she didn't know he was,' came the reply. 'Apparently, he never turns up with a wife at any of the staff parties: not his wife, anyway. As for Tom, he said he didn't think to mention it. Typical male!'

Although Madeleine had disappointed Cameron where his amorous expectations were concerned, she had the satisfaction of knowing she had not disappointed him in any other way. He surely could find no fault with her work. Totally committed, she had taken pleasure in fulfilling her obligations to Belle Laurie. If Cameron and his team had encountered any problems along the way, they had not been of her making.

'Jeremy's doing well,' Samantha told her, changing the subject. 'On the strength of his reviews, he's already received two commissions for portraits.' Seeing her friend's face light up, she went on, 'He says the portrait of you brought him luck and he regrets having sold it. If you ask me, he's still in love with you and that's the real reason he regrets the sale.'

'Has he been seeing anyone else since we broke up?' Madeleine asked.

'I don't know,' Samantha shrugged. 'Haven't seen him recently . . . he just phoned a couple of times to inquire after you. He knows you're back, by the way.'

Before the week was over, Madeleine visited Ravenswood, where she once more reverted to the name of Katherine. Since she had originally regarded her involvement in the modelling profession as no more than a temporary interlude and knowing the parochial views of Mrs Johnson where her mistress was concerned, she had not taken the trouble to explain her reasons for being at the Paris Trade Fair. Her sudden move from Veronique Couture to Belle Laurie had also been allowed to go unmentioned. No one at Ravenswood had thought to question her occasional telephone calls from abroad, but had simply assumed travel went with her respectable work as a designer.

Now she saw the advantages of keeping her double life a secret for as long as possible. Until the launch of the publicity campaign, at least: Alexis was unlikely to hear the name Madeleine Harcourt mentioned on one of his infrequent visits to her home. For a while, she could feel safe from discovery.

Not having been home for some considerable time, the difference in Katherine was pronounced. No longer perceived as a youth, she was treated by all, from the farmers and their families to the household staff, with fond respect. She noticed that even Ellie seemed to go in awe of her, but doubted deference from that quarter would be of long duration.

'Hasn't Miss Katherine changed – she's so sophisticated an' all,' Ellie said to the housekeeper when they were alone together in the kitchen. 'Maybe if I went to London and got m'self a posh job and some nice clothes, I'd come back looking like that.' She gazed dreamily off into space, the silver she was supposed to be cleaning quite forgotten.

Mrs Johnson looked scornfully over the top of her glasses. 'It would take a bit more than a posh job and nice clothes to make a lady out of you, my girl. You'd have to learn to speak properly for a start, acquire a few manners and an education.'

Coming back to earth, Ellie thought about that for a moment and then, remembering her new boyfriend, said, 'Well, maybe I won't go to all that trouble. My Ted likes me the way I am.'

'So do we all, Ellie . . . so do we all,' the housekeeper said kindly.

The name of Alexis Drew came up only once and that was when Mrs Johnson told Katherine he had phoned to say he would be abroad for a few weeks and would let them know when he returned.

'He didn't say where he was going or for what reason but, if my memory serves me right, he should be back any day now.' She went on to say, 'We haven't seen him for a while, so I expect he'll make one of his fleeting visits. Such a nice, conscientious young man.' Then, suddenly, right out of the blue, Mrs Johnson snapped her fingers and exclaimed: 'Fruit cake!'

Raising her eyebrows, Katherine turned amused, questioning eyes in her direction.

'He likes my fruit cake,' she explained defensively. 'He's

always very complimentary about it. I'd better have a fresh one baked and put by ready for when he comes.'

Mrs Johnson did not volunteer to look in her diary for the exact date of Alexis' return and Katherine did not want to evoke curiosity by pressing her to do so. She had planned to leave for London the following evening, but just to be on the safe side, she decided to vacate Ravenswood a little earlier. As much as she wanted to see Alexis again, it would not do for him to find her here.

Paris now seemed a lifetime away and Alexis just a memory. Time, distance and all the many things that had occurred since their parting stretched endlessly between them. She knew only that he had gone off to Milan and would be returning from there to England . . . he had not said exactly when.

'You've got his number, you can always call to see if he's back,' Samantha said brightly over supper, soon after her return to London.

'You know very well I can't do that, Sam,' Madeleine replied in exasperation. 'To him, I was just a casual dinner date and someone he accompanied around the sights of Paris. Hardly grounds for a chatty telephone conversation. Besides, how on earth would I explain having his number: he's not listed, remember?'

'And neither are you. Not as Madeleine Harcourt anyway,' Samantha reminded her. 'Why didn't you give him your number?'

'I told you . . . he never asked for it. I guess he wasn't interested enough.'

Within 24 hours Alexis proved her wrong. When his telephone call came, Samantha was still at work and Madeleine was alone in the apartment. She recognised the cultured, self-assured voice instantly and her stomach turned a somersault.

'Alexis.' Her own voice trembled slightly. 'How did you get my number?'

'Earl and Harrow,' was the only explanation he offered.

Knowing that they had at one time handled his advertising, that he had friends within the agency, she accepted his answer without question.

Hearing an echo and a little static on the line, she inquired with some surprise, 'Are you still in Milan?'

'No. I'm in New York but I'll be back in London tomorrow. Will you keep the evening free for me?' he asked.

'Yes,' she replied, her heartbeat quickening.

'My flight is scheduled to land mid-afternoon,' he told her. 'I'll call you as soon as I get home . . . about five or soon after.'

All the next day Madeleine went around in a state of impatient euphoria. At frequent intervals she glanced at her watch and several times counterchecked it against the kitchen clock, as if, by doing so time could be willed to pass faster. The thought of being in Alexis' company still had the power to make her nervous, a condition that did not improve with the approach of the hour. She questioned why a man of his calibre, who came into contact with so many beautiful, sophisticated women should be showing an interest in her. It could not be for her worldly assets since he had no knowledge of them.

Madeleine tried on every appropriate garment in her wardrobe before making a final choice. Despite the numerous changes, she was still ready far too early. Time passed slowly, five o'clock came and went and still he had not called. She began to have doubts.

Samantha returned from work. One look at her friend's face was enough to tell her Alexis had not yet been in touch.

When the telephone did eventually ring, Madeleine had to restrain an impulse to pounce on it. And about time too, she told herself! Her feelings of elation turned to guilty disappointment when she realised the call was not from Alexis.

'Hi. It's me . . . Jeremy. Welcome back,' she heard him say. 'Look, I want to hear all about your trip, but I can't talk right now, I'm in a bit of a hurry,' he apologised. 'I hate to ask, but I'm hoping you can do me a favour. I've a canvas that needs delivering to Harrington's Gallery and I promised to have it over there tonight. Unfortunately, the place closes at six-thirty and there's no way I can get it there in time.' He sounded harassed. 'I forgot about the tutors' meeting scheduled for this evening. I wonder if you could find time to rush it over for me?'

'Where's the canvas now?' she asked, trying hard to keep her lack of enthusiasm from reaching her voice.

'Just inside the door of my apartment,' he replied. 'Sorry to have to ask you, but you're the only one with a key.'

Madeleine quickly calculated that by the time she collected it from Saint Martins, took it over to the gallery and returned home, no more than 45 minutes would have passed. Knowing Samantha was not seeing John until later and would be in the apartment if Alexis rang, she made a decision she was later to bitterly regret.

Madeleine was through the door of the gallery five minutes before it was due to close for the night. Taking the painting into Mavis's office, she deposited it against the wall.

'Madeleine. You're quite a stranger these days,' Mavis accused her, with a welcoming smile. 'If it wasn't for the publicity you've been getting, I'd have forgotten by now what you look like.'

'What publicity?' Madeleine queried. The Belle Laurie campaign had not yet been launched and her modelling debut in Paris was now old news.

From a drawer, Mavis produced a newspaper cutting, which she passed across the desk. It showed Madeleine and Alexis happy in each other's company. From the Eiffel Tower in the background it was quite clear where the photograph had been taken, and Madeleine could easily guess by whom. She made a mental note to strangle Tom with his own camera strap the very next time she saw him.

Her attention went to the short article beneath the picture. *Together for a weekend in Paris: Alexis Drew with Madeleine Harcourt, the new girl in his life and on the modelling scene. . . .*

The report mostly concerned itself with his involvement in the much publicised film premiere. It said a little about her new career, touched on his tour, and mentioned the couple had recently been seen together in Paris.

The photograph and article were innocuous enough, and although Madeleine wondered how Alexis would feel about having his name linked with hers, this was the least of her worries. Fervently she prayed that no one would recognise the picture of Madeleine Harcourt as being in reality that of Katherine Drew. Above all, she hoped no one would point this out to Alexis, or she would have some explaining to do a lot sooner than expected.

Feeling the best way to deal with Mavis's curiosity was to play down the article, she laughed, 'Believe it or not, we hardly know each other.'

Mavis did not believe it, which, as things later turned out, was just as well.

If Madeleine had known she was going to run into Harrington on the doorstep, she would either have left sooner or stayed with Mavis a little longer. Instead, all she could do was swear under her breath.

In the middle of a dispute with Susan, he looked as stormy as the early-evening sky.

'I'd like to help out but I can't,' Susan was saying. Stoically, she stood her ground.

This was obviously not the answer Harrington expected to hear from a member of his staff. He was about to give further verbal abuse but, on seeing Madeleine, thought better of it. Now, as he turned his back on Susan, the scowl slowly faded away, to be replaced by a charming smile. Susan continued to hover, uncertain whether to stay or go.

'I hope you've got an umbrella,' Harrington commented to the new arrival in a tone now all concern. 'It's throwing it down.'

Madeleine obviously had not, and she viewed the unexpected heavy downpour with dismay.

'Never mind. My car's here, I'll give you a lift.' Ignoring her hesitation and Susan's look of alarm, he took Madeleine firmly by the arm and, sharing the shelter of his umbrella, ushered her to the nearby car.

To her surprise, Harrington said he did not need directions, he knew where Marlow Place was. Through the heavy rain, with the windscreen wipers working overtime, they travelled in the general direction of her apartment. As they wove through the rush hour traffic, he inquired after her new career and asked when he might expect to see her advertisements appear. Both the interest and charm, although surprising, seemed genuine enough. This was a side of the man she had not seen before.

The weather was now so appalling that Madeleine was beginning to feel grateful to Rodney for having saved her from a thorough drenching. All the special care taken over her appearance would have been wasted if she had walked home.

Visibility had become so poor, it was a full five minutes before Madeleine realised they had by-passed the turn-off for Marlow Place.

'I thought your apartment was just after Knightsbridge,' Harrington said, looking and sounding most apologetic. 'I'm so sorry, I don't know how I could have made such a mistake.' He glanced at his watch. 'Oh dear. It's already getting on for six-thirty,' he said, in a troubled voice. 'I'm running rather late for some clients. I really should be there to welcome them. Would you mind if I brought you back later?' Expecting opposition, he quickly added, 'This won't take long, really.'

Madeleine did mind. In fact, she minded very much. She

wanted to be at home for Alexis. For a moment she considered asking Harrington to drop her off at the nearest tube station but then remembered she had come out without a purse. Intending to travel no great distance, she had not foreseen the need to carry money, credit cards or chequebook. All she had with her were the door keys, which, out of habit, she had picked up on her way out.

All was not yet lost, she told herself, brightening a little. 'If you wouldn't mind lending me some money, I could find my own way home,' she suggested. 'I'll return the money to you tomorrow,' she promised.

'I wouldn't dream of doing such a thing,' he scowled reproachfully. 'My conscience wouldn't allow it. I offered to drive you home. Under the circumstances, that's the least I can do. Be patient,' he insisted, 'this won't take long.'

They drove on for a while, neither speaking. When they began to leave the heavy city traffic behind, Madeleine's agitation increased. Glancing at her out of the corner of an eye, Harrington broke the silence to apologise and reassure her yet again that they were nearly there. More time and miles passed. Her agitation continued to increase, along with her fear, as did his apologies and apparent remorse. Although Madeleine wanted to believe in the sincerity of his words, that the mistake really had been genuine, there lurked a strong suspicion Harrington had known all along what he was about.

At one stage, when they stopped for a red light, on an impulse, Madeleine tried to open the door, only to discover Harrington had applied the central locking system.

'Security,' he smiled, soothingly. 'We can't have you falling out of the car.'

With a sinking heart Madeleine realised that, short of trying to attract attention through the window, she was totally reliant on this man keeping his word. She wondered who, anyway, would hear or notice her cries for help. Traffic had noticeably thinned and those few left on the streets had run for cover.

Entering Richmond, they made a short journey through

an exclusive residential area before the car turned in through an open gate and onto a drive. The car's main beam illuminated a large ultra modern house of unusual architectural design situated in the middle of an extensive mature garden. The property was surrounded by a wall and topped with a railing – the kind intended to keep unwanted visitors out.

The fact that the house was in darkness and therefore likely to be deserted added to Madeleine's feelings of insecurity, as did the isolating distance between the property and its nearest neighbour.

After deactivating the burglar alarm system, Harrington led the way through the hall and into a large split-level reception room. There, he took Madeleine's coat and, telling her to make herself at home, left the room.

Searching for a telephone, her worried gaze swept over the modern, expensive decor, with its straight, clean lines and light colours. Becoming distracted for a moment by the valuable paintings and fabulous free-standing artwork, Madeleine found herself thinking that under any other circumstances it would have been a pleasure to view treasures such as these.

Her eyes settled on a covered table. Approaching it, she raised a corner of the sheet to discover an appetising and substantial cold buffet had been laid out in the type of serving dishes favoured by outside caterers. Here was indisputable proof that Harrington had deliberately misled her. He had definitely not come all the way out to Richmond for a quick meeting with clients. This was planned entertainment for up to a dozen people. She was now quite sure he had no intentions of taking her home, not yet awhile anyway. On one score her anxieties were laid to rest: he had not lied about expecting guests. At least, there would be safety in numbers.

On a glass-topped occasional table was a telephone. With a sigh of relief Madeleine reached for it. Money or no money, she was going to call a taxi, after which she would ask Samantha to stand by at the other end to pay the driver.

She could have wept with frustration when she realised there was no dialling tone.

The telephone was still in her hand when Harrington entered the room. She raised hostile eyes. 'It doesn't seem to be working. Is it the only phone in the house?' she asked him, now making no attempt at politeness.

'Here, let me see,' he said, strolling towards her, his voice unruffled. Taking the phone, he listened to the continuous hum for a moment before replacing it on its cradle. 'You're right, no dialling tone,' he agreed. 'There's another in the hall and one up in the master bedroom,' he told her, 'you can try those.'

As Madeleine quickly left the room, an artful smile spread across his face. He knew they would all be the same. Anticipating her move, he had been into the study and, taking the receiver off the hook, had hidden the phone behind the desk. Until the receiver was replaced, all three phones would seem to be out of order.

What bad luck you're having this evening, Madeleine my dear, he mused to himself, perfectly satisfied with his own good fortune.

When she returned looking distressed, he said with mock concern, 'I expect the heavy rain brought a line down. But cheer up, someone may already have reported it. Try again later.'

'No! I can't wait until later,' she snapped irritably. 'Would you take me to Richmond station and lend me some money for the train fare back to town. I had plans of my own for this evening.'

In her absence he had put on soft background music, removed the cover from the table and brought in an ice bucket containing a chilled bottle of champagne. He had already drawn the cork and was in the process of filling a couple of glasses.

'I can't do that,' he purred, dropping all pretence at apology. 'That would interfere with my plans.' He put one of the glasses in her hand. 'The others should be arriving at any minute, and what a bad host I'd be if I wasn't here to greet them,' he smiled smugly. 'I'll take you as soon as I can, if you're sure that's what you really want, but in the meantime, while we wait, why don't I show you some of the artwork?'

The triumphant smirk he turned towards her further infuriated Madeleine. With admirable restraint she curbed a strong desire to put the ice bucket, complete with contents, over his head. But what would that achieve? she asked herself. It certainly would not ensure her a lift to the station. Maybe one of the guests would offer to take her.

Biding her time, she allowed him to lead her on a tour of the downstairs rooms. By keeping distance between them and focusing his attention on the artwork, he hoped to lull her into a false sense of security.

Although desperately disappointed with the outcome of the evening and furious with him for his interference, Madeleine began to feel less threatened by the situation. She told herself that Rodney Harrington was just a spoilt man who expected to get everything he wanted in life.

If Harrington could have read her thoughts, he would most certainly have agreed with her unflattering opinions. He was a man without moral conscience who believed that Rodney should always get whatever he wanted – one way or another.

27

Despite the dismal English weather, Alexis was pleased to be home. His flight from the States had departed late and then, to add to his frustration, the torrential rain had caused an accident on the motorway, reducing the flow of traffic into London to a snail's pace. By the time he reached Linnet House and was able to call Madeleine, she had already gone out for the evening.

'Madeleine isn't here right now,' the girl who introduced herself as Samantha Scott had told him. 'She's delivering a picture to an art gallery for a friend. It's not far – she shouldn't be much longer. Madeleine said to ask you for your number so she can call you back.'

He had left his number but that was already more than two hours ago and his call had still not been returned. When he had tried the number again, no one had answered.

Lounging back in his favourite armchair, he gazed moodily at the glowing logs in the iron basket. The warm, colourful flickering of the flames had an almost mesmeric effect on his tired senses. The excessive amount he had travelled of late, and the long strenuous hours of work, were beginning to take their toll.

Wryly, he told himself a good night's sleep would be more therapeutic than a night out on the town. He would call Madeleine again in the morning. However, before he could finish the contents of his glass, there came a ringing of the doorbell. He was not expecting anyone, but then, not all his friends believed in giving prior warning of a visit. Unhappily, it crossed his mind that, while it could be any one of a number of people, it was unlikely to be Madeleine.

As far as he knew, she had never been to Linnet House. He was not sure she even knew where it was.

The very last person he expected to find on his doorstep was Mavis Ford. She looked guilty, as if caught playing ring-and-run.

'I hope you don't mind my calling on you, but it is important,' she insisted apologetically.

'Of course not. It's an unexpected pleasure,' he assured her, wondering what on earth would bring her, of all women, to Linnet House on such a filthy night and at such an hour.

Mavis accepted his invitation to enter the house but, he noticed, did so with some hesitation. Entering the house of a bachelor, he guessed, was probably a daring adventure for someone as ultra-respectable as Mavis appeared to be.

He led the way across the hall and into the drawing room. Her eyes, he noticed, were bright with curiosity, as they flickered appreciatively around the room.

'May I offer you a drink?' he asked, when she was seated. 'A glass of sherry, or wine, perhaps?'

'Oh, no thank you, Mr Drew,' she replied. 'I can't stay more than a few minutes. I've asked the taxi driver to wait for me.'

Intrigued by her unexpected visit, Alexis settled once more into the armchair he had recently vacated and, picking up his half-empty glass, regarded her meditatively over the rim. Mavis Ford, no longer on familiar ground, had none of the confidence formally displayed at Harrington's Gallery. She appeared shy and insecure.

She sat very upright, on the edge of her seat, her knees firmly together and her hands clutching the bag perched on her lap. In the bag was the newspaper cutting that stated this man and Madeleine were more than just acquaintances; only today, Madeleine had talked about him and, at the exhibition, had said their friendship went back a long way. But for that knowledge, Mavis would not have had the nerve to bother such a celebrated personality.

'It's Madeleine I've come to see you about,' she flustered.

'I'm worried about her, Mr Drew. I should have warned her . . . given her the benefit of my experience. She doesn't know men like I do.' She paused, as if to reconsider what she had said.

Alexis was hard pressed to keep the smile from his face. He tried to see Mavis in the role of femme fatale, but failed completely. He let the comment pass.

'Of course, you might think it's none of my business but if anything awful happened to her, I wouldn't want it on my conscience,' she told him. 'I shouldn't talk about my employer, I know – loyalty has always been a rule of mine – but under the circumstances . . .' She broke off lamely and looked at him for encouragement to proceed.

At the mention of her employer, his eyes narrowed. Now what has he to do with this? Alexis wondered warily.

Seeing him nod, Mavis took it as approval to continue. 'Mr Harrington sometimes entertains male clients and friends at his house in Richmond. When he entertains, he gets outside catering sent in buffet-style, and self-service so no staff are required.' She lowered her eyes. 'He arranges for an escort agency to send a few girls over and then – well, what goes on out there isn't hard to imagine.' To prove her point, a blush spread across her face. Quickly, she hurried on. 'Mr Harrington organised such an evening for tonight. I know he did because the escort agency phoned when he was out wanting to know if Paula, Cindy and somebody-or-other would do, and tonight was specifically mentioned.

'Also Mr Harrington tried to talk Susan into going with him but she had an excuse prepared. Unfortunately Madeleine came along just at the wrong moment . . .' Here Mavis hesitated. Her host, she noticed, had gone unnaturally still.

'Are you telling me that Madeleine was fool enough to go with him?' he asked in a voice deceptively mild.

'Yes,' confirmed Mavis, timidly. 'Madeleine was delivering an oil painting for her friend, Jeremy Grierson. We were just about to lock up for the night, so she only stayed a few minutes. Mr Harrington was on the doorstep, just about to leave, when Madeleine came out of the gallery. Her timing couldn't have been worse.' Agitated, she fidgeted with the clasp of her bag. 'He offered her a lift home. Well, it was pouring down with rain,' she hastened to explain, as if seeking an excuse on Madeleine's behalf.

When Alexis did not comment, she went on, 'Susan watched them drive off together and because she was worried, came in to tell me about it.' She paused, took a deep breath. 'I got Madeleine's telephone number out of our files, intending to call her when I got home, just to make sure she was all right and Mr Harrington hadn't pulled any of his funny tricks.'

Mavis stopped, looked embarrassed, and then, as if she felt she owed him further explanation, said, 'There were some nasty rumours about him a few years ago . . .'

It was not necessary for her to elaborate. His memory had long since stirred.

'By the time I made the call, she'd had plenty of time to get home,' Mavis went on, 'but she hadn't arrived. I didn't want to worry her friend so I just said I'd call again later but, when I did, there was no one there – her friend must have gone out. So then I called Jeremy Grierson, but he wasn't in either, and that was when I decided to come and see you.' She looked at him apologetically. 'You're her friend, so I thought if . . .' Mavis paused, uncertain. 'You are, aren't you?' she asked.

'Yes, Mavis, I am,' he assured her. To himself, he added, and a lot more besides, as Harrington will find out to his cost if he's been the cause of any grief.

'I thought if I told you, you'd know if anything ought to be done about it . . . might know what to do, I mean.' She was looking to him for approval.

'You did the right thing,' he reassured her. 'Where is the house?'

He had spoken quietly, unemotionally, but there was now a hard set to his mouth. The warmth had gone from his eyes: they glittered, dark and menacing. Mavis shifted uneasily.

'I would have phoned,' she told him, 'but the house is rather isolated; not at all easy to find without this.' Opening her bag, she took from within a neatly folded page. 'The address and directions – I've written them down for you,' she explained. 'You'll need them. I hoped . . . thought you might . . .'

Somewhere out in the street a car horn sounded briefly.

'Oh! My taxi! I'd forgotten all about it,' she gasped, hurriedly coming to her feet. 'I must go.'

At the main door she hesitated, wanting to be assured that he really did plan to do something about Madeleine. But Alexis, now impatient for her to be gone, had preceded her down the steps to the waiting taxi and was holding the door open.

On his mind were words, spoken by Hugh in Nikolai's Greek restaurant, *Some rich bastard who owns an art gallery. Unfortunately, he's the type who will do it again.*

Before the taxi turned out of Belgrave Square, Mavis looked back along the lamplit street. Alexis Drew was no longer on the steps. The door to Linnet House was closed.

28

'What do you want to know about trains for?' slurred Rodney Harrington. 'I said I'd take you home when I'm ready.'

'I don't want you to take me home, I want you to take me to the station,' Madeleine replied, trying to keep her voice calm. 'It's late and my friends will be worrying about me.'

Nervously she watched Harrington, now very unsteady on his feet, stagger over to the sofa to sit so close, she could feel the heat of his fleshy thigh pressing against the full length of her own.

He turned his wrist to peer at his watch, spilling drink from his glass. He ignored the spillage. 'If you must know, the last train leaves in ten minutes,' he smirked.

'Ten minutes!' Madeleine gasped, coming rapidly to her feet. She had long since realised that there was no hope of salvaging her evening with Alexis, but even so, she was not going to spend one minute more with Harrington than she absolutely had to. She headed for the door.

'And where do you think you're going?' Harrington challenged. Reaching out, he caught hold of her skirt, and then, when she tried to pull it away, transferred his grip to her wrist.

'There's not much time – let me go,' she cried angrily, rotating her hand in an attempt to break his hold. She now no longer bothered to hide her impatience. 'I want my coat. I'm going home, with or without your help!' she yelled at him angrily.

'You don't need your coat. You're not going anywhere.' He bruised her wrist. 'I've already told you, I'm not driving you to the station and it's too far to walk. Anyway, that would spoil the little finale I have planned for our evening.' His laugh was unpleasant.

For a moment, Madeleine ceased her struggle. Wide-eyed with comprehension, she stared at him. Icy fingers of fear crept up her spine. A voice screamed in her head, 'Run! Get out, quickly, while there's still time.'

'I see we finally understand each other,' he smirked. Effortlessly, intentionally, he twisted her wrist so that the pain forced her against her will back onto the sofa. Then, with a sudden jerk, he pulled her into his arms.

'Relax my pet,' he coaxed, holding her hard against him. 'All I want for now is a kiss of appreciation.'

His tongue wet on her neck made her flesh crawl; his breath reeked of alcohol. Frantically, she struggled to push him away. '*Appreciation*?' she repeated, unable to believe her ears.

'Of course,' he purred. 'One good turn deserves another.'

'What are you talking about? What good turn?' she gasped, struggling to get her hands up to push against his chest.

'I haven't been wining and dining you for nothing,' he mumbled, tangling his fingers painfully in her hair while his moist mouth sought her lips. 'I think it's time you started to show a little gratitude for all my efforts.'

With the arrival of the guests, Harrington had singled her out for himself. When any of the other men had shown more than a passing interest in Madeleine, he had possessively let it be known she was already taken. At first she had thought he was being protective, but later, when it became apparent he was warning them off for his own selfish purposes, alarm bells had rung in her head.

The evening had gone progressively from bad to worse. From what she could see, all four men were as bad as each other: it would have been quite useless appealing to any of them for help. When the escort agency girls arrived, their questionable dress, make-up, hairstyles and conduct spoke volumes about what they were, and why they had come.

All Harrington's guests ate, drank and smoked too much. The subject of art was hardly touched upon and, as the evening advanced, the quality of conversation deteriorated further into coarse manners and smutty jokes. Apart from their first names, Madeleine learned nothing of interest about any of the people present and made no effort to do so. Disgusted, all she wanted was to escape the house and unsavoury company.

When, soon after the buffet, everyone partnered off and drifted out of the smoky lounge, Madeleine came close to panic. She was afraid to be left alone with Harrington. He had been drinking heavily all evening and the more he drank, the more unreasonable he became. Long gone were the feigned charm and promises to do the right thing by her.

Madeleine's mind was racing; she tried to control her thoughts. She had to think of some way to escape this loathsome man. Only one solution sprang to mind. She prayed it would work.

As if resigned to the inevitable, she changed tactics and said softly, with a sigh, 'You're absolutely right, Rodney. The last train has gone, the telephones are still out of order, and you can't really be expected to desert your guests on my account. We might as well make the most of our time together and enjoy what's left of the evening.'

Harrington became still. With his hand still tangled in her hair, he drew his head back so that he could regard her through narrowed, suspicious eyes.

Her ploy seemed to be working. Deliberately using her husky voice to tantalise, she continued as if warming to an idea. 'Why don't you be an angel and fix us fresh drinks while I go to the bathroom and then,' she said, forcing herself to look him squarely in the eyes, 'when I get back, we'll really get into the mood.' She smiled seductively.

Careful to hide her revulsion, she traced a finger slowly, almost caressingly, down the side of his face.

Putting pleasure before reason, Harrington loosened his hold. 'Now you're talking, sweetheart.' His voice was thick, his breathing laboured, as he visualised the evening of licentious pleasure ahead.

To the soft background music, Madeleine came slowly, provocatively to her feet. Running hands down over her hips, smoothing out imaginary creases, she purred, 'I won't be a moment, Rodney.'

Hips swinging, she calmly crossed the room to the hall, but once through the door and out of sight, she dropped all pretence and hurried across to the main entrance. There, with heart pounding, holding her breath, she paused to listen. Over the music of the stereo came the sounds of ice clinking against glass as Harrington replenished their drinks. Whispers and giggles floated down from one of the nearer bedrooms.

Quietly, with shaking hands, Madeleine slid back the latch. Afraid the sharp noise would alert Harrington, she carefully secured it so that it could not click closed behind her. Stepping out into a bitterly cold blast of night air, she hesitated, remembering her coat. Too late, she dared not take the risk of returning for it.

Long suspecting the telephones had somehow been tampered with, Madeleine intended to solicit the help of a neighbour. She had, however, badly underestimated her abductor's state of awareness and the danger he posed. Before she could take more than a few paces, the front door flew open and Harrington, like a raging bull, lumbered down the drive.

Panic stricken, with hands outstretched to ward him off, Madeleine backed away. Viciously he knocked them aside. 'Bitch!' he bellowed. 'Lying bitch!'

A powerful hand clamped roughly over her mouth stifled the terrified shriek that rose in her throat. With strength she had not known he possessed, Harrington dragged her struggling and kicking back into the house. He did not loosen his grip until they were once more in the lounge, where he flung her onto the sofa.

'So you thought I'd fall for that one, did you?' he jeered, breathing heavily as much from anticipation as from the unaccustomed exertion. Towering over her, he glared triumphantly through small unfocused eyes. 'Thought you'd leave without paying your dues? Well, we'll see about that.' Watching her closely, deriving maximum pleasure from the moment, he slowly took off his jacket and tie. Then he began to undo his shirt. Losing patience with the last button, he ripped it apart.

Madeleine watched. Traumatised, she was incapable of movement until the sight of exposed white flesh, broke her trance. She moved to rise but was quickly knocked back down again. To prevent any more attempts at escape, Harrington brought the full weight of his sweating body down on top of her.

Pinning her wrists above her head, with wine-soaked breath full on her face; he brought his mouth down on hers. Sick with disgust, trying to avoid contact, Madeleine rolled her head from side to side. The struggle, she realised, only served to incite him further. Smirking, he tightened his grip. The uneven fight and her fear were going to work on his senses like a powerful aphrodisiac.

'Don't stop, sweetheart, put up a good fight,' he encouraged, delighting in his ability to dominate and hurt. 'An easy conquest isn't much fun,' he jibed. 'So much for those haughty airs and graces. By the time I've finished with you, you'll be willing and eager, just begging me for more.' He laughed coarsely.

'I'll never be willing. I hate you – you disgust me,' gasped Madeleine, turning her head again to avoid his repulsive kisses.

'No matter,' he sneered, breathing heavily, a twisted smile on his face. 'It makes no difference to me. I'll have you anyway, just as I've always intended to.' He sniggered. 'Thanks for making it so easy for me.'

This was her worst nightmare coming true. 'That's rape,'

she breathed, her throat suddenly dry, her voice hoarse. 'Don't think you'll get away with it,' she threatened on a trembling note of hysteria. 'I swear I'll report it to the police.'

Sounding very sure of himself, he smirked, 'No you won't, I've witnesses to say you came with me willingly and more witnesses to say whatever I ask them to say.' With a sly smile, he added, 'Think of the publicity, the disgrace – it would ruin your lovely new career.'

He saw the doubt in her eyes, felt the slight hesitation, and was satisfied that the truth of his words had hit home. 'Now be a sensible girl,' he grunted. Wasting no more time on words, he shifted his bulk to force her legs apart so that now he lay between them. Through their clothes, she could feel his erection pressing against her, hard and throbbing.

Taking advantage of a moment's inertia, he forced a hand down the front of her dress and, cupping a breast, kneaded it cruelly with brutal fingers, taking pleasure in the punishment and humiliation they were inflicting. Suddenly, becoming irritated by the restrictions imposed by the garment, he stopped to rip the fabric from neckline to waist. Triumphantly, he raised himself up for a better view of her nakedness. The tip of his tongue darted across his lips, a lascivious smile spread over his face.

'As lovely as your portrait, my dear, and all mine for the night to take as often as I want, in whatever way I choose,' he purred, taking pleasure in her look of horror.

In all her life, nothing Madeleine had ever experienced had come anywhere near to preparing her for this moment. Trapped and helpless, she was unable to control the sickening panic rising within. With a rush of adrenaline, she made a frantic all-out effort to fight off her attacker, but again her struggles were ineffectual. She was no match for this man and, as his weight slowly squeezed the air from her lungs, she weakened, resistance draining away, leaving her spent and white.

In a small trembling voice that did not sound like her own, she heard herself plead with him to let her go. In her heart, Madeleine knew it was too late for pleading, he was too far gone on alcohol and lust. But still she pleaded anyway, and hated herself for doing so.

He paid no heed but, instead, shifted his bulk so that he could, with fumbling fingers, unfasten his trousers and push them down over his hips.

This can't be happening to me, she told herself over and over. With the blood pounding in her temples, she felt herself slipping into a state of shock.

'Harrington!' Cracked an angry, whiplash voice from the far side of the room.

Harrington's attack came to an abrupt halt. With unfocused eyes, he turned to see who had dared to interrupt at such a moment.

'Bugger off! You can see we're busy,' he said nastily, thinking the interruption came from one of the guests. Turning his attention back to his victim, he failed to see the man's swift advance across the room. The next instant, he felt himself brutally hoisted by the scruff of the neck and hurled violently through the air. Impacting painfully with the floor, his limbs sprawled ignominiously in all directions.

Through the haze of his inebriation, he recognised the dark, menacing face of Alexis Drew. 'Who the bloody hell let you in?' he blustered, crawling behind the wide glass-top table for protection. With its aid, he managed to scramble unsteadily to his feet.

'No need to fight over her,' he grumbled, keeping the table between him and his powerful assailant, 'there are plenty of other tarts around the place . . . help yourself to one of them . . . In any case,' he rushed on, now using a placatory tone, 'you wouldn't want this one, she's not very amiable.' His gaze momentarily slid across to Madeleine. 'But if you insist, you can have her when I've finished with her,' he offered with a benevolent smile.

With strength born of rage, Alexis heaved the heavy table out of the way. To the sound of shattering glass, he came at

Harrington, who, reeling and flailing wildly, threw the first punch. It failed to connect. With a sickening smack, Alexis' fist slammed into Harrington's fleshy face, sending him careering across the room. His head hit the wall and he landed in an untidy heap on the floor.

'Damn you to hell, Harrington!' Alexis exploded. Wanting to thrash the man within an inch of his life, he willed him to his feet. Harrington lay still, the impact had cast him into merciful oblivion.

Becoming aware of a throbbing in his hand, Alexis cursed softly and flexed his fingers for damage. Satisfied no bones were broken, he turned his attention back to Harrington and had the pleasure of seeing the early promise of an embarrassing black eye. Stooping to find a pulse, he muttered, 'He'll survive,' and then, with contempt, added, 'A pity.'

He quickly crossed the room to Madeleine, who was, with shaking hands, unsuccessfully attempting to rearrange the tattered remnants of what had once been an attractive and expensive dress. Removing his jacket, Alexis placed it around her shoulders.

Shock, or maybe pride, prevented her from crying in front of him. He did not know which. But the sapphire eyes she raised to his were bright with anguish and unshed tears. She did not speak. Instinctively, he knew that to offer sympathy right now would be a mistake. It would destroy her tenuous self-control.

Gently he pulled her to her feet, and putting protective arms around her, held her tightly until her trembling subsided. 'Time to go home,' he murmured, turning her towards the door.

Madeleine allowed herself to be led but, as they drew alongside Harrington, she paused to look down with loathing on his crumpled, inert form. Fury and an uncontrollable urge to lash out replaced impotence. With blazing eyes and clenched fists, she honoured that urge by giving Harrington an almighty kick in the ribs.

'He's had enough,' Alexis said, drawing her away.

'I missed my target,' she complained bitterly, her eyes still on Harrington. 'I was aiming lower.'

Harrington groaned and stirred but did not regain consciousness.

'I wanted him to feel it,' she hissed viciously.

Alexis was quite certain he had heard the snap of bones. Harrington would be aware of her retribution – later.

29

Something awoke her. A pigeon perhaps, landing on the window ledge and fluttering against the glass, or maybe it was a car backfiring in the street below.

Madeleine sank down further under the duvet, as if by doing so she could shut out the world and the nightmares of the evening before. Becoming aware of aches and pains, particularly around her wrists, she pushed the cover back and held an arm up for inspection. Blue and purple bruises stood out in sharp relief against their ivory background. Sincerely hoping the other aches came more from pulled muscles than unsightly bruises, she hid it again from view. Her physical injuries, she knew, would heal faster than the memories.

When she recalled what Rodney Harrington had done, and the further sickening violation he had intended, her stomach churned. She thanked God for Alexis' timely intervention but was mortified that he should have been a witness to such a humiliating scene.

'Damn, damn, damn!' she groaned aloud.

'If that's Rodney Harrington you're banishing to purgatory,' Samantha said, sticking her head around the door, 'I'll come and give my blessing to his damnation.'

Still in her dressing gown, fair hair tousled from sleep, she entered the room carrying two mugs of steaming coffee, one of which she set down for Madeleine, on the bedside table. Although Samantha had spoken lightly, her feelings did not match her tone of voice, and her eyes wore a worried expression.

'How are you feeling?' she inquired, perching on the edge of the bed.

'Physically or mentally?' Madeleine asked, coming out from under the covers.

'Both.'

'Abused and abused,' came the answer, with a feeble attempt at humour, 'but it could have been worse.' She showed Samantha the bruises on her arms.

'Not much worse, by the look of those,' Samantha commented, appalled. Intentionally switching to a lighter note, she said, 'But I'm pleased you don't intend to let Harrington get you down.'

'Bad choice of words,' Madeleine grimaced sourly. 'He already did get me down and, if Alexis hadn't come to my rescue when he did, he would have done a lot more than that.'

'I didn't get too much out of you last night,' Samantha said. 'Want to tell me what happened?' She did, in fact, have some idea, but thought the best therapy for Madeleine was to talk the experience through.

Hesitantly at first, Madeleine told her all, and when she had finished, said, 'Imagine, if I hadn't left the front door on the latch, Alexis would have had to find an alternative way into the house, and would have arrived too late.' Her eyes were huge, horrified at the appalling possibility. 'He might even have come into the room while Harrington was actually . . .' Unable to finish the sentence, she put her hands over her face. 'It was bad enough that the top of my dress was in shreds and my skirt had ridden up around my waist, and that fat bastard was on top of me . . . mauling me. Oh Sam!' she wailed.

Samantha recalled the shock she had felt on first seeing the garment. The ringing of the doorbell so late at night had frightened her. The image of a uniformed policeman had flickered across her mind as she whispered to John, 'It can't be Madeleine . . . she's got a key.' It was with considerable relief that the door was opened to Madeleine and the man she immediately recognised as Alexis Drew. Although his features had long been familiar to her, never had the camera caught him wearing such a turbulent expression: eyes bright with controlled emotions, grim hard set to mouth and jaw. He had said little, waited only long enough to see Madeleine safely over the threshold. Before Samantha could ask any questions, he had turned away, leaving behind him the sound of footsteps receding down the dimly lit stairwell.

The state of the dress had not been immediately apparent as the worst damage was covered by Alexis' jacket. But, just one look at her friend and she knew something was terribly wrong. Without word or pause, Madeleine had brushed past and gone straight to her room.

Waiting only long enough to whisper a hasty goodnight to John and to secure the door behind him, Samantha had followed her friend. By this time the jacket was hanging on the back of a chair, the dress in a crumpled heap on the floor near the bin. Madeleine was under the shower, trying to wash away the memory and the odour of Harrington, the nauseating feel of his body on hers and the remembrance of an evening, unforgettable for all the very worst reasons.

There was something about the way the dress had been discarded that drew Samantha's attention to it. Last night, she had not learned much from Madeleine, only the bare outline of what had passed, but she was satisfied that Harrington had been unable to carry his vile intentions to their full conclusion.

Madeleine relived the journey home. She had, initially, been unable to look at Alexis, let alone talk to him. From his stern concentration on the road, the way he gripped the steering wheel, and the speed at which he drove, she was able to gauge the depth of his anger. She had wondered what he was thinking but, for some minutes, had been afraid to ask for fear he would criticise her naivety in going with such a man as Harrington.

Might he think she had gone willingly instead of waiting in for his call? And how had Alexis known where to find her?

Tense and on the defensive, she eventually turned to him. 'Aren't you going to ask how I came to be with Harrington?'

'No,' he replied, 'There's no need . . . I already know.'

'I didn't go with him willingly,' she insisted, doubting the accuracy of his knowledge.

He slowed the car and relaxed his grip on the wheel so that his knuckles were no longer white. 'Madeleine, I already know all I need to know,' he said, taking his eyes off the road to glance at her.

'But how do you know? How did you know where to find me? I don't understand,' she said, unable to keep the agitation from her voice.

He pulled the car into a lamplit lay-by and turned off the engine. Turning to face her, he gently pushed a tussled lock back off her face. Then, taking her hands in his, picking his words with care, he explained in a soothing voice, 'Susan saw you leave with Harrington and told Mavis Ford. The party was common knowledge to the staff, and knowing what debauched affairs these parties are, Mavis was concerned for your safety. Later, she phoned you at home but Samantha said you had not come back, and so she came to see me.' He paused, then added: 'No great mystery.'

After a moment of thoughtful silence, Madeleine asked, 'But why ever did Mavis come to you for help?'

'She seemed to think we were . . . *close* was the word she used.' His face was turned from the light. She could not see his expression clearly, but it seemed he was smiling.

Confused, she asked, 'But why would she think that?'

'She didn't say. She may have seen us talking at the exhibition or maybe saw a photograph of us together in Paris which somehow found its way into a couple of magazines. The captions suggested we're more than just good friends.' A warmth had crept into his voice and again, there was that smile.

She paused, looked down at their entwined hands. 'Oh, so you know about the magazines . . . well actually, you're right, Mavis did see one of them. In fact, she showed me a cutting when I was in her office.' Knowing Alexis was not listed in the telephone directory, she next asked, 'How did she know your address?'

He remembered the card he had given Mavis on his last visit to the gallery. But he merely told her, 'I'm on Harrington's guest list. She must have a memory for numbers.'

Still feeling intensely vulnerable, raising unhappy eyes to meet his, she said in a small voice, 'Thank you, Alexis. It's obvious what would have happened if you hadn't come when you did.'

She had felt the inadequacy of her words but been unable to think of anything further to add.

There was the sound of the main door closing and Samantha's bare feet padding up the hall. She re-entered the bedroom carrying a huge bunch of red roses enclosed in cellophane and artistically tied with a huge bow.

'For you,' Samantha sighed, looking at them enviously before passing them on.

Attached to the ribbon was an envelope with Madeleine's name on it. Recognising the writing, her eyes brightened. 'They're from Alexis,' she murmured, a lump in her throat.

The enclosed card read: *If you feel up to it, come to a party with me this evening. Love, Alexis.*

'Will you go?' Samantha asked.

Cradling the roses and staring at the card, Madeleine hesitated. 'No . . . I don't think so.' There was a catch in her voice. His thoughtfulness was bringing her dangerously close to tears.

'I think you should,' Samantha said, gently. 'The sooner you put the whole thing behind you, the better. Yes, I know,' she said in a hurry, 'easier said than done, and it wasn't me it happened to.' After a moment, she suggested, 'Don't decide about the party now. See how you feel later.'

Reaching for the flowers, she added, 'I'll just go and put these in a vase for you.'

'Sam,' Madeleine called after her. 'Whatever you do, don't tell Jeremy what happened, or anyone who might tell Jeremy. It would only make him feel guilty about sending me over to the gallery and I don't want him to fall out with Harrington over this.' She twisted the sheet between agitated fingers. 'If Harrington decided to turn vindictive, he could destroy Jeremy's career as easily as he's built it up.'

Reluctantly, Samantha agreed, and then asked, 'Are you going to report him to the police? You should, you know. He needs stopping, before he can do it to someone else.'

'No I can't, Sam. I wish I could, really I do,' she replied, her voice contrite, 'but it might get into the papers and I don't want the publicity for Alexis or for myself, and I'm sure neither Earl and Harrow nor Belle Laurie would thank me for it.' She gave a dispirited sigh. 'I hate the thought of Harrington getting away with it, or doing the same thing to someone else, but they wouldn't lock him up, you know – after all, he didn't actually succeed in . . .' She could not finish the sentence. *Rape* was a word she would never be able to say or hear again with impunity.

The telephone rang. Madeleine answered the call while Samantha hovered at the door, waiting to know if it was for her.

'Ah. Just the person I want to talk to,' said the angry voice of Rodney Harrington. 'I'm going to sue your boyfriend for breaking and entering and for bodily assault. He cracked a couple of my ribs.' Too humiliated, he omitted to mention the outsized lump on the back of his head and the enormous black eye.

The colour drained out of Madeleine's face and her whole body shook with fury. 'He did not break your ribs,' she hissed through clenched teeth. 'I did, and I'd have broken a few more if Alexis hadn't stopped me. As for suing, there are witnesses who heard you offer me a lift home and saw me leave with you in all good faith. I've an independent witness to your attack and another who can testify to the bruises you inflicted on me. If anyone's going to sue, it will be me.' Before he could interrupt, she went on to speculate, but in a calmer voice, 'If I went public with this, I wonder if any other victims would come forward.'

There was silence on the other end of the phone.

'Anything else you want to say to me?' she asked with biting sarcasm, knowing she had scored a direct hit and wondering who his other victims were.

'Yes,' he answered, disgruntled but using a more reasonable tone. 'You left your coat and keys behind. Just to show there are no hard feelings, why don't you come over tonight and collect them, and I'll take you out for supper.'

'I'd only be tempted to accept your invitation if I thought I might have the pleasure of breaking a few more of your ribs,' Madeleine snapped at him before slamming the phone down.

With incredulous disbelief, she stared at Samantha.

'The nerve of the man,' she cried. 'Would you believe, he wants to take me out tonight?'

Samantha grimaced. 'I think you adequately expressed your feelings on the subject.'

Going over to the full-length mirror, Madeleine stripped off her nightgown and inspected her body for bruises. There were a few discolorations but, fortunately, they were not nearly as bad as they felt. The worst bruising proved to be around the wrists where Harrington had gripped her, and particularly around the one he had twisted so viciously. She would have to wear long sleeves for a few days at least, she told herself. Her muscles had stiffened up overnight, but a soak in a hot bath would probably sort out that problem.

It was while Madeleline was towelling herself dry that Samantha informed her Alexis was on the phone. 'Shall I tell him you'll call back?' she asked through the bathroom door.

'No. Don't do that. I'm coming.' Wrapping the towel around her, she padded out to the extension in the bedroom.

'Alexis?' she asked shyly.

'Yes. I hope I haven't woken you up,' he inquired.

'No. I've been awake for some time,' she replied. The pleasure of hearing his voice put warmth into her own. 'Thank you for the lovely roses . . . and the note.'

'And what is your answer? Will you come tonight?' His voice was gentle, persuasive.

When she hesitated, he did not press for an answer. 'Samantha tells me Harrington phoned this morning. What did he want?'

'Just to let me know he's got a couple of cracked ribs,' she told him, not bothering to hide the elation in her voice. 'He also asked me to come over to the gallery to collect the coat and keys I left behind last night.'

'Anything else?' he queried.

'Yes. He invited me out to supper tonight to show there are no hard feelings,' she retorted, obviously incensed by Harrington's audacity. 'I hung up on him.'

'I'll get your coat and keys back for you,' he told her, 'but in the meantime I think you should arrange to have the locks changed on your door.'

She agreed to do so.

'I'll collect you tonight at eight,' he said firmly.

'But – ' The line went dead. He had already gone.

True to his word, Alexis was at the door at eight, devastatingly attractive in dark shirt, Levis and suede jacket. He had brought her coat, from which he had removed the keys for safekeeping. These he handed to her separately.

'I don't think you'll be hearing from Harrington again,' he told her. Although she looked in inquiry, he did not elaborate on what had further passed between them.

Madeleine knew she should invite him in but, since she

was alone in the apartment, was reluctant to do so. Harrington had seriously undermined her confidence in men.

Seeing her hesitate, sensitive to her feelings, Alexis suggested, 'If you're ready, we'll go out for a drink, give the party an hour or so to warm up.'

By the time the taxi dropped them off outside the mews house in Chelsea, the party was in full swing. The house appeared to be filled with fascinating extroverts and it was plain to see that, like Alexis, most of them were in some way involved in the arts.

Initially feeling a little out of her element, Madeleine stayed close to his side. It seemed to her, he knew and was known by everybody. This was his territory, these his type of people, and he moved among them with comfortable ease.

Conversation and laughter flowed as lavishly as the drink and in one part of the house guests were dancing to loud rhythmic music.

Madeleine had not long been at the party when the inevitable happened. She found herself looking into the shrewd eyes of Hugh Bradford. Because they had met only once before, she had not instantly placed the familiar face. By the time enlightenment dawned, it was too late to turn away. Holding her breath, Madeleine suffered the introduction as best she could. They shook hands, and only when it was apparent he had not recognised her was she able to breathe freely once more. He had accepted the name Madeleine Harcourt as easily as Alexis had done.

Just then a woman pushed through the crowd. 'Alexis darling,' she called in a theatrical voice. 'I heard you were here. Do come and dance with me. It's bad form to refuse the hostess,' she warned, laughing.

Taking him by the hand, with determination she pulled him in the direction from which she had come. With good-humoured resignation, Alexis allowed himself to be led away.

'Look after her,' he managed to call over his shoulder to Hugh before disappearing into the crowd.

'Care to follow suit?' Hugh asked Madeleine.

The volume of sound made conversation impossible, which was a relief since Madeleine now felt even less comfortable than usual with the problems of having two personalities. Losing herself to the music, the worst of her aches and pains evaporated. No doubt the warmth of the room, the medicinal effects of the alcohol and the exercise had something to do with the cure.

Hugh soon got elbowed out of the way by an amiable friend. 'You've been dancing with the best-looking woman in the room quite long enough. It's my turn,' he grinned tipsily.

With an apologetic smile, Hugh said, 'Madeleine, meet Dan.' Allowing himself to be ousted, he moved off in search of the glass he had put aside.

Madeleine danced well: her subtle movements provocative. Whether on the dance floor or off, she was never without company. When Alexis was not at her side, Hugh kept a discreet watch on her. He had heard about her brush with Harrington.

Alexis was an attentive partner: although not always at her side, he was never out of sight for long. Whenever his reassuring gaze came to rest on her, it was as if he was saying; *I'm here if you need me.*

As the evening progressed, Madeleine's inhibitions dropped away leaving her more light-hearted than she felt she had a right to be so soon after Harrington's attack. She knew she had Alexis to thank.

That he was immensely popular had become clear within minutes of their arrival. Madeleine did not begrudge the popularity that took him away from her, until later, when, with a twinge of jealousy, she noticed the effect he had on women. Hanging on his every word, they seemed to come alive, their eyes acquiring extra sparkle, their gestures and speech more animation. She wondered if he was aware of the seductive qualities in his voice.

A Drew trait, she smiled complacently to herself.

When the buffet was finally announced, Alexis slipped an arm around her waist and, drawing her away from those with whom she had been discussing one of London's current musicals, murmured softly, 'It will be a while before we can get near the food. Come and dance with me.'

For the first time that evening, she wished the music slow and romantic so that her partner would hold her close

Later, when Madeleine was once more involved in a discussion, and Alexis had drifted away into the smoky atmosphere, she noticed there was one woman more often at his side than any other. She did not recall having seen her earlier and thought she must have been a late arrival. Whilst Alexis did not actually treat her with disdain, there was an apparent lack of warmth in his response. Each time he moved on, although not encouraged, the woman followed. Madeleine's curiosity was aroused.

Her attention was diverted when she was asked to dance and when, 15 minutes later, she returned to collect her glass, neither Alexis nor the woman was anywhere to be seen. Madeleine had never before thought of herself as being particularly suspicious, jealous or possessive by nature. But now, she realised she was having a taste of all three sentiments, and did not like herself for it. She told herself to be reasonable; Alexis had not seemed flattered by the woman's company. But then, where were they now?

Feeling the need to be alone with her insecurities, Madeleine threaded her way through the noisy crowd and, leaving the hot stuffy room, went up the dimly lit stairs, past silent lovers partially concealed in the shadows, to a room and en-suite bathroom assigned to the use of guests. Bypassing the bed piled high with an assortment of coats and jackets, Madeleine seated herself before the dressing table mirror and, cupping her chin in her hands, gazed moodily at her reflection. When had she become so dependent upon Alexis for her peace of mind? she asked herself. Disconsolately, she shook her head and, making a mental effort to rise above her suspicions, set about the task of repairing her make-up and restoring some semblance of order to her tousled hair.

Satisfied but not yet ready to return to the party, Madeleine stepped over to the window and, perching on the wide sill, opened it slightly to admit the cool, fresh air.

Instantly, her attention was arrested by the sound of nearby voices and, looking along the cobbled street below, she saw, between two cars, the silhouette of a couple deep in conversation. The woman's voice, being shrill with agitation, carried more clearly in the crisp night air.

'But he never was the right man for me,' she was saying. 'There hasn't been a right man since you. How could there be . . . we had something so special, something I've never found with anyone else.' With feline grace, she moved towards the man and, leaning her curvaceous body against him, put her arms around his neck.

Taking hold of her wrists, he disengaged himself. Putting distance between them, he moved back, to lounge, with arms folded, against the bonnet of one of the cars.

Madeleine felt sorry for the woman. He was not responding as a lover should. She was about to remove herself from the window when the resonant voice she recognised as belonging to Alexis, said: 'It's been over a long time, Henrietta, and at the risk of sounding ungallant, it was never that good between us.'

The woman gasped and said with feeling, 'But we were great in bed. You know we were.'

'I've never found great sex that hard to come by,' he returned, with a laugh not altogether pleasant. 'It seems to me we were a bit short on the other requirements for a lasting relationship.' When Henrietta did not immediately reply, he went on to remind her, 'Besides, it was your decision to move on, remember?'

'Only because you made it impossible for me to stay,' she accused him. 'Seven years! How could you expect me to wait seven years?'

'As I recall, I didn't expect you to wait seven years,' he responded.

The woman ignored this. 'You'll be free soon – the seven years are nearly over . . . I've always loved you Alexis. It's not too late . . . we could try again,' she pleaded. Taking a step towards him, she placed a hand on his arm.

Alexis straightened up. 'It was all over between us a long time ago. Accept it,' he said firmly but not unkindly.

'You don't intend to go through with the divorce, do you?' Henrietta asked, suspicion in her voice. 'I've always known it. It's her money you're after. You don't want me any more because I can't give you what she can.' She laughed on a slightly hysterical note. 'That's it, isn't it, Alexis? You can't fool me, I know you too well.'

Alexis did not answer.

'Stay married to her if you must and have her money. But have me too. We can both enjoy spending it.' She laughed again.

Turning away, Alexis began to walk towards the house.

'That girl you've brought with you tonight,' she hissed after him, 'does she know you're a married man?' A truly vindictive note had crept into her voice.

Alexis did not answer or look back but, in the light cast by a passing car, Madeleine saw the question had put a curious smile on his face.

Madeleine returned to the party shocked at what she had heard and ashamed of having eavesdropped. She remembered when she had done so before, and no good had come of it then either. Now after all these years she had seen Henrietta, knew what the woman looked like, and wished she did not. Henrietta was lovely, like a china doll.

Alexis was once more in the room, the woman too, but no longer at his side. Hardly aware of the conversation around her, Madeleine let her troubled gaze rest on him while she brooded on the little she knew of the woman who had, for a while, shared his life. Her train of thought was broken when she became aware that Henrietta had unexpectedly materialised at her side.

Following the direction of her rival's gaze, Henrietta said, 'Ah. Alexis Drew. So you're another of his conquests. You're wasting your time, you know – he's already married.' Seeing that she had Madeleine's full attention and being in a spiteful mood, she continued, 'Oh, I'm sorry. Didn't you know he was married? He got himself a child bride worth a lot of money – an heiress – about six years ago.' She laughed unpleasantly. 'Her money was the only thing that attracted him, so he left right after the wedding and hasn't been back since.'

Out of large, seemingly innocent eyes, Henrietta watched for an adverse reaction. Had she known she was in fact speaking to the child bride, she would have been ecstatic, but not quite so pleased to realise she had turned into this undeniably beautiful woman.

Madeleine deeply resented this former lover knowing so much about their private lives. But more than ever she resented the element of truth in Henrietta's words. Right about so much, could she possibly be right about all? Alexis had indeed married for money, but not her money . . . surely?

Henrietta was not only stirring up old resentment, but also presenting her with new ones. Well, nearly new. She recalled Samantha had once suggested something along similar lines. She had been as much disturbed then as she was now, but she was damned if she was going to give this woman the satisfaction of knowing it. Making an effort at composure, she responded coldly, 'That's all nonsense; nothing but malicious gossip!'

'Fact, my dear,' Henrietta countered, undaunted by Madeleine's tone of voice. 'Believe me. I know . . .'

'In that case, you only know half a story,' she interjected, and then, managing a smile quite as feline as Henrietta's, she purred, '*Believe me, I know!*'

'Well, he certainly didn't marry her because he got her pregnant, if that's what you mean.' Henrietta now sounded nettled. 'He's far too experienced to fall into that trap,' she added with conviction.

Madeleine had not meant to imply any such thing, but before she could say so, Henrietta continued, 'Besides, a country mouse would not interest him in that way – not at all his type. He likes his women experienced. I should know,' she smiled smugly.

At that moment Alexis happened to glance in their direction and, seeing the company Madeleine was keeping, excused himself and began to manoeuvre his way towards them.

Henrietta had seen that look on his face before. Having no wish to cross swords with him, she made the wise decision to beat a hasty retreat. 'If it's marriage you want, you're wasting your time. He won't marry you; he's already married to her money – and he won't give it up. Believe me, I know what I'm talking about. So nice to have met you,' she smiled sweetly before hurrying away.

'I see you've met Henrietta Maison,' Alexis said, at last gaining Madeleine's side.

'Oh. Is that her name?' she asked a little too nonchalantly. 'We never got around to introductions.'

'And what did you get around to?' he asked, studying her closely.

'Nothing of any consequence,' she replied.

Hearing the slight tremble in her voice, he swore under his breath and determined not to leave her side again so long as his former lover remained at the party.

Henrietta did not stay long.

It was one o'clock before the crowd began to show signs of thinning. By two, half the guests had drifted away. Someone called to Alexis to play something on the piano. He declined but the cry was taken up.

'None of your nocturnes and concertos, Alexis,' called a young black American from the back of the room who, Madeleine thought, looked as if he might be a jazz or blues musician. 'Something we can dance to.'

'No. For goodness' sake, don't play his kind of music,

Alexis,' someone else called. 'He's the only one who likes that rubbish.' She laughed heartily, as did his other friends.

'Here we are,' said their hostess, whom Madeleine now knew as Margot. 'Choose something from one of these.' She handed him a couple of thick books.

'OK. You choose, I'll play,' he offered.

'One of the oldies,' someone called out.

'"Unchained Melody,"' Margot suggested. 'Think you can play that?'

There was a chorus of laughter at the absurdity of the question.

'I think I can just about manage it,' Alexis teased her. Taking the books, he strode over to the piano.

'Before you do,' said an eccentric-looking old gentleman standing near Madeleine, 'play your own music . . . from the new film.'

Someone turned off the hi-fi and the loud hum of conversation died away as the word was passed around that Alexis was going to play 'Where Shadows Fall'.

Glancing around the room at his happy, inebriated audience, he laughingly declined to play it, saying, 'It's not a party piece. Too emotional, it would probably reduce you all to tears.' Looking at them again, this time with a more critical eye, he smiled broadly, and added, 'In any case, it would be wasted on you tonight.' He was adamant. 'It will be out on release soon.'

To put an end to further attempts at friendly persuasion, he began to play, as formally requested, 'Unchained Melody'. And then, to an appreciative audience, he went on to play one of his own modern pieces which a new vocalist had recently taken into the charts.

Here he would have ended his recital if he had been allowed to do so, but no one wanted him to leave the piano.

'Where's Diana?' he asked. 'I'll play "On My Own" if Diana will sing.'

Diana came forward to stand just behind Alexis where she could look over his shoulder at the music and lyrics. She had a lovely voice which might have been trained for the stage and Madeleine wondered if she had ever played the part of Eponine. Nothing about these people would surprise her. So many of them seemed to be connected with showbusiness in some way.

Diana sang one more song, also from *Les Misérables*: 'I Dreamed a Dream', and then she would sing no more, but the pianist was not to be let off so lightly. Jerry Lee Lewis music was called for and Alexis played to a great deal of drunken accompaniment, 'A Whole Lotta Shakin' Goin' On', followed by, 'Great Balls of Fire'.

Madeleine had never seen or even suspected that there was a much lighter side to the personality of Alexis Drew. Nor had it occurred to her that the boundaries of his interests extended beyond the classics.

This enigmatic man of many talents and moods was her husband but she was the only one in the room who knew it. With fascination, she watched him perform and knew she was hopelessly in love.

30

For the past couple of weeks, Alexis had not been much in evidence. Madeleine met him once for lunch but it was a rushed affair – time snatched between appointments. The long run-up to Christmas was, inevitably, a busy time in the entertainment world, and it looked as if there would not be much let-up until after the New Year.

Cameron Knight called to invite her to lunch, during which he brought her up to date on the advertising campaign, gave her an itinerary and discussed her future participation. All was on schedule for the big launch set for the following week. It was, he said, coming together like clockwork.

'Want to meet for a quiet candlelit supper one night?' he asked, with a show of optimism but little real hope.

'Only if we're making up a foursome,' she answered, smiling sweetly. 'Always wanted to meet Joanne.'

He returned her smile, though a shade on the wry side. 'I'll see you on Monday.' he responded, non-committally. 'Get lots of rest in the meantime. You're going to need it.'

A couple of times, she called in on Jeremy. He showed her several canvases that were in readiness for Harrington's next exhibition. Not a word did he say about her abduction to Richmond; it seemed that both Harrington and Mavis had kept silent on the subject.

She called Mavis to thank her for her discretion and for her part in Alexis' intervention. It was then that she heard, in muted tones, what had transpired in Harrington's office when Alexis had gone to collect her coat. Mavis had heard it all from her office opposite and, since Susan had been with her at the time, she too had heard.

'We didn't miss a word,' Mavis admitted, unashamedly,

'and it confirmed a thing or two we'd previously only suspected.' She paused a moment, but finding her employer no longer worthy of loyalty, went on to whisper into the phone, 'Mr Drew accused him of having been on trial for date rape a few years back. Mr Harrington didn't bother to deny it, but said he'd been found not guilty.'

Madeleine was not surprised to hear there had been another victim, but she was surprised that Alexis had known and not told her.

'Mr Drew reminded him that this time there was a reliable witness,' Mavis continued, 'and another to testify to the injuries he'd inflicted. He warned Harrington to stay away from you and said if he heard so much as a hint of a new scandal, he'd come back and cut off . . .' Mavis faltered.

'Ouch! Sounds painful,' laughed Madeleine.

'Mr Harrington must have thought so. For once, he was lost for words and hasn't been quite himself since,' Mavis continued cheerfully. 'I expect you already know he's got an enormous black eye?' She did not wait for an answer, but chortled on, 'You should see him – he's gone into hiding behind an equally enormous pair of sunglasses. Honestly, Madeleine, sunglasses at this time of year!' She paused, 'No need to ask how he came by the black eye. I can guess.' Mavis then said with a sigh of admiration, 'Your Mr Drew is not a man I'd care to cross.'

Me neither, Madeleine thought, wondering how he was going to react when he discovered she was keeping secrets from him. Remembering the explosive temper, she shivered.

On schedule, the Belle Laurie promotion was launched worldwide. Madeleine was guest of honour at a gala dinner at the Ritz Carlton and, soon after, at a number of receptions. Before she had time to draw breath, she was whisked off to tour and promote on the Continent.

Simultaneously, all over Europe, the television commercials began to appear with regularity, posters went up in busy public places, and advertisements went into popular glossy magazines. The new range had, for some time, been selling in the big stores, but now the counter advertisements were also on display. Madeleine, a picture of exquisite beauty, confidence and success, smiled out at shoppers all over the world.

For weeks now, the high spot on Madeleine's horizon had been the film premiere to which Alexis had invited her. One of the fleet of limousines hired by the studio for the occasion took them to Leicester Square, where it came to a stately halt outside the cinema. The red carpet laid from pavement to main entrance had been cordoned off. The press was out en masse and an inquisitive crowd of star-spotters jostled for a glimpse of the famous. As Alexis had forewarned, it was a formal affair, a showy parade of fashion, wealth and fame.

As the composer of the music, Alexis had been one of those interviewed for the documentaries of the movie in the making. The documentaries had gone worldwide, promoting not only the film shortly to be released to the public, but his music too. The melodies were so captivating they became an instant success and were already out on release. Sales had rocketed and it had already made the charts.

As Alexis and Madeleine alighted from the limousine, a ripple of excitement ran through the crowd and the name Alexis Drew was murmured over and over.

Nearby, a little girl stood staring at the lady in the long black lace. Tugging on the hand that held hers, she said, 'Oooh, is she a princess, mummy?'

Flash bulbs exploded in their faces, and microphones, aimed at Alexis, were accompanied by a whole string of questions. Madeleine could not avoid the cameras nor could she prevent Alexis giving her pseudonym to the reporters.

Making room for the arrival of other celebrities, they proceeded up the red carpet and were soon through the cinema doors and out of sight. They had made an elegant and distinguished couple and the eager flock of onlookers had not been disappointed.

At the reception, Alexis introduced her to a number of colleagues, many of them well-known artists themselves, after which they moved en masse into the auditorium to take their seats. It was a romantic film which brought tears to the eyes of the soft-hearted. Madeleine was unashamedly one of them. That it managed to bring out such depth of emotion was due, in large part, to the dramatic, atmospheric music.

There, in the darkened theatre, while she watched and listened, Madeleine was very much aware of the charismatic man at her side. She wondered again at the strange entanglement of their lives.

A late-night party had been planned at a nearby nightclub for those who had worked closest to the film and it was expected that Alexis would attend, bringing with him his beautiful partner, over whom there had been considerable curiosity. In the back of the limousine, Madeleine noticed his strange restless mood.

'Would you be disappointed if we gave the party a miss?' he asked in a voice low and brooding.

She imagined he was feeling the anticlimax that sometimes follows on the heels of the build-up and completion of so important an event. She gave the assurances he wanted to hear, but secretly was sorry to have the magical evening come to an early conclusion.

It was, therefore, with mixed emotions that Madeleine heard him say, 'Instead, will you come back to my place for coffee?'

The poignant tone he used left her in no doubt his

invitation was for more than just coffee. There followed a moment of tension while he waited for her reply, his dark, questioning eyes impatient for an answer.

With a flutter of butterflies in the pit of her stomach, Madeleine placed her hand in his, knowing that in doing so she was giving her consent.

Raising her hand to his lips, he kissed the open palm. Then, leaning forward, he slid the glass partition across and gave new directions to the chauffeur.

So far, Madeleine reminded herself, Alexis had done little more than drape an arm casually around her shoulders. After Margot's party, she had thought he would at least kiss her but, as in Paris, he had seen her safely to the door and left her there feeling frustrated and unappealing.

Now, as the car moved down The Mall and along Constitution Hill, she began to wonder if she had read too much into the invitation. The thought both calmed and deflated her.

By the time the car came to a halt, Madeleine found she was looking forward with considerable curiosity to seeing the interior of Linnet House. When he handed her out of the car and she walked up the steps at his side, she said none of the things she might have said if truly in ignorance of Alexis' background. She did not comment on the wealthy address, nor the splendour of the house. She did not wish to compound the lie that stood between them.

Preceding her through the door, Alexis quickly turned on the lights and disarmed the security system. Then he crossed to a gilded wall table to lay his keys in a celadon bowl. There he paused to surreptitiously watch her through the mirror.

Her eyes, bright with interest, swept around the reception hall with its panelled doors, elaborate cornice ceilings, Venetian chandelier and wide curved staircase. Her admiring gaze flickered over the exquisite antique Italian furniture and over the fabulous art treasures. Only a fool would think of turning his back on this, with or without the temptations of the Steinway, and Alexis, she told herself, was anything but a fool.

Turning, Alexis placed an arm lightly around her waist and led her across the pale marble floor, into the drawing room. He felt her slight intake of breath and was pleased with her reaction to the size and splendour of the palatial room. It was clear she had never before been through the doors of this, their great-grandfather's house.

Excusing himself, he went to check the answerphone pulsing in the distance, deliberately leaving her alone.

Madeleine had always been intrigued by the history of Linnet House and had become even more so since the overheard conversation between Alexis and Hugh regarding the black sheep of the family. Now she felt as if she had taken a step into the past. It was all she had imagined, and more. An exquisite chandelier and wall sconces threw a myriad of lights over ornate, sculptured cornice ceilings and a room rich in shades of blue and cream. At the tall sash windows hung luxurious swag and tail drapes.

There appeared to be little that was not antique. Silverware, mostly Georgian, was on display in a corner cabinet, and on the other side of the window was a tall leafy fern – no doubt the same one she had seen from the pavement below when passing with Samantha two years previously; only now, it was taller and fuller. On a long low table in front of a window stood a seven-branch silver table candelabra made in the Spanish style. Madeleine was momentarily startled by its presence. She knew it to be one of a pair: its twin was at Ravenswood.

On a small mahogany table near the sofa was a silver cigarette box. The engraving on the lid read: 'Presented to Frederick Drew by the members of Summerton Lodge, on the occasion of his marriage, 18 December 1880.' It was, she knew, typical of her great-grandfather to think nothing of bringing one of his wedding gifts to the house where he had installed his mistress. Turning, she let her gaze wander to the far end of the room.

There were handsome pieces of oriental porcelain and,

mounted flat along the largest expanse of wall, was an antique six-panelled Chinese screen depicting a colourful scene of warlords on their horses, ready to do battle.

In front of this screen stood a magnificent grand piano. She did not need to read the golden lettering to know that this was the famous Steinway, the treasure for which Alexis had sold his freedom.

Slowly, Madeleine crossed the room and gazing meditatively down on the shiny wood, ran her fingertips along its cool surface. Her memory flashed back through the years to when she was four and had, from the dim landing, listened for the first time to the enchantment of Alexis' music. Following the path of time, she remembered the night she had lain on her bed, devastated by her grandfather's will, when sounds from the piano had floated up to her room and soothed her into an exhausted sleep. Her recollections moved on to the Royal Albert Hall, where Alexis had again stirred her emotions and she had felt the beginnings of a restless new love.

Surely it was understandable – quite natural, even – that he would want this piano. After all, music was his first love, his life's work. Was it not appropriate that her grandfather should leave it to the one person who would appreciate and value it above all else: to the great-grandson of Frederick Drew, to Alexis, who had inherited Frederick's talent and with dedicated hard work turned it into genius? But was this Steinway, together with Linnet House, enough to tempt Alexis, against his will, into seven years of marriage? Or was Katherine's fortune his ultimate aim? she asked herself.

Henrietta's accusations and Samantha's earlier suspicions were now never far from Madeleine's thoughts. Only if he kept his side of the bargain, did not obstruct the divorce when the time came, would she have the answer to her question: the answer she hoped for. Only then would she be able to completely trust him.

With a lingering look at the piano, she sighed and turned to move away. A sound caught her attention. Looking up, she became aware that Alexis had returned and was, from the doorway, watching her intently.

'I was just admiring the piano.' She said, feeling guilty, as if caught doing wrong.

Moving to the centre of the room, she quickly sought an object on which to transfer her attention. Her eyes came to rest on a magnificent portrait hanging over the marble fireplace.

'Who is she?' asked Madeleine, studying the lovely features of the Victorian subject.

'Arabella Haste,' he said, following her gaze but not entering the room. 'She lived here at the end of the last century. All this is her taste.'

'She had beautiful taste,' Madeleine approved.

'I agree. That's why I left it very much as I found it.'

'Who was Arabella Haste?' Madeleine asked, hoping he would embellish on the fascinating information she had overheard him relating to Hugh.

'She was the mistress of my great-grandfather.' He smiled indulgently. *And yours too,* he added, but only to himself.

'Will you tell me about them?' asked Madeleine.

'If you like,' he replied, wondering how much she already knew with regard to the old reprobate and his lovely mistress. 'I'll tell you over coffee.'

While waiting for Alexis to return, a group of silver-framed photographs on the mantelpiece claimed her attention. One contained a head-and-shoulders studio picture of her grandmother. Another, a youthful Aunt Caroline, holding a small dark-haired child who could only be Alexis. Madeleine did not recognise the man with them but, from the Drew dark good looks, she guessed he was Nathan Drew, Alexis' natural father. With a sharp intake of breath, she recognised a picture of herself as an infant in arms. Taking it closer to the light, she studied the faces of her beloved parents, and as she did so, reminded herself that they too had once stood in this same room and been familiar with all its many treasures. It was with relief that she saw there were no recent photographs of herself.

Hearing the approach of Alexis' footsteps, she hastily returned the frame to its former position. Looking around for some other object on which to fix her attention, she spotted, hanging from the ceiling to one side of the mantle-piece, a thick gold cord. She recognised it as a household bell, not unlike those in the rooms at Ravenswood. With a show of interest, and a genuine curiosity to know if it still worked, she took it in her hands.

Seeing what she held, Alexis, looking very haughty, asked in a very proper butler-type of voice, 'You called, madam?'

'I didn't pull it,' Madeleine laughed, releasing it and going to sit on the sofa. 'But if I had, would you have obeyed the summons?'

'That depends on your reasons for summoning me,' he replied. As he crossed the room, the appealing aroma of fresh coffee wafted in the air.

She watched him set the glasses on the table. 'If you didn't come, you wouldn't know my reasons,' she pointed out playfully.

'In that case, I'd have to come if only to find out,' he agreed, going to sit, not beside her, but in an armchair opposite.

'That doesn't sound too obliging – you'd make a terrible butler,' she complained.

His eyes swept the length of her graceful limbs. He smiled at his thoughts. 'On the contrary,' he countered, 'you might find me very obliging . . . but that would depend on what you wanted me to do for you.'

Lowering her eyes, she said softly, 'We seem to have come around in an interesting circle.'

Changing the subject, he asked, but in a voice grown deeper with desire, 'I hope you like Irish coffee?'

Unsettled by what she had read in his eyes and voice, she smiled doubtfully at the glass in front of her. 'Yes, but I shouldn't,' she demurred. 'It usually goes straight to my head.'

He sincerely hoped so. He wanted her relaxed, with her defences lowered. He had waited long enough – longer than he had ever waited for any other woman and with more patient restraint than he knew he possessed. It amused him to think that tonight he planned to seduce his own wife. He wondered if she would consider his actions a betrayal of Katherine; after all, he was not supposed to know she was Katherine. The whole situation had turned into an Elizabethan comedy. How could he have allowed himself to be drawn into such a ludicrous situation? he asked himself with perverse humour.

Breaking into his thoughts, Madeleine reminded him, 'Now, will you tell me about Arabella Haste and your great-grandfather?'

He had no intention of wasting too much time on a history lesson, the details of which, quite likely, she already knew. He had other plans for their evening together. And so he gave her only a brief outline, telling her nothing she did not already know.

His voice was harmonious and intoxicating, and if he had told her nothing new in ten times as many words, Madeleine would have listened with just as much rapt attention.

At the end of the narration, in the ensuing silence, an atmosphere of intimacy developed which Madeleine found strangely disconcerting. There was again a brooding impatience in Alexis' mood. She realised that at some time he had dimmed the lights, probably when returning with the coffee. Nor had she noticed the removal of his jacket and tie and the top two studs from his white dress shirt.

There was a charged expectancy in the air. The butterflies returned to her stomach and she swallowed nervously. They wanted the same thing and they both knew it, yet she needed time.

Looking towards the piano, Madeleine asked in a hesitant voice grown husky with desire, 'Alexis, will you . . . play something for me?'

'What would you like me to play?' he asked, aware she was stalling but willing to indulge her just a little longer.

'You choose,' she murmured.

For a moment, he held her gaze with his own. Then, silently, he went to the piano and began to play Schumann's *Romance.* There was no score before him. He played from memory and, as soon as his fingers touched the keyboard, he became absorbed in the music, as she knew he would.

In the soft glow of the lamplight, with heart beating fast, Madeleine studied the man who had come to mean so much to her. Her gaze traced the strong, well-defined line of his jaw and the sensual lips. She saw the wide shoulders, the straight back, the unconscious sway to harmonious sounds brought to life by those long fingers moving so confidently over the keys. Mesmerised by those supple, beautiful hands, Madeleine longed to feel them on her body, gently, knowingly caressing her.

Her love for him was growing, seeking expression and she grew weak with desire, but mingled with that desire was also apprehension. She had known intimately only one man, a man she had been attracted to but now realised had never really loved. With Alexis it would be different and she wanted desperately to please him. There was no doubt that he was a man of considerable experience. Had he not said to Henrietta, 'good sex is easy to come by'? Might he find her inexperience disappointing?

And then, there was the problem of her true identity. Should she not put an end to this foolish charade: do the right thing, tell him who she really was, before their involvement went any deeper? Would he be pleased, or angry at having been duped? More likely the latter, she warned herself – he had the Drew pride. Her silence had gone on too long, what excuse could she now offer? She could hardly tell him she doubted his motives for marrying Katherine: that she had been waiting to see if he would go through with the divorce. The magic would surely disintegrate leaving the evening in ruins. She again baulked at telling him.

Seeking excuses for her cowardice, Madeleine tried to resurrect other old grievances: his opinion of Katherine, his publicised romances, Vienna with Henrietta . . . But, it was already too late for that. Blinded by love, she no longer had any desire to think ill of him. Indeed, at this moment, she could remember no good reason for ever having doubted him.

The sounds that filled the air were gradually soothing away her contradictions. She should have known better than to ask him to play. Alexis, of all people, would be aware of the power of music to influence someone as susceptible as herself. He must know he had only to play the right piece at the right time and she would fall hopelessly under his spell.

Wrapped in the medley of her reflections, only now did Madeleine become aware that he was watching her through half-closed eyes, his desires as transparent as her own. She grew weak under his gaze. If he wanted her tonight, she would not have the will to resist, but would be his for the taking.

The music came to an end and for a moment all was still. Slowly, Alexis arose and crossed the room. He took the empty glass from her trembling fingers and placed it on the table.

'I – I should go,' she stammered, coming unsteadily to her feet.

He did not answer her. Either he had not heard or did not choose to hear. Instead, he put his hand to her hair and, removing the clasp, allowed it to spill down her back. Entwining his fingers into the thick curls at the nape of her neck, he drew her into his arms and kissed her: at first tenderly, and then, teasing her lips apart, more passionately.

Although tense, Madeleine did not resist. She wanted him, had wanted him for a long time. However, instinct must have warned him to move slowly for it seemed he made an effort of will to relax his embrace and to make his kisses less demanding, more tender.

He soothed her with caresses, causing delicious sensations to travel along her spine. She felt her tension melt away. Gradually, hesitantly, her arms came up and around his neck. Without her realising, her response became more ardent. A moan escaped her lips.

Softly coaxing, she heard him murmur in a voice thick with desire, 'Stay the night with me.' He did not seem to expect a reply; did not wait for one. Instead, he sought her lips once more, and this time there was an insistent urgency in his kisses. It was as if, through them, he was seeking her consent, and meant to have it.

As passion grew within, so did her response, and Madeleine knew that with such a response, she was giving him the answer he wanted. Having given it, there would be no turning back.

He did not ask again.

Taking her by the hand, Alexis led her out of the room, up the stairs and along the landing to a large bedroom that she took to be his own. He did not turn on the light, but waited with his back to the closed door, a hand resting on the handle.

At first, she could not see details, only outlines, but, as her eyes became accustomed to the dark, she was able to make out a large Spanish bed. Her eyes went to it, then, quickly, nervously, turned to his face.

Alexis had known that he was taking a chance breaking the mood of the moment. With her recent traumatic experience still fresh in her mind, she might still try to draw back. He could not let her do that, not now. He wanted her too much; had waited too long. Reaching out, he drew her into his arms and kissed her before she could speak. Again, his caresses aroused her until her needs were as great as his own, any thought of resistance soon forgotten.

His practised fingers went to the zip of her gown. The heavy lace fell free to the floor. While his touch became bolder and his kisses more demanding, he adeptly removed her few remaining garments, and with her help, his own.

He laid her on the bed. All prudery forgotten, she put her arms out to receive him. A whirlwind of pleasurable sensations swept through her at the feel of his long naked limbs against her own. He cradled her in his arms; kissed her eyes and temples and then, as light as a feather, stroked the side of her neck. Slowly, his fingertips moved over her shoulder. Not stopping there, they continued on down, causing erotic, searing sensations wherever their touch lingered on her skin. As they brushed over a breast she took a sharp intake of breath and trembled beneath him.

Her hands on his back, at first moved hesitantly, as if afraid of doing wrong. Slowly, gaining in confidence, they grew eager to touch and explore. One hand moved over his hip, and when her fingertips came to rest on his thigh, he stifled a moan.

Slowly, slowly, Alexis was warning himself, fighting for self-control. He was ready too soon. He had been with no one since his discovery of Madeleine, preferring to wait for her, knowing she would be worth the wait. Being constantly in her company, having to bide his time and knowing it would be unwise to move too fast, he had gone through daily torments. He had denied himself a long time, too long, and now he was paying the penalty of abstinence.

He brought his lips down to her breast and, in doing so, shifted his body away from her, giving himself temporary respite. With the tip of his tongue, he teased a nipple erect. She gasped; her senses suddenly overwhelmed by a surfeit of pleasure, but did not draw away.

His hand, moving down over her abdomen, was followed by his lips. It was as if his kisses burned her flesh. She writhed beneath him, her breathing erratic, her response ardent and almost beyond control. There was a deep ache within, a throbbing excitement, a yearning for fulfilment.

Wanting to give as well as receive, to touch as well as be touched, Madeleine enticed his lips back up to her own. Obedient to her demands, he thus placed his body once more within her reach and at her mercy. But his hand stayed where it was, stroking the inside of her thigh until it moved to where she most wanted to be touched, and where it could wreak the most tantalising havoc.

Stroking her hand from abdomen down to groin brought sweet torture that was so nearly his undoing. With a quiver and a deep moan, he caught her hand to halt its progress as, with great effort, he strove again for self-control. This time, aware of his reaction, her eyes flew open and he saw bewilderment in their exquisite depths.

'Witch!' he murmured.

She caught the amusement in his voice. With the dawn of understanding, Madeleine smiled a knowing, provocative smile, pleased to have so aroused him.

Only later, knowing the man, would Madeleine realise the effort it had required to restrain the violence of his needs as, patiently, he strove to bring her back to him again and again, and each time closer to the brink of ecstasy.

Pleasure rose gradually until, bombarded by heightened sensations far greater than any she had experienced before, she tried to pull away, to escape those hands. With a soft moan, she called his name.

Parting her limbs with his own, he brought the weight of his body down on hers. Waves of rapture swept them up higher and higher, carrying them both to the ultimate peak.

Sated and breathless, a warm exhaustion came over the lovers and it was some time before they drew apart. Stroking the curls back off her moist face, Alexis tenderly kissed her brow.

Her languid smile mirrored the deep contentment and well-being flowing through her. He had been an ardent lover, caring before and after, neither cool nor indifferent. With her head on his shoulder and an arm resting across his chest, she fell asleep.

Madeleine awoke to the grey light of dawn to find Alexis bending over her. That he had left her side and was already dressed was a vague disappointment.

With sleepy, questioning eyes, she put out a hand towards him, wanting to bring him back to her.

Taking her hand, but resisting the temptation she offered, he kissed each fingertip in turn. 'No, my darling,' he laughed down at her. 'It's time to get up, unless, of course, you've no objection to my cleaning lady finding you in my bed.'

Although neither said so, both knew no one had more right to be in his bed than she did.

31

For Madeleine, the lead-up to Christmas passed in a dream, with Alexis dominating her every thought. They had met whenever possible and exchanged Christmas presents before his departure for New York. He and Irvine were negotiating deals on his new releases, after which Alexis would be flying on to give a concert in Washington. While Madeleine mourned his loss, the temperature in England plummeted and snow blanketed the countryside. It tried to settle in the city, but quickly turned to grey slush.

Reverting once more to the name of Katherine, she and Samantha followed their annual custom of spending Christmas at Ravenswood.

Reginald Johnson, proud in uniform, drove to the station to collect them. Their arrival at the manor house provoked the usual bustle of excitement from Mrs Johnson and Ellie. While their comforts were being seen to, they were regaled with the local gossip followed by a torrent of questions.

It didn't take the gregarious Ellie long to get around to asking, ''Ave you seen that new TV commercial . . . the Belle Laurie one?' She peered at Katherine over the tea trolley she was positioning next to her mistress. 'Tha' girl looks ever so like you,' she added cheerfully, 'only maybe a bit better-looking.' Cocking her head on one side, she examined Katherine more closely, and then, evidently having second thoughts, went on to allow, 'Bu' maybe with the right clothes, the same 'airstyle, an' more make-up, you could pass as 'er.' She moved the trolley a little closer to Katherine, then ran a practised eye over its contents, making sure she had not forgotten anything.

Under their eyelashes, Katherine and Samantha sneaked

peeks at each other. It was all they could do to keep from collapsing into fits of laughter.

Without noticing anything amiss, the girl rattled on. 'I'm not the only one to notice the likeness, miss.'

Forewarned, Katherine put her hair up in a ponytail, wore little make-up and simple, unsophisticated country clothes. Even so, she and Samantha found they could not walk down the village high street without drawing comment on her likeness to the girl in the television commercial.

When accosted on the subject by Reverend Martins, Samantha could not resist chipping in with, 'I can't see the likeness myself.' With mischief in her eyes, she peered quizzically at Katherine. 'Her nose is too big, and as for her ears . . . well, anyone can see, they stick out too much.'

'Well, now you mention it,' responded the Vicar, who was in an agreeable frame of mind. As if bestowing his blessing on such unfortunate defects, he said affectionately to Katherine, 'Under the circumstances, I think you're looking remarkably well, my dear.'

Christian duty done, sure that somewhere an important matter awaited his immediate attention, he prepared to move on. 'My goodness, is that the time?' he said cheerfully, looking at his watch. 'Must go. Must go.' He turned to hurry away. 'I'll see you two in church on Christmas Eve,' were his parting words.

'Got you safely out of that one,' Samantha congratulated herself smugly.

Katherine inspected her reflection in the post office window. 'I didn't know I was such a reject,' she said in mock wonder.

Arm in arm, the friends continued their stroll through the village.

At first, Katherine was on her guard but, as the days passed and the subject of the Belle Laurie girl was mentioned with less frequency, she began to relax and enjoy the Christmas festivities.

She and Samantha tobogganed on the white slopes near the lake, threw snowballs at each other and anyone who came within range, built an enormous snowman, and generally behaved like overgrown schoolgirls until the novelty of the first snowfall of the season began to wear off.

On Christmas Eve, the traditional party was thrown for the children of the tenant farmers, and for the staff – a tradition the girls particularly looked forward to. After tea, Mr Johnson, playing his annual role of Santa, distributed the presents from under the tree. Since in height and shape he looked the part, and all that was verbally required of him was the occasional merry, 'Ho! Ho! Ho!' he was perfectly comfortable in the role.

Later, the two girls attended midnight mass at the village church and, with sparkling eyes and controlled good humour, sat through one of Reverend Martins' more inebriated sermons. Somewhere midway, his message got hopelessly and irretrievably muddled. Undaunted and in a thunderous voice for so small a church, he kept on to the end, spilling fire and brimstone over the heads of his captivated congregation, thumping the edge of the pulpit one minute and throwing his arms out the next, to add emphasis to his words.

'He's practising for Westminster Abbey,' Samantha giggled.

'Too much brandy on his Christmas pudding, more like it,' Katherine whispered back, then, tilting her head to one side, added, 'He's much more interesting when he's talking nonsense, don't you think?'

It was not until the morning of Christmas Day, as they were finishing breakfast, that Ellie happened to comment, 'There's a picture of that Madeleine 'arcourt in this week's *Woman's Own*.' No one appeared to be interested. 'You know, the Belle Laurie girl what looks like you, Miss Katherine,' she persevered.

Mrs Johnson paused in the process of removing a plate from the table. Through narrowed eyes, she stared at her young mistress. Katherine and Samantha held their breath. So far, although the commercial made it clear the name of the model was synonymous with the new range of cosmetics, there had been no mention of the name Harcourt.

'Madeleine *Harcourt*, you say? Is that her name?' asked Mrs Johnson.

'Yes. There's an article about 'er. She was at some film premiere with Mr Drew.' Carrying a vase of wilting flowers, oblivious to the undercurrent she was leaving behind, Ellie disappeared out the door.

'*Madeleine Harcourt* . . . I seem to have heard that name somewhere before,' the housekeeper muttered, looking piercingly from one girl to the other, while both girls looked mutely at nothing in particular. 'Quite a coincidence, wouldn't you say?' Mrs Johnson did not continue to labour the point; it was not her position to do so, not now her charge had reached maturity, but she could not help wondering at the strange turn of events and the reasons for Katherine's secrecy.

That evening, in the comfort of her own little lounge, she was able to think up quite a few convincing reasons why Katherine should want to keep her private and professional life separate. Her husband, as always, sagely agreed with everything she said. Satisfied that she and Reg were of one mind, she determined that, if that was the way her young mistress wanted it, there was nothing more to be said on the subject to either Katherine or anyone else, and certainly not to that chatterbox of an Ellie.

But still, she couldn't help one last baffled comment, 'Katherine keeping company with Mr Drew . . . well I never. Who would have thought it, Reg?'

*

Katherine had purposely not placed her present from Alexis under the Christmas tree. Questions would have been asked and, in any case, she had wanted the pleasure of opening the parcel later in the privacy of her bedroom.

It was only just still Christmas Day by the time Katherine finally got her wish. Prolonging the suspense and moment of pleasure, she first prepared for bed and then, taking up the precious gift, she carefully removed the ribbon and wrapping, to disclose a small green leather book, exquisitely tooled in gold leaf. It was *The Rubaiyat of Omar Khayyam.*

She ran her fingertips lovingly over the cover, knowing Alexis had chosen the book especially for her and had only recently held it in his own hands. Between its fine pages was a bookmark. On it, in his distinctive, artistic hand, Alexis had written one of the quatrains:

> Ah Love! could you and I with Him conspire
> To grasp this sorry Scheme of Things entire,
> Would not we shatter it to bits – and then
> Re-mould it nearer to the Heart's Desire!

For a moment, Katherine pondered the beautiful words. Alexis could not possibly have known how appropriate his choice of verse. She supposed he meant it to allude to regret that they should be apart at such a time as this. To her, of course, the quatrain held quite a different message – a message so much deeper, so much closer to her heart.

She remembered the day the fates had brought them together, and thought of the secrecy of her own foolish making – a secrecy that now clouded her happiness and put at risk their future together.

'Oh Alexis,' she sighed sadly, 'if you asked me to return a verse, I would have to reply:

The Moving Finger writes; and, having writ,
Moves on: nor all your Piety nor Wit
Shall lure it back to cancel half a Line,
Nor all your Tears wash out a Word of it.'

Samantha returned willingly to work. All day, she looked forward to seeing John, but his office remained empty. By the end of the afternoon, when he still had not appeared, she assumed he had extended his Christmas break in order to stay longer with his mother at their family house in Herefordshire.

She had, several times, phoned his apartment, but on each occasion his recorded voice had invited her to leave a message. Still he failed to return her calls. Repeatedly, she reassured herself that if anything awful had happened to him, it would be hot news in the office. His continued silence hurt her.

Although it had not once been mentioned, Samantha had taken it for granted that they would be seeing the New Year in together. Now she began to wonder.

She gazed with unseeing eyes out of the office window. A frown of discontent creased her brow. Casting her mind back to their last couple of dates, she remembered that John's strange moods had been uncharacteristic. Or *had* they been uncharacteristic? she now asked herself. She wasn't sure. At the beginning of their relationship, in an attempt to win her over, he had been on his best behaviour: all charm and thoughtful attention. Recently, she had been allowed to glimpse a less pleasing side to his personality. She had made excuses for him; put his unpredictable mood swings down to stress. But, just maybe, this was the real John: selfish, arrogant, conceited – and, come to think of it, not the world's most considerate lover either.

She had been dissatisfied with their relationship for some time, she now realised, so why had she taken so long to put that dissatisfaction into constructive thought?

There was a knock on the door. Emily, one of the

secretaries, entered. Thinking she had come to collect the mail, Samantha reached for the out-tray. Something in Emily's expression stopped her. The girl had something on her mind.

Uneasy, Samantha asked, 'What is it, Em?'

'You sure you want to know? You're not going to like it.' Emily warned her. She was from Lancashire, usually outspoken to a fault, but well meaning.

'I'm listening,' Samantha said, fixing her with wary eyes.

'John had a bit of a wild time while you were out of town,' she said, not mincing her words.

'He said he was spending Christmas in Hereford,' Samantha said, puzzled.

'He did, but he didn't leave London until Christmas Eve.'

'Two days after me,' Samantha calculated. 'So?' she queried.

'So, he went out on the town with Carol.'

Carol was the new girl in the typing pool: pretty, brunette and, Samantha had thought, uninterested in John. That anyone should be uninterested in the boss's attractive son would certainly be a blow to his ego. Carol's apparent lack of interest would be her main attraction, she surmised.

'Tell me more,' Samantha demanded coolly.

'The way Carol tells it, he took her to Carnegies, got smashed and danced on the bar.'

'Nothing new about that, he does it all the time,' Samantha pointed out.

'Yes, well, this time he sat in the ice bucket, got his pants wet and, er, decided to take them off right there and then.'

Samantha stared in disbelief.

'The full Monty, in front of a full house!' Emily failed to suppress her mirth. 'I'm sorry,' she said, 'but I can't help it. God, I wish I'd been there to see it.'

Samantha started to laugh too. 'You didn't miss much, Em. If the audience had paid admission, they would have been entitled to a refund.'

Relieved at Samantha's unexpected reaction, Emily now chortled openly. 'He knows you're going to hear about it. I expect that's why he's taken the day off to give you time to cool down.'

'He knows the whole office is going to hear about it, more like. Too embarrassed to show his face,' Samantha suggested. 'By now, there won't be a member of staff Carol hasn't told.'

Emily nodded, confirming this as fact. 'Carol walked out on him, said she'd never been so embarrassed in her life. Serves the silly cow right!' Emily said, without a hint of sympathy. Then she added, 'Says she won't ever have anything to do with him again.'

'Well, that makes two of us!' Samantha pulled the telephone towards her and dialled John's number. In her mind, she was preparing a message; one quite different to those she had previously left.

'An original way to terminate a relationship,' Alexis laughed over the phone, when Madeleine had finished telling him about John's antics at Carnegies. 'The man's got style.'

'Originality, maybe. But, from what I've heard, his act was totally devoid of style,' Madeleine corrected.

'Just as well it wasn't Samantha he had in tow at the time,' Alexis pointed out. 'How is she taking it?'

'Philosophically, most of the time,' she replied.

'It would be a pity if she stayed in alone tonight of all nights. I'll call David, to see if we can manage to squeeze in one more around the table. I'll call you back.' Alexis hung up.

Ten minutes later he rang again. 'I've told David we're dropping out. It seems our numbers have already expanded from twelve to sixteen – too many for the original booking. By dropping out, we're solving problems not causing them,' he told her. 'Do you think Samantha will agree to dine at Linnet House?'

'No, I don't think so,' she said, sounding uncertain. 'She'll think she's playing gooseberry.'

'She won't be. Since Hugh's date's gone down with the

flu, he's on his own. He's volunteered to join us.' With humour, he added, 'And he promises to removes his clothes only on request.'

Madeleine laughed, but still she hesitated. 'You and Hugh shouldn't give up your evening on our account,' she mildly protested. 'I'm sure you'd much rather dine out.'

Before she could protest further, he added, 'Got to go – pick you both up at eight.' The line went dead again.

At seven o'clock, when Samantha had made no move towards getting ready, Madeleine took control of the situation. Earlier in the week, her friend had shown her a matching crepe skirt and top, bought especially to wear on New Year's Eve. When Madeleine had commented that the neckline was uncharacteristically high and the hem at least 2 inches lower than any of Samantha's other daringly short skirts, her friend had light-heartedly agreed. 'I guess it is a bit staid for me, but John doesn't like me to wear anything too revealing. He's a bit conservative where I'm concerned.'

Madeleine could now smile at the man's hypocrisy.

'Since when have you allowed yourself to be influenced by the opinions of any of your dates?' Madeleine had questioned with raised eyebrows.

'Since John,' had been the reply.

Only then had she realised John meant more to Samantha than just another date.

Taking the new outfit from the wardrobe, Madeleine laid it on her friend's bed. Next, she picked out an assortment of jewellery and a favourite pair of shoes. Her eyes kept returning to the new garment, an expression of uncertainty in them. Was she being tactless, laying out this particular outfit? After all, Sam had bought it especially for tonight, an evening she fully expected to spend with John. After a moment of indecision, Madeleine decided strong measures were called for.

The humour of John's fall from grace had soon been replaced by the realities of her loss. Now Samantha's moods swung between relief at having put an end to a bad situation, anger at having taken so long to do it and depression over having lost a lover she had genuinely cared about. 'A bit like withdrawal symptoms from a bad habit,' Samantha had said, describing how she felt.

It was a bit early to expect Samantha to put the affair behind her, but the sooner she made the attempt, the better.

When Samantha came in answer to her call, she was momentarily stunned. 'I can't wear that,' she objected, her troubled gaze going from the outfit to Madeleine.

'Then what would you prefer to wear?' Madeleine asked her gently.

'Nothing,' Samantha muttered.

'Wonderful. Not even a G-string? You'll cause a riot but, if you insist . . .' Madeleine smiled.

The hint of a dimpled smile appeared, 'No, I mean I'd rather not go,' she said.

'OK, then we'll stay home and be miserable together, if that's what you want,' Madeleine said, with a resigned shrug.

'No, that's not what I want,' her friend protested. 'I want you to go out and enjoy yourself and stop worrying about me.'

'Sorry . . . can't do that. It's New Year's Eve. Either we both go out or we both stay in,' came the adamant reply.

'All I want is to be left alone,' Samantha snapped irritably. 'I don't need a babysitter.'

Damn! She's going to be difficult, Madeleine told herself, and quickly decided tougher measures were called for. 'So you can revel in self-pity? No, Sam!' she said firmly. 'I've made up my mind. You're not staying in on your own. As I said, either we both go or we both stay, but if you insist on us staying in, I promise to be miserable enough to satisfy the pair of us!'

Madeleine rarely spoke in so decisive a tone, and Samantha stared at her. After a short silence, she grumbled ungraciously, 'In that case, I suppose I shall have to go.'

Madeleine gave an inward sigh of relief, thankful that her usually indomitable friend was not up to a fight.

'Alexis is collecting us at eight,' she informed her, deliberately neglecting to mention Hugh Bradford.

Definitely not the best time to tell her she's going on a blind date, Madeleine told herself.

The girls were not quite ready when Alexis arrived. At Madeleine's invitation, he entered the apartment for the first time, and accepted the offer of a drink. While he waited, glass in hand, he wandered around the lounge, studying the artworks on the walls. He was immediately drawn to a landscape, painted in the grounds of Ravenswood: the magnificent manor house clearly recognisable on the distant rise beyond the lake. The name *K. Drew*, was just legible in the bottom right-hand corner.

Alexis studied the oil painting in detail. Good . . . very good, he acknowledged to himself, a slight smile softening his features. So, the artist's model is herself an accomplished artist. It gave him pleasure to know that Smith's reports had not exaggerated her talents. On hearing footsteps in the hall, he quickly drew away. It would never do for Madeleine to know he had seen that tell-tale landscape and signature.

He saw her eyes dart past him to the wall beyond and then quickly return to focus on his face. Seeing nothing in his expression to cause alarm, she calmly said, 'We're ready whenever you are.'

He knew that particular picture would not be on display when next he came to call.

Hugh was already at Linnet House. He had been left temporarily in charge of the kitchen. Although he was brandishing a wooden spoon and making an attempt at competence, he was, in fact, feeling totally inadequate in the position of duty chef. Fast losing control, he was thinking that, unless someone came to the rescue soon, dinner would be beyond redemption.

It was with considerable relief that he welcomed the arrival of Alexis, Madeleine and Samantha. If it had not been for Samantha's quick reactions to the bubbling gravy, it would have been necessary to serve it off the top of the cooker. As she stood before him, holding the saucepan and looking for some heat-resistant surface on which to rest it, Hugh studied her through appreciative eyes. 'You must be Samantha,' he purred.

By the time supper appeared on the table, Samantha and Hugh were chatting like old friends. The meal that Alexis had skilfully begun, which Hugh might have wrecked had not Samantha come to the rescue, was cooked to perfection.

Throughout the evening, the wine flowed freely, as did the conversation and humour.

Taking advantage of Samantha's brief absence from the table, and with her friend's welfare at heart, Madeleine inquired of Hugh, 'The girl you were supposed to be taking out tonight . . . is she your girlfriend?'

'Just good friends,' Hugh responded airily, then added, 'I'm between girlfriends . . . Resting, you might say.'

'*Resting!*' Alexis scoffed. 'If you were between girlfriends, I doubt you'd be resting.'

Since it was clear which way the wind was blowing, Madeleine was relieved to hear there was no one special in his life. If Samantha was going to rebound, then she was happy for her friend to do so in Hugh's direction.

When Samantha returned to the room, Madeleine was amused to notice her skirt was a good two inches shorter, having been turned up at the waistband, and that the two top buttons at the neckline had been attractively left undone.

*

The candles burned lower and, when they arrived at the coffee and liqueur stage, they agreed to move into the drawing room. While Alexis played softly at the piano, they waited for the approach of midnight. With the arrival of the hour, they turned on the television to hear Big Ben strike out the time and herald in the New Year.

As they joined hands to sing 'Auld Lang Syne', Madeleine looked at Samantha's radiant face and knew it was going to be a happy year for her, after all. But sadly, for her own future, she had doubts.

She and Alexis were already in their seventh and final year of marriage. With the arrival of the New Year, the threatening divorce seemed to have suddenly, ominously, taken a giant leap nearer. Very soon, Mr Fairfax would commence proceedings that would give them back their freedom – a freedom she now no longer wanted.

32

Through the worst of the winter months, until the completion of her contract, Madeleine was kept fully occupied by Belle Laurie. Before she had time to worry about her future, London's top model agency begged her to register on their books. She did, and within a short space of time found herself dashing from one assignment to another, with hardly a spare moment between. In the spring, honouring her obligation to Veronique Couture, she once more packed her suitcase for the Paris Trade Fair. Despite all, Madeleine was enjoying her success and no longer had any immediate desire to return to her old career. Success had come to her through a different door and sent her self-esteem soaring. Added to this, she was a woman in love. Life was full, sweet and, oh, so heady.

While so much was going on in Madeleine's life, Alexis was caught up in his own demanding world. He had begun work on a new musical with a highly talented team of artists, and was now never without a pencil and notepad so that whenever a piece of music came into his head, he could jot it down to be worked on at the piano later. To help out an old music academy friend who had started his own music supply agency, Alexis occasionally passed on his lesser compositions, and was often amused to hear one of his familiar jingles hit the charts.

While Samantha and Hugh were constantly in each other's company, Alexis and Madeleine had to be content with moments snatched between business commitments.

Not a day passed when Madeleine did not ask herself if she should tell Alexis the truth about her identity. But success was exacting a high price and all too often, she found, when one was in the country the other was just leaving. Finding the time to be together was a constant and frustrating problem, and because those meetings were few and often in the company of friends, the time to tell him was never quite right.

It wasn't long before a reporter, thinking her obscure background rather mysterious, asked too many searching questions. Although she chose her words with great care, and he went away seemingly satisfied with her well-practised answers, she was uncomfortably aware that the next inquisitive reporter might feel justified in digging a little deeper.

When she voiced her concerns to Samantha, her friend said with some impatience, 'This whole business is getting out of hand. You should have told Alexis ages ago, then you wouldn't have to be so secretive.' When Madeleine made no comment, she went on, 'This has gone beyond you and Alexis. Do you realise, I have to be very careful what I say to Hugh in case I drop you in it?'

'Has he ever mentioned Katherine Drew and that day at Ravenswood?' Madeleine asked, her curiosity piqued.

'No, never,' Samantha retorted. 'And I have to be careful not to mention it either, because I'm not supposed to know anything about it. The whole thing's getting very complicated.'

'What's so complicated about it?' Madeleine wanted to know, trying to ignore the pangs of conscience. 'As far as you and Hugh are concerned, I'm just Madeleine, Alexis' latest girlfriend. If he ever mentions Katherine, all you have to do is change the subject.'

'But I'd rather *not* change the subject. I'd much rather be able to talk openly about the past,' complained Samantha. 'I'd like to be able to tell him I've known about him for years and, if he's ever heard mention of Katherine's friend Samantha, then he's known about me for years too. It's so romantic, or would be if only I could talk openly about it.'

'I'm sorry, Sam,' Madeleine said, looking apologetic. 'I'll tell Alexis, when the time's right . . . Promise.'

'And when will the time be right?' Samantha pressed.

'When he's honest with me and tells me he's a married man,' was the stubborn response. With an angry scowl, she added, 'And I would like to hear him say he loves me, just once, and wants to marry me, before he learns I'm the one who has the other half of the Drew fortune.'

She had not meant to voice her fears aloud. A stunned silence followed. The girls stared at each other, both remembering vividly the time of the concert at the Royal Albert Hall when Samantha had unwittingly sown the seeds of doubt in her friend's mind.

Are you sure he'll give you a divorce when the time comes? she had asked. *He has the Steinway, Linnet House, Ravenswood and his and your finances under his control. Furthermore, he has a presentable wife to give him children, and all the mistresses he wants.*

Now, silently, Samantha asked herself that same question that had, for some time, been bothering Madeleine. Would a man with a driving force as powerful as Alexis', a man with the single-minded ambition to take him to the top of his chosen profession, settle for half his great-uncle's fortune when he could have it all?

Samantha was the first to speak. Shaking her head, she said, 'Now that I've met Alexis, I can't believe he'd refuse you a divorce.'

'Oh Sam,' Madeleine whispered, 'I don't either. I don't really believe he'd allow himself to be influenced by gain.' Both were thinking of Linnet House and the Steinway.

She paused; thought for a moment, and then, looking up at Samantha with large tragic eyes, said, 'I can't tell him – not yet, anyway. I really must know he loves me for myself alone, before the truth comes out.'

It was the day before Good Friday and late in the afternoon by the time they drove over Henley Bridge and into the cobbled centre of the old town, where, at Madeleine's request, they did a quick circuit.

'You'll have lots of opportunity to look around later,' Alexis assured her. Leaving the streets and shops behind them, they followed the river to the west. It was an ideal time to introduce Madeleine to his country home and retreat, and he wanted her to see the cottage while the daylight still held.

The world was awakening from a harsh winter. The fragrant smell of spring hung in the air, and all around was evidence of rebirth. Bushes and trees, heavy with fresh new leaves and buds, rustled gently in the crisp April breeze. Spring flowers had opened to face the sun, and soon the rhododendrons would be in full bloom, turning England once more into her colourful best.

Leaving the road and an assortment of country dwellings behind them, they drove a short distance along a track until they arrived at a large picturesque cottage set in extensive grounds which sloped down to the very edge of the River Thames.

Whilst Alexis took their weekend bags into the house, Madeleine stood in the drive, enchanted by her surroundings, waiting for him to rejoin her.

'Oh Alexis, it's lovely,' she rhapsodised, her eyes shining.

He was surprised at just how much her approval meant to him.

'Please, can't we walk around the garden before we go in?' she pleaded. Taking his hand in both of hers, she pulled him in the direction she wanted to go.

They strolled along paths, passing thick clumps of colourful spring flowers, through a mature, well-stocked garden and on down to a small timber boathouse and jetty. There, by the water's edge, with the breeze on their faces and in their hair, they turned and looked back up the gentle rise towards the cottage.

'Now I know why you spend so much time here,' Madeleine said. Her gaze travelled slowly over the handsome brick and timber structure, with its elaborate leaded windows, thatched roof and profusion of climbing plants. 'It's beautiful . . . and so peaceful.'

Her interest was held by what appeared to be a large extension added to the rear of the cottage – an extension carefully designed to blend in with the rest of the building, its double sliding doors opening onto tiered patios.

Following her gaze, Alexis explained, 'I had it purpose-built for meetings and rehearsals. Music needs space and good acoustics.' With a grin, he added, 'Great for soireés and parties too. You'll see when we go in.'

They sat on the edge of the jetty and, watching the boats go by, talked of all and nothing, as lovers do, until the shadows grew longer with the arrival of dusk and the temperature dropped too low for comfort.

Alexis led her on a tour of the ground-floor rooms, coming last to the extension. It stood on a slightly lower level to the rest of the property, to compensate for the slope of the land towards the river. Descending the steps into its interior, Madeleine saw that this spacious room, with its Indian rugs and large Sri Lankan batiks, had a personality quite different to the other rooms through which they had passed.

'Well,' she teased, 'it's plain to see where your interests lie!'

An extensive and complex-looking music centre had been installed in a corner. Along one wall a custom-built unit housed countless CDs, records, cassettes and videos. It was also home to piles of music scores. Rows of books, judging from their titles, were nearly all to do with music. Propped against a wall was a violin case and music stand, and suspended high in the corners of the room were sophisticated speakers. In another corner, facing into the room, was a piano, on top of which were scores showing signs of having been worked on recently. She guessed that this was the piano at which Alexis preferred to work. It must have been his most treasured possession before he set his sights on the Steinway.

Following him to the centre of the room, turning slowly on the spot, she said, 'I see what you mean when you say the extension's great for soirées and parties.'

'Parties on warm nights are the best. We slide back the doors so that we can spill out onto the patios and lawn. We make our own music and usually end up skinny-dipping in the river.'

Madeleine laughed. 'Shocking!' she said, then asked archly, 'Can I come to your next party?'

Remembering vividly their nights of lovemaking and the portrait that hung in his study at Linnet House, he drew her into his arms. 'You can skinny-dip for me any time you like,' he said, a smile on his lips, 'why wait for a party.'

Bending his head to hers, he kissed her passionately. 'You haven't seen everything yet,' he said, his voice made vibrant by the stirring of desire. 'I've saved the most important room until last.'

Taking her hand, he drew her back through the drawing room with its beams and inglenook, brasses and chintz, to the hall beyond. With an impatience to match his, she followed him up the stairs to one of the rooms, where he stood back to let her pass.

The dark-grained furniture, the masculine colour scheme, left one in no doubt that this was a man's room. A cufflink box lay open on a tallboy beside an antique silver and ivory clothes brush, a familiar jacket hung on the back of a trouser press, and a tall mirror was adjusted on its stand so that it tilted at just the right angle for Alexis' height. The scent of his cologne hung in the air, filling her suddenly with a strong sensual yearning to be in his arms. Turning towards him, she sought his lips, while her fingers went to the buttons on his shirt.

He laughed at her eager impatience for love. 'Wanton!' he teased and, sweeping her off her feet, carried her over to the bed, where he allowed her to have her inventive way with him.

For the four days of Easter, while they had the cottage to themselves, they did whatever pleased them.

They took a long walk along the river towpath, ending up in a secluded corner of a quiet pub, oblivious to other customers and so obviously unsociable lovers. With the intention of feeding the water-birds, they walked to a nearby bakery, but absent-mindedly ate most of the bread themselves whilst talking and strolling their way back to the river. With the toss of a coin, Madeleine won the right to choose between taking the rowing boat or the motorboat out on the water. She chose the rowing boat. With eager high spirits, she insisted on taking a turn at the oars and succeeded only too well in soaking them both to the skin.

Late on the Saturday afternoon they drove into Henley. Coming out of the car park, they were accosted by friends of Alexis. While the men cast eager, inquisitive eyes on Madeleine and the females looked hopefully at Alexis, the couple only had eyes for each other.

Escaping, as quickly as good manners would allow, they entered the first confectionery shop they came to which had not already locked its doors for the night. There they purchased two mammoth Easter eggs.

The following morning, being Easter Sunday, Alexis carried them into the kitchen.

'Bags that one,' called Madeleine, pointing at the one prettily wrapped in silver and pink paper.

'It's yours only if you can catch it,' he agreed. With a mischievous grin, he promptly tossed it to her across the room.

Unprepared, she squealed, fumbled the catch, and let it slip through her fingers, to drop at her feet with an ominous thud.

Stooping to retrieve the flattened heap of silver and pink paper, Alexis regarded it with mock disdain. 'You missed,' he pointed out with a doleful shake of the head. 'I guess that makes this . . . eh, mess, mine.' With a grin, he handed her the undamaged one. They dissolved into fits of laughter.

By the evening, the eggs had been totally demolished and neither cared if they never saw chocolate again.

By mutual consent, evenings were spent alone in the cottage, where they dined by candlelight to soft background music. For this weekend at least, the lovers could behave as if they were the only two people in the world.

On the last evening, after supper, Alexis went to the piano. This time he did not ask Madeleine for her request but began to play a piece of music she had never heard before.

Silently, she listened, and when he trailed off, asked the title.

'It's Moussorgsky's *Pictures at an Exhibition*,' he said. Softly, he began to play again.

After a moment, above the quieter strains of the music, she heard him murmur, 'Madeleine Harcourt was first revealed to me through pictures at an exhibition. It shall be our tune.' Glancing up, he asked in a languid voice, 'Have you any idea what became of that portrait?'

'Only that it was bought on the first night by an anonymous collector who took it abroad the next day,' she replied.

'Are you not curious to know who the buyer was, or on what wall it now hangs?' he asked.

'No,' she replied, a little too sharply, her gaze dropping away.

Seeing her heightened colour, he said, 'The buyer, then, was a man.' After a reflective pause, she heard him say, 'It must be daily torture to know that somewhere in the world is the flesh and blood reality and that all you may ever have is a constant reminder of her existence.' She looked up; saw the wistful, enigmatic smile. 'Never would I settle for just the portrait,' he said.

*

Later, when they lay before the roaring fire, sated and glistening with perspiration from love's labours, Alexis murmured, 'I know so little about you . . . after all this time, you're still a mystery to me.'

He felt her stiffen in his arms. 'There's little to tell that you don't already know,' she replied.

That was true. He did already know all there was to know about her. Her choice of words amused him, but at the same time he was baffled by her lack of trust. He wanted the facts to come from her, not out of a file. Silently, he willed her to speak. She shifted uneasily, but did not confide.

'I love you, Madeleine I can't imagine life without you,' he murmured, looking deep into her large, anxious eyes.

These longed-for words wrapped themselves around her heart, filling her with acute happiness. Too choked to speak, she nestled close, burying her face in the curve of his neck. At last, one of her dearest wishes had come true. Now, if only he would admit to having a wife already, confirm his intention to divorce her in September, and ask her, Madeleine, to wait for him, her happiness would be complete – or would it? For then, somehow, she would have to find the courage to tell him the truth: to tell him who she really was.

Where will I start, and how will I ever manage to explain? she wondered in an agony of doubt. *I'm Katherine Drew, the woman you want to be rid of,* would be an appropriate beginning.

She turned over so that now she was looking down on him, her long curls tumbling around her troubled face like a thick, dark veil. Bringing her lips down fiercely, passionately, on his, she effectively put a stop to any further conversation. Her arousing caresses grew demanding until he made love to her once more.

Again, Alexis let his questions go unanswered but, he told himself, he would not do so for much longer. She would tell him the truth if he had to drag it from her.

*

Although it was well after midnight, they still lay in front of the fire, talking softly of whatever came to mind.

'Move in with me, Madeleine,' Alexis suddenly said, taking her by surprise.

Madeleine wanted to move in with him. Oh, how she wanted to say yes, but instead, she hesitated, wondering at the wisdom of doing so. He had said he loved her and, at that moment, she did not doubt his sincerity. Alexis was not a man to intentionally use such words lightly. But they had made love in a romantic setting, and it was a small progression from tender thoughts to ardent words. Just how reliable were his feelings for her? she wondered. He had said, 'I love you, Madeleine,' but she was not Madeleine, she was Katherine. She already knew what he thought of Katherine; had known since their wedding day. When he discovered how he had been deceived, would he not think even less of Katherine?

With a jolt, she realised he was still waiting for her reply. 'Move in here? You mean, give up the flat in London?' she asked, playing for time to put her thoughts in order.

'Yes. Why not?' His voice was soft, persuasive. 'Samantha spends so much time with Hugh, they're practically living together. She wouldn't mind.'

Turning on his side, he raised his head to rest on his hand so that he could study her face. 'Neither of us has a nine-to-five job to worry about and there's a good train service to London. But, if you prefer, we can get you a car.' He thought of the Mercedes, garaged at Ravenswood for the exclusive use of *Katherine*, and smiled inwardly. 'We would have more time together,' he pointed out.

She thought for a moment. To live with him would be heaven but it would complicate matters further: yet another lie to add to their lives, and more opportunities for her to slip up. Besides, she did not wish to be his live-in lover. She wanted to be his wife – in the true sense of the word. 'No. I don't think it's a good idea,' she eventually said, looking away evasively.

A frown creased his brow. 'Why not?' he asked. Using his

free hand, he turned her face towards him so that she could not avoid eye contact. 'Give me one good reason,' he persisted.

Feeling pressured, she let slip that which for some time had so dominated her troubled thoughts. 'Because you're married, Alexis,' she said sharply. The minute the words were out: Madeleine realised what she had said.

There followed a poignant silence. A voice in her mind urged, 'The truth . . . now tell him the truth.' Instead, she stammered: 'H – Henrietta told me at the party . . . you have a wife.'

'I see,' he said. 'How kind of Henrietta to be so informative. No doubt she had our interests at heart.' His silky voice was heavy with sarcasm.

Furious with herself for her unguarded words, Madeleine moved as if to get up. But with a hand on her shoulder, he firmly held her down.

With mischief on his mind, he owned, 'She's right, I am married and have been for over six years, to a second cousin.' He went on to explain, 'It's a marriage of convenience, nothing more.' Taking her hand in his, he raised it to his lips and kissed the open palm. 'And just as well,' he added, keeping his eyes lowered lest she see the laughter in them, 'since she was the last person on earth I would have chosen for a wife.' He heard the sharp intake of breath, the gasp of indignation. Seemingly unaware of her reaction, he blithely continued. 'In order to inherit from my great-uncle, I was coerced into a seven-year marriage with his sixteen-year-old granddaughter.' He dredged up a deep sigh; looked into her eyes as if in search of sympathy.

Madeleine had none to offer. She pulled her hand away.

'From the beginning,' he confided, 'Katherine and I have had an unspoken agreement to stay out of each other's way . . . until the divorce, that is.' She couldn't argue with that, he told himself, suppressing the urge to laugh aloud. It was the truth. He was playing the game according to her rules.

'If you felt like that about it, why did you agree to this marriage?' she asked, between tight lips.

'For the same reasons as Katherine,' he replied. 'For gain, of course! A property the size of Linnet House situated in the heart of fashionable London is no small temptation to turn one's back on, and . . . it contained the Steinway.' He paused, but when she offered no comment, continued, 'Linnet House and everything in it had originally belonged to my great grand-father. I felt, and still feel, I have as much right to it as any other member of the family.'

And what of Ravenwood and the Drew fortune: did he consider them also his by right? she wondered.

As if in reply to her thoughts he repeated, 'As I said, I had everything to gain and nothing to lose.'

'So it would seem,' she responded, a little too sharply. 'But, your cousin had *everything* to lose . . . and still does.'

'Meaning?' he asked, suddenly alert to her strange choice of words.

Madeleine was uncomfortably aware she had said more than she intended. Searching for an alternative meaning for her words, she improvised, 'She lost the opportunity to marry for love.'

Your cousin has everything to lose, she had said. Like a thunderbolt, it hit him. She suspected his motives for marrying Katherine; doubted his intention to relinquish control over her estate.

There followed a seemingly interminable pause. Picking up a lock of her hair, he played with it, letting it curl around his fingers. Aware that some playful demon was now working within him, he replied, 'Not true. She could have married for love at any time . . . *if* I had been willing to give my consent to an early divorce. But,' he smiled, 'that would have meant my losing *everything*. Asking rather a lot, don't you think?'

She ignored the question. With narrowed eyes, she asked, 'And what if *you* had met someone you wanted to marry; would you have asked for an early divorce . . . forfeited *all* for the woman you loved?'

He took time to consider. 'Maybe, for the *right* woman,' he finally said, glancing at her out of the corner of an eye.

Infuriated by his glib reply, Madeleine fought to keep her temper under control. She recalled that, in the time he had known her as Madeleine, he had not once volunteered the information that he was married, nor had he asked her to wait for him, neither had he loved her sufficiently to apply for an early divorce in order to marry her. The subject, until now, had simply never come up. It was becoming quite obvious to her that Alexis did not consider Madeleine to be the right woman. Even now, she fumed, he was not offering her his name, only accommodation as a live-in lover.

To hell with you, Alexis Drew, she raged to herself. I'm no Henrietta!

Apparently unconcerned by the turmoil he was causing in her mind, he asked, 'Now you know all, will you move in with me?'

'No, Alexis,' she replied through tight lips, 'I will not.' Sharply she moved her head so that the curl dropped from his fingers. 'Nothing has changed, you're still a married man.'

'Then September cannot come too soon,' he smiled cheerfully, 'and then I'll be free to ask you to marry me.'

She stared at him, her rage dissolving in an instant. 'Marry you!' Madeleine gasped. Throwing her arms around him, she knocked him over onto his back. 'You're going to ask me to marry you? Oh Alexis, I didn't know.'

'Well, if that's the response I get from merely threatening to propose, when I actually get around to it, I'd better be prepared to be savaged,' he laughed, pretending to defend himself.

33

‘At last. Now the truth will out. Right?’ Samantha asked, over lunch in a little Italian restaurant in Soho.

‘It’s not that easy,’ Madeleine demurred, picking uninterestedly at the food on her plate. ‘I’ve left it a bit late to tell him who I am. He’ll want to know why I kept silent for so long.’ She raised worried eyes. ‘What will I tell him?’

‘The truth?’ Samantha suggested, practical as ever.

‘And what exactly is the truth?’ she scowled. ‘That initially I lied because I was embarrassed that *he* of all people had seen me baring my all in a portrait?’ She paused. ‘Should I tell him I thought he would go out of my life again, never having to know that Madeleine Harcourt, the artist’s nude model, was really me, Katherine Drew: twice related?’

‘Why not?’ Samantha wanted to know. ‘He would probably have laughed.’

‘Wish I had,’ she said mournfully. ‘But now, after all this time, he’ll want to know why I kept quiet for so long.’

‘Well, why did you?’ Samantha asked, a little exasperated. ‘I keep asking that question myself.’

‘Because of all those awful things he and Hugh said about me,’ she snapped. ‘Unforgivable things – or so I thought.’ After a short pause, she groaned, ‘They don’t seem so bad now – I seem to have got it out of all proportion.’ Looking dejectedly down at her plate, in a small voice, she added, ‘Shame had something to do with it too, I suppose. I would have had to admit that my low opinion of him came from having eavesdropped on a private conversation.’ She spread her hands helplessly. ‘Anyway, how was I to know we’d fall in love and want to spend the rest of our lives together?’ She looked at Samantha for understanding. Seeing none, she said defensively, ‘Well, he obviously didn’t find marriage to me an appealing proposition. That I could have forgiven: after all, it's true, I wasn't very appealing. It's the other bit I find hard to forgive.'

'What other bit?' asked Samantha, wondering if she was referring to the piano.

'You know, him . . . and Henrietta.' Now thoroughly put off her food, she pushed her plate away. 'He said Henrietta was going to join him in Vienna – on what should have been *our* honeymoon.'

Samantha stared at her and started to laugh. 'You're being ridiculous. You didn't want to go with him, remember? You would have run a mile if he had even suggested taking you on honeymoon.'

'But that was then,' Madeleine pointed out. 'I wasn't to know I was going to fall in love with him.'

Now Samantha was all sympathy. She knew the emotional traumas love could inflict. Had she not recently been through a few of those traumas herself?

'I wish I'd never laid eyes on Henrietta,' Madeleine grieved. 'Now I keep seeing them together, when it should have been me. Well, maybe not, under the circumstances . . . but the point is, she shouldn't have been with him in Vienna – not on that occasion. It's the principle of the thing.'

'I seem to remember you telling me Alexis was very cool towards Henrietta at that party of Margot whatever her name was.' Samantha reminded her. 'If he was still interested in Henrietta, then you'd really have something to worry about.'

'Yes, I suppose so,' she agreed half-heartedly.

'Well, I'm pleased we've managed to get that problem into perspective,' Samantha said airily. 'And now, no doubt, you're going to bring up the little matter of having been married for a Steinway.'

Madeleine smiled. She had long since decided the Steinway had gone to the right person.

*

On several occasions Madeleine came close to avowing the truth to Alexis. But on each of those occasions, at the last moment, the opportunity was lost.

When asked again to move into the cottage, she stalled, saying, 'When you divorce Katherine . . . if you still want me . . .' Although she had smiled and spoken lightly, there was something about the look in her eyes, the tone of her voice, that suggested a meaning he did not care for. Was she still questioning his intentions to go through with the divorce? he wanted to ask, but since there was much he was not meant to know, he refrained from comment and made no further effort at persuasion.

When free of other commitments, they now regularly spent their weekends together in Henley. Although Madeleine was aware of his secretary's part-time existence, their paths never crossed. Late one evening, provoked by a couple of glasses of wine into feeling curious and just a little jealous, she asked for a description of Jenny Simmons.

'Oh, she's short, fat, sixty and has a moustache,' Alexis joked.

Such a reply was sure to fuel Madeleine's suspicion that Jenny was young and attractive. 'Oh really?' she retorted hotly. 'And I suppose next you'll be telling me Katherine has bandy legs and . . . and . . . crossed eyes!'

'Katherine, crossed eyes?' Much amused by her jealous response, he smiled. 'Not that I remember. In fact, I seem to recall she had the most beautiful, sensitive eyes I've ever seen.' He paused, and tilted her chin to search her face. 'Not unlike yours, really . . .' Then he shook his head, and said, 'But she was nothing like you in any other way. If she had been,' he laughed, 'I would not have parted with her so willingly, and I would not now be talking of marriage to Madeleine Harcourt.'

While she was at the cottage, a letter arrived from Mr Fairfax, reminding Alexis that he and Katherine could now commence divorce proceedings.

Seemingly elated, he showed the dreaded missive to Madeleine. Her expectation of such a letter did not lessen the shock of its arrival and for a moment she felt as if the room was closing in around her.

'He asks if my cousin and I wish his firm to deal with the matter. What a question!' Alexis exclaimed, eyes gleaming. 'Of course Fairfax must deal with the matter, and the sooner the better.'

Although tremendously relieved to hear that he did not mean to hinder the divorce, Madeline now found herself unreasonably provoked by his enthusiasm to be rid of her other self. Tartly she asked, 'How do you know Katherine will want him to deal with this matter? Doesn't she have any say in her own affairs?'

'Katherine and I have waited seven years for this – she will be as eager as I to get it over with,' he replied. 'She must be . . . let me see . . . twenty-three by now,' he calculated. 'She could be thinking of marriage – a real marriage.'

The irony of his words was not lost on Madeleine: Katherine was indeed thinking of a real marriage, and to this very man.

Going to sit at the piano, Alexis began to play a tune in keeping with his buoyant mood. With his attention supposedly focused on the music and careful to keep a straight face, he went on to tease, 'Maybe I should call Fairfax and suggest he apply for an annulment on the grounds that the marriage was never consummated. Might be easier and quicker than a divorce.' Startled, Madeleine could not prevent her eyes darting in Alexis' direction. They connected with his but quickly, evasively, slid back to the letter in her hands. Knowing that his marriage with Katherine had indeed been consummated made her feel most uncomfortable.

'Well, perhaps not.' He took up where he had left off. 'After all, at twenty-three, she's unlikely to still be the little innocent I remember. In which case, non-consummation of the marriage will be hard to prove.'

He was silent while he accomplished, with his usual flare and finesse, a particularly intricate piece of staccato.

'I'm not an authority on the subject of divorce,' he drawled, the demon in him once more taking over, 'but I believe a couple may also have a strong case for divorce if they have refrained from intercourse and cohabitation for two years.' With a thoughtful smile on his face, he said airily, 'I must remember to ask my solicitor about that. It might help progress.'

Alexis was having trouble hiding his amusement. Of course, he had no intentions of questioning Fairfax on the finer details of the law but it would not hurt to let her stew awhile.

Cheerfully, he continued to tease. 'Fairfax will probably suggest incompatibility.'

'Incompatibility!' she snapped, now irritated beyond endurance. 'If you've never lived together, how do you know you're incompatible?'

'I don't think anyone at the wedding was in any doubt about our incompatibility,' he replied airily.

If Madeleine had had the courage to look again, she would have seen the glint of merriment in his eyes. But instead, laying the letter down, she turned her attention to rearranging a vase of flowers she had already earlier arranged to her complete satisfaction.

The suggestion that he and Katherine might still qualify for an annulment was laughable, as was his plan to divorce Katherine and marry Madeleine, but she did not feel much like laughing. Soon, whether it came from her or not, Alexis would know the truth. She had no way of knowing how he would take it. It was probable that the link that had kept them joined for the best part of seven years would be severed, and that anger and pride would take him out of her life for ever.

In his letter to Katherine and subsequent telephone call, Mr Fairfax assured her that, with both parties being in ‘eager and harmonious agreement’, he saw no reason why the divorce proceedings should not run smoothly in accordance with everyone’s wishes.

Everyone’s but mine, she thought, not sure whether to laugh or cry at the absurdity of her situation.

As predicted by Alexis, Katherine gave her consent for Mr Fairfax to begin divorce proceedings. However, her consent was not given with quite the degree of eagerness Alexis had anticipated when sharing his thoughts with Madeleine.

In the study at Linnet House, Alexis wrote:

Dear Katherine,

According to the terms of your grandfather’s will, we have now fulfilled our obligations and may apply for a divorce. As you are probably already aware, Mr Fairfax commenced proceedings some time ago and has now written to advise me that the necessary documents are ready for us to sign. I have asked him to forward them to Linnet House.

You will remember, it was your grandfather’s dearest wish that, for the sake of Ravenswood, we remain together to perpetuate the family name. I want you to know that, since there is no one else in my life that I wish to marry, nor is there ever likely to be, I would be very happy to waive the divorce and fulfil your grandfather’s wishes.

I look forward to seeing you at Linnet House at 2 p.m. on the 28th so that we can discuss the possibility of a future together.

Yours always,
Alexis

Alexis laid the pen down beside the letter. A machiavellian smile hovered on his dark features. Picking up a small open jewel box, he turned its sparkling contents to the light.

Embedded in the velvet interior was a diamond solitaire engagement ring.

His thoughts were interrupted by a knock on the library door, followed by the appearance of Mrs Stewart's head.

'You've got a visitor,' she announced with her usual lack of enthusiasm and with a face that would do credit to a poker player. 'It's Mr Bradford,' she sniffed.

Hugh was unceremoniously ushered into the room and the door closed behind him.

'At a guess, untrainable,' he grinned, referring to Mrs Stewart's manners, or lack of them.

'As the saying goes: you can't teach an old dog new tricks,' Alexis replied. 'Not a lot of charm, but she does an excellent job and, in her own funny little way, takes my welfare very much to heart.'

'A one-man dog then? Lucky you!' Hugh quipped. His eyes alighted on the open letter on the desk. 'Caught you at a bad time?' he asked, and then, noticing the box in Alexis's hand and its sparkling content, exclaimed admiringly, 'Nice little bauble. Must have set you back a bit. I can see it's not exactly your style, so who's it for?' he inquired.

'Madeleine – as a token of my affection and good intentions,' he smiled complacently, flicking the lid closed with a snap.

Picking up the letter he had just finished writing to Katherine, he passed it across the desk and then, while he waited, Alexis watched with some amusement as a broad smile spread across his friend's face.

'You're looking for trouble,' Hugh accused, his eyes alight with speculative good humour.

'Just thought I'd stir things up a bit,' Alexis agreed.

Hugh laughed. 'What's the idea?'

'This way, whether Katherine or Madeleine, she will know I want her to be my wife,' Alexis explained. After a moment, he went on, 'Not once has she said how she feels about me. Now the onus is on her to say what *she* wants.' He paused to take back the letter. Folding it, he placed it in an envelope and then, smiling roguishly, said, 'I fly to Salzburg tomorrow and won't be back until the twenty-seventh. Maybe, by then, she will have made up her mind about our future.'

'By then,' Hugh laughed, 'her estimation of your character will have reached rock-bottom!'

'Yes, quite likely,' Alexis agreed. On a more serious note, he continued, 'By the time Katherine comes to Linnet House, my signature will already be on the divorce papers. Maybe then, she'll realise I have no intentions of blocking the divorce. The final decision to sign will be hers.'

Later that evening, as arranged, Madeleine joined Alexis in a club in Chelsea. Knowing he had an early morning flight to catch, they stayed only for a short time before returning to Marlow Place. Finding a space near the entrance, he parked the car and put on the interior light.

'I've something for you,' he said. Taking the jewellery box from his jacket pocket, he placing it in her hand. 'Open it,' he invited.

Madeleine raised the lid and immediately the light caught in the facets of the diamond ring. Completely taken by surprise, she gasped. 'Oh, Alexis, it's so beautiful. I c-can't accept it. I mean . . . I shouldn't,' she stammered. Her conscience pricked her, guilt never far from the surface.

He looked at her questioningly but, when she remained silent, let the comments pass. Instead, he said, 'A little early, I know. I was going to keep it until after the – well, never mind that. I want you to have it now, before I go to Salzburg, as a constant reminder of my love for you.'

Lifting the ring from the box, he slipped it on her engagement finger. Tenderly, he kissed her. 'Don't take on any bookings for the two weeks following the twenty-eighth. I thought we'd go to Vienna to celebrate.'

'I don't believe this!' Madeleine gasped, staring at the letter in her hand.

Samantha turned inquiring eyes on Madeleine and then, seeing the stunned expression and the pallor of her face, stopped what she was doing to ask anxiously, 'What's happened?'

Madeleine passed her the letter that had just arrived in the morning post, forwarded from Ravenswood. Her hand shook uncontrollably. 'You were right about him all along,' she whispered. 'He doesn't want a divorce.'

Not since the reading of her grandfather's will had her mind been in such painful confusion, and Alexis Drew had been the main cause of her anguish then, as he was now.

'*There is no one else in my life that I wish to marry nor is there ever likely to be*,' she mimicked Alexis's treacherous words. '*I would be very happy to waive the divorce and fulfil your grandfather's wishes.* How obliging of him!' she railed, her voice heavy with sarcasm.

'I don't believe it,' Samantha muttered, staring at the letter. 'There must be some mistake.'

'Oh yes. There's some mistake all right,' Madeleine agreed, bitterly, 'and it's all his. He's slipped up, given himself away. He sends this letter to Katherine and at the same time gives Madeleine an engagement ring. He's overplayed his hand and made it quite clear he doesn't intend to give either of us up. Obviously, he's not satisfied with just the Steinway and Linnet House, he wants Ravenswood, a wealthy wife, and a mistress too. Why settle for half when you can have it all,' she ranted on, tugging the ring from her finger. 'He once told me, for the right woman he'd give it all up and get a divorce. Well, I'm obviously not the right woman. I can see that now and, as for love, he doesn't know the meaning of the word. How could I have been such a fool as to put my trust in such a man?

'It would appear he inherited more than musical genius from dear unscrupulous great grand-father Freddy – he also inherited his complete lack of morals!' Angrily, she dashed a tear away with the back of her hand. 'Yet, he seemed so sincere . . .' She trailed off, a catch in her voice.

After a short pause, her eyes again glittered with a

resurgence of anger. 'He said he was going to take me to Vienna to celebrate the divorce,' she recalled. '*Vienna* of all places! First he takes Henrietta there on what should have been my honeymoon, and now he wants to take Madeleine. Does he take all his lovers to Vienna?' she wailed.

Samantha could only shake her head in bewilderment and listen while Madeleine poured out all her grievances. Finally, when it seemed there was nothing left to say, she fell silent, but only for a minute. Suddenly coming to a decision, Madeleine turned to the table. With mutiny on her mind, she reached for the offending letter and jewellery box and, dropping them into her bag, stormed, 'I'll be damned if I'm going to let Alexis Drew have his cake and eat it.' She headed for the door.

Alarmed, Samantha called after her retreating back: 'Where are you going?'

'Home to Ravenswood. I need to be alone for a while,' Madeleine flung over her shoulder.

'Call me when you arrive and let me know you're all right, 'Samantha called after her. The door had already closed.

Although Katherine had planned to visit Ravenswood while Alexis was away, she was not due to arrive for another couple of days. Her early appearance threw the household into a flurry of excited activity.

'Your bed's not aired yet, miss,' Ellie said in her usual guileless manner. 'You've put Mrs Johnson in a tizzy,' she giggled, totally oblivious to her mistress's cheerless mood.

Alone, Katherine once more gave herself up to melancholy. She saw, stretching endlessly before her, a bleak and empty future.

It did not take Mrs Johnson long to realise that all was not well with her young mistress. She had lost her sparkle, her zest for life. Nothing held her attention for long, except the problem that gnawed away at her mind. To the cause of her unhappiness, Katherine gave no insight. To all inquiries, she insisted she was fine.

'She'll be all right, Reg,' Madge said, more for her own peace of mind than for her husband's. 'A bit of home cooking and some clean country air will put the colour back in her cheeks.'

To appease the housekeeper, Katherine made an effort to eat but, with the approach of the 28th, her appetite deteriorated badly, her solitary walks increased and her nerves grew noticeably more jittery.

In the privacy of their own little living room, the anxious Madge asked her uncommunicative husband, 'Whatever can be wrong with her, Reg? She spends all her time either walking down by the lake or locked in her bedroom. Katherine's got something on her mind and I don't like the effect it's having on her. I wish she would tell me what's wrong.'

The housekeeper cast her memory back to the day she realised Katherine was keeping secrets – the day Ellie had said the name of the girl in the commercial was Madeleine Harcourt. She could find no fault with her using her great-grandmother's maiden name, nor with her wanting to keep Ravenswood a private retreat. But that Katherine had never raised the subject of her dual life with either her or Reg did seem strange indeed. Or was it so strange? Madge asked herself; after all, Katherine was no longer a child. She was mistress of the manor, and they merely her employees. Why should she confide in them?

Almost seven years had elapsed since the death of her former employer. For a while she reminisced over the days when the house had been full of music and laughter, when there had been people constantly coming and going, parties and picnics to arrange and sometimes even a ball. It had all come to an end slowly, like a clock running down, giving its final tick when Katherine had gone off to live in London. These days, their mistress spent little time at Ravenswood.

The manor house was just a shell of its former self. Maybe later, Madge told herself, when the young mistress marries and has children the house will reawaken. Whatever was she thinking? she asked herself with a start. Katherine was already married.

It was at this point that Madge remembered the correspondence from Mr Fairfax, dutifully forwarded to Marlow Place. Comprehension dawned, brightening her eyes. For a moment she considered, and then asked, 'You don't think Mr Drew's refusing to give her the divorce, do you, Reg?'

Hearing his name mentioned, Reg managed, for all of two seconds, to drag his eyes away from his motoring magazine.

Taking her husband's lack of proper response as the affirmative she sought, Madge gave a slight nod. 'You're right, Reg, that's what's wrong. Well, who would have thought it of him.' Madge pondered a while longer and then, feeling happier than she had for a while, sighed, 'They make a lovely couple.'

The day before Katherine was due to call at Linnet House, Samantha telephoned. Knowing Alexis was due back from Salzburg that day, Katherine could not help wondering if she was calling with news of him.

'Before you ask, no, Alexis hasn't phoned,' Samantha volunteered. 'I just want to know you're all right, that's all.'

'I wasn't going to ask,' Katherine said untruthfully, trying to keep the annoyance out of her voice. 'And yes, I'm all right. Thank you for asking. How's everything with you and Hugh?' she inquired.

'Fine,' Samantha replied, not wanting to sound too enthusiastic about her own accelerating love life in view of the crisis in Katherine's. 'I hoped by now Hugh would have told me something enlightening about Alexis and the two women in his life. But so far, he hasn't told me anything I don't already know.'

'What is there to tell?' Katherine retorted. 'It all seems fairly obvious to me.'

Hearing a resurgence of anger in Katherine's voice, Samantha asked cautiously, 'What do you plan to do?' Quickly, she went on to clarify the question. 'I mean, are you going to sign the papers?'

'Of course I'm going to sign the bloody papers,' Katherine snapped. 'For all his scheming, he'll not get either Katherine or Madeleine – I'll see to that. Nor will he get anything that isn't rightfully his.' With bitter scorn, she added, 'And to think my grandfather was worried about fortune hunters. Little did he know he was marrying me off to one!'

Samantha sighed at the hopelessness of the situation. 'Want me to come with you to Linnet House for support?' she asked.

'No, Sam,' Katherine replied after a short pause, the heat going out of her voice. 'I'd rather see this through on my own.'

The following day, Katherine drove to Belgrave Square, where she parked along side the familiar burgundy Jaguar. It was the first time she had driven the Mercedes into London since the beginning of her affair with Alexis. There was now no longer any need to keep the car out of sight and no need for her to hide behind an assumed name. She was keeping her appointment with Alexis as herself: Katherine Drew. But for the hurt, the honesty would have been a blessed relief.

Tall and erect, head held high, she marched across the street and knocked purposefully on the door of Linnet House.

You're in for a nasty surprise, Alexis Drew, Katherine told herself as she waited for him to open the door.

The door, however, was not opened by Alexis but by Mrs Stewart.

'I'm Katherine Drew. I have an appointm—' she started, but got no further.

'You'd better come in then,' the woman cut in, looking Katherine up and down. 'You're expected,' she said dryly.

Strains of Liszt's *Rêve d'Amour*, sensitive and intimate, floated through from the drawing room. *Dream of Love*, she translated to herself. How appropriate that he should welcome Katherine with this particular piece of music, she thought with bitter irony. Dream all you like, Alexis Drew, for dreams are all you'll ever get from Katherine – empty dreams and nothing more.

Interpreting Alexis' mood from the manner in which he played, she judged him to be feeling pensive and maybe a little vulnerable. Soon, he was going to feel even more vulnerable, Katherine promised herself, as, triumphantly, she visualised the moment when he would look up from the Steinway to see her, Madeleine, enter the room.

'What are you doing here?' he would ask warily, surprised by her unexpected appearance and displeased because Katherine was due to arrive at any moment. 'I wasn't expecting you.'

'But I'm Katherine Drew,' she would tell him simply and then watch with vengeful pleasure his shocked reaction to her words. But, she realised, such pleasure would be short-lived: for the shattering of his dreams would mean the shattering of her own.

With a heart threatening to break, she followed the housekeeper, not to the drawing room, as she had expected, but across the marble hall to the library – a room she had never entered before; a room always kept locked because, she had been led to believe, it was Alexis' private domain.

The door was not locked now, and Mrs Stewart pushed it open. 'You'd better wait in there,' she said, before walking away.

Madeleine hesitated on the threshold; reluctant to intrude where she had not been invited by Alexis. The surreal effects of the background music lent her the courage to go forward.

Entering the room, she was greeted by the faint smell of leather upholstery and musty antique books. Her eyes went immediately to the large, handsome desk in front of her; to the cream vellum document and pen, which lay on the tooled leather surface, so obviously placed in a prominent position for her attention. Mesmerised by this treacherous document, she approached the desk. The black ink of Alexis' bold, intricate signature stood out starkly against the cream background.

That he had not come forward to greet her, had already signed, could only mean he did not, after all, wish to discuss a future with Katherine. Then he intended to stay true to Madeleine – or did he? She recalled again his written words, 'There is no one else in my life who I wish to marry . . .' Confused by all that had recently passed, she no longer knew what to think. A sob caught in her throat.

'Oh God,' she murmured, 'please give me the strength to get through this and out of here with dignity before I completely go to pieces.'

Katherine picked up the paper, but her hand shook so much, she could hardly read what it contained and so she quickly replaced it. Bending over the desk, she read it where it lay. She despaired of being able to hold the pen, let alone write her name next to his, but, somehow, she managed to sign herself Katherine Drew and date the signature.

'Stay married to you! Like hell I will!' she said with bitter resentment, but now there was no fury behind the words, only desolation. Laying the pen aside, she next took from her pocket the black jewellery box containing the diamond solitaire and wedding band. Opening it, Katherine emptied its contents onto the document where they would instantly be seen. Throwing the box aside, she said aloud, 'Now work that one out, Alexis Drew!' But, there was no pleasure to be had from either the action or the words. She was losing all she valued most in life. It was the end of a beautiful dream.

Through a shroud of misery, Katherine was vaguely aware the music had reached a climax. The earlier quality of vulnerability was now no longer to be heard in the playing.

Slowly, taking a deep steadying breath, she turned away from the items she found so painful and offensive and was about to leave the room, when her eyes came to rest on a portrait hanging on the wall opposite. With a jolt, Katherine realised she was looking at a picture of herself. The painting was the very same one Jeremy Grierson had exhibited at Harrington's art gallery.

In stunned disbelief, she stared at it. It had been bought by a foreigner and taken abroad, or so she had been told. Confounded by its presence, she questioned what it could possibly be doing here, in this of all houses: hidden from view in a room usually kept locked.

Her attention was claimed by something affixed to the lower part of the frame that had not been there before. A small engraved silver plaque. Going closer, she saw it bore her name. Not the name Madeleine Harcourt, as might have been expected, but the name Katherine Drew – her true name.

Full understanding came slowly. He must have known her identity all along. With such evidence as this, there could be no doubting that Alexis had been the mystery man who had bought the painting; in which case, only he could have been responsible for the silver plaque.

Now the carefully chosen words in his letter began to take on a whole new meaning. He had surely known Madeleine and Katherine were one and the same person when he had written: 'there is no one else in my life who I wish to marry nor is there ever likely to be', and when he had said: 'I would be happy to waive the divorce'. She now realised that, by signing the divorce agreement, Alexis had offered her unconditional freedom. By relinquishing any claim to her and her fortune, he had proved his love was for her and herself alone. The final decision of their future had been left for her to make and now, in her ignorance, she had signed away her happiness. After all that had passed between them, all the bad she had allowed herself to think of him, how could she ever bring herself to face him again?

Her throat ached painfully with the effort of holding back the tears. Released, they coursed silently down her cheeks. Alexis could not possibly want her now. It was over. No point in prolonging the agony of parting, better to leave, and quickly.

In a panic to be gone, Katherine turned away from the portrait. But, instead of rushing from the room, she came to an abrupt halt. Her way was barred, the door now closed. With his back against it, Alexis stood still and silent, watching her.

Numbly, all she could think was, 'When did the music stop? Why didn't I notice the quiet?'

He seemed in no hurry to break the silence between them. Katherine was the first to speak: 'You knew all along,' she whispered in an unsteady voice.

'Yes, Katherine. I knew all along,' he agreed.

She was aware he had used her real name. It had rolled off his tongue quite naturally, as if he had never known her by any other. 'But you didn't say.'

'Nor did you, although I gave you every opportunity,' he pointed out, quietly, calmly.

He did not smile. She assumed he was angry and felt he had every right to be. 'I didn't mean to deceive you, it just happened and grew out of control,' she said in a small, anguished voice. 'I wanted to tell you . . . tried to so many times. Not at the beginning, perhaps – too much stood between us: your opinion of me, Henrietta . . .'

He turned his gaze towards the desk. He seemed disturbed by what he saw. When he raised his eyes, she tried to read the expression in them, and thought, for a moment, she saw pain.

'I should go,' Katherine murmured. She could not bear to be the cause of his hurt.

'Before you do,' he said, putting out a hand to stop her, 'are there any more grievances I should know about?'

'Yes,' she replied honestly, with a wan smile, 'many.'

'Then it could take a long time to . . .' He sighed. 'No matter. We have our whole lives to sort out our differences.' His voice touched her like a caress.

She turned her head to look at him. 'You mean, you still want me?' she asked, afraid to hear the answer.

'For ever,' he replied, and then, with a glimmer of humour, added, 'and by any name you choose to call yourself.'

Taking up the rings, Alexis asked, 'Shall we please your grandfather?'

Without waiting for a reply, he took her left hand in his and slipped first the gold band and then the solitaire onto her finger.

'But I've signed the divorce paper,' Katherine wailed, her beautiful face a picture of tragedy.

'That's a mistake easily rectified,' he smiled down at her. Turning to the desk, Alexis took up the document and slowly, deliberately tore it into little pieces.